RENEGADES

A GROWER'S WAR
BOOK 2

D.J. MOLLES

The characters and events portrayed in this book are fictitious. Any similarity to real persons, living or dead, is coincidental and not intended by the author.

ISBN-13: 978-1548073176

CHAPTER ONE

It's been three days since Carolyn was taken from me.

Three days since the CoAx purged my hometown.

The room smelled like the military. Like rubberized metal that has been sweated on and then cleaned, a thousand times over. A cross between a machine shop and a gym.

There was a bed. There was a toilet. There was a sink and a mirror. There was a little shelf to store personal items, which was currently barren—a reminder to Walter Baucom that he had nothing anymore. Nothing but the life that was still in his chest.

Forty-eight hours since I found out my long-lost brother was still alive.

Thirty-six hours since I found out that my father is headed for DTI.

He stood, gripping the sides of the sink, like he might fly off the face of the earth if he let go.

And if we don't come up with a plan in the next twenty-four hours, we're going to lose Pops forever.

He stared at the image in the mirror.

His short brown hair was messy. Pressed to his head on one side, cowlicked on the other. The angular features of his face were interrupted on the left side by the NeoSkin that was still meshing to his burn, and it gave his face a half-formed, puffy look. The NeoSkin glistened like it was oily, and was an angry red like a sunburn. It didn't match the right side of his face at all. The right side had a two day beard. The left side was smooth and hairless.

Not even a five o'clock shadow. His hair follicles were probably burned out and dead.

His left eye had no visible white in it. The blood vessels had burst, and his iris was surrounded by a creepy red halo that made him look insane.

Small, but surprisingly painful in light of everything else: A notch in his right ear where a bullet had clipped him.

You look like a fucking alley cat.

It was going to be a bad morning.

He could already tell that. He could *feel* it, like an old man feels a weather change in his arthritic knees.

Time was running out to get intel on when and where the CoAx was going to ship their prisoners out of District 89—which was their one, long-shot opportunity to rescue Pops. And today would be the day when he knew that he was either going to launch himself into a mission that could very likely take his life, or he was never going to see his Pops again.

And all he could do was wait.

And the pressure of the waiting hung on him, as hot, and cloying, and itchy as a wool sweater in July.

Made him want to move.

Made him want to hit things.

Kill things.

Rip the sink out of the fucking wall.

Do *something* for God's sake.

After fighting for his life in District 89, the past few days spent hiding in the mining town of Kanawha 3, somewhere in the mountains of West Virginia, felt like torture. Felt like a little tiny box that he'd crammed himself into. And every fucking hour it was getting smaller.

He rattled the sink.

He ground his teeth.

He'd found himself doing that a lot, lately.

And his jaw was hurting. His teeth ached in the beds of his gums.

But it was clean pain. Clarifying pain. It kept him from releasing that thing that was growing inside of him that he knew he shouldn't release, but that he also didn't know how to keep from growing.

Where was Carolyn right now?

He didn't know. The not knowing was the worst. Every time he thought of it, it felt like he was running a cheese-grater across his brain. It made him sick with worry. Sick with longing. Sick to his stomach. Sick, sick, sick.

But at least he knew that Carolyn was someplace safe.

She was not currently in the custody of the CoAx, about to be sent to DTI, as was his Pops.

It felt weird to Walter to have to prioritize his family. But that was exactly what he was required to do right now. Who needed his help?

Not Carolyn. As badly as he wanted to see her, she didn't need him at that moment.

His Pops did.

And here he sat.

Useless.

Waiting.

For intel.

Fuck.

He blew a breath.

It came out unsteady.

Fogged the mirror, then disappeared.

Evaporated.

"Fuck this place," he mumbled to his reflection. "Fuck everything."

Then he pointed very deliberately. Crammed his index finger into the two-dimensional version of his face. Pressed it in until his knuckle was painfully back-bent and he thought the glass might crack.

"And fuck *you*."

Not sure why he was so pissed at himself.

He wanted to do things. He wanted to fight.

He wanted to find his father.

He wanted to find his wife.

But he couldn't do those things. He had no way off this fucking mountain. Aside from just hiking out and hoping the resistance didn't catch him. Which they probably would. The entire place was ringed with a sensor grid. They owned the checkpoints out.

Hell, they'd even tapped into the local Network Hub, so they could monitor what everyone was saying.

Stop any incriminating communications before they ever got transmitted.

What's that? You want to tell Aunt Bea about the strange men hiding in the slurry cisterns?

Nope. That message ain't gonna send.

Want to call Aunt Bea after that?

You'll notice a slight delay. And if you start talking about the slurry cisterns again, your call's gonna drop.

Strangest thing.

Yes, the "renegades" had a tight hold on Kanawha 3.

Necessarily so.

But it meant that Walter was stuck.

Stuck with this new thing that he'd birthed in himself—*changing tides, changing polarities*—and no idea of how to control it. Only that he wanted to fight. God, but he wanted to fight anyone, anything, would even take a throwdown with one of the locals.

Except they weren't supposed to talk to the locals.

"I gotta get out of here."

He pushed away from the sink and shook himself out, like a dog shaking off wet fur.

He was already dressed like the locals. Here in Kanawha 3, denim was similar to tans in District 89. It was what all the workers wore. Denim pants. Denim jacket. Sometimes denim overalls. Denim, denim, denim.

Nice, blue, close-stitched denim.

Walt slipped into his denim jacket and went out of the room, hoping to God that there would be some news—some *good* news—but steeling himself for the fact that he was now living in a world of longshots, where the odds were against you, and the stakes were always more than you wanted to pay.

CHAPTER TWO

A line truck is a one-ton truck with knobby, off-road tires used for getting around in the mud, in order to service the regulator stations that keep the hydroponics pumped into a field. It has about a half ton of equipment on it. Its front bumper is black, diamond plate steel.

This all would become very pertinent in Brad Hughes' life, momentarily.

At the moment, Brad Hughes was in a GUV, though. In a leather-upholstered GUV. And he was making the leather dirty. Actually, he was making it *bloody.*

Brad Hughes' face had seen better days.

Typically he had a lean, Roman face. Now it was puffed up and cut and bleeding. He couldn't see out of his right eye. It'd gradually become swollen shut over the course of the last half hour.

His lips still throbbed. His ribs ached with every breath.

His hands were bound behind his back and he was starting to lose feeling in them.

With his one good eye, he looked to his left, out the window, at the fields of Agrarian District 89 as they flew by him. Morning was dawning on the third day of the purge.

Not much of a purge anymore. The purge was pretty much over. But the borders were still closed. To the outside world, AD89 was still a little black hole of mystery for the time being, as the

CoAx sorted out everyone that they now had captured. Sorted them out like it was Judgement Day. The sheep from the goats. The redeemed from the damned.

DTI being hell, of course. Where all the damned were to be sent.

Which made Brad Hughes what?

Lucifer, he supposed. A fallen angel.

Sent to do the Fed's bidding, but then he decided to think for himself.

He'd made a good go of it, though. Ran when he knew he was outed. But he had certainly chosen the wrong place to run to. Jesus, what fucking luck.

Anywho, he'd taken out five of them before they'd finally gotten him.

Should've eaten that last bullet, Brad thought to himself, growing sick in his stomach as he considered what lay in store for him. *Rather die than DTI.*

And he would be a special case in DTI. Oh, yes he would. He knew it, and he knew what they would want to know. And he knew how desperately they wanted to know it. Desperate enough to cross whatever boundaries of decency they still had left, which wasn't much.

They would want to know where Colonel Wainwright had taken ten percent of their military. They would want to know where those defected troops were hiding. Or, as they'd been dubbed by the media, *renegades.* Probably because it sounded ominous and out of control.

Defected made it sound like they had a *reason* for rebelling.

Renegades made it sound like they'd lost their marbles and would drive a tank through your kid's kindergarten classroom just for the fuck of it.

"It's all such a goddamned stage play," Brad mumbled through fat lips.

"What's that?" asked a gentle voice beside him.

Brad turned to his right. He was in the middle seat. An agent to his left, and an agent to his right. He knew both of them. He'd been their colleague up to about seventy-two hours ago.

The one to his left he only knew passingly.

But the one to his right was Agent Farrell, and they'd been partners earlier in their careers.

Farrell looked at him with a mix of bitterness and pity.

He just couldn't quite believe that Brad had turned coat. Couldn't quite believe he'd been feeding intel to the resistance. Couldn't quite believe that he had to send this man to DTI, who'd been to his daughter's fourth birthday party only six months ago.

And pity, because he knew what they were going to do to him.

"I said," Brad licked his lips and tasted blood. "'It's all such a goddamned stage play'."

Farrell sighed, long and heavy, and looked out the front windshield.

"Why'd you do it?" Farrell asked, quietly.

Brad just sat there, staring at the side of Farrell's face. Seeing the clean-shaven skin. The neatly trimmed blond hair. How he smelled of sweat under a layer of aftershave. Sweat, from the exertion of beating the fuck out of Brad.

It almost made Brad want to laugh.

Such a stage play.

Eventually, when Brad didn't answer, Farrell turned to look at him again.

Brad smirked at him with his broken face. "Why do you *keep* doing it?"

Farrell sneered. "You gonna try to take the moral high ground here, Brad?"

Brad looked away. "You gonna try to tell me you're okay with seven hundred dead civilians, Tony?"

"Militants," Farrell said, aloofly. "Seven hundred dead *militants.*"

Brad shook his head, but said nothing.

A crossroads approached. A four-way stop.

The driver didn't even tap the brakes.

They sailed through the intersection.

Brad shifted slightly, tried to feel his hands, but it was no good. They were probably dead blue right now.

"I'll do this for you," Farrell said, quietly, but very seriously. "Because you're a friend."

"Yeah?" Brad said, not much caring, because it was all such bullshit. "What's that?"

"I'll pull over to the side of the road right now," Farrell said, looking at him with an intense honesty. "You tell me where Colonel Wainwright and the renegade troops are hiding. We've got strike teams on standby to probe any location we get. We'll know within thirty minutes. You tell me, I confirm it with the strike team, and then I'll..." he swallowed here, then worked his jaw. "I'll just execute you here."

Brad stared back at him.

Surprisingly, he felt nothing.

The GUV kept rolling on.

The two former friends looking at each other.

"One to the back of the skull," Farrell said, almost a whisper. "You can watch the sunrise. It's a beautiful scene. Good way to go. Far, far better than what they got planned for you at DTI. You know that, right? You *have* to know that."

Brad turned to look at the sunrise.

"It is pretty, isn't it?"

And for just the breadth of a second, everyone in that GUV glanced to the left, out that window, into the east where a yellow sun was rising into a puffy white sky, like an egg that's just been cracked into a skillet.

No one saw the line truck coming.

It hit the back, right quarter panel. Rammed it with that big, diamond plate bumper, and sent that outsized GUV flying, twirling like a thrown boomerang. The GUV did three full revolutions, each one bouncing a little higher off its wheels, until the third one came down at too much of an angle and the vehicle overturned and went sliding on its roof into the ditch on the side of the road.

Brad never observed any of this.

One second he was looking at the sunset.

Then, a noise like someone had let off with a shotgun inside the vehicle.

And the next second he was raising a wobbly head and trying to interpret what he was seeing and why he hurt so much worse now than he had before. He was staring at the ceiling, he thought, but it was weird because there was beads of broken glass all over it, and his face was bleeding again, and instead of running down to his chin, it was flying up off his face and pattering on the ceiling—

Oh, I'm upside down. No shit, Sherlock.

They'd been hit. They'd been in an accident.

Brad was still dangling by his seatbelt, as was everyone else.

Brad struggled to turn his head to the right, to look at Farrell, and he was supremely shocked with himself that he was registering a sort of concern for Farrell's well-being. But maybe Brad was just a softer person on the inside that he'd ever suspected.

Maybe that was why he couldn't look at all those dead folks as militants.

Farrell was blinking rapidly, his mouth working, coughing.

The interior of the GUV smelled like the acrid smoke that's expelled when an airbag goes off.

Probably because every damn one had gone off.

"Fuck!" was Farrell's first word. Then, "What the fuck just hit us?"

He was struggling to get his seatbelt.

Actually, no.

He was trying to pull his gun.

But then his head exploded.

And his chest, right after that.

"Jesus Christ!" Brad shouted, flinching back as his mouth was sprayed with blood.

The other agents in the vehicle were just starting to stir, except for the driver, who seemed unconscious or dead. But it didn't matter whether they were moving or not.

Brad heard the gunshots and watched every single one of their chests and heads burst.

"Fuck! Fuck!" Brad was trying hard to get his seatbelt undone.

His brain was foggy, almost punch-drunk, but he was able to reason that if they'd just been ambushed, then the ambushers would probably assume he was a Fed like the rest of them.

It was very difficult to get his seatbelt undone because, for one, his hands were secured behind his back, and second, he couldn't really feel them. But he was going to try, for God's sake!

"Brad Hughes!" came a voice.

Big. Burly.

Almost merry.

He froze in his convolutions.

Looked to his left, where the voice had come from.

A New Breed's helmet, visor, and battleshroud was in the window, looking right back at him. Then a big paw of a hand—ungloved, which was unusual for a uniformed New Breed—reached up and flipped back the ballistic visor and undid the battleshroud.

The New Breed was indeed merry.

He had sharp blue eyes that twinkled with some Viking happiness, and a wolf's grin that was framed by a fiery red beard.

"Yeah?" Brad said, weakly.

"I'm Chief Kozlowski," the Viking said. "We're gonna get you out of here."

CHAPTER THREE

A memory.

The two of them, lying in bed next to each other. The dim twilight comes through the window, coloring their skin an unearthly shade of blue. Every inch of it laid out in the privacy of their bedroom.

Sweaty, and spent, and pleasantly warm.

On their backs, looking up at a blank ceiling.

Walt turns his head to look at her. He has a smile on his face. But she is pensive. Her eyes are far-off. Her finger absently traces a pattern between her breasts.

Walt looks back at the ceiling.

"You know," Carolyn says. It is almost a whisper. Because the house is so quiet, it seems wrong to talk at full volume. "We don't need children."

Walt turns towards her again.

She rolls on her side, faces him. Looks at him.

"What do you mean?" he says.

"We have us, right?"

"Of course."

"Well...you know...maybe that should be enough."

"Yeah," he says, almost as though he doesn't believe her. Almost as though he is waiting for her to make an addendum to this statement.

"This isn't so bad," Carolyn says, rolling back to look at the ceiling. "What we have. Right? I mean, it's you and me. We can

build a nice life. Quiet. Grow old together. Kids would only complicate things. I should be happy."

Should be.

But perhaps she wasn't.

Walt watches her, and even from out of the corner of Carolyn's eye, she can see that his expression is strange. A slight frown creasing his brow.

"Yeah," he tells her, his voice oddly hollow. "We have it pretty good."

***

Two nights ago, Carolyn Baucom had come home from her shift at the messhall, normal, sane, and unafraid. For what did she have to be afraid of? She and Walt lived a quiet life, doing what they were told. They did not rock the boat. They did not break the rules.

So the wind blows.

Her feet were tired and sore, but that was normal. Ten hours standing and rushing about in the madhouse of the lunch and dinner hour had made sore feet a thing that she barely noticed anymore. It was simply a way of life.

They could only afford one vehicle, and that was Walt's truck, which he used for work. So she used the SoDro vans to get to and from work. They picked her up at ten in the morning, and dropped her off at about 8:30 at night.

Their usual dishwasher had come down with the flu, or something akin to it. But that was the third time that it had happened in the last couple of months, and she and everyone at the messhall were quietly thinking that he was on the outskirts of full-blown redlung, and maybe was trying to keep it quiet.

His absence meant that everyone else had to chip in to get the plastic dishes and meal trays rinsed and into the industrial cleaning machine.

Carolyn, being the more conscientious of the bunch, had spent her time hurrying back and forth between the crowded serving line and the dishwashing station, and as she rode home her hands were raw and chapped from the hot water rinse and they smelled vaguely of old food and dirty water.

The next day was the magical and mythical Day Off, and what made it even more magical and mythical was that it had fallen on Walt's day off as well. Which was something akin to the rarity of a solar eclipse.

The house was dark when the van had dropped her off, but the floodlights were on.

She scooted her way out of the van, the very last passenger of the night. She said goodnight to the driver, an older man named George who talked of little else besides his upcoming retirement. He was nice though, better than the other driver she had on Wednesdays and Thursdays which was a surly young woman that never talked at all to her passengers—as though they were some cause of great inconvenience to her.

Polite and old-fashioned as ever, George sat in his van as she traversed the gravel parking pad to her front door, stepping in and out of the circular glow created by the floodlights. She unlocked the front door and went inside. Only when she closed the door behind her did George conduct a tight three-point turn and head on down the long dirt road away from her house.

The second that she closed the door behind her she sensed something was off. She still couldn't put her finger on what it had been. Maybe she'd made out the shape that was sitting on the couch. Maybe she'd smelled the smell of someone that didn't belong.

Maybe it had just been the tingling of some sixth sense. A woman's intuition.

Her guts immediately felt jumbled and electric.

She reached out and slapped the lights on, feeling simultaneously scared and foolish, in the way a kid feels scared and foolish when they jump into bed to avoid hanging their ankles over the dark space beneath their bedframe.

The feeling of foolishness disappeared.

Someone was sitting on her couch.

For the briefest of moments, she thought it was Walt.

The figure on the couch stood up quickly, but didn't advance. It was a man, and he turned to face her with his hands up, as though to show that he meant no harm, but that did nothing for her in that moment. Carolyn felt *very* threatened.

She fought the urge to scream, knowing it wouldn't do her any good.

"Who the fuck are you?" she said, hoarsely.

The man stood in the middle of her living room, with his hands upraised, showing his palms, and his face was very serious, very intense, but not threatening.

And then everything changed for her, all in a sentence.

"Carolyn Baucom, your parents sent me for you," he'd said, his voice urgent. "The CoAx is on their way here for you right now and we need to get you out."

She'd been scared then. Scared out of her mind.

But it was the fear of a person that knows nothing. A bland sort of overarching fear, and not with any specific object to pin it on. The fear of a person that has simply been overwhelmed.

Now, she found her fear had coalesced into something more specific.

Over the hours and days that had passed since that first harried, surreal conversation in her living room, her knowledge had grown. And with it, the blind nebula of panic had collapsed in on itself and become the white-hot focal point of an ugly star that pulsed fear into her.

Very real, very tangible, very *articulable* fear.

Now, Carolyn was on a southbound Maglev train, sandwiched between two armed strangers.

She was on her way to meet her parents.

And things were about to get much worse.

CHAPTER FOUR

There's a battle outside
And it's ragin'
It'll soon shake your windows
And rattle your walls
Oh, the times they are a-changin'.

Those were the words rolling around in Bobbi's head. In the darkness of her head. Dark, even with her eyes open.

The whole world was dark, and it smelled like dirty laundry.

Like *other people's* dirty laundry.

Not even the familiar semi-comfort of your own stink.

It was the sack that was over her head. It smelled of other people's sweat. Other people's fear. And she began to wonder how many of the people that had worn it before her had died. How many had gone to DTI? What had they looked like? What did their families think now that they were gone? Or were their families taken alongside them?

And then she began to wonder about this black sack.

Why did they do this?

Why was it necessary?

And also, did every fucking New Breed carry a black sack around with them? Like a cop carried handcuffs? Were they standard issue? And who was manufacturing the black sacks? And what were they sold as? What were they labeled?

DTDD, she decided. Domestic Terrorist Disorientation Device. Because the Fed was a sucker for a good acronym.

She'd been in the belly of a gunship, that much she knew. She'd felt them drag her aboard, shortly after the black sack and the plastic restraints went on. She'd felt the rotor wash. Felt it lift into the sky.

Then they'd moved her to someplace else.

There were a lot of people in this place, and she got the sense that it was crowded. Crowded with a lot of unfortunates just like herself. She could hear them moaning and groaning and crying. Men and women alike. But Bobbi herself remained quiet. She tried to listen. To pay attention to what was going on around her, even though the DTDD was doing its job—disorienting her.

There was someone beside her. She thought that it was a man, by the voice. And he wouldn't stop squirming, bumping into her all the time. And he wouldn't shut up. Kept saying he was a loyalist, and when he'd say this a few of the brave souls that didn't care that they were found out, or had simply lost all hope, would shout him down, calling him a traitor and telling him to go fuck himself, and also, fuck the CoAx.

He was either ignoring them, or he couldn't hear them through his own panic.

"I'm loyal to the Fed!" he shouted for what must've been the hundredth time, his voice cracking. "I don't belong here! I don't belong here!"

He was making it very difficult for Bobbi to hear, and she was struggling to hold onto her temper.

She was fairly certain through her listening that there were soldiers of some kind in the room with them. She didn't know whether they were New Breeds or not, but she figured it didn't matter. They would be armed, and she was not.

She knew they were there, because occasionally they would shout at someone to shut up or sit down.

"Please!" the man beside her shouted. "I can tell you who the resistance people are! I can tell you their names! I can point out the collaborators!"

"You fucking traitor!" Someone shouted.

And another person: "Choke on a dick, you fuck!"

Then a bellowing voice that reminded her of a roaring bull: "Everyone in here better pipe the fuck down!" it shouted. "Next person to speak will be shot, as will the person next to you."

The voice was American.

A Fed soldier.

They wouldn't, a part of her thought.

But then she pictured the smoking rubble of the 8089 Town Center.

Yeah, they would.

The room became suddenly quiet, save for some sniffling and whimpering.

The man beside her continued to squirm about, jostling into her.

"Sir! Sir!" The man next to her shouted suddenly.

He was trying to shout to the roaring bull, she thought.

Her stomach did a flip flop.

She whispered, as loud as she dared, "Shut up!"

"Sir! I'm with you!" the man continued. "I can help!"

There were the sounds of boots approaching. The heavy, careless tread that someone uses when they are entirely angry. A sort of childlike stomping.

The boots were getting closer to her. To the man next to her.

Oh, Jesus. I'm right next to him.

The boots stopped directly behind her.

"You just don't get it, do you motherfucker?" Someone said coldly, and she thought it was the roaring bull, but his voice was quieter this time.

"I'm loyal to the Fed!" the man proclaimed again, heedless, stupid, panicked beyond being able to think his words through. "I can help!"

Shut up shut up shut up she willed him, but didn't dare whisper again, because they were right behind her. *They're gonna kill us both!*

Maybe he didn't think they would. Maybe he hadn't seen the Town Center.

Maybe he was just mad with terror.

There was the sound of scuffling.

Right beside her.

"Sir!" the man pleaded.

There was the *whuh-POP* sound of a suppressed gunshot.

Oh, JESUS!

The jostling beside her stopped.

She could feel something flop to the ground directly to her right. But it didn't move anymore.

She realized she was now hyperventilating. Even in the darkness she could see the sparkling of over-oxygenation beginning at the corners of her black vision.

They're gonna shoot me next.

She had a picture in her head, a black and white picture of a long-ago massacre called the holocaust, where they'd lined people up single file and shot through them to conserve bullets. And she'd always wondered what possessed the people at the back of that line to sit there and wait for the bullet and not at least *try* to do something.

She understood now.

It was that rare occasion when hope was the thing that killed you.

Whuh-POP!

She jerked.

Then huddled on her knees.

She hadn't felt a thing.

Somewhere to her right, the sound of another body slumping down.

Someone cried out and another whimpered.

"No more talking!" the bull roared again.

And no one did.

The room became very silent.

In Bobbi's black existence, it was just the sound of a rushing river, and she knew it was the blood in her ears, in her head. Pumping so hard now that she thought her head might explode.

She was too terrified to breathe.

To move.

How could they? she thought with her stomach twist-turning, all her guts like a writhing pile of snakes.

But she knew how they could.

Because…they could.

But it wasn't so simple as that, was it? No. Of course not. Nothing is ever so simple.

Everyone thinks they're doing God's work.

And if she ever got out, and she ever got a rifle in her hand again, then she would remember this, and she'd believe she was doing God's work too, wouldn't she?

There's a difference, she told herself. And maybe that was true.

But in that moment it didn't feel like it.

In that moment she stayed curled in her little ball on her knees, and she felt that she was at the edge of a precipice, or that she was standing before some raging hurricane, something that was far beyond her control.

It'll soon shake your windows

And rattle your walls.

Oh, the time's they are a-changin'.

Who had they killed next to that man?

Father? Mother?

Someone she'd seen when she'd been operating in District 89?

Someone that'd smiled at her and sold her a cup of coffee?

Some sad sap grower that'd been on a planting tractor only a few days ago, whose biggest concern at the time had been whether or not his family could make ends meet?

It didn't matter now, she supposed.

Time passed in the darkness.

She listened to the sounds, and she thought of the words of that song.

Who had written that song?

It began to rub at her like a rock in her shoe.

She knew she should know.

But as frustrating as it was not finding the answer in her brain, it became a welcome distraction from the never-ending moment she found herself in.

She almost didn't want to think of the answer, because when she thought of the answer, then what would she have to think about?

More time passed.

She listened to the boots stalk around. They would stop somewhere in the room. Someone, possibly the bull, would say, "This one."

There would be some rustling.

Silence.

"Katie Gillespie. Negative ninety-nine."

Or it would be,

"Roger Pule. Ninety-nine."

And when they said "ninety-nine," the bull would say, "roger, go ahead."

And then the other voice would say, "Sir, stand up and come with me."

More shuffling.

Sometimes a whimper.

But no one spoke.

Not Katie. Not Roger.

Not those labeled "negative ninety-nine," or those labeled "ninety-nine."

On and on it went.

"This one."

Oh, the times they are a-changin'.

Who wrote it?

"Phillip Decken."

It was right on the tip of her brain.

"Ninety-nine."

"Roger. Go ahead."

"Sir, stand up and come with me."

As a side thought, Bobbi found it so strange that they kept saying "sir" and "ma'am."

What was the point?

They were cattle in a cattle car.

"This one."

Ah, she thought she had it.

Bob Dylan.

Yes. That was right. She was positive of it.

Her heart sank.

"Walter Baucom. Ninety-nine."

What?

"Roger. Go ahead."

Had she heard that right?

"Sir, stand up and come with me."

Shuffling.

She had the urge to shout.

It almost came out of her but she clamped down at the last second.

Was he here? Was Walt here? She felt like the floor had suddenly dropped out from under her.

He'd been on the gunship, hadn't he? They'd escaped, hadn't they?

Her breath was coming fast again.

How had they got him?

Maybe she hadn't heard it right. But she knew that she had.

Did that mean that Getty and Rat were here too?

There was a horrible sense of relief. Horrible because she should not have been relieved that they were captured, but it meant that she wasn't alone. She wasn't alone. And that meant everything to her in that moment. Like finding a piece of driftwood to cling to after your ship is destroyed and you're out floating in a storm.

But *horrible*.

Oh, no. No, Getty. No, Rat. Please don't be here.

One thing was for certain: she knew that "ninety-nine" was not a good thing.

The boots were walking again.

They stopped behind her.

"This one."

She felt someone take her right hand. It wasn't harsh. It was surprisingly gentle. As surprising as the use of the words "sir" and "ma'am." She felt the hand that had taken her manipulate her right thumb so that it was sticking out. Then she felt something cold and hard press against her right thumb.

It was held there for a moment.

A moment in which she couldn't breathe anymore.

Then her thumb was released.

"Alice Corning."

The name shocked her.

She hadn't heard that name in a very long time. It was so far in her past that she had to think for a moment if there had been some mistake, but no. That was her name, wasn't it? It was her name in the time before she'd been a part of the Linklater outfit. Before she'd been given the false identity of Bobbi Novak.

A bloom of hope came alive in her chest, the way a plant withering in the heat will suddenly perk up when it's watered.

She hadn't been called Alice Corning in ten years. When she'd been Alice Corning, she'd been honest. She'd been straight. She'd never broken a rule in her life.

Surely they didn't know…?

"Ninety-nine," the voice said.

"Roger. Go ahead."

The hope died in her chest. Left a foul black spot behind to remember it by.

"Ma'am, stand up and come with me."

CHAPTER FIVE

Roy Baucom made it to the checkpoint thirty seconds behind the marshal.

Apparently, there was a problem.

The checkpoint was a paved road out.

The *only* road out.

Most of these mining towns had only one access point, and West Virginia's Kanawha 3 was no different. The checkpoints and their hydraulic spike strips were supposed to keep these important infrastructure operations safe from domestic terrorists.

Now, it seemed, the checkpoints were keeping the domestic terrorists safe from the CoAx.

Or at least from anyone telling the CoAx that they were there.

Which pretty much meant that no one was allowed to leave.

Desperate times and all that.

The barricade arm was lowered down over the spikes, which were still up and threatening, and sitting plaintively in front of them was an old, tan GUV that had seen better days in its thirty-year life. Its siding was crunched in several places, the paint broken and the steel underneath rusted. Its tailpipe muttered steamily into the air.

To the left, a guard shack.

All around them, the mountains, the forest.

Strong, yellow sun bouncing off of spring-green leaves.

Roy could see that the vehicle was full. He could count at least four heads, two adults and what looked like two older children, possibly teenagers. But it was also full of belongings.

Marshal Dixon, short, lanky, and flint-faced, had reached the lowered driver's window and the two checkpoint guards were taking a step back, their hands still on their pistols. One of them glanced up at Roy, and there was a flash of worry in that gaze.

Roy quickened his pace.

Don't say anything stupid, Roy willed at Dixon.

Dixon, the Marshal.

For all of two days now.

The *real* Marshal was lying in a shallow grave with his two deputies. Hands still bound behind their backs. Bullet holes in their skulls. Fed loyalists.

So the wind blows.

Dixon was supposed to have kept them detained, as they'd done with the others. But the reason Dixon was such a staunch supporter of the resistance was the same reason why he was volatile. His teenage son had been disappeared only two years prior, and now there was a cold spot in that man's heart, and it was into this barren place that he swept every Fed loyalist, whether he'd grown up beside them or not.

Roy gritted his teeth as he came up beside the man with the face made out of sharp angles and bitterness.

"Marshal Dixon," Roy managed, amiably enough. "What's the problem?"

Dixon pushed up off the driver's side of the vehicle, still eyeing the man in the front seat. "It's the Kenners," he said, and it came out like he was describing an unpleasant bodily function. "Trying to make a trip down the mountain."

"Ayuh, I can see it's the Kenners," Roy said.

Mr. Kenner looked out of his driver's window, eyes wide and full of fear and anger. "Look. I don't want any trouble. It's not about that, okay? I got my family to think about. We're just…just going to stay with an aunt for a while."

"Joe," Roy smiled, and he tried to make it look kind. "Nothing bad will happen to your family. I promised you that, didn't I? I promised you that at the outset."

Joe Kenner shook his head hotly. “Things haven’t gone like you said they would.”

Roy felt his smile strain on his face. “Things progressed quicker than we expected.”

“What happened to the O’Briens, huh?” Joe Kenner demanded suddenly, the anger edging out the fear for a just a moment. “What about the Parsons? And the Mullers?” He looked venomously at Dixon, whom Roy knew Joe Kenner had little love for. “And where’s the *real* marshal? And why is this hack wearing his fucking shirt and badge?”

Dixon’s face contorted. “Marshal Bowers and his lackeys were fucking fascists!”

Roy cringed at the word, which held behind it such violent political dogma. He stepped forward before Dixon could continue yelling at the family, which he looked like he was about to start doing, with his hand fidgeting anxiously on the butt of the pistol strapped to his leg.

“Marshal Dixon,” Roy said loudly enough to drown the man out. “Is the marshal at this time, and some respect would go a long way, Mr. and Mrs. Kenner.”

In the momentary silence following what amounted to an unspoken threat, the Kenners stared at Roy, and Dixon stared at the Kenners, and Roy let his eyes waver into the backseat, where the two children were sitting watching this all happen with the quiet and indistinct discomfort of the ill-informed who perhaps do not understand the true stakes that are being played for in the sudden joust of a few hotly spoken words.

A boy that looked to be about fourteen. A girl of about ten.

The girl was looking at Roy.

She was a pretty child. Her face was flushed. Her dark hair tousled, like she’d been piled into the car immediately after waking.

Had the Kenner children been awake all night, their parents’ voices murmuring urgently to each other in muted argument, trying to decide which was the greater risk: to stay here in Kanawha 3, which had, over the course of twenty-four hours, gone from a simple mining town to a place where renegade Fed troops were being hidden away in unused slurry cisterns?

Or to make a run for it?

"Marshal Dixon," Roy said, this time looking at the man. "Can I speak with you for a moment?"

Dixon looked at Roy resentfully. This unforgiveable encroachment on his newly found authority. But he nodded, brittle as a dried twig.

The two of them stepped a few paces away from the Kenner's vehicle.

"We can't let them leave!" Dixon immediately hissed.

"I know that."

"We don't know what they'll say!"

"Dixon."

"All it takes is one person! One person to report what's happening here—"

"Hey! Fuckhead!" Roy spat, but managed it quietly enough that he didn't think anyone but the fuckhead in question heard it. But Dixon's cheeks burned mightily. "Reign that shit in, do you understand me?" Roy was leaning towards Dixon now. *Over* him.

Dixon wasn't cowering back. He wasn't giving an inch. That was not who he was.

Hothead, perhaps. Murderous, cold-hearted sonofabitch, perhaps.

But not a coward.

"We're on the same side," Roy leveled his tone out a bit, now that he'd achieved silence from the other man. "But if you keep going around icing these motherfuckers, it's not going to help us, do you understand that? You've got fucking hate in your heart, and I get that. I have it to. But some of these people don't understand it. They've never lived it. They don't see it on the level that you see it, or I see it. And for now, they'll go along with the resistance, because they agree on a head-level with what we're doing, even if they don't understand it on a heart-level. But if you keep imprisoning or hurting their friends—loyalists or not—things are going to spiral out of our control here. You do understand that, don't you? This is a thinking man's game. Not a purge, for fuck's sake."

Dixon bared his teeth for a flash and he stared up at Roy with his little narrowed eyes like nubs of ice, and he wasn't afraid of Roy, not one fucking bit. "What the fuck do you want me to do then? Because if I let them go back to their house, how long is it before they try to make a run for it again? Maybe this time on foot?" He shook his head and sneered. "No, those fuckers are done. They're *done*."

Roy clenched his right fist in an effort to control himself. "Dixon…"

"We're never going to be able to trust them."

"Would you shut up and listen, for God's sake?"

"Fuck 'em."

And Roy wasn't sure whether their voices had mistakenly carried, or the tension of the moment had simply been too much for Joe Kenner, but the next thing that reached Roy's ears was the sound of a revving engine.

Tires chirped.

Someone shouted.

Roy spun just in time to see the Kenners' old GUV rear back like a spurred horse, its chunky, squarish nose rising up, Joe Kenner with both hands on the wheel, hunched over it, and the vehicle charged forward, its rear tires spitting up a bit of smoke as it crashed through the barricade arm.

The two checkpoint guards had their pistols drawn, but they weren't firing, they were simply yelling impotently.

But Dixon was running. Sprinting. He had his gun in his hand.

The Kenners' truck ripped across the spike strip, the tires tearing and spewing out air, a stupid panicked decision. First the front tires, then the back tires, while the engine roared and the bits of the broken barricade arm were still clattering back to the ground.

Dixon staggered to a stop and leveled the pistol at the vehicle as it thumped forward on flapping, shredded tires.

"Dixon! Don't!" Roy shouted.

But he did.

Dixon began firing into the car.

And with the noise of those first few shots, the two checkpoint guards began firing too.

Roy watched clouts of dust fly off the truck. The back window disintegrated. Pock marks and holes sprouted up all across the back of it. He saw the heads ducking down inside of the vehicle, but he couldn't hear anything over the sudden, earsplitting crackle of guns.

The brake lights never came on.

The truck simply stopped accelerating.

It rolled forward from its own momentum, the engine downshifting itself automatically. It listed to the right, tumbled off the road, and slouched into the ditch with a hollow crunch.

The gunfire had stopped.

The two guards stood with their pistols still in hand, but their feet frozen to the ground like they couldn't quite believe what they'd just done. Dixon, however, seemed not to be encumbered by such thoughts. He raced forward towards the vehicle.

Someone inside was mewling pitifully.

Roy's stomach lurched and squeezed.

He wanted to draw his own weapon, and put Tanner Dixon down like the rabid dog that he was. It would be a goddamned relief, not only for Roy, but for every person that lived in Kanawha 3.

But no.

He didn't do anything.

Because Dixon had been hand-picked to take over the marshal's office. By the Eudys.

Why would someone call the Eudys extremists?

Because of shit like this, he thought to himself bluntly.

But he couldn't stop it from happening. He couldn't be a dissenting voice.

To dissent would be to shake the structure that was already doubtful, but that you so fervently hoped would hold together. It was easy to cry out against something you knew would not fall as a result of what you did. But they were in such dire straits that Roy felt he could not afford to utter a single word. It was that fragile.

And he did not want it to fall apart.

He wanted to win.

He wanted to kick this fucking CoAx out of his country.

He wanted to be a free man again.

Two rapid gunshots drew him back to the moment.

Marshal Dixon was standing at the driver's door, his pistol held out, still smoking in the cold morning air, and the pathetic sounds of dying had ceased.

Dixon spent another moment staring into the vehicle with cold, calculating eyes and Roy had no doubt that what he'd just done was not touching anything inside of that man. It was all corralled into the barrens.

Then Dixon holstered his pistol and turned quite abruptly. He marched back up the road. The Kenners had made it all of fifty yards before rolling into the ditch. When Marshal Dixon had made up half that distance back to the checkpoint, he called out to the guards.

"Clean this shit up before people see it."

Roy stared at him and felt hatred fill him up to the very top, but the surface tension held. It never spilled over. He couldn't afford to let it. He couldn't just go buck wild like Dixon was apparently allowed to do. He had to be controlled.

He was about to go down a dangerous path, and it wouldn't do to make any more enemies. He'd have plenty of them before the week was out.

His Personal Device vibrated gently on his forearm.

He turned stiffly away from the checkpoint, and started trudging back towards the heart of the mining town. He flipped up the monitor and read the message while he walked.

It was from Koz.

Just got back. Have intel.

Roy snapped the monitor shut and quickened his pace.

CHAPTER SIX

"Why are we doing this?" Walter whispered.

This was a day ago. The last time he'd talked to Roy.

Roy looked at him with a frown. "What do you mean?"

They were walking, away from other people. In the warm morning sunshine. No one else was around. Still, they both spoke quietly. That was the nature of the subject.

Walter looked away from his brother. Down at his feet. Crunching through the gravel. His hands were shoved into the pockets of his denim jacket. His thumbs and forefingers were nervously prying at each other.

"Even if we succeed," Walter said. "Even if we get Pops out of there, we're fucked."

Roy sniffed. Flared his nostrils. Stifling a knee-jerk response in favor of a more measured one.

Walter could imagine what Roy had *wanted* to say.

Something along the lines of "How could you even say that? He's our father!"

But Walter *could* say that. Because there was a war going on.

"You say I need to fight," Walter continued. "You say we need to win this war. But this is counterproductive to that." Walter grimaced, hating himself for the words he was saying. "I'm not…shit. I'm not saying I don't want to save Pops."

"Sounds like it," Roy snipped.

Walter sighed. "No. I'm not."

He stopped. There in the dusty gravel. Turned to his brother.

The two of them looking at each other, slipping in and out of the past. Old feelings of camaraderie. New feelings of discomfort. A sense of distance. Something neither of them wanted, but neither wanted to close the gap either.

Roy shook his head. "I can't explain it to you, Walt. I just..." he looked momentarily stricken. "Look what they did to us."

Walter's brow creased. Confused.

"To you and me," Roy clarified, and there came in his voice a tremor that shocked Walter, and shook him. "They took it away from us. They took away what we had." He shook his head, and Walter could tell that he was shaking off the emotion. "I just can't. I was there, Walter. I was there in that place. I lost ten years of my life to it. Ten years of hell. I just can't let Pops go into that. I know what it's like. Not academically. I *know*. And I just can't let them put Pops in there."

Walter watched his brother. He swallowed. His throat felt thick.

"You know he's dying."

"What?" Roy looked surprised.

"Redlung." Walter nodded. Couldn't speak anymore after that.

They stood, silent for a time.

"Doesn't matter," Roy said, quietly.

"Okay." Walter nodded. Put his hand on his brother's shoulder and squeezed him. "We're gonna get him. We'll figure out a way."

That'd been a day ago.

They still hadn't figured out a way.

***

After two days in Kanawha 3, Walter no longer had to be escorted. Which was good.

He hadn't been much of a fan of his babysitter, Sergeant Mason. The man clearly viewed Walter as something akin to a leech, or a garden slug. Something whose purpose in the circle of life is inscrutable. Perhaps just there to be bothersome to others.

Walter didn't care for the way he looked at him.

Dumbfuck grower.

Fuckin' knocker.

That's what the looks said.

Walter had already fought his way through hell and back. He didn't need anyone's praise or back-slapping. But a bit of quiet deference would have been nice.

Apparently, fighting your way through a CoAx purge, going head to head with New Breeds and Lancer cannons and actually managing to make it out alive…apparently that didn't mean shit.

Even Roy, Walter's brother, was still treating him like a knocker.

Like *little brother.*

Like he still had to prove himself.

Fine, Walter thought angrily as he stalked down the hall of the sleeper module where he and Rat and Getty were housed. *Give me a fuckin' chance. You said you wanted me to fight, but you haven't given me a chance.*

So far, Roy'd mostly kept him in the dark.

Kept telling him to be patient.

They were "working on things."

It was difficult to describe the relationship there, between Roy and Walter.

Strained?

No, it wasn't strained. Not in the traditional sense.

But it was like their brotherhood had happened to some past version of themselves, and they'd both become different people in the intervening ten years when neither thought they'd see the other again.

Mostly, they operated as those different people, because it was habit now, the people that they'd become without having to grow around each other, as constant companions do. And who they'd become…well, their personalities clashed a bit.

But deep down inside they were still family. Deep down Walter knew that he'd do anything for Roy, and he knew that Roy would do anything for him—and already had, by pulling his ass out of the fire in District 89.

But…

In way, they were also strangers.

Walter hadn't seen much of Roy since their talk in his room when Roy had told him two very unpleasant truths. One: if he ever wanted to see his wife again, he was going to have to learn to fight so that they could win this war. And two: their father had been captured by the CoAx simply because he was immediate family to Walter.

Walter, whose face had been broadcast to the world for all of one minute and four seconds before the CoAx managed to pinpoint the signal of the terminal he was transmitting from, and shut him down.

But in that one minute and four seconds, Walter had told the country what they needed to do.

If you were ever thinking about doing something, if you'd ever considered saying 'enough is enough,' then maybe you should do something about it right now. Because the situation is only getting worse. It's only going to get harder and harder to fight them.

Of course, the Fed-controlled media sources brought on "experts" that debunked the entire thing, saying that there was no purge happening in District 89 (just a minor skirmish), that the broadcast hadn't even been a live feed, but had in fact been recorded months ago, and lastly, that a man named Walter Lawrence Baucom III did not actually even exist.

The last part was actually partially true.

Walter didn't exist anymore. Not in any sort of public record.

The only place he existed was in slot #17 of a CoAx "Most Wanted" list.

Walter just had to shake his head at the whole giant fuckupedness of it.

He didn't stop at the doors to Getty or Rat's rooms.

They would not be inside.

It was almost eight o'clock. Which meant that their breakfast ration was only being served for another half hour.

To Walter, being hungry was cleansing. Like a hunger strike that only he knew about. It helped him focus. Kind of like the pain of grinding his teeth. It made it a little easier to control himself.

He'd eat dinner, but times were tough for a bunch of renegade troops hiding out in the mountains. And besides, Walter wasn't doing much besides standing around, hating life. So he figured he didn't need many calories to do that.

Meanwhile there were two teams of New Breeds that had defected to this location, and those motherfuckers needed almost four thousand calories a day just to stave off starvation. And they were actually working. Going out. Hitting supply caches. Disappearing like ghosts.

They really creeped Walter out, having them around, but they were doing good work.

He exited out of the sleeper unit, and into the dark cavern of the defunct slurry cistern that had become his home as of two days ago. There were six cisterns in all. Big, fat, squat cylinders. But the mining operation had gone to natural gas a decade ago, and so the cisterns were no longer used to hold coal slurry.

Now they held renegade Fed troops.

Six sleeper units in this one. And it was only about a third full.

The main cistern, where the renegade command was set up, looked like an underground city.

There was one entry point. Technically, a "washway." But it looked like two massive sliding doors. They could open wide enough to let trucks easily in and out, but now they were just cracked. Just enough for one person to get through.

There was a light that was stationed next to the exit. It was blinking red.

There were about a dozen people stacked up next to the exit.

Rat and Getty were among them.

The scent of cigarette smoke wafted over Walter as he approached them. Made him want a cigarette. And it was better than the damp coal-and-cement stink of the cistern.

Getty turned as Walter approached them. He nodded, giving Walter's face a once-over, which had become standard procedure.

"Lookin' better," Getty observed.

Rat pretended to just notice Walter standing there, then pretended to jump out of fright. "Jesus Christ!" He exclaimed, then smiled, showing his rat-like front teeth. He slapped Walter on the shoulder. "Just kidding, buddy. How are you this fine morning?"

"Good," Walt lied. He nodded towards the red light. "How long's this been goin' on?"

"Fifteen minutes," Getty said. "Or at least fifteen minutes since we got out here."

Rat shuffled anxiously. "Gonna miss breakfast."

Walter stared grimly at the light. "Getty. Got a cigarette?"

Getty took out his pack and held it out to Walter.

It took a few tries for Walt to pinch one out.

"Yeah," Getty said as he watched Walt fumble. "Get your dick beaters all over them."

Walter got it out, stuck it in his mouth. Grunted a single-syllable laugh.

Getty pocketed his cigarettes and got out the lighter, which he lit, and held for Walter. He seemed to like to do this for others. Like he considered it a gentlemanly thing to do. "You know," Getty said around his own smoke. "The Pop Shoppe is open to us after twenty-one-hundred. They'll sell a pack to you, too."

The Pop Shoppe was a local convenience store. The owner had agreed to let them come in after-hours and use his store as a sort of commissary.

Walter tasted smoke. Enjoyed it. Blew it out. He eyed Getty. "I'm not a smoker, Getty. I'm not gonna buy a pack of cigarettes."

Getty chuckled and shrugged. "I'm keepin' a tally, you know."

"Alright," Walter said.

The stood and smoked in silence for a minute.

The others waiting on the light to go out talked quietly amongst themselves. There was even a few bouts of laughter.

"Think they're really up there watchin' us?" Rat asked, looking up.

Walter looked up too, even though he knew that he would only see the black ceiling of the cistern. But he knew what Rat meant. He was visualizing the sky beyond. Satellites. Drones. Aircraft with high-resolution imagers. Searching. Looking for any sign of where that little 10% of their military had wandered off to.

Walter shrugged. Looked back down.

"Or," Rat continued. "Do they just turn the fucking lights on any time they get a chill up their back?"

Getty stubbed his cigarette out. Sighed the smoke out of his nose. "Well. I'd rather miss breakfast than get a bomb dropped on me. Know what I mean?"

"Yeah," Rat admitted. "I know what you mean."

Less than a minute later, the light went out.

"Thank God," Rat murmured.

They exited the cistern, single-file.

The bright morning sunlight was blinding after the dim interior of the cistern. The mountain air was cool. The sun felt warm, but if you walked through a shadow, it was downright chilly. The air had that crisp blueness to it that is the sole property of higher elevations.

The messhall was located in a neighboring cistern. Back into the smelly dark, with one last look over their shoulders, wishing they could be out in that nearby town where the sun shined and a pretty waitress could bring them coffee and waffles, rather than freeze-dried toast and rehydrated eggs.

Not that Walter could complain.

He wasn't going to eat the shit anyways.

The messhall was on the tail-end of busy. As Getty and Rat stood in line, most of the people were getting up and clearing their trays. Walter avoided the line. Staked out a seat at a table where no one else was at. Told Rat to snag him a coffee, if he could. Rat was not a coffee drinker and they'd give you a water and one other beverage—either coffee or orange drink.

Orange *drink*, not orange *juice*.

Orange-flavored vitamin C in liquid form.

Walter brushed toast crumbs and a bit of stickiness from the table. Probably from a spill of orange drink. He sat back and waited.

Sergeant Mason and his usual entourage entered. Two other NCOs that were more or less indifferent to Walter's presence. At least they didn't seem to disdain it the way that Mason did.

Mason scanned the room and found Walter, like he'd specifically been looking for him.

Walter just stared back. Wondered if today was the day he was going to get locked up for beating the fuck out of Mason. Did they have a jail here amongst all these modulars hiding in the dark? At first it seemed like a superfluous thing, but then Walt figured they must have one.

Maybe I'll find out today.

Or, another possibility: Mason just waylaid him and left his broken body on the ground.

That was always a possibility.

And that was okay too.

Walter was comfortable with that.

They eyeballed each other for a bit.

Mason stayed with his group. They went to the line.

Eventually Mason rolled his eyes and looked away.

And what was that, just before he'd rolled his eyes?

A tiny flaring of the nostrils?

A twitch of the lips?

Walter smirked.

"What are you smiling about?" Rat said, setting his tray down beside Walt.

Walter shook his head. "Oh, nothing."

"Here's your coffee."

"Thanks."

Getty sat across from them. Immediately started shoveling rehydrated eggs into his mouth.

Walter took a sip of the coffee. It was exactly what you'd expect. "How's breakfast this morning?"

"Just like mother used to make it," Getty replied.

Walter leaned back, watched his compatriot for a moment.

"Getty, tell me your secret."

Getty didn't even look up. "How's that?"

"How are you always so…unflappable?"

Now he did look up. "Un-what?"

"You're always just so level-headed," Walter explained. "You're a cool hand. How do you do it?"

Getty kind of straightened up, as though the question seemed a bit odd to him. He tapped his plastic spork on the serving tray a few times. Sucked some egg from a back tooth. He looked like he was considering saying something. Something actually meaningful.

But then he just shrugged.

"I dunno," he said. "It's just one of my many talents, I guess."

He went back to eating.

Walter sipped coffee.

"Hear anything from your brother?" Rat asked around a mouthful of dry toast.

"Not yet."

"Koz and them were supposed to be back today. Right?"

Unless they got killed.

"Right," Walter nodded.

It wasn't two seconds after that when Walter's PD vibrated on his arm. He felt a little jolt inside of him.

He flipped the monitor up. Read the message.

Felt his heart rate ramp up.

He stood, leaving his coffee.

"Speak of the devil," Walter mumbled, then discreetly: "Come on. They got intel."

CHAPTER SEVEN

The Maglev stopped in Georgia.

At first, Carolyn was able to feel the deceleration of the train.

It was very slight, but she noticed it and she looked out the window. There was nothing around to see. They were passing through countryside. An Agrarian District, by the looks of it.

Which one? Well, she knew they were in Georgia, which meant that it could be any of the Georgian districts, which were 49 through 55.

The fields lay quietly in their neat blocks, under skies that were beginning to threaten, surrounded by trees and striped with hydroponics lines and tractor rails. It looked like Agrarian District 89. Probably most of them did.

She leaned forward.

The man sitting next to her—bodyguard, she supposed—shifted with her, as though he hadn't expected her to move and was suddenly made uncomfortable by her doing so. She leaned slightly across him to see out the window to her left. She looked in the direction that the train was going. Then looked back in the direction that it had come.

Nothing much to see.

Two days in a safe house in Charlotte.

And then, this morning, they'd gotten on this train.

Now, they were reaching their destination, and Carolyn still didn't know where the hell it was.

Definitely not the Agrarian District they were passing through now. Not at the rate that they were decelerating. But something nearby, on the other side of this district.

Atlanta, maybe?

She wasn't familiar with where the Maglevs ran. She'd never been on one before.

"When the train stops," the bodyguard said. "You come with me." He nodded across her to his counterpart. "He's going to split off. Don't worry about him. Don't look at him. Don't look at any of our other elements on board. Don't look at anybody. Just walk with me and act like you're supposed to be here."

Carolyn could no longer feel the deceleration of the train. She looked to the man on her left. "What's your name?"

"I'm John," he responded curtly.

She wondered if that was really his name.

The guy at the safe house had been named Tom. The woman that was with him was Jennifer. Carolyn was starting to think they were all a bunch of made up names. Not even imaginative ones.

She wanted to ask the other bodyguard what his name was, but figured that fell in the "don't even look at him" column, and she remained silent. She decided to think of him as Jason, for no particular reason. He just looked like a Jason to her.

So far, neither John nor Jason had looked at her for more than a flash of the eyes. Their eyes were up and always scanning. But they didn't hold eye-contact with her. As though they were averting their eyes out of respect. Which was very odd to her.

Carolyn looked down into her lap and realized that her hands were gripped together there, the fingers wrestling with each other.

"And my parents?" she said, quieter now, because her stomach was tightening.

Out of the corner of her eye, she perceived that John had finally turned his reticent gaze upon her. She turned to him. His eyes were a cold shade of blue and his face was inexpressive, and unlined, as though he'd gone through life that way, never bearing anything but this still-water calm.

"You'll see them soon," John said, then looked away from her again.

Out the window.

Carolyn followed his gaze.

The countryside was no longer flying by in a blur. Now she could see the individual trees along the Maglev tracks. And in the distance, to where the tracks were gradually and gently curving, a conglomeration of structures completely foreign to her, but which she immediately somehow recognized.

It was not Atlanta.

Not really a city at all. At least not the tall, distinguished line of skyscrapers that she associated with a city.

This was a sprawl of short squat buildings that jumbled together, none of them more than four stories. They spread out across the land in the distance like some body of water that had overflowed its banks with red mud and detritus. It looked from this distance like some vast refugee camp, like all of those buildings were nothing more than shanties all crammed in together.

But the center of the ramshackle sprawl told her everything she needed to know about where they were headed.

It was a square that rose up above the city all around it, like the castle that rises out of a village, and the walls of that square were higher than any other building in the sprawl.

At the corners of those walls, and along it, she could see the gun emplacements. And the small black specks that she knew to be flights of gunships skirted across the horizon, and rose up from out of the walls and went out to do their business, while others came back and settled. The rain created an ugly, foggy haze that sat over the whole picture.

Carolyn's feeling of misgiving ramped up like feedback in her brain, becoming a single, screeching note of alarm that she felt from her chest all the way into her head and seemed to make her mind white hot and her vision snowy.

"CoAx County?" she blurted out. "You're taking me into *CoAx County*?"

"Ssh," John said.

The speakers of the Maglev dinged softly, and a polite, automated voice announced that all passengers disembarking for Hillsboro, Georgia, should now move toward the exits.

John nodded for the small door out of their private cabin. He rose with a briskness that caused Carolyn to rise as well.

Jason remained in his seat, looking out the window as the trees and fields turned to a spotted slurry of old buildings.

John opened the door to the cabin and stepped out, looking conscientiously in both directions. He turned left and started moving towards the front of the train.

Carolyn followed.

In the hallway, she heard other cabin doors opening and closing.

At the end of this car was the connector, and through the clear doors she could see a crowded passenger area with many people beginning to rise from their seats and pull their luggage from overhead racks, or stretch their arms and backs. Others remained seated, glad to be rid of their close neighbors and looking forward to more leg room.

Carolyn took a glance up and down the hall, but saw no one immediately within earshot. She hurried after John. There wasn't quite enough room in the hall to walk abreast, so she walked close behind him.

"Shouldn't we have some sort of story?" she asked under her breath. "Like you're my husband or something?"

John shook his head once. "The less you talk the better."

Carolyn burned a bit. Felt it in her cheeks and knew her face was flushing. "So just let you do all the talking? Wouldn't want the country bumpkin fucking shit up."

John gave her a sidelong glance that showed a shred of surprise—heavens to Betsy, the man could have an emotion!—but it was gone just as quickly and he tapped the button for the sliding door to the car connector.

"No," he said in a quiet tone that wished to leave it be and not draw any attention. "*None* of us are going to talk if we can help it."

The sliding doors opened and they stepped into the connector. The door closed behind them. The air in the connector was cooler, but also more humid. For a brief moment, they were in that small space, and both doors were closed.

John turned fully to her. "Carolyn…" he said, and then stopped, and his brow furrowed. "Do you prefer Carolyn or Stephanie?"

For a moment, Carolyn was about to tell him that the PD they'd given her bore the identification of one Jessica Ballantyne, but that would have been just a childish dig and she felt their time growing taught, and knowing that she was balanced on it made her want to limit her speech.

"Carolyn," she said.

"Fine," he said, his voice clipped. "Carolyn. Listen. Don't forget that five of our operatives—good people—died getting you out of that district. I treat you with the deference you deserve as a Eudy, but let's be clear—my job is to get you back to them. If I have to knock you unconscious to do it, I won't have a problem with that. We've made it ninety-percent of the way there without getting killed or captured, so please don't fuck it up at the very end, okay?"

Carolyn clenched her jaw. But she nodded.

What could she say?

What could she do?

Oh, she wanted to give him an earful. And all of the words that she was thinking still managed to pile up in her brain. But she hadn't the time or the impetus to spew them out, so she kept them to herself, and she felt that that was wise.

She was in John's world right now.

What was she outside of this world?

Well, not too long ago, she'd been a woman with sore, tired feet, wearing clothing that smelled of fryer grease, looking forward to taking it easy and finally having a night off with her husband. Looking forward to a night that would never happen, because the second the key turned in her door, her life had been turned upside-down.

And now she was here.

Okay.

Adapt.

She could do that.

A long time ago, she'd adapted.

She'd been a kid when Benjamin and Jean Eudy had been taken from her. Taken to DTI, where people *do not come back.* And they'd both been taken in the same night. So in one moment she'd had everything taken from her—her parents, her house, her school, her friends—and she'd been dumped in the care of the Fed.

A ward of the state.

And shipped to a new Agrarian District in North Carolina that she'd been completely unfamiliar with.

District 89.

And she'd adapted then.

Even though she thought that her life was over, she'd managed to adapt.

That was what she needed to do now.

She never did give John a response, but he took her silence as affirmation, and he pressed the button to open the other side of the car connector.

As it slid open, the sounds of the people on the other side drifted in, and it wasn't as abrasive as Carolyn had been expecting. There was very little conversation, and what there was seemed quiet and reserved.

She immediately noticed that most of it was not in English.

The cadence of it was off.

The sound of it was skewed.

She took a better glance at the people as John led her down the aisle, being careful to stay with him as they dodged between people that were interjecting themselves out of their chairs and into the paths of others, many of them bleary eyed and wrinkle-faced from sleep.

Most of them were Russians, she thought. There was a distinctness in the manner in which they dressed that was neither grower, nor urby, nor anything else American. Somehow, as close as their cultures had become intertwined, they'd never quiet synced up when it came to how they dressed.

But that was the nature of CoAx County—more Russians and Chinese than there were Americans.

A few generations ago, it had just been a section of national forest in Georgia.

But since then it had been requisitioned by a Sino-Russian partnership. Because they didn't want to set up shop at any of the extant Fed military bases. They didn't want their troops quartered directly alongside the American troops, whose loyalty to the Coalition was often questioned.

So they procured themselves a piece of soil, and that chunk of Georgia became a base for both the Chicoms and the Russians. A sort of hub for all of the troops and supplies and equipment that arrived in the Continental United States from points abroad.

All around this hub had sprung up the haphazard growth that has accompanied every military base since the dawn of militaries—an entire economy and society based upon the military, with the base as its core, its nucleus, the center of its universe.

Because soldiers needed entertainment. They needed booze. They needed sex.

Hell, they even needed families.

There was no small amount of American women who'd born sons and daughters to Chinese and Russian troops, only to weep when they finished their long tours and went back home to their *real* families. And now all those faux-families lived in the shadows of the walls of CoAx County and scratched a living out of catering to the constant influx of Russians and Chinese.

So the wind blows.

And so was born the sprawling dismality of CoAx County, which had the look from afar and from up close, of something from a mediocre country that has suffered greatly under a tide of refugees.

And here, walking the aisles of the Southern Maglev as it made its final, slowing approach towards CoAx County, she listened to the foreign tongues being spoken and felt that she was no longer in her own country.

There were a few Chinese in the mix as well, but this car at least was mostly Russians, and the Chinese that were there kept quiet, standing and waiting dutifully for the train to stop.

John looked neither right nor left.

Carolyn mimicked him and kept her gaze straight ahead. Fixed on John's back.

They reached the end of the train car.

Into and out of another connector.

Into another passenger car, just like the last, except that in this one the aisle was mostly jammed with people, the line to exit now having been formed by forty or so tired humans who swayed back and forth on their feet.

John sidled up very close to the man at the end of the line. An older man in a glistening shirt that was some sort of Tartan pattern imbued with gold thread. He had a single paper bag that he held by corded handles and stared blankly forward. He did not notice John, or bother to look behind him when John's shoulder rubbed his.

In fact, they were all packed in quite closely.

Carolyn didn't like it. She wanted about an arm's length of personal space, but that wasn't going to happen.

More people poured into them from the back. The shifted close to her, bumping elbows and shoulders. They seemed to spy the gap between her and John, and, based on the tone of their mutterings, she gathered that they disdained such a waste of precious real estate. That two-foot gap could possibly keep them from the timely discharge of their schedules.

Suddenly self-conscious, Carolyn moved forward to where she was shoulder-to-breast with John.

The couple behind her filled in the gap quickly, and muttered no more.

Carolyn was not quite sure why she felt so enormously uncomfortable touching John in that moment. After all, they'd been shoulder-to-shoulder in the cabin seats only moments ago, and she'd been too lost in thought to care.

She turned to her right, to the window that showed the outside world, and she watched the cityscape creep by. It had a run-down look to it that seemed both sad and darkly amused by itself.

Like a disfigured man that has made peace with his appearance.

The gloomy scene outside was wet with a cold, weary drizzle that came out of the gutters and downspouts looking like dirty bathwater. It moved by slowly now, at almost a parade-speed, and still slowing, gradually slowing, until suddenly it stopped, and the image that she saw beyond that window was of a collection of short buildings with disastrous metal stairs circling their outside walls and power cables running haphazardly to and fro.

A projected sign provided a stark golden glow in the rain. The sign was on the side of a building, directly in front of her field of view. It manically blinked and declared

LUCKY'S DOUBLE-O RANCH
GET LUCKY!!!

And then alternately,

XXX

GIRLS GIRLS GIRLS
LUCKY LUCKY LUCKY

The second that the train came to a full stop in front of Lucky's Double-O Ranch, there was a polite little hydraulic hiss, followed by the same dim voice declaring, "Thank you!" repeatedly.

The foreign conversation in the train car grew from a murmur to a roar, and the line began to move forward, and the profuse gratitude of the train's computer was drowned out in the rude babble.

John and Carolyn started forward at a shuffle, as though it would be the worst sin to allow any sort of space to grow between themselves and the man with the gold, Tartan shirt. The shuffle continued at an annoying pace until they reached the end of the train car, hung a right, and found the open doors that were issuing this procession of people out into the sodden cityscape.

All their faces blinked gold and red with promises of LUCKY and GIRLS.

Just before they hit the bottleneck of those doors, the man in the glittering Tartan shirt held his arm back behind him. And John's hand was immediately there to intercept his. The movement was so fast and close—something exchanged between them—that even though it was right in front of Carolyn's face, she almost missed it.

Then the door came, and the world opened, and the glittering Tartan shirt went left, and John and Carolyn went right, along a surprisingly affluent-looking train station. Or maybe it only looked like that because it was juxtaposed to the muck of CoAx County.

Out of the train car, Carolyn let her personal space return to normal.

John kept walking straight forward.

The air hit her. It was warm. Almost muggy. It smelled like exhaust and fried foods.

Ahead of them, the crowd from the train was dispersing, and further down the station, other train cars with other exits were still dribbling out their passengers. Hundreds of people, all walking in different directions, some of them forming little currents as they headed towards certain shared points.

John was angling to the left a bit, away from the train.

Carolyn followed and saw that they were headed for a rack of lockers.

"We're being followed," John said.

CHAPTER EIGHT

We're being followed.

"Oh?" Carolyn replied, because she could think of nothing else to say.

"I'll handle it," John said.

His hand brushed hers.

Carolyn felt a little tingle of shock—the thought that he was trying to hold her hand, and she almost jerked away—but then she realized he was passing her something. She took it without looking. It felt like a piece of metal attached to a rubberized tag.

"Key to a locker," he said. "I'm going to split up. Get whatever is in that locker and keep walking toward exit C. I'll catch up to you."

"You're going to split off?" Carolyn asked, her voice tightening.

But when she turned, he had already done it, and was melting into the tide of people.

Sonofabitch...

Her heart clawed its way up her throat, then jumped back down into her stomach.

Son of a BITCH!

She wanted desperately to look around, to see if she could spot the follower, or maybe see where John had gone.

Instead, she remained eyes forward, fixated on the wall of lockers.

She felt the key fob. Felt the key.

She looked down at it.

Her knuckles were white. She was gripping it with her finger tips and her fingers were aching with the pressure of it. She needed to relax. She could feel her gait becoming awkward with tension.

The key was a typical coded maglock. The number on the fob was "23."

The lockers were clearly marked and she spotted number 23 without having to look for it.

It was one of the tall lockers. About four feet tall. On top of the tall lockers was a row of short lockers that were only about two feet square.

What the fuck was in the large locker?

And then, since she'd asked that question of herself, she couldn't dismiss the image of a body in a black bag, although surely, surely, surely, that was ridiculous.

Still…the size and color of those lockers made her think of the steel boxes where most growers were crammed upon their deaths and turned into ashes to adorn their family's mantles forever.

She reached locker 23.

Passed the little maglock tab over the cheerful yellow circle, which blinked green and beeped so loudly she thought she'd draw attention until she realized that there were about fifteen other people accessing lockers at that moment, and the air was filled with those insistent beeps.

She yanked the locker door open.

Inside was a black bag.

Her heart skipped a beat.

It was a large bag. It filled up the locker.

Oh, holy fuck…

But no. This was a narrow bag. And it wasn't rubber. It was canvas.

It was a sports duffel. Long and durable.

She grabbed it because there was nothing else to do, and she yanked it out of the locker and froze, staring at it. It weighed heavy in the straps that she held it with, and she heard something clank and rattle inside and she did not like the sound of it. She thought maybe she knew what it was.

You get caught with this…

But of course, that was a silly thought.

If she got caught at all, the contents of the bag wouldn't matter.

Her identity would be the thing that mattered.

And if they found out who she was, then it would be off to DTI with her, never to return again.

She closed the locker door at which point another automated voice spoke up, telling her to return the key to the key box on the front of the door, and that if the key was not returned, the cost of the replacement key would be billed to a guy named Jonathan Scharner. Then the computer announced an exorbitant amount of money for a replacement key.

She put the key in the box as instructed.

The computer thanked her cheerily.

She turned back in the direction that she and John had originally been heading. To her right, the train had already closed its doors and begun moving again. At the end of the concourse, she saw a large, white and blue sign projected in the air that read EXIT C.

She began walking for it.

Each step was a second counted in an interminable hour.

She was waiting for John to rejoin her, *needed* for him to rejoin her, because he'd only told her to go to Exit C, which she was doing, but there weren't any instruction that had followed that, so once she got to Exit C, what the fuck was she supposed to do?

A million possibilities started branching out in her brain.

She began to wonder if this was a mistake.

She began to doubt the competence of the individual who had introduced himself as John.

No one was infallible. Everyone made mistakes.

Maybe this was his mistake.

Maybe Carolyn was now walking with her proverbial ass in the wind.

Maybe she was now abandoned in CoAx County without a friend or a dime to her name.

She realized that her own train of thought was causing her heartrate to spike.

She kept counting the steps to Exit C, and it was drawing terribly close.

Right about the point when she was convinced that all was lost, John fell in step with her, although his pace was slightly more rushed than hers had been, and again, he spoke in that calm, conversational tone that completely contradicted his words.

"We're gonna need to make a move. Are you ready?"

Carolyn swallowed and realized her mouth was dry as a bone.

But she still managed to croak out, "Yes."

The station platform was elevated above the ramshackle city around them.

Exit C was the last exit off the platform. The clean white concrete and steel formed a staircase that led to the road below. The road was paved, but poorly, and the red Georgia mud seeped up through the cracks and seams. The staircase grew rustier-looking the further down it got, until you could hardly distinguish it from the mud-slogged road below.

John took the stairs, this time pulling Carolyn along with him. They were no longer walking, they were jogging now. Their feet fluttered down the stairs with a little staccato rhythm. An old, fat woman laboring up the stairs with a suitcase nearly as big as herself stopped to let them slip by. She gave them a reproachful look.

"Do you see that storefront?" John asked, his voice trembling with his footfalls as they went down the stairs. "The blue sign."

Carolyn glanced up and saw it.

Two buildings down, to the right.

A blue sign that read "Seller's Consignment."

She read off the name and looked left at John.

He nodded. "We're going inside. As soon as the door closes, we run for the back. Understand?"

She nodded. That was about all she could manage.

For a half a second, there upon the third or fourth step from the ground, she had a minor split from reality and she hovered above herself, saw herself being towed along by this stranger named "John"—*bullshit, his name's not John*—and herself carrying a duffel that was full of things she didn't want to think about.

Guns

She wanted to be anywhere else.

It was the feeling that things were so outrageously off-kilter, that it couldn't possibly be reality.

When your day-to-day reality consists of a steady schedule and the same drive to the same place to work with the same people and cook the same food for the same customers, every day for nearly a decade…well, then your world is pretty cloistered, isn't it?

This sharp new reality was jarring and uncomfortable, like plunging into an ice bath when you're fresh out of a hot shower.

The only thing that kept her sane in that moment, the only thing that kept her feet moving and her eyes focused on the door to "Seller's Consignment," was the fact that the stress of the last two days had inoculated her.

She'd almost become accustomed to this surreal, floating sensation.

Then her feet hit the rust-colored puddle at the bottom of the steps and she felt the cold, dirty water in her shoes. The same damn shoes she wore to work. The ones with the non-slip soles so she wouldn't wipe out and bust her ass on a patch of fryer grease.

She came back to herself.

Adapt!

They moved down the street.

John had released his guiding hand on her elbow. He was more circumspect now, his head swiveling back and forth, checking every corner, staring down every shadow. More than once he looked behind them, but he did it casually. He disguised it with other movements, like crossing the street or pointing out a sign.

Were they still being followed?

Right now?

If she looked behind her, would someone be looking back?

They'd exited the staircase on the left side of the street, and had now crossed the two lane road. The road was just a spur—a dead end—that terminated in the station platform. Taxis and shuttles rumbled back and forth, trying to make their bread for the day.

John and Carolyn dodged between them and made it to the other side of the street. The cracked and pitted sidewalk flew under their feet. The sign directly ahead of them, splashing the wet sidewalk with glowing blue.

John slowed them to a walk.

Businesslike. Purposeful.

They reached the door. John stepped forward and held it open for her, and even gave her a jaunty smile as she passed him by, as though they were a couple out to do some shopping. Somehow, she managed to smile back, though she felt nothing at all in her soul except a queer sort of thrill.

She stepped into the consignment store without breaking her stride.

There were mountains of crap everywhere, and it was poorly organized.

Some antiques, some tech, some toys, some clothes.

The place smelled musty and disused.

She looked to her right and saw a counter that was obviously the checkout, and a man behind it, who stared back at her with a stiffness and intensity that was awkward, but then the jingling of the bell over the door brought his attention back and he seemed to recognize John.

The two exchanged a nod.

"Run," John said.

Carolyn darted forward. He'd told her to run to the back, and that's what she intended to do.

She dodged around piles of clutter and shelves holding bric-a-brac of what use she couldn't begin to imagine. But her ears, her ears were exquisitely attuned for the ringing of that bell, wondering if it was going to ring again, if someone was going to follow them into the store.

She reached the back.

A wall.

A door.

Clearly marked EXIT.

She started for it, and realized that John was right there, already pushing through it.

The back of the store was dark, but when he hit that push-bar on the door, even the pale glimmer of sunlight that was managing to make it through the clouds seemed to blind her.

From the front of the store, the bell rang.

"Hello!" the clerk called, over-loud. "Can I help you find something?"

John and Carolyn slipped through the back door.

More chilly air. More humidity.

It only took a moment for her eyes to adjust.

She was in an alley that smelled of natural gas and also vaguely of spoiling meat.

There was a black car idling directly in front of her.

John was already on the back passenger's door of the car, which he ripped open, not sparing a glance in Carolyn's direction, or a word to instruct her. His eyes stayed fixed on the door to the back of the store.

Carolyn tumbled into the car.

Fake leather that had long since gone to waste and ruin. Gone was the gas-and-meat smell of the alleyway and here now was the smell of a car's heated air, re-warming the ghost of French fries long passed.

Carolyn turned to look.

John was now at the side of the back door of Seller's Consignment, and he had drawn something that she hadn't noticed on his person before, but with a flick of his wrist she saw it extend into a mean little sliver of metal, and he held it low, but close to his body.

What the hell's he going to do with that?

Carolyn was still clutching the duffel, and she let it slough out of her arms. It hit the floorboard with a metallic clank and clatter that made her cringe.

She got a vague impression of the driver as he craned his neck to see her.

He was older, white-haired, and had a look in his eyes that was nothing short of wonderment.

The back door burst open.

A woman stood there.

A young lady, actually. Fair-faced, and red-haired. A wholesome look about her that said that she could have been pulled from any Agrarian District in the States, told to dress in the fine gray peacoat that she wore, and she would have fit the bill perfectly.

The young woman's eyes hit the car, then the door—which was still open—and then found Carolyn, who was sitting inside.

Perhaps the young woman's eyes had needed a moment to adjust, just like Carolyn's.

It was odd, but seeing her standing there in her posh, urby attire and her wholesome face, her fine red hair framing her features nicely, Carolyn almost smiled, almost wanted to ask her what was wrong, why she had been following them, *had* she even been following them?

But Carolyn was never able to ask any of those questions because John swept up behind the young lady and he hooked his arm firmly around her chin and neck and then he made a thrusting movement with the other hand, right into the base of her skull.

The young, pleasant-looking woman went rigid, and then limp.

Carolyn couldn't help herself. She cried out and reached for the young woman, like she might save her from John.

John bore the entire weight of the limp body, as you might bear a drunken friend, and he tumbled the whole package into the car. Then he got in himself.

Carolyn backpedaled as the young woman sprawled across the seat.

John wrenched out whatever he'd planted in the back of the woman's skull.

There was a sickening sound—metal scraping on bone.

John reached out and closed the car door.

Carolyn stared in horror, her mouth working.

The red-haired woman was half in the seat and half out, and her head was twisted in a limp, dead-animal way, and her eyes were half-open, and though they clearly were not seeing, Carolyn felt like they were seeing *her*.

Carolyn belted out a yelp and did the only thing she could think of doing in that moment.

She struck the face hard with the palm of her hand, shoving it way, shoving it back, shoving it so that the head was now at an even *more* awkward angle, but at least the eyes were looking somewhere else.

John slapped the front passenger seat and spoke loudly, stress coming out of his voice like the first waves of a bad storm as it begins to shake your windows and rattle your walls: "Go, Brady! Get us the fuck out of here!"

The small car rocketed forward, carrying them towards the train station for a single block and then taking a hard left turn and delving into the cesspool of CoAx County.

Carolyn kept trying to get away from the body, but she was already against the opposite door. She knew the answer to the question, but felt the imperative need to ask it anyways, almost as irresistible as some automatic physical function like blinking or breathing.

"Did you kill her?"

John was looking ahead at the road and the buildings. And then he looked behind them, craning his neck this way and that in order to see. And then finally, almost irritated, as though it was somewhat of a bother for him, he looked down at the body that was laid across the seat between himself and Carolyn. He reached out with his thumb and his forefinger and he touched her neck for a moment.

John retracted his hand and went back to looking around. "She's dead," he announced.

Carolyn felt like vomiting. It came on her very abruptly and she only barely avoided doing it.

"Is she a Fed?" Carolyn croaked. "Who the hell is she?"

"Someone that was following us," John said sharply.

Carolyn felt a sudden bloom of rage. She reached forward—across the body—and she wailed out a punch, which was the same type of punch she would give to Walt when he was being an ass.

John took the hit with a look of minor offense. "What?"

"That's a fucking *person*!" Carolyn shouted. "Is she Fed? Who the fuck is she? Don't you think you should know before you fucking *kill* them?"

John frowned at her. "No. I don't need to 'know' a goddamned thing. You wanna stay alive, don't you? Well, then don't wait around to ask questions." John looked forward, but Carolyn saw the sidelong glance at the body, a hesitancy, a discomfort that belied his callous attitude.

Carolyn wanted to continue to argue, but she stopped herself. She leaned forward and grabbed the body with a resoluteness that seemed to surprise John, and she heaved it up from where it was slouched onto the floorboards.

The head lolled and Carolyn struggled not to be sick.

She pulled open the pea coat and stuck her hand inside with her teeth gritted, hating how the body was still so warm, the flesh so soft. She felt like a pickpocket that could, at any moment, get caught.

She touched what she'd been feeling for.

In the waistband, at the small of the woman's back.

She grabbed it and drew it out.

It was a small, subcompact pistol. Barely bigger than Carolyn's hand.

John looked at it. He did not seem surprised.

He glanced at Carolyn as though to say *See?*

Carolyn slumped back in the seat.

The car took a sharp right turn. Now heading directly towards the heart of CoAx County.

John looked behind them, then tapped the front seat. "Okay, Brady. Slow up."

The car slowed to a more reasonable pace, though it still jockeyed around other cabs and cars and came close to mowing down pedestrians more than once. Though, in Brady's defense, this didn't seem an uncommon occurrence on the streets of CoAx County.

John leaned over the body and began rummaging through the pockets. He found nothing. Not even a scrap of paper. He seized the PD that was biometrically attached to the inside of the dead woman's wrist and pulled it from her skin with a slight sucking-peeling sound.

"Clean body," John announced. "Not a shred of any regular-person shit on her. Just a gun and a PD." He looked at Carolyn from under his brows. "Still think she was asking for directions?"

Carolyn looked down at the pistol in her hand. "No."

John gestured to the pistol. "Do you mind? Best not to hang onto these things. Never know what might be tracked."

Carolyn handed it to him like he'd told her it was diseased.

John had the gun and the PD in his lap now, and he was pulling on a pair of rubber gloves. As he worked, he nodded to the duffel bag on the floorboard. "Open that up. We might need what's inside."

Carolyn bent for the bag, but kept an eye on John.

With the rubber gloves on, John took the two items from his lap and arranged them in his palm. Then he pulled a small bottle from his inside jacket pocket and spritzed something that smelled strongly chemical over the two objects. Then he flipped them over. Then he spritzed the other side. Then he opened the window and tossed them out.

"What about the body?" Carolyn asked.

"We'll take care of it," John said, then looked at her, then at the duffel again. "The bag, Carolyn."

She grabbed the tabbed zippers and pulled them in separate directions. Like eviscerating some animal's gutsack. Three subguns shifted as the duffel holding them tightly together came open.

"You ever used one?" John asked.

Carolyn shook her head grimly.

John reached over the dead woman's body and grabbed one. "Well, you'll figure it out. Go ahead and take one. CoAx County is not a safe place for us."

Carolyn looked at him with furrowed brow. "Then why the fuck am I here?"

John actually laughed at her as he chambered a round into the subgun. "Carolyn, there's nowhere in the world that's safe for you right now."

CHAPTER NINE

Roy was tapping an imaginary watch on his wrist.

Walter stopped as he came into the common area that existed in the center of three sleeper units erected in a triangle. He stared at his brother, honestly puzzled for a moment, because they'd come straightaway after receiving the message.

"We came as soon you told us," Walter said.

"Time's wasting," Roy said sharply.

Walter's face darkened. He parsed through a few likely responses, all of which ended in some version of telling Roy to cram it. He decided not to say anything. That was best. He couldn't control the blackness in his head, but he could control his actions.

Getty glided past him into the common area, giving him a light hand on his shoulder, as though to express that he felt Walter's pain.

In the common area was a metal picnic table that had seen better years, and had likely been stolen from some local playground, and a propane heater, because if there was one thing they had plenty of here in Kanawha 3, it was propane. The heater was hissing and blazing busily away.

At the picnic table, Chief Kozlowski—Koz, informally—sat with a bare back to the propane heater, hunched with his elbows on the table. He looked like nothing so much as a grizzly bear that has found a park bench with some old picnic leavings on it.

The big New Breed stroked his prodigious beard and nodded to Walter silently.

Roy was standing off to the side of the picnic table.

Walter and Rat and Getty stopped at the other side of the table, facing Koz.

"This a safe place to talk?" Walt asked.

Koz cast a glance over each shoulder, then waved the concern away. He had no tattoos, unlike a lot of the other New Breeds. Just a lot of muscle that coiled and jumped as he moved, under skin so dusted with freckles it was almost tan.

"The others are still in debrief. I managed to slip away. It's safe enough."

Getty swung his leg over the bench seat and sat down. "Did you find her?"

Koz eyed the man like perhaps he had committed a grave sin by sitting at the table. But then he nodded, just once. "Yeah."

Rat stepped up to the table. "Is she okay? She's not…" He cut himself off.

Koz shook his head. "No. She's not dead. Not that the lists say anyways. Keep in mind, the list we got was off one of the dead agents. We have no way of knowing how accurate that list still is. It could be outdated."

Getty leaned back and clasped his fingers together. "So she got captured."

"M-hm. That's what she's listed as. Under the other name. Not the Bobbi name you gave me. The Alice Corning one."

Getty nodded, then, as an aside to Walter: "Bobbi was an assumed name. Alice was her real name. Before she got involved in the Honeycutt organization."

"So they knew that name?" Walt asked Koz.

The New Breed nodded. "She was hot-listed under it."

"Fuck-all," Rat mumbled. "Wonder how many of our names they have?"

Koz shrugged. "I was only looking for Alice. Or Bobbi. Whatever you guys call her. And yes, they have her. If she's still alive, anyways."

Now Walt turned and faced his brother. "Is it possible to get them both? Pops and Bobbi?"

Roy put his hands on the table and leaned on them. "I think so. Long shot, but it's better than no shot." He looked at Koz and prompted him with a nod.

Koz took a moment to stretch his back. His neck. It was visually impressive. “Car accident,” he said, cryptically. “Need a fuckin’ masseuse.” When he settled back down to the table, he looked at Walt. “Yeah, we can get ‘em both. We got good intel off the guy we just rescued. It’s solid and reliable. He says that there’s only going to be one convoy for those captured in District Eighty-Nine. They’re doing it in one trip in order to limit exposure. Don’t want constant caravans of poor doomed fucks flowing out of the district for anyone with a PD to broadcast on a live feed.”

“So one convoy,” Walt said, nodding. “Which means that we can possibly get both Pops and Bobbi in one hit.”

Koz smiled broadly, as though he found Walt’s naïveté endearing. “Possibly.”

“I know it’s a long shot,” Walt said, grudgingly.

“Real long.”

“But is it unreasonable?”

Koz shrugged. Then threw a thumb over at Roy. “Depends on what your brother can get his hands on.”

Roy made a face and stared intensely at the tabletop.

Walter read him easily and fluidly. It’d never been hard. Ten years of not seeing each other had changed Roy’s face somewhat, but it was still easy for Walter to read him.

Ten years in DTI had given him some scars, too.

But he still looked like Roy.

Which was to say, he looked like their mother—God rest her soul. Rounded features, almost soft—particularly in the mouth and nose—as opposed to Walt who favored his father’s hawkish nose and angular face.

If Roy wasn’t such a perpetual asshole, he might’ve been perceived as a pretty man. But he frowned all the time and flattened his lips. Something he’d done since childhood, Walt remembered. Something that a teenaged Virgil used to refer to as “Grundle Face.”

Grundle Face or no, this was the face that Walt knew.

And what Roy was saying on his face was that he had something, some ace up his sleeve that could solve their problems, he was just very hesitant about using it.

“Roy,” Walt said, trying not to sound reprimanding. “If you got something that’ll help us…”

Roy gave Walter the quintessential Grundle Face. "It's not that simple."

Walter raised his eyebrows. "Okay. Can you tell me why or do you just want to keep us all in the fucking dark a little while longer?"

Roy stared at him, not giving an inch. Doing his level best to chop Walter down to size with his all-powerful gaze. Walter just stared right back.

Rat fidgeted. Cleared his throat.

Eventually, Roy turned to Koz, and his expression changed, and Walter saw that he was at the cusp of a decision. Actually he was making. Yes. There it was.

Decision made.

"It ain't just me," Roy said. "It'll land you in hot water too."

Koz suddenly laughed. A gut-busting laugh. A booming laugh. It seemed like it was going to rattle the sleeper units and blow the propane heater out. "The three biggest super powers in the world want me dead," he said, stifling himself. "You think I'm worried about Colonel Wainwright?"

Roy smiled mirthlessly. Leaned back. Stuck his hands in his denim jacket pockets. "I suppose not."

Koz straightened his face out amid a few sniffs. Then he grew very serious, putting his elbows on the table top. "Besides. Father for a father. I owe you this."

Roy held the New Breed's gaze. Very intensely.

"What?" Walter interjected quietly. "What's that mean?"

Koz diverted his sharp eyes to Walter. "We all know the CoAx likes to hit the family of a detractor. Well…I have parents too. And I didn't want them in DTI when I decided to defect." Koz nodded his head in Roy's direction. "Your brother made sure they got out clean and safe. And so there's essentially no way I can say 'no' to this operation and still have a set of balls."

Walter looked at Roy neutrally for a moment.

Roy seemed uncomfortable under his gaze. "I would've done the same for Pops, but…things moved too quickly. I had a lot more forewarning with Koz's parents. And besides. The Eudys were much more willing to devote resources to convince New Breeds to defect. They wouldn't have done the same just to protect a couple of growers, if you know what I mean."

Roy took a steadying breath and focused himself back on Koz. "Anyone else from your team?"

"Javon," Koz said. "That crazy fucker'll do it. For the love of violence, he'll do it. I probably won't even hassle the rest of the guys. Two New Breeds will bring you plenty of trouble and attention. Any more than that I don't think we'll be able to move about unseen."

Roy nodded. "Okay. I like Javon."

"Good. Me too."

Roy looked at Walter. Then Rat, then Getty. "There's only a small window. We only get one shot at that convoy."

It felt like the box that Walter was crunched inside of had just fallen to pieces and Walter was able to stretch himself. It was the relief of standing after a long car-ride.

"We're ready," Walt said, not even trying to disguise the eagerness in his voice. "I can't take another day of this place."

"Good," Roy said. "Because we're going to have to leave tonight."

Koz nodded. "The convoy moves tomorrow night, if everything goes on schedule. We gotta hustle if we wanna make it, or we're gonna be way behind the ball."

Getty raised his hand, as though he were a kid in a classroom. "Real quick, gentlemen," he said, probingly. "We kinda glossed over the part where you explained how exactly four busted resistance fighters and two New Breeds were going to take on a whole convoy." His eyes tracked between Roy and Koz. "I mean, don't get me wrong. I'm on board. But…you know…I'd like to know what I'm walking into."

Walter kept his eye on Roy the entire time, because he was easier to read than Koz—not that Koz was particularly difficult. Just different, really. The New Breeds were all a little different.

Roy did not particularly like being questioned, that much was obvious. He wanted everyone to have blind faith in him. He wanted to be some old school general whose orders were obeyed simply because they'd come out of his mouth. He had little patience for explaining himself.

But he was also reasonable—mostly—and Getty had a point.

Roy took his time considering and framing his response.

"I may have access to a weapon that could…" he waffled his hands. "…level the playing field a bit."

Getty's lips pursed. He sniffed. Then started fishing out a cigarette. "Okay. Level the playing field. That sounds great. What is it?"

"Something the Eudys have been working on for a while now." Roy grimaced. "And they're gonna be real pissed if they find out we used it." He quirked a thoughtful eyebrow. "On the other hand, we could articulate our actions as proof of concept. You know. Proving that the weapon actually works before the Eudys put all their eggs into that basket. Which could possibly mitigate how pissed they'd be. Possibly."

Getty lit his cigarette and shrugged. "That don't befront me much, Roy. I worked for the Honeycutt organization up until you pulled me out of Eighty-Eighty-Nine. I'm sure the Eudys don't like me much anyhow."

Walter leaned forward, concerned about another aspect of the situation now. Because they were talking about a *weapon.* A weapon that the *Eudys* had created. And the Eudys were *extremists*, at least according to everyone outside of their organization.

"What about collateral damage, Roy?" Walt asked. "This gonna wipe out a bunch of civilians, too?"

"No," Roy replied. "It's designed only to affect New Breeds."

Walter rocked back on his heels a bit. "That's why they've been kidnapping the New Breeds. They're doing testing on them, aren't they?"

Roy only nodded. Then he turned to Koz. "We need a way out of this place. I'll leave that to you and Javon. You figure out how to get us out. I'll meet back up with you around…when?"

"Make it twenty hundred."

"Twenty hundred then." Roy turned and disconnected himself from the picnic table. Then he looked Walter, Getty, and Rat square in the eyes. "You three come with me. Don't say a fuckin' word. Just follow."

Walter didn't care for Roy's brusqueness, but for the moment, his curiosity outweighed his irritation, and he found it easy to brush aside.

Koz got up from the table and went to one of the sleeper units.

Roy started walking out of the triangular common area.

Walt and his two companions followed.

Roy didn't say a word to them. He just marched out. Hung a hard right onto what could only be described in Walt's mind as "Main Street." It was a large space, wide enough for two trucks to drive abreast. It ran the length of the cistern, and bisected the clusters of modulars and temporary buildings like the dusty main drag of an old-timey Western town.

This place was organized chaos. The right half of the cistern—as divided by the "Main Street"—was mainly sleeper units, all crammed in together. The left side was command modules. Generators abounded, filling the air with noise and diesel exhaust. Power cables ran everywhere over their heads, and also across the ground.

People milled back and forth. The movement was constant.

On the left side of the street, two soldiers in uniform walked with purpose.

To their right, a group of five sprinted past in some competitive workout. Getty watched them over his cigarette like he thought they were silly.

Further down, a trio of New Breeds sat outside of another set of sleeper units. All three of them were dressed in what looked like skivvy shorts. Nothing else. Their body-modded forms hulked there in the harsh stadium lighting that set the air aglow and made the shadows black.

They lounged, the way big cats lounge when they are conserving energy. Leaning on walls. Sitting on stairs. The only one standing was smoking a cigar and peering through the smoke, straight at Walt.

Walt stared back, unbowed. But he couldn't stop feeling like they might try to kill him at any second.

It was hard to accept. Like trusting a biting dog that has recently returned from obedience school. Looking at that one lounging there, smoking that cigar, his mind threw him back to an unpleasant childhood memory that existed, isolated, in a sort of mist of forgetfulness.

He and Roy were kids. In bed. It was late. They were supposed to be asleep. But someone was at the front door, and they could hear their parents talking to them in low tones. And someone was outside their window, but the curtains were drawn and all they could see was a hazy half-form in the moonlight, and Walter was terrified.

Walter remembered going to that window like a kid in a trance. He didn't want to pull back those curtains, but then, he felt like he had to.

He'd pulled them back suddenly, as though expecting something to jump out at him.

And in their backyard was a New Breed. A Russian. He was kneeling on the ground, his battlerifle propped up on his chest, smoking a cigarette. He saw the movement at the window and twisted in that direction quickly, bringing his slung rifle to bear, but when he saw it was just a kid, he relaxed a bit.

Out in the distance, there were the sounds of gunfire.

The Russian New Breed kept on smoking. Cast an eye out towards the horizon.

Then Walter had heard the muffled sound of their front door closing again. A conclusion to whatever conversation had just occurred.

The New Breed in their back lawn rose up and looked at Walter and gave him a wink. Then he had tossed the cigarette into the dew-wet grass and disappeared into the night.

Walt was grinding his teeth as he looked back at the New Breed.

They're friends now. They're allies. Just like Koz. You like Koz, don't you?

Yeah. Koz seems okay.

Walter became aware that they'd stopped in front of modular.

He tore his eyes from the New Breed down the stretch and looked at Roy.

"We're here," Roy said, gesturing to the modular. "We call it the Sleep Lab."

CHAPTER TEN

Roy led them into the Sleep Lab.

He closed the door behind them, and the hinges squeaked under the weight of it.

The door was thicker than it should have been. It looked like it belonged on a vault. And when it thumped closed, there was the sound of latches locking back into place. A slight suction sound.

Walt regarded the door with a single quirked eyebrow and a knot in his stomach that he didn't let show.

All four men were now standing in a small, square entryway. Surrounding them was a cage of bars fit for a super-max prison—or, say, a DTI. Backing the bars was a thick layer of ballistic glass. Besides the vault-like door they had just come from, there was another, equally-serious looking door across from them. It had a passkey slot with a red light on it.

The square cage seemed to be sealed. Looking through the bars and the thick ballistic glass, he could see that there were people on the other side. Some of them were conversing, but he couldn't hear them. Couldn't hear anything but his breathing, and the breathing of the three others. The swish-swoosh of their clothes as they fidgeted.

There were four people that Walt could see.

Two of them wore white lab coats, and the other two wore simple Fed uniforms.

The two in uniform were armed with pistols and subguns strapped to their chests, but they wore no armor.

The two in white lab coats—a man and a woman—huddled down at the far end of what appeared to be a bank of monitors, and they were conversing with each other in a casual and relaxed fashion. The woman's mouth opened in a silent laugh. She touched the man's shoulder, as though he had cracked some hilarious joke.

The two guards in their brown Fed uniforms watched the group in the entryway, but they did not move to open doors or assist them.

Roy produced a white card from a pocket on his denim jacket and stuck it in the passkey reader. The red light on it turned green. Roy removed the card, and the door made a *chunk* noise, and drifted inward an inch or two on well-oiled hinges.

As it did, the noise came in as well.

Nothing boisterous.

Just a mutter of light conversation. A hum of recycling air.

Roy pushed the door open and stepped into the cramped confines of the facility. As he did, Walt took a look up at all the bars that surrounded them and he saw the weld-points in the ceiling and when he looked down, he could see them on the floor as well. Not weld-points from a factory.

They were well-done, but it was still obvious that there had been extensive retrofitting.

"Y'all built this thing?" Walt asked, stepping out of the entry cage.

"Like I said," Roy nodded along, holding the door for Getty and Rat. "It was a field hospital. Now it's a lab. It took some modifications."

Walt rapped an evaluating knuckle on the inch-thick ballistic glass. "Little worried about the lab rats escaping?"

Roy smiled as he let the cage door swing shut again. It latched and sealed on its own. "Ayuh. Sure. Wouldn't you be?"

Walt swallowed, nodded. "Ayuh."

The cage that they'd just exited appeared to be in the last quarter of the rectangular modular. The rest of the facility stretched out to the left, and to the right appeared to be what counted as a break room of some sort—a small refrigerator unit, a table, a coffee machine.

To the left, where it seemed the actual "lab" was situated, were a series of stainless steel workbenches that were crowded against the front wall of the modular, and these were stacked with all manner of important-looking electronics.

He mentally categorized what he saw as *Fancy Shit.*

For some reason when he'd heard "lab" he'd pictured test tubes and beakers and strange colored fluids boiling with white vapor. Scientists dressed in full body suits peering into high-powered microscopes and silently noting their discoveries.

What he found instead was jumbles of tech, two bored security guards, two lackadaisical scientists—well, he assumed they were scientists, since they were wearing white lab coats—and the rest of the space was taken by a big metal block that sat upon the opposite wall of the modular, directly across from the tables of technology. This big metal block had the same retrofitted look to it as the cage they'd just stepped out of.

As Walt followed Roy into the section of the modular that appeared to be the actual lab, he noticed that this block of welded steel plating was, in fact, four cubes, each nestled next to the other.

Cells.

Of course.

Small cells, Walt noted.

They couldn't have been more than 12-by-12.

Roy nodded to the two guards like he knew them, and they nodded back. No questions asked.

Walt looked over his shoulder at Getty and Rat. "You guys are awfully quiet."

Rat was looking at the cells the way a museum-goer might look at an old torture device from the Middle Ages. Something used to get a confession from a heretic. He frowned when he looked at Walt. "What the fuck do you want me to say?"

Getty's expression remained placid. "I'm just…taking it in."

None of the cells had windows in them. They were just steel boxes, painted the dull gray of a warship's interior. There were wires and ducts leading to and from them, and even though Walt knew this was likely just environment control, it gave the boxes a malicious feel.

Walt couldn't see inside of them, but he did observe that on those tables filled with technology, there was a bank of four monitors. A monitor for each cell, showing a vid-feed of the interior.

Each cell contained one occupant.

The interior of those boxes was the same gray as the outside, but it was, at least, well-lit.

Each of the monitors showed the hulking figure of a New Breed soldier, dressed only in what appeared to be a hospital gown that looked several sizes too small for them. Two of the New Breeds were lying on narrow cots and staring at the ceiling.

They were oversized for the cots too.

A third was in the middle of his cell, occupying himself with an endless string of pushups. The hospital gown didn't close in the back, and his bare ass was fully camera-facing. The soldier didn't seem to really care.

The fourth was sitting with folded legs on the floor of his cell, as though in the midst of meditation.

"Walt."

Walt looked up from the monitors. Getty and Rat were there with him, and their expressions matched his on the level of their discomfort, intertwined with strong curiosity.

Roy was further down, standing beside the two apparent scientists. Or doctors. Whatever they were. He was looking at Walt, and so were the man and woman in the white coats. The two of them bore curious expressions. Roy, a tired, impatient one.

Roy held out a hand and flicked his fingers a few times.

Walt moved away from the monitor, not liking being beckoned like a child, but then again, he didn't seem to come up with any words to say about it.

The tigers in their cages.

He drifted along the stainless steel table with all their *Fancy Shit*, and he found himself standing in front of the two scientist and his elder brother.

Rat and Getty continued their tense silence behind him.

Roy waved a hand casually between Walt and the two individuals in white. Walt noted they were dutifully wearing denims underneath their lab coats. "Walt, this is Kevin and Stacy. They're in charge of this little operation we call Sandman. Kevin, Stacy, this is my brother, Walt."

Kevin came up out of his position, reclining back against the steel table and reached out an eager hand to Walt. "No shit.

'Walter Lawrence Baucom—the third, if it matters'," he quoted, with a smile that bordered on star-struck.

Walt took the offered hand and pumped it one, firm time. Then he released it, not quite sure what to think. He just nodded back, then nodded another time to the woman in the lab coat, and said, "Stacy," to acknowledge that he'd heard her name.

Roy glanced over Walt's shoulder. "These are two of Walt's associates. They go by Rat and Getty." Roy raised an eyebrow. "You don't mind if I introduce you that way, do you?"

Rat gave Roy a sharp look, but smiled, showing the teeth that had earned him half of his name. "Of course not."

Walt turned to look at the steel boxes across from them. "Sandman, huh?" he said quietly. "Sleep Lab. What is it that you guys are actually doing here?"

Stacy and Kevin exchanged a look. Kevin nodded to her, and she joined Walt in gazing at the featureless steel boxes. "You ever hear of Project Torrent?"

Walt shook his head.

Stacy tucked a bit of black hair behind her right ear and turned to Walt and Getty and Rat. She had a kind face that looked like it belonged to a bright-eyed youth. But Walt could see her age around her eyes.

Up-close, he could see that despite her otherwise flawless, round face, her eyes said she was about thirty, maybe a bit older. Still, there was a youthful twinkle in them as she spoke, and her eyes flitted from Walt to Getty to Rat, enjoying her captive audience, and speaking about something that must've really got her motor running.

She started to say something again, but Getty spoke up, his voice still plain and quiet. "The exosuits, right?"

She nodded with enthusiasm. "Right! The only reason it's not common knowledge, like the New Breed program, is because Project Torrent was a dismal failure. The concept was basically to take a normal man and use tech to turn him into a super-soldier. They made these horrendously expensive exosuits that responded perfectly to input from the wearer, gave them armored protection from projectiles, gave the soldier the strength to overturn cars, or crash through a concrete wall. Stronger than a locomotive. Leaping tall buildings in a single bound. All that good stuff. The only problem with the whole concept was that right around that time the Directed EMP was being put into use by militaries the world over. And whenever something hits the world's militaries…it gets out. It inevitably gets pirated. So it wasn't long before the first bands of insurgents started to figure out how to cobble together DEMPs. They were large and unwieldy, but if they managed to tote that thing out onto a battlefield where Torrent soldiers were operating, it would shut down the entire system. And then you'd have soldiers that were locked in a metal coffin, unable to move. Sitting ducks."

She turned away from them and looked at the steel boxes again. "It was during that time that the resistance actually managed to gain some steam. But then the Fed got one over on us, and that was the New Breed Program." She tossed a hand out in the direction of the boxes. "Why strap a normal man into a four million-dollar exosuit that's vulnerable to a DEMP some farmer cobbled together from tractor components, when you can take the normal man and manipulate his DNA into superhero DNA?" She cut herself off with a wave and a momentarily flustered look. "Sorry. Everyone knows about the New Breeds. I didn't mean to insult your intelligence. The point I was trying to make was that the military abandoned the techno-soldier, and went back thousands of years to, essentially, knights. The biggest and the baddest human beings around, clad in armor a normal man would collapse in. A warrior class. And that's how they've kept us under thumb since we were kids. Because they've created a better man. Strip away the weapons and the technology, and even if we were fighting with fists and rocks, the New Breeds would still beat us every time. They're simply superior." She held up a finger. "But…what if we can do to the New Breeds what the DEMP did to the Torrent soldiers?"

Rat spoke up. "That'd be a dream."

Stacy smiled. "Well, that's what we've been working on here."

"I'd like a demonstration," Roy said firmly.

Now Stacy looked suddenly off-balance. "Well. I…uh…"

"I'm vouching for these three," Roy said, gently.

The way he said it to her caused Walt to glance at him. His eyes. His mouth. The way he was looking at Stacy. The way that he'd said the words. How he was standing across from her.

Shit.

He's fucking her.

Kevin stepped forward now. The star-struck look had left his face, and when he looked at Walt again, it was a very different look. It was an evaluating look. And he gave the same look to Getty and Rat.

But, at the end of the day, Roy was vouching for them. And Roy was trusted by the Eudys themselves.

After a moment, Kevin put his hand on his hips and nodded with a pursed expression. "Alright then. Come with me."

He shouldered gently between Roy and Stacy and passed Walt and his two compatriots. The group turned and after a moment, they followed him a few steps back—back to the monitor with the four screens, showing the four New Breed soldiers, each in their own cage.

Kevin eyed the monitors for a moment, like he was picking the ripest produce. Then he motioned to the individual who was on the floor of this cell. The one that had previously been doing a marathon of pushups, and now appeared to be doing a marathon of situps.

"Dmitri," he said, simply, and then nodded to Stacy.

Stacy was now standing at a terminal and she activated the monitor, which sprang into the air and illuminated her face. Walt eyed the monitor but saw nothing on it but graphs and controls that made no sense to him at all. She made a few selections, and then, with a short breath, looked back to Kevin.

"Okay. Ready."

Kevin sidled over a bit so that all of those present could see the monitor—specifically the one with Dmitri, in the middle of his unbroken set of situps. "You'll want to watch here," he said. "And I will warn you, Dmitri is not a fan of our experiments." A slight smirk crossed his lips. "When he wakes up, he's probably going to have a bad attitude."

"Go ahead," Kevin said to Stacy.

She tapped a single command on the monitor in front of her.

Walt turned his attention to the monitor, where Dmitri was sitting up, then leaning back, then sitting up…and then suddenly stopped.

The hulk of a man sat there in the middle of his cell. He was not taking a break, that much was immediately apparent to Walt. He was frozen in place. His hands still up next to his ears, his elbows pointed out towards his knees. Slowly, his arms began to lose tension, they began to drift down.

Walt was able to see the expression on Dmitri's face. Or, more accurately, the complete *lack* of an expression. His mouth hung open, his eyes half-lidded, every muscle in his face lax. Like someone in a state of catatonia.

Walt had never seen someone in a catatonic state before. He'd seen people in shock. He'd seen vacant looks. But even in those shocked faces, they'd had the appearance of a pond with a still surface, but which you could tell teemed with life below.

This was more like the pond had been suddenly and completely frozen over.

There was no perceivable thought going on there.

And Walt felt confident, based on his own unique talents, that if there had been thought, he would have been able to see it.

He ground his teeth together absently as he watched.

Roy leaned in, seeming to pick up on exactly what Walt was wrestling with: "What's he thinking right now, Walt?"

"Nothing," Walt said flatly.

The two scientists looked at him with a bit of confusion.

"Exactly," Roy stated.

Rat spoke up, his voice wondering. "What the fuck did you do to him? Is he brain-dead?"

Now Kevin smiled the same sparkly smile that had been on Stacy's face earlier. "It's the chink in the armor," Kevin said. "It's the weakness in the machine. But he's not brain-dead. He's in a state of *hippocampal desynchronization.*"

Walt, Getty, and Rat, all looked at the smiling man in the lab coat.

He singled out Walt. "You ever walk into a room and forget what it was you went in there for?"

"Yes," Walt said, guardedly.

Kevin turned his eyes to the monitor, where Walt found that Dmitri's face was no longer a complete blank, but was registering an enormous amount of confusion. For a second it struck a chord deep in Walt's psyche, and he felt pity for the soldier. Because in that moment that soldier didn't look like a soldier at all. He looked like a child that had been completely overwhelmed and had no idea what was going on.

"That's what is happening to Dmitri right now," Kevin said, with no trace of sympathy, only fascination. "At this moment he can't recall where he is, what he was doing, how he came to be there, or even what his name is. He can't recall anything. The lines between his logical brain and his memory have been completely interrupted."

"Tell them how," Roy said

"Sound." Kevin's smile showed teeth.

"A combination of high frequency sounds," Stacy added, as though she was reading it from a textbook. "Which elicit a strong hypersonic effect and cause hippocampal desynchronization."

"We call it ECHO," Kevin continued, right on the back of Stacy's last syllable. Then he gave a self-conscious shrug. "It stands for Electronic Concussive High-frequency Otolysis. We made it up." Then, with a note of disappointment: "Everyone just calls it Sandman, though."

Getty spoke quietly, scrutinizing the face on the monitor. "You said he'll wake up. How long?"

"It varies," Kevin said. "Sometime within the next few minutes. Sometimes as short as thirty seconds. As far as we can tell, he won't remember anything about it. He'll just get really pissed and start trashing his room and yelling at us." Kevin put his hands on his hips again. "Conceivably, though, during that minute or so that he's out of it, you could walk right up to him and…do whatever."

"Do whatever?" Walt questioned.

But Getty overrode him. "How do you know he's not faking it?"

Kevin indicated the monitor which Stacy was standing in front of. "You can't fake brain waves. He's not a functioning individual right now."

"And you've tested this out?" Getty said in that half-amused, prodding way of his. "You've walked in there and tried to provoke him?"

Kevin chuckled derisively. "Of course not. That'd be way too dangerous."

"Hmm," Getty said.

Kevin looked briefly defensive. "We just don't have the resources and facilities capable of safely testing that—"

"Thank you," Roy interrupted. "That's all we needed to see."

Roy was already heading briskly for the exit.

Getty and Rat peeled off to follow, almost as though they were relieved to be free of the Sleep Lab.

Walt took an extra moment to look at the man's face in the monitor and saw that it was not a child's face anymore.

He gave a glance to Kevin and Stacy and he saw only excitement—maybe with a little bit of defensiveness. After all, it is always difficult to see the flaws in the products of your own mind.

As the four of them entered the cage again, just before Roy closed and sealed the door behind them, Walt heard what must have been a horrendous crash inside one of the cells, but came through only as a muted *thump*, and then the hoarse yelling of a man's voice.

CHAPTER ELEVEN

"Jeff, you can do this. You have *to do this."*

Another memory.

This time from before.

From the time before she was Carolyn Baucom.

Back to a time when she only knew herself as Stephanie Eudy.

She is young. Perhaps nine or ten. She understands what her parents do. She understands what they are involved in, though they've never directly told her. She's pieced it together from astute observations, as children can often be astute. However, also like children, she doesn't have the full picture.

She is standing outside of the doorway into their kitchen.

Benjamin and Jean Eudy—only known as Mom and Dad at that point—are in the kitchen.

There is a man in there with them.

The man is crying.

Stephanie knows this because she can hear him sobbing and it makes her so incredibly uncomfortable. She's not sure she's ever been in the presence of a grown man who is crying. She also knows it because she occasionally takes a peek around the corner.

The man is red-faced, tear-stained, head hanging.

She recognizes him, although from where, she can't remember.

Her parents are social people.

They have friends over all the time.

They come and go at weird hours.

Have strange conversations.

Like this one.

"I don't know if I can," the man says, his voice half a whisper and half a groan.

"You can," Mom insists, her voice comforting. The voice she would use when encouraging Stephanie to rip a Band-Aid off quickly. "Think about what they took from you. That's what you should focus on."

"But the people," the man says, his voice growing louder.

"Ssh," Dad says in a stern sort of fatherly way. "You're going to wake our daughter."

Stephanie is supposed to be in bed. It's late at night.

She stays hidden behind the corner of the door and listens.

"The people," the man says in a more controlled tone. "The innocent people."

"Some collateral damage is expected, Jeff," Dad says calmly.

"Besides," Mom says, her voice holding an edge to it now. "There are no innocent people in that pack of wolves. This is the Office of the Liaison to the Coalition Forces. Half of them are traitors to the core, and the other half are guilty by association. They know who they work for. They know exactly what their employer is guilty of. And still they go, because a paycheck is more important to them than freedom or the lives of their fellow countrymen."

There is a long pause.

Mom speaks again.

"Jeff. It was people like this that looked the other way when the bombs were dropped on Tammy and your boys. It was people like this that didn't care enough to say something, when they knew an atrocity was about to occur. They look the other way. They do not deserve your pity, Jeff. They're as guilty as the rest of them."

Another long silence.

There is a sniff from Jeff, but he's no longer crying.

"Okay." He says quietly. "You're right."

"No, Jeff," Dad says. "You're *right. You're making the right decision here and now. You're doing what you have to do. And even though they will call you a terrorist on the news—and they will, Jeff, they will—the future will know the truth about you.*

They'll know that you fought for freedom. They'll know that you fought for your countrymen."

"Where do I pick it up?" the man asks. "Is it too bulky to hide under a jacket?"

"You let us worry about the details," Mom says. "You just be ready."

Stephanie fidgets.

The floorboard creaks.

There is silence.

Stephanie thinks quickly.

She immediately steps out from behind the doorway.

Her heart is slamming in her chest. Not because she fully understands the ramifications of what she's just heard, but because she feels like she's about to be in trouble. But she might not be in trouble if she can play it off.

She can play it off.

She's always been pretty good at manipulating her parents.

So even though her throat feels suddenly ragged and her heart is going wild, she puts on a sleepy face and shuffle-walks into the kitchen.

She stands there for a moment, blinking blearily in the bright kitchen light.

Her Mom and Dad and the man called Jeff stare at her, alarmed.

"Stephie-Bug," Dad says cajolingly, "What are you doing up?"

"Thirsty," she mumbles. "Can I get some water?"

Her mother pulls herself quickly out from the table where the three of them are huddled like conspirators—which is exactly what they are, actually—and she crosses to the kitchen sink where she grabs a plastic cup with flowers printed on it and pours her daughter some water.

Stephanie stands there rubbing her eyes theatrically.

Heart still uncontrolled.

Lungs burning a little.

"Here you go, Sweetie," Mom says, putting the cup of water into her hands and gently turning her away. "Now go on back to bed."

"Okay," Stephanie says, bringing the water to her lips and taking a sip. It is so cold it almost hurts. It tastes metallic. "G'night."

"Good night, Stephie-Bug," Dad says.

And then strangely, the man called Jeff: "Good night."

Stephanie stops in the doorway and looks back at him for a beat or two.

In that one or two seconds she knows, and he knows, somehow, he knows that she knows.

But no one says anything.

She just turns silently and goes back to bed where she will lie and not sleep for another two hours, long after the mumbles of perfunctory goodbyes are heard through the walls, and the opening and closing of the front door, and the starting of Jeff's vehicle, and the headlights splashing across her bedroom wall, and the rumble of the engine fading into obscurity.

A week later on a bright Monday morning at about 9:15 a.m., a man walks into the Offices of the Liaison to the Coalition and detonates a suicide vest, killing himself and nineteen others, and wounding thirty-four.

Two of the dead are American military officers.

The rest are civilians.

That night, Mom and Dad drink a bottle of red wine and they toast the bravery of a man named Jeff.

***

It had taken nearly forty minutes to make a trek that Carolyn suspected would have taken only twenty if the driver, Brady, hadn't made so many turns.

In the back of the car, she sat behind Brady, and John was across from her, on the passenger's side of the back seat. The dead body was no longer with them. John and Brady had disposed of it in a dumpster in a quiet alleyway, somewhere in CoAx County.

She'd felt nauseous as she watched from the back seat.

Then she couldn't watch anymore and she stared straight ahead with her mouth sweating, and she began to wonder if she was going to puke in the back seat. She laid her hand on the door in case the urge became stronger. Then she began to think about running.

Brady and John returned before she made up her mind.

They drove on without a word to each other.

Brady and John both were breathing heavily with the strain of their efforts.

More twists and turns. Doubling back. Making circles to see if any other cars behind them would complete the same nonsensical maneuvers. John kept his eyes to the side, watching the buildings that passed. Brady kept his eyes on the mirrors.

Who had she been? The lady that they'd unceremoniously dumped into a garbage bin?

What was her name? Was she Fed?

Something else?

Had she even meant them any harm to begin with?

Too late now to ask those questions.

The subgun between Carolyn's legs felt heavy and uncomfortable. As she jostled in the back seat, its corners and edges ground into her inner thighs, like an overexcited lover that doesn't know what the fuck he's doing.

At first it seemed that they were driving closer and closer to the actual base. In long streets that ran towards it, the walls of it loomed up higher and higher, closer and closer. But gradually they began to turn away from it. Tacking like a ship against the wind. And now, if she looked out the right windows, occasionally she would see the walls and the gun emplacements, but they were further off.

They were heading for the north end of CoAx County.

The north end appeared to be no different from where they'd started out.

Apartments, bars, peep shows, pawn shops, bazaars. All low and squat, like homeless men hunkering against the rain that was still coming down putridly.

They slowed in front of a seedy looking motel that offered daily rates. The gaudy sign showed brightly in the dreary downpour and proclaimed it The Royale.

There was nothing Royale about it.

They didn't stop at the front. They took an alleyway just past it and drove to the back of the building. There were two other cars back there. Neither was occupied. There were no people around.

John twisted in his seat. He yanked down the armrest that was between him and Carolyn, and she saw that there was a trunk access there. He pointed into the dark hole.

"Slip the subgun in there. Brady will take care of them."

She hesitated for a moment, looking at John.

"I'm still armed," he reassured her.

That's great. But I'm not.

She didn't truly want to be rid of the thing. The words that he'd said to her were still rattling around in her skull, finding new and inventive ways of making her heart and stomach do-si-do around each other.

"There's no safe place in the world for you right now."

"Come on," he said, gently. To show his goodwill, he put his own subgun into the trunk and then motioned for her to do the same.

She felt childlike in that instant.

With a huff, she shoved hers into the trunk. Not hers, really. But when it left her fingers she missed it. She felt defenseless. She didn't want to rely on John to defend her. But he had a point in getting rid of them, and she knew it.

They couldn't just waltz around with the damn things strapped to their chests.

CoAx County might be as seedy as they came, but it wasn't *lawless.*

He closed the trunk access and opened his own door and got out.

Carolyn scooted across the seat and exited out the same door.

John offered his hand, but she did not take it.

This was no date, and she wasn't in the mood for chivalry.

Thinking of dates made her think of Walt. Made her think of the day off together that they'd never got to enjoy. Made her think of the other rare occasions when they'd had that opportunity. She questioned whether she'd truly made good use of them, or if she'd taken them for granted.

If I ever get back to you, Walt... she thought. But she didn't even finish the sentence in her own head.

John closed the car door, and as soon as he did, Brady pulled off, destination unknown.

They went in through the backdoor of The Royale. It wasn't locked.

Inside, Carolyn found herself in a hallway. It branched off to her left, and also went straight ahead. The two views looked identical. Just a bunch of hotel room doors. Green carpeting with smears of mud across it that seemed to coalesce where she was standing, into some sort of abstract painting of people's shoe prints. Then the shoeprints all went their individual ways, trialed off, and disappeared.

Immediately to her right was a cubby with a trashy-looking drink station. It smelled of over-cooked coffee. A single occupant sat there. An old man who read the projected monitor of his PD with intense concentration, as though trying to translate it from a foreign language.

He looked up at them, and his eyes lingered a moment longer than they would have if they'd been strangers.

A lookout if I ever saw one.

The old man returned to his reading with a wet sniff.

John was already continuing down the hall. He hadn't waited. Had not passed a greeting.

Carolyn followed behind him. Down the worn out green carpeting that smelled the way all seedy hotels smell, like they've soaked up the essence of the thousands of downtrodden that have passed through it.

Were her parents here? In this place?

She wasn't sure what she'd expected. In her mind's eye, perhaps she'd pictured these two heroes of the resistance—or extremists, depending on who you were talking to—in some sort of command bunker.

Now she created a much sadder picture.

Benjamin and Jean Eudy, huddled in a dark and foul-smelling room. The shades drawn. Their faces drawn. Worn out. Lined. Sagging.

Christ, what would they even look like?

Would she recognize them?

Would they recognize her?

A decade spent in Sweetwater DTI.

They would not be the people that she remembered from her childhood. But for some reason she could not stop picturing them that way, even though she knew that was not how it would be. How else could she picture them? It was the only image she had to go on.

So she steeled herself for what she might find.

The end of the hall opened into an atrium. The front of the place.

A clerk sat at his desk. A younger man. Very skinny. With dark eyes and hair that looked like it needed a wash. The desk was enclosed by safety glass. Like he was a bank teller. And that told you everything you needed to know about the type of place this was.

The exact same thing occurred as had occurred with the old man at the backdoor.

The clerk, also engrossed—or seemingly engrossed—in his PD, glanced up and looked them over. Except this time there was a slight nod. And John nodded back.

They approached a door that said "Employees Only."

The clerk reached under his counter and touched some control. There was a buzzing sound, and the door unlatched and John went through. He held the door for her, then let it close on its own. She heard the thing latching back behind them.

They found themselves at an unmarked door that had the look of a storeroom. Here, John stopped for the first time and appeared to draw himself up a bit. Carolyn watched this as she'd watched all of his movements—with acute interest.

How else was she supposed to know what the hell was going on? She was taking her cues from him, as few as they seemed, and as inscrutable as they were. Otherwise she would've gone mad with the powerless feeling of simply being towed behind him like a piece of luggage.

John knocked on the door.

No secret knock. Just three firm raps with his knuckles.

Then he stared down at his shoes.

Carolyn realized that her heart was pounding.

The door opened without any particular caution, as though those on the inside already knew who they were.

A large man with a shaved head looked at them. Again, first at John, and then at Carolyn.

But when he looked at Carolyn, his eyes held. And there was something in his eyes. Something almost misty about them. Did she know him? She didn't believe so. He was young. Her age, if she were to take a guess. He would've been too young to be one of her parent's associates from the time before they were disappeared.

After a moment, he blinked rapidly and drew himself up.

"John," he said. "Glad to see you made it safely. Any trouble?"

"A little bit," John said.

The man moved out of the doorway and invited them in. He cast an outward glance as though to see if anyone else was in this private area that the clerk had buzzed them into, but it was just the clerk, still at his counter, with his back to them now, still looking at his PD monitor.

John and Carolyn entered the room.

It was not a storeroom as had been Carolyn's first impression. It was something more of a spacious office. It was in an L-shape, and Carolyn could not see around that corner. But she could hear someone moving there. Like a chair being rolled, and her heart caught and her throat seized up and she wondered who was behind that corner.

The man with the shaved head closed the door and before saying anything else he produced a small device from a pocket, which he appeared to aim at both John and Carolyn. Like he was scanning their bodies. After a moment of scrutinizing what Carolyn guessed was a monitor, he pocketed the device again and smiled at John.

"Congrats. You're not bugged. What type of trouble did you run into?"

"We were followed off the platform by a female," John said.

"Fed?"

"We don't know for sure."

"Did you take care of her?"

"Yes."

"Any other followers?"

"No. Not that we saw."

"Good."

The three of them stood in silence for a brief moment, and then the man turned his head towards the corner of the room that Carolyn could not see, and he spoke to whoever was there. "It's all clear."

There was the shuffle of footsteps, and that same rolling sound.

A man stepped out from around the corner, older than she remembered, older than she had expected, but he stood erect with a powerful bearing, and she did remember that. It was that way that he stood that she recognized, more than his face, which was scarred and lined and the straight, equine nose was bent and broken.

Beside that man that was like a ghost of her memories rolled a chair. An electric wheelchair. The type that was used for paraplegics. Slumped in the chair was a withered female form with lank gray hair. The woman in the chair goggled up at Carolyn and her face contorted, and her mouth trembled, and tears were already in her eyes, but now they spilled over down a craggy face.

Carolyn was not breathing.

What did they do to you? She wanted to ask, but could not find the air to say it, and was glad that she could not.

It was not merely the passage of time that had changed them. No one could have aged so much in only a decade. The passing years that produced these two people, that had produced the sad form in the chair, had been as harsh and cruel as a ten-year winter.

"Stephanie," her father said with a voice that broke at the end of the word.

And Carolyn stared back at him, for a moment, lost.

Who was Stephanie?

She was, of course. Stephanie was her, a decade prior.

Her father took a step toward her, tentative like one might step toward a wild animal that they feared might flee, but which they wanted desperately to touch. His hands were halfway raised, as though he wished to embrace her but was scared to do so.

He must've seen the look of confusion that passed over her face when he used that old, bygone name. His face looked pained for a moment, grieved.

"I know you must think of yourself as Carolyn, after all these years." A shadow of some madness passed over his features and for the first time, but not the last time, Carolyn felt a twinge of fear. Fear of her father. Of what was in his heart. "That is the name that *they* gave you. Those beasts." He spat the last word like a bitter rind in his mouth.

But the name of Carolyn was more than just the name she'd been given by the Fed when they'd relocated her to District 89. It was so much more than that, wasn't it?

It was the name that Walt knew her by.

It was the name that he called her.

It was the name under which she'd married him.

And she had become Carolyn Baucom.

That was who she was at the core of her.

Or was that only what she believed?

Was she something else in the darkest parts of her? The parts that had been left like a temple in the jungle to be overgrown, once used, but now considered abandoned and unexplored.

"May I call you Stephanie?" her father asked, quietly, and the anger was gone from him. "May I call you the name that we named you? I know it must be strange to hear now. But at least for now. At least until I can wrap my head around this. Can I call you Stephanie?"

She did not want to be called Stephanie.

She did not want to be called Jessica.

She wanted to be called Carolyn.

"Yes," she said. And she had taken a step forward, and that was all it took.

Benjamin Eudy crossed the distance almost frighteningly quick, but then pulled himself up at the last second, and rather than throwing his arms around her as she'd thought he was going to do, he simply took her by the shoulders and began to weep silently.

Carolyn was crying herself. Crying with her eyes wide open. Looking over her father's shoulder at her mother.

The chair lurched forward with the same aggressive quality.

"Mom?" Carolyn choked out.

She noticed for the first time, the small device attached to Jean Eudy's left temple. A flesh-colored nodule that was not quite the same color as the skin around it.

Benjamin followed Carolyn's gaze. "She has trouble with speech," he said, coldly.

Jean reached up with a frail, left hand, and with a trembling finger, touched the nodule. The voice that came out was not the electronic terror that Carolyn had half expected, but a soft, feminine voice that was pleasant to the ears, but strange to her because it was no version of her mother's voice that she'd ever heard.

"Will you come closer to me?"

The voice did not impute the emotion on her mother's face. Like it had come from some unassociated interpreter.

Her father released her shoulders, and Carolyn took a halting step to her mother's chair.

Jean reached up with her free hand, her left still touching the nodule on her temple.

"I want to touch your face."

Carolyn bent down. She watched a tear drop fall from the tip of her nose onto Jean's withered lap.

Her mother's hand touched the side of her face, lightly. The skin of it was warm and dry. And the touch told the tale that the voice modulator could not, as no technology could ever fathom the depth of this most human emotion.

"You are beautiful," the calm, pleasant voice said. "Isn't she beautiful, Ben?"

"Yes," her father said with a tremor. "She is very beautiful."

"Such a beautiful young woman that you've turned into." A rueful smile broke out over Jean's face, lighting up eyes that were still quick and fiery and intelligent. "I hate this goddamn voice. She sounds like such a bitch."

Carolyn suddenly laughed, almost a cough through her tears.

The laugh rippled through the room, breaking the tension of so much emotion.

"It was the best we could do on short notice," said the voice that was not her mother's. "But it serves its purpose well." Jean's eyes widened a bit. "And married now, too, yes?"

Carolyn straightened up, grew serious. "Yes. Walt. Do you know where he is?"

In the absence of any vocal inflection that the modulator did not provide, Carolyn found herself paying special attention to her mother's eyes. And here, they bore a certain clinical curiosity that she did not care for.

"Ah yes, Walt," Jean said. "The voice of District Eighty-Nine."

"Mom. Dad," Carolyn said, and for the first time those words felt strange to say, and they made her feel small and childlike and supplicating. "I need to get a message to Walt. I need to tell him I'm okay."

Her mother's head moved slowly back and forth. A negative shake.

"Such a thing is not possible right now," the voice said. "We are in a war, my dear. We are in a war for things much more important than that. But don't worry. We will see what your Walt is made of soon enough. We will see if he is worthy of our beautiful Stephanie."

Carolyn stared at her mother. Then looked at her father. But words failed her.

Worthy? She suddenly wanted to scream. *He's my fucking husband!*

Instead, she swallowed thickly and said, "Can you tell me where he is?"

Jean's eyes flicked to Benjamin's. He cleared his throat and reached out and put a hand on Carolyn's shoulder again. "He is relatively safe. As safe as can be expected. He's with his brother."

"What?" Carolyn almost choked. "He's in DTI? I thought you said—"

Benjamin raised a hand to calm her. "Roy was in Sweetwater DTI with us. We chose to extract him during the raid to free us. He'd proved quite smart and resourceful in DTI. Become a close ally of ours. He's one of our most valuable assets."

Carolyn couldn't do much there. She just stood, stunned like she'd been rocked in the jaw.

Roy was free too. A man she only knew from photographs.

Walter was with Roy.

They were safe.

She supposed that was all that mattered.

Right?

Her mother cut off any more questions she might've asked. "And now, my dear, we need to talk about the war."

Carolyn looked back into Jean's eyes and saw the thing that she had seen in Benjamin, the thing that had frightened her and turned these two people that were just beginning to awaken some vestiges of familial remembrance, into strangers she did not know.

It was the cold, glittery look of insanity that marked them.

"Oh, my dear Stephanie," that calm, bitch voice said. "We are going to make them pay for every year they took from us."

CHAPTER TWELVE

Roy knocked on the door of the sleeper unit.

He took a glance around him, but the halls of the unit were abandoned. It was just past midnight. Almost everyone was asleep. The only people awake would be those manning the command module, keeping their eyes peeled for drones and reconnaissance flights. But the nightshift was a skeleton crew, and none of them were out and about.

From inside the sleeper unit, he heard the shuffles of someone moving around.

He waited patiently.

The door cracked open.

Stacy peered out at him.

"Roy," she said, quietly. Then she opened the door all the way.

He slipped in, and she closed it behind him.

Her unit was organized chaos. To the right, her cot sat up against the wall, the blankets neatly covering the thin mattress, as though she made her bed under the pretense of a surprise inspection.

A white, plastic set of drawers stood at the base of her cot. Inside would be her neatly folded clothes.

On the other side of the room stood her desk, and there was where the majority of the chaos lurked. A single lamp hung over her desk, casting it in a stark white glow. Strewn across the desk was all manner of technology that had been pirated and dissected and cobbled back together in some new and ungodly form.

The room smelled strongly of soldering.

Roy turned his attention to Stacy, who was looking up at him with some apprehension.

"You sure about this, Roy?" she whispered.

Roy nodded. "Were you able to do it?"

Stacy's dark hair was pulled back in a haphazard pony-tail that had since gone to tatters and was now hanging loosely at the back of her neck, strands of her hair having come free and wispy around her drawn and tired face. She had bags under her eyes.

She rubbed her face vigorously. "Yes," she said, slightly muffled by her hands. When she removed them from her face, she was looking at her desk. "Yes, I think so."

Roy walked over to the desk and looked down at five cylindrical objects that were standing in a neat row amongst the wreckage of the things they'd been built from. Like tiny towers rising up from the mess of a construction site.

"Is that them?" he asked, gesturing to the five objects.

Stacy hurried to his side. "Yes, but..." her voice was distraught. "But I can't promise that they work, Roy! You're about to risk your life on something...something I just *cobbled together*! They haven't been tested!"

He picked one of them up and looked it over.

It was a light item. It didn't have the weight of a munition. The bulk of it was a thin aluminum body that she'd rubberized. Two bulbous endcaps. Also rubberized. But on the endcaps he could see where she'd bored through and installed small, high-output speakers.

There was a red switch on the side of it with a little safety paddle drawn over the top. He ran a thumb across it.

"You could test it on me right now," he said.

"Christ! No!" She grabbed the object out of his hand, held it away from him. "Are you fucking kidding me? What if I didn't program it right? What if it scrambles your fucking brains? What if you go into a coma right here in my sleeper...? No. Absolutely not. Besides, they're not supposed to do anything to regular humans. Not *supposed* to anyways."

He smiled at her, as though through a fever. "Tell me how it works."

She looked down at it. "It works like you asked. Or…at least…it's *supposed* to."

"No delay?"

"No delay. Just flip up the safety paddle and flip the switch." Her face screwed up. "Oh, Jesus. You sure about this?"

Roy nodded and unslung a simple black pack. It was empty. He laid it on the chair next to the desk and opened it up. Then he held out his hand to the device that Stacy was holding. "It's okay, Stacy. I have faith in you."

She chuffed at him, but handed the device over. "That's nice. That's more than I can say."

Roy took the device and stuffed it into his bag. "Those safety switches. They're pretty sturdy?"

She nodded miserably. "Yeah. Yeah. You have to force them up. They won't flop open on their own."

"Good," Roy said, taking the remaining four from the desk and bagging them as well. "Be a shame if they went off at the wrong moment."

"Oh, Lord…"

"What about the ear pro?" Roy asked.

"Well," she said, walking around to the side of the desk. "I was only able to make two sets."

Roy let out a low sound of disapproval.

"What the fuck do you want from me?" Stacy snapped suddenly. "I'm doing all this shit by myself. I'm not a goddamned factory. You're lucky I was able to do any of this stuff at all!"

Roy reached out and laid a reassuring hand on her shoulder. "Alright. It's fine."

Stacy shook his hand off with a huff. She grabbed two small boxes and shoved them into Roy's hands. "Here. I'd suggest you give them to your New Breeds, if you have any. They're most at risk for the effect. It should *only* affect them. But…maybe if you have regular guys, they should wear ear plugs. Just to be on the safe side."

"That's going to be cumbersome," Roy remarked, opening one of the boxes and looking inside.

"Well, it was the best I could do on a day's notice, Roy."

He looked up at her, his face placating. “I know, Stacy. Relax.”

“Relax,” she said with some disgust. “You know I could get shot for this? If Major Pallen finds out that I helped you…” She suddenly looked terrified, as though it was the first time the thought had occurred to her. “He’ll execute me on the fucking spot.”

“He won’t,” Roy said, and he was being honest there, at least. “You’re too valuable to him. We’re not exactly flush with scientists.” Roy closed the box and shoved both sets of ear pro into his bag, this time zipping it up.

“Right, right.” She was not convinced.

Roy picked the bag up and slung it onto his shoulder. “Like I said, Stacy. I have faith in you. You should have more faith in yourself.”

Stacy ignored him and pointed to the bag. “One more thing, Roy.”

“Ayuh?”

“They’re one-time use, okay? Those high-output speakers are going to bleed that battery dry within a few minutes—I had to keep the battery small to fit it in. So…use them wisely.”

Roy nodded. “Got it.”

“Good luck,” she said, forlornly.

“Hey,” Roy said, smiling again for her just so that maybe she would be able to sleep. Then he gave her a quick, dry kiss on the mouth, and it felt oddly spousal to him. “Have some faith.”

***

Walt did not sleep.

And he figured that Getty and Rat didn’t either.

He didn’t even bother with the pretense of it. He never even laid down on his cot.

Fully clothed, he paced the room. Then he would go sit on the edge of his bed until the stillness was unbearable, and then he would go back to pacing.

He thought of his Pops.

He thought of Bobbi.

He thought of Carolyn.

Mostly of Carolyn.

It is easy to be strong in the distraction of daylight.

In the still expanse of nighttime, however, the soul wants comfort, and a man will drive himself mad thinking of his wife.

The knock finally came shortly past midnight.

Walt wanted to go to the door with cool aplomb, but he simply couldn't handle it. The solitary cell-like nature of his room had begun to grate on him, to become little more than a box, and each passing minute had taking a bit longer to pass, and he'd begun to feel a manic sort of energy come up in him, like he was growing too big for this box and would have to kick his way out.

So he ripped open the door with no reservations.

Roy stood there, his lean face regarding Walt with the very coolness he'd wished he possessed in that moment. He wore a simple black backpack, and for a brief moment Walt was transported to a summer so long ago, and the feel of it was the same—the feeling of sneaking out under Grandpa Clarence's nose—the feeling of going off to do something that Walt knew would get them in trouble.

What's in the backpack? He'd wondered then, and he wondered now.

God, but life worked in circles, didn't it?

Walt leaned out of the door and looked both ways down the hall. It was empty. No babysitting detail. But more than that, no New Breeds.

"Where's your friends?" Walt asked.

"They're going to meet us," Roy said. "Come on."

Walt stepped out and closed the door behind him.

"What about *your* friends?" Roy asked, pointedly.

"They're coming."

Roy seemed momentarily pleased. "Good. Get them."

Walt went down to Getty's door and found Getty was waiting as eagerly by the door as he had been. He exited out wordlessly with a glance and a nod of greeting both to Walt and then to Roy.

Walt knocked on Rat's door.

And waited.

There was the sound of shuffling.

Murmuring.

Walt fidgeted in place.

The door opened, privately cracked.

Rat's narrow, rodent-like face protruded, blinking blearily in the light. "Yeah? Is it time?"

"Christ, were you sleeping?" Walt asked.

Rat rubbed his face, frowned at them. "Well, yeah. It's fucking midnight. What're you, a fucking party boy?"

Walt waved at him impatiently. "Just come on."

Rat shuffled out with a tired grumble, like an old man awakened late. He was fully clothed. His hair was rumpled from sleep. He closed his door behind him and turned to Walt. He gestured at his clothes. "I slept in my shoes, you know."

Walt wasn't sure whether Rat felt that this was a great injustice that he'd had to endure, or whether he was trying to defend himself by demonstrating how ready he was.

The four of them exited the sleeper unit into darkness.

The big stadium lighting that had lit the darkness so starkly had been turned down to a tepid glow. Walt supposed that they didn't want light pouring out of cisterns that were supposed to be dark and derelict. Little details like that could give away the resistance presence in Kanawha 3.

Roy led them through the dark, to the door that opened out into the world beyond. It sat there in the darkness, pale and blue in the moonlight that was coming from beyond.

The air had chilled even more in the hours since Walt and Getty and Rat had been outside to hold their private meeting.

Roy looked both ways, up and down the gravel road that led from the town to the mining operations. And then he walked nonchalantly across that road, and stepped off of it and onto the soft shoulder that quickly turned into mountainside and trees.

Walt figured that they were hitting the edge of the woods to keep concealed, and would skirt it around to a vehicle. But then the little foray into the woods became a trek, all of it downhill, and when he looked behind him he could no longer see any of the buildings or cisterns.

"Where the fuck are we going?" Walt whispered in the darkness.

"Just a little further," Roy said over his shoulder.

Walt looked back. Getty raised his eyebrows and shrugged, but kept walking. Rat was busy staring at the ground, threading his way between deadfall and around small saplings.

They reached a steep section and Roy began to switchback down, holding onto the sides of trees for support. Walt's feet threatened to slip out from under him several times, and he heard a few curses from Rat.

At the bottom of the steep section, Roy stopped. He looked around in the darkness.

The woods were still. Still in the night, still in the cold. No crickets or bugs to sing to the moon. No little animals moving about. Just the sigh of the wind through the trees, the deep black carpet of the ground under their feet, and the slim, moonlit sides of the trees all around them and ranking out deep into the woods where they disappeared in a slurry of shadows.

Roy let out a low whistle.

About ten yards in front of them, two shapes rose out of the ground like goblins out of holes in the mountainside. Walt restrained the urge to jump back, because Roy stood there and watched them, as though this was expected.

The two shapes were huge.

Walt wondered how two men so big could have hid themselves right in front of his eyes like that.

Roy walked casually up to them. He raised a fist to them and the two giants tapped it with fists of their own. Then Roy turned and looked at Walt. "You guys wanna join us?"

No, not particularly.

But Walt walked over to them and looked up at the two Goliaths in front of him. New Breeds, but they were not in their armor. Neither appeared to be armed, but they both had large packs on their backs that Walt guessed contained weapons.

He recognized one of them.

The Norse God with the fiery red beard and the perpetual mischievous smile on his face. He extended a hand to Walt that was roughly the size of a ham hock, and Walt took it. He expected it to be a crushing grip, but the Norse God apparently knew his strength and spared Walt a broken hand.

"Koz," he announced, quietly. "Good to formally meet you, Walt. Sorry about everything that happened on the gunship."

"Ayuh," Walt returned, hollowly.

The other giant was a little shorter than Koz, but what he lacked in height he made up for in pure width. He was roughly the size and shape of a refrigerator. His skin was black in the half-light of the moon, but he had a broad smile that he showed them all, flashing very white teeth in the midst of a scraggly beard.

"Javon," he rumbled, offering his hand as well.

Walt gave it a single pump and again escaped with a working appendage.

"You've disabled the perimeter sensors?" Roy asked them.

Javon nodded. "For the next ten minutes. Hole closes up after that."

Roy nodded.

"Were you able to get the things?" Javon asked back, eyeing Roy's backpack.

"Ayuh. I got 'em." He took a step back and motioned Walt, Getty, and Rat to join the circle. When they had, he spoke again, keeping his voice low. "We couldn't drive out without raising suspicions. So we're hiking out."

"Fuck-all," Rat said with a tired huff.

"We have some transportation at the bottom of this mountain," he continued. "But time is short, so let's go."

Quietly, in single file, the six of them set off down the mountain and out of the protection of anyone that could help them.

CHAPTER THIRTEEN

It was midnight and Tanner Dixon sat in the Marshal's car, backed into the Petersons' driveway on a quiet and mostly-dark street jam packed full of old tract housing built nearly a century ago, and every damn one of the houses was the same floorplan, the same house, just replicated, one after the other.

The Petersons were asleep, Dixon believed. The house was dark, and there'd been nary a peep from them. He wasn't particularly worried about them, though. They were collaborators all the way. Dixon was friends with Harlon, the man of the house, and he knew that even if Harlon were to see the marked car out in his driveway, he would not have anything to say about it. Harlon would assume that Dixon had his reasons for being there. Official reasons. And nothing would be said.

Harlon Peterson was one of the few people that had been glad to see the old marshal disappear like so much dust in the wind, and smiled a knowing smile when he'd first seen Dixon wearing the uniform.

Besides, it was not the Petersons' house that Dixon was concerned with.

He stretched his legs. Stretched his back. Grunted quietly to himself.

The old marshal—a tall, heavy, white-haired man by the name of Prior—had been a slob. His legacy of slobbery had continued in the form of the shitty patrol vehicle that Dixon now had to use.

And no matter how Dixon had cleaned the thing out and practically damn fumigated it, the vehicle still smelled like Marshal Prior.

Like old cheese and beefy farts.

Dixon had the windows down in the patrol vehicle. The outside air was cold, but Dixon refused to turn on the heat inside the vehicle. The heat seemed to exacerbate the smell. Dixon preferred to simply be cold.

He rubbed his hands together and blew into them, and cast his eyes down the street at the house that was the subject of his ongoing scrutiny. But not after tonight. No, he would put a stop to this bullshit tonight.

A block down the street, and across it, stood the Hoffman residence.

Unlike every other street on the block, the lights were still on.

Craig Hoffman was a first shifter. Which meant his ass should be asleep. His shift would start in five hours. Most first-shift families were lights out by ten o'clock at the very latest.

Oh, yes, Dixon had done his homework.

He'd gone to the foreman—a sketchy man that Dixon couldn't pin down as being either collaborator or loyalist—and asked in about Craig. The foreman had pansied around a bit, but eventually told him that Craig had called in some sick time a few days prior. The very same day, as a matter of fact, that all this shit had gone down and the renegade forces had moved in and hunkered down in those defunct slurry cisterns.

Craig had claimed the flu. Said he was going to be out of work for a few days.

He was an old hand. So not much fuss was made. The man had accumulated hundreds of hours of sick time, being the usually hale and hearty individual that he was. So, while the flu was uncommon for the Hoffman family, the foreman certainly wasn't going to begrudge him a few sick days on an otherwise spotless career of working his ass off.

That was the story that Dixon had got, anyways.

But here was the problem.

Dixon hadn't seen hide nor hair of *any* of the Hoffmans in two days.

Not since the day that Craig had allegedly called in sick.

Michelle Hoffman had not gone to the pharmacy for flu meds.

Their two snot-nosed kids had not been to school.

No one that Dixon trusted to actually tell the truth could say that they had seen any member of the Hoffman family.

And yet…the lights went on at dark. And come early morning, they would be off.

Same times, every night.

Dixon had made a note of it.

The sick guy with the flu was burning the midnight oil.

How odd.

He should be resting.

Perhaps there was a reasonable explanation for this, but Marshal Dixon had a gut feeling, and he trusted his gut. One of the many things that he believed made him far more qualified for this position than the loyalist hack who was rotting alongside his two deputies in a ditch outside of town.

Dixon checked the time on the dashboard clock.

It was five minutes past midnight.

He looked back down the street at the Hoffman residence.

And just like clockwork, the lights started winking out. One by one.

Not all at once, as though the lights in the house had been put on a timer.

One at a time, with a few moments between, as though someone was inside, turning them off.

Dixon coolly shifted the car into drive and pulled out of the Peterson's driveway. He left his headlights off. Drifted down the road, just as quiet as could be, and pulled up in front of the Hoffman residence.

He left the car running, parked at the curb. Stepped out. Quietly closed the door behind him. He drew his pistol and held it low, next to his leg.

The upstairs lights were still on.

All the downstairs lights had been shut off.

Dixon pursed his lips and stepped quietly down the driveway. The family car was present—an old, rust-red GUV. But that didn't convince Dixon of shit. The car hadn't moved in two days. He was positive of that.

Dixon went to the backyard. It was very dark. The few streetlights didn't reach this far back, and the small patch of grass was a swamp of black shadow. A few children's toys were scattered about, their bright colors the only distinguishing landmarks in the darkness.

He went to the back door. It was ajar.

How fascinating.

He gently pushed it open.

Slipped through. Slid it shut behind him until it latched.

The house was cold. The heat wasn't running.

He stood there in the quiet, dark kitchen. There was no smell of recent cooking. No dishes in the sink. No evidence of life. Just dead quiet darkness.

Over his head, a floorboard creaked.

Dixon's eyes looked to the ceiling.

He waited to feel any sort of apprehension. But he didn't. His heart was steady. It never did get riled. Always seemed to tick at the same rhythm, unless he was exerting himself. Dixon was not a man given to panic or fear. What was there to fear, anyways?

There was much for others to fear.

But not him.

Mostly, he felt a grim sort of satisfaction.

Satisfaction, because he'd known and now he was going to prove it.

Grim, because it meant that there was yet another set of dirty loyalists, putrefying his proverbial barrel of apples.

Another creak in the darkness. Then another.

Light footfalls coming down the stairs.

Dixon reached behind him and dead-bolted the back door. Then he moved quietly further into the kitchen. He did not want to be seen when the person, whoever it was, immediately entered the kitchen. They might panic and attempt to run. That would cause things to be messy, and Dixon hated a mess. Oh, yes, he fucking despised them.

He put his back to the pantry door. To his right, the kitchen. To his left, the small dining nook where the Hoffman's had broken bread together every night—until recently, anyway.

The footsteps were coming down the hall now.

Dixon waited patiently.

A figure entered the kitchen. A man. Dressed in denims.

Dixon didn't immediately recognize him, but he knew for sure it wasn't Craig Hoffman.

The man had his shoulders up, and his gaze was locked on his target—the back door. He was not very aware of his surroundings. He was not looking into the shadows. He just wanted to get out of the house, apparently. The stupid little sneak.

As the man shuffled past, heading for the back door, Dixon raised his pistol and took a step towards him.

The man whirled.

His eyes were bright and liquid in the darkness.

He froze in place, staring at Dixon, his arms tensed comically at his sides.

"M-M-Marshal Dixon?" the man stuttered.

Dixon squinted at him.

Ah. He recognized the man, alright. Hell, Dixon knew every motherfucker in this town. Unlike his inept predecessor who'd been sent to rule over them by the Fed and still, after a goddamned decade, couldn't get everyone's names right.

"Junior," Dixon said quietly. Then he shook his head and tsked with his tongue. "What would your father think of you right now?"

Junior McCarroll just stared silently for a moment, then stuttered again, not quite understanding the situation. "My pa's dead, marshal. What are you doing here?"

Dixon nodded. Took another step forward. "Yeah, I know your pa died. And how'd he die, Junior?" he didn't allow Junior to answer. "He died fighting the Fed, didn't he? To think, such a hero could've raised a fucking loyalist."

Junior began shaking his head vehemently. "No, no, no! I'm not a loyalist!"

"Sure. Where're the Hoffman's, Junior?"

Silence.

Dixon sniffed, irritably. "Where are they? Not snug in their beds, I'm sure."

"I don't know where they are."

"I think that you do."

"I really don't!" Junior's voice was getting whiny. "I'm just doing them a favor."

"Tell me about it."

Junior's hands found each other at the center of his chest and began wringing together nervously. "I…uh…well…Craig asked me to watch the house. Asked me to turn the lights on and off."

"Where'd they go?"

"He didn't tell me where they went. I swear."

"I know where they went," Dixon said, feeling heat rising on the back of his neck. "They went down the fucking mountain to tell the Fed about what's happening up here, didn't they?"

"No!"

"Yeah, they did. And you're fucking helping them out. Helping them keep it a secret from me. From *me*." Dixon flashed an unpleasant smile. "You can't fucking keep secrets from *me*!"

"Jesus, marshal, I'z just doin' them a favor! Bein' neighborly, that's all. If a neighbor asked you to take care of his house, you would, wouldn't you? I know you're a neighborly guy, too."

Dixon sneered. "I don't associate with loyalists, Junior. You shouldn't have either."

"No, marshal…"

Dixon shot him in the chest.

It was incredibly loud in the enclosed space. The flash of it was bright.

Junior jumped back with a little muffled cry and then his feet tangled up and he tumbled to the left, right into the little dining set. There was a loud clatter of wood as he tried in vain to hold himself up on the chairs, but he'd run into them too hard and they toppled over under his grip. He went down with them.

Dixon kept the pistol trained on him, but decided not to take another shot. He felt confident he'd hit something valuable inside of Junior. He didn't need another bullet.

For a moment, Junior kept trying to raise himself up on the legs of a toppled dining room chair. But he didn't have the strength anymore. His mouth was hanging open wide and he was making grunting piggy noises. He wasn't looking at Dixon. He was staring off into the darkness with panic in his eyes.

Junior slumped against the legs of the chair. His arms were uselessly tangled now. One of them flopped off to the side like a dead fish. The other kept trying to grasp the chair leg, like he was desperate to have something to hold onto. His head was cranked up so that his chin was to his chest and the piggy noises continued with struggling snorts.

Also, there was a wet, raspy sound, and it wasn't coming from Junior's mouth.

Dixon stepped over to him and squatted on his haunches. His elbows on his knees. The pistol hanging in his grip, between his legs. He tilted his head to listen to the wet sucking.

"See, that bullet went through your chest cavity," he told Junior. "Broke that vacuum that your lungs live in. Now air is getting into that chest cavity every time you try to breathe. They call it *tension pneumothorax.* Your lung is collapsing."

More noises.

Dixon squinted at him, genuinely curious. "Can you tell which one it is?"

No answer.

Of course not.

Dixon shook his head, disappointed. "I don't abide loyalists, Junior. Your father would be ashamed of you."

Junior expired a minute or two later.

Dixon took the time to make sure he was dead. He even felt a brief pang of regret. Not for what he'd done—no of course not, this was a fight for freedom, a fight against tyranny—but for the fact that yet another one of these people in Kanawha 3 had forced his hand.

Did they not see what was going on around them?

Did they not see the tyranny of the CoAx?

Disgusting of them to be so blind.

They earned what they got, but it still irked him that they were left with one less person to help the cause.

He left the body where it was. Left the house. Drove quickly up to the cisterns. The headlights of his patrol vehicle flashed across the pale concrete monoliths. He parked it and got out and stalked purposefully towards the one where he knew Roy resided.

He would be discreet about this. There was no need to go pulling any big red handles at this point. But Roy needed to know the danger that the entire operation at Kanawha 3 was in. If the Hoffmans had run, that meant that they were loyalists. And if they'd made it off this mountain, they were going to end up telling someone about what was going on in this quiet little mining operation. And then things were going to get very bad for them.

He found Roy's sleeper unit and went inside. It was Dixon's opinion that they should have guarded the sleeper units, or at least the cisterns. But manpower being as low as it was, Major Pallen felt that they would be better served by placing their sentries in an outwards-facing manner—in other words, have them watch the perimeter, and not the interior.

When Dixon had pointed out there might be CoAx sympathizers from the civilian population that might try something, Pallen had made it abundantly clear that he considered this Dixon's problem.

What if I were a saboteur? Dixon thought as he walked up to the door to Roy's room. *I could assassinate Roy while he was sleeping. Hell, I could put a bomb in here and take out the whole goddamned unit.*

Lucky for them, Dixon was for the resistance. And also, lucky for them, he was swatting CoAx sympathizers like flies. Soon enough he'd rout every damn one of them out, and then Kanawha 3 would be completely safe for the resistance—at least from the inside.

He knocked lightly on the door and waited with his hands clasped behind his back, considering this a fairly good representation of "parade rest."

He listened carefully, but heard nothing.

Perhaps Roy was asleep. He had avoided knocking loudly in hopes that he wouldn't garner the attention of any of the other people sleeping in this unit.

He knocked again, harder.

Waited.

Still no sound from inside.

He frowned at the door.

Felt a quiet little note of unease.

Pulse still steady, though. Always steady.

Hm.

He thumbed his PD to life. He hadn't wanted to speak over the PD. Not only was he not completely sure that these devices were safe to speak over, but he thought this issue would be better handled in-person.

He put a call into Roy's contact.

He listened carefully.

No ringing from inside.

No buzzing.

No shuffling of someone coming awake.

Well. This was odd.

Then a polite, artificial voice informed him that the PD he was attempting to reach had been disconnected.

Dixon didn't even wait for the artificial voice to finish. He snapped his PD shut. The monitor hovering in the air over his arm winked out. He clenched his teeth together.

It was no longer just a quiet feeling of unease.

Now it was his gut telling him something.

And he always trusted his gut.

***

Craig Hoffman drove along a dark and winding mountain highway. Not too far at all from where Dixon was coming to grips with a mess of suspicions.

Craig's stomach was fluttery. Not what you would call butterflies, though. Nothing so lighthearted as that. No. He would probably call them bats. Bats in his stomach.

He was running the heat in the borrowed van, but his fingers were still ice cold.

He didn't want to do this.

But a deal was a deal.

He could've avoided it. Could've simply lost himself. Hid himself. And his family, of course. But he believed Roy. And Roy had been very clear with him.

Two days ago, Roy had smuggled them out of Kanawha 3 in the back of a civilian bread truck that had just dropped off a load at the convenience store in town. It had been broad daylight when Craig, his wife Mora, and his two children were huddled at the back of the truck, behind a stack of boxes. Despite their hiding place, Craig had felt exposed simply because it had been daylight.

Escapes were supposed to happen at night. Not when everyone was walking around.

In their quiet little hide, he'd heard Roy speaking to the driver. Roy had never explained his relationship to that driver, and perhaps that was for the best, but it worried Craig nonetheless. Was the driver just some guy that Roy had slipped money to? Or was he part of the resistance too?

He couldn't hear what Roy and the driver were saying to each other. Just the murmur of their voices. Then the voices had stopped. There was the sound of the truck's cab opening and closing, and the truck rumbled to life.

Roy swung up into the back of the bread truck.

Craig peered between two loaves of white bread.

Roy saw him, made a beckoning motion with his hands.

Craig slipped out of the spot, laid a staying hand on his wife's shoulders. Mora was knelt down, her arms around their two kids, and she was looking up at Craig with a determined sort of fear that made his heart break for her, but also filled him up with love.

God, they were being uprooted. Their entire lives. But at least they were together. At least they were getting out of the line of fire. At least they would be safe. Relatively safe. And she was handling it well. She was handling it bravely.

He had a good woman there.

Craig left her and his kids and walked to the far back of the truck.

Roy stepped up close to him, their faces just a foot apart, if that. Over the course of the last day or so, Roy's face had become stern and drawn. He'd learned some things that he didn't like, and he never communicated those things to Craig, who he'd picked up a passing friendship with, but Craig could see that those things weighed heavily on Roy.

Now Roy's eyes were as cold and hard as little chunks of granite.

"I'm doing this for you," he said very quietly. "And you're going to do something for me, when the time comes. Do you understand that?"

Craig nodded with a frown.

They'd already been through this. Why was he saying it again now?

"Craig," Roy whispered. "Say that you understand that."

"I understand."

"Promise me that you're going to answer when I call."

Craig frowned deeper, but said, "Yes. I promise."

Roy's jaw muscles bunched rapidly. He looked over Craig's shoulder at his family. Leaned just an inch or two closer, and spoke even quieter, to be sure that Mora and the kids didn't hear him. "I know you have to think about your family, Craig. And I respect that. You get them safe. Don't get them involved. But I swear to God, if you leave me high and dry when I call for you, I will find a way to kill you. Do you understand that too?"

Craig leaned back. Felt heat on the back of his neck. "Jesus, Roy!"

Roy was not to be appeased in that moment. "This ain't fucking marbles, Craig. We're playing with lives, and we're playing for keeps."

Craig had never seen Roy so intense before. In that moment, the friendly relationship seemed dried up. It was all business now. And he was slightly afraid of Roy. But he was more afraid of Tanner Dixon. And at the end of the day, Roy was getting them out from under that psychopath.

Craig nodded stiffly. "I'll be there, Roy."

And then, with nothing further to say, Roy hopped down from the back of the truck and closed the sliding door. And a moment later he heard the thump of a hand on the side of the cargo area and the truck started moving, getting the Hoffman family out of Kanawha 3.

And now, here he was. Craig Hoffman. In control of a big, cream-colored utility van with an empty backend, except for two benches along each side, so that when anyone sat in them, their back would be to the wall. They weren't even real bench seats. They were made out of wood, and covered with industrial gray carpeting to pad them.

He'd received the van from a shady character in Charleston, West Virginia only hours before.

And now he was driving along a highway that ran across the bottom of the mountain on which Kanawha 3 had been built.

He flipped up his PD for the umpteenth time.

He could see the little blue arrow of his dot on the map, and now it was fast approaching a little red waypoint.

He drove perhaps another tenth of a mile until the two icons were on top of each other.

Then he slowed down, and he pulled to the side of the road, the bats in his stomach going crazy, and his mouth going dry.

How long did he have to wait here?

What if someone saw him on the side of the road and started to inquire?

Worse, what if it was a CoAx patrol that found him? Those fuckers were damn near everywhere now. The last few days, they'd been flying about like hornets on a kicked nest. Oh, bad things were happening. The world around him was going to shit.

But he'd only been there on the side of the road for about a minute before he heard a tap on glass and he nearly jumped out of his skin.

He looked to his right, and saw Roy's face looking at him through the glass of the passenger window.

Craig's stomach did flip-flops.

He touched a button and the door unlocked.

Roy didn't hesitate. He ripped the door open and swung inside and closed it behind him all in one fluid motion. The chill air came in with him, smelling of exhaust and mountain air and faintly of Roy's own sweat.

"Everything okay?" Roy asked him.

"Yes," Craig said, shakily.

Roy fixed him with a stern, calculating glare.

Shit. Craig was supposed to say something.

Something to prove he wasn't under duress.

It was failing him now. That very obvious thing that you should have been able to remember but for some reason, you can't grasp it…

"You want some coffee?" Craig blurted out.

Roy appeared to relax marginally. He sat back in his seat. "Nah. I'm good."

Then he raised his hand up to the window and gave a big thumbs up to the glass.

Then he settled completely into his seat.

A few seconds later, the van's side door slid open, and five others tumbled into the back of the van, one after the other. The first three were regular people, and they didn't say a word to Craig, just kind of looked at him with a quick, knowing glance, and found a place to sit on the floor. But the last two that came through had to squeeze just to get through the door.

Fucking New Breeds!

Craig almost panicked and drove off at the sight of them.

But they were not in their armor. And they gave him the same cursory glance that the others gave them. And Roy didn't seem to care.

The last one in was a massive black New Breed with a pleasant smile on his face, his white teeth almost glowing in the darkness. He slid the van door shut and slapped Roy on the shoulder. "All in," he rumbled.

Roy pointed forward without looking at Craig. "Get us out of here."

CHAPTER FOURTEEN

Walt sat on the floor directly behind the driver's seat. To his right, Getty, and then Rat. And directly across from him, Koz and Javon filled up the passenger side.

Walt kept an eye on his brother, who was seated in the front passenger seat. From his vantage, he could not see the driver—Craig—but he could hear his voice clearly enough.

Tone and cadence told almost as much truth as tics and fidgets.

"Is your family safe?" Roy asked quietly. Almost apologetically.

"Yes," Craig said. Wooden.

"Good. Any trouble getting here?"

"No. Everything was…fine."

Silence for a moment.

Walt felt Craig shift in the driver's seat and could almost see the man's discomfort. He had something else to say.

Which he did: "You have any idea what the hell's going on out here?"

"Yes, we have a good idea," Roy replied.

"Never seen so many goddamn patrols," Craig mumbled. "They're everywhere now. Flights going overhead at all hours. You guys really kicked the nest. You pissed 'em off solid. You brought this whole thing back two generations. It's gonna be bad again. Like it was when our fathers were kids."

"It had to happen at some point in time."

A light huffing noise from Craig.

If Walt were to venture a guess, he would say that Craig was one of the silent majority that went along with the CoAx, despite the fact that he hated them. He wanted to see the resistance win, but felt it was a pipe-dream. And he certainly didn't want to risk his own life to make it happen.

If Walt were to venture a guess, he would say that Craig believed they were all dead men.

"There's rumors of a troop surge," Craig said.

Roy looked out the windshield. His expression didn't change. The corners of his lips twitched downward. He didn't respond.

"Fuckin' media won't say shit. They've already forgotten about your boy Walt. They're focusing on terror attacks in the north. Boston. Richmond. New York. A few of the Agrarian Districts up there."

Roy looked over at the driver. "You consider them terror attacks?"

Craig shifted in his seat again.

"Depends," the man said.

"On what?"

"Whether they're killin' civilians."

"And the purge on District 89? The civilians that died there? Was that terrorism?"

Walt could see the fire burning in Roy's eyes and knew he was hanging onto his temper, but just barely.

"What about all the people in DTI?" Roy continued. "Is that terrorism?"

Roy was looking for an abject apology, or a fight—he'd take either in that moment. Walt considered intervening, but then, he was thinking about Carolyn. He was thinking about the arm that he'd seen in the rubble. He was thinking about the bombed out buildings in his hometown and how there wasn't a camera around to see that shit and now it was simply being denied, being reframed, being dressed up for public consumption.

And he thought, *No, let Craig pull his own ass out of the fire.*

He'd begun to grind his teeth again.

Craig kept his mouth shut until Roy simmered himself down and looked back out the windshield. Their headlights plummeting ahead of them as they wound their way down the mountain and out of the valley.

"They're purging more districts as we speak," Craig said.

Roy nodded, cold now. "Ayuh. We've heard."

"Where are you going?"

"The less you know, the better off you are. Just take us to where I told you."

"Durham, right?" Craig asked.

Walt watched Roy carefully here.

Roy looked up at Craig a bit sharply, blinked a few times, and frowned just slightly. He didn't respond. He looked out the windshield again, his lips tightening down.

Walt's gut clenched suddenly.

Roy shifted in his seat, and as he did, he dropped his left arm down briefly to the side of his chair and twiddled his fingers slightly. He immediately disguised this into a stretch, but Walt had seen it.

Walt's eyes shot to the two New Breeds in the back.

Javon was staring back at him and he lifted one finger up to his lips.

Koz rose up from his seat with a grumble. Moving casually. "I gotta piss, man. You got a bottle up there or anything?" he shoved past Walt's legs and wedged his bulk in between the two front seats, but Walt could see his right hand pulling something out of his waistband.

Javon was still holding his finger over his lips.

Walt ground his teeth together sharply.

Pain.

When it happened, it happened quick.

Koz thrust out with the object in his hand. There was the light *pop* sound that Walt had come to recognize as a stun gun. He knew the sound, because it'd been used on him.

The van lurched, but then Roy came across, grabbed a hold of the wheel with both hands, and used his left leg to shove Craig's feet over and take control of the pedals.

The van righted itself.

There was the click of a safety belt being disengaged, and then Koz simply hauled Craig's limp body into the back like he weighed nothing, and laid him gently on the floorboard.

As this happened, Javon coughed loudly, then harrumphed and spoke conversationally. "So, Walt, what'd you do in District Eighty-Nine?"

He was twirling his finger in the air. *Keep it going.*

"Uh…Um…" Walt blanked for a moment. "I was a tractor driver."

"Oh, man. One of those big-ass things?" Javon said lightly. "The ones that go on the rails? What are they called again?"

Walt was staring at Craig. His eyelids were closed, his eyeballs twitching rapidly beneath. On the side of his neck was a small, black ball that appeared to be encased in some sort of sticky gel that had adhered it to his skin. A tiny blue light flashed manically on the ball.

"Ayuh," Walt said thickly, like a man trying to remember his lines as he's being heckled by an audience member. "Span planter."

"Right," Javon said, snapping his fingers. "Span planter. That's a bigass machine. How much training do they give you for that?"

"Training?" Walt asked, still unable to look away from Craig.

In the front, Roy had navigated himself into the driver's seat.

Koz had liberated a long, wand-like object from a side-pocket of his backpack and was turning it on. It made a low hum and a whistling tone.

Javon laughed. "Yeah, training, man! What? Do they just give you the keys and tell you to figure it out? Ha! That's fucked up, bro."

"No," Walt swallowed. "You have to have a mentor. For a year."

"Well, I guess that's better than a bunch of boring-ass classes."

"Ayuh."

Koz waved the wand carefully over every limb on Craig's body—up and down the legs, up and down the arms, all around the torso, and even the head. The thing continued to make the same low, hum-whistle.

"You know," Javon said languidly. "I always preferred a mentoring to classroom session. You know what I mean? I feel like classroom shit is just theory. Half the time it ain't even important.

Nothing they can't teach you in a mentoring session. And then you get to actually see it put into action. You know?"

"Ayuh." Walt scrambled for something else to say. "I feel the same way."

Koz had moved on from Craig. Abandoned the man's body to sit there with his eyes wiggling behind the eyelids. He started at the back of the van and ran the wand in broad, spiraling circles, covering every inch of ground.

A few times, the wand made a little high-pitched squeal, like a bitten animal, but Koz appeared to ignore this and keep moving.

Walt could feel him losing his grip on the conversation.

Rat jumped in: "You know, when I was in school, they told me I had *learning deficiencies*. Tried to give me a bunch of meds to keep up. But I'll tell you what, when it came to learning things with my hands, I'd learn faster than all the other kids." He laughed ruefully. "Now, isn't that some bullshit? When it came to learning things with your hands, all the other kids were *learning deficient*, but they never had to take meds. So who decided that sitting in a fucking class and regurgitating facts was the litmus test for your learning capabilities?"

"Preach on, brother," Javon said solemnly.

Koz had made it to the cab now, scanning under seats, around the console. He was very careful now. Going very slowly.

"We of the infamous *program*," Javon continued. "Are cured of any quote-unquote learning deficiencies."

"Right, right," Rat grumbled. "When they turn you into fucking superman."

"Never gave me my laser vision," Javon said. "I feel gypped. Hey, Koz, they ever give you your laser vision?"

"Nah, man," Koz said as he worked. "Fuckers ripped me off."

"I did get an eighteen-inch dick, though," Javon said, then laughed boisterously.

To Walt's right, Getty had found himself a cigarette and was lighting it. He was smiling over the flame at Javon. "Oh, come on. You had that before the body mods."

Javon stopped laughing and made a face of innocence. "No, I swear." He held up his hands. "It was only a foot long before the body mods."

Then they both laughed.

Walt was still caught up in the absolute strangeness of the moment, how suddenly it had come upon them. He stared at Getty, and Javon, and now Rat who was laughing too, and he realized his expression was one of marveling at how fluidly they'd all adapted to this situation.

It was like showing up to a party where everyone is in costume except for you.

I need to learn to think quicker on my feet, he said, and he wanted to say something, but feared that it would come out stupid and awkward.

At that moment, Koz turned off his whining wand. "We're clear."

The congenial smile immediately fell from Javon's face. "What are we gonna do with this motherfucker?"

"How much time left on that stunner?" Roy asked.

"A minute or so," Koz said.

Walt noticed that the little flashing light had gone from blue to yellow.

"Well, he wasn't bugged or wired," Roy stated.

"He shouldn't be asking those questions," Koz said.

"He was nervous," Walt suddenly put in. "He was talking to fill the silence. I don't think he thought twice about it, Roy."

Roy took a moment to consider this.

"You feel confident about that, Walt?" he asked.

Walt suddenly realized that the responsibility for what they did with Craig had suddenly been shifted deftly to Walt's lap.

Hot potato.

And then he simultaneously realized that it wasn't just an issue of what was best for them as a group. It was now a question of whether or not Craig was going to live through the night.

Walt sniffed loudly. Then breathed out through his mouth. "Ayuh. One-hundred-percent."

Roy nodded in the driver's seat. "Okay. If Walt says he believes it, I'm with him. Craig gets to make it through this one."

Walt felt a wave of pride at how little hesitation Roy had shown. And then he boxed that shit up and threw it away from him. He didn't need approval from anyone.

They didn't drop Craig in the middle of nowhere.

Roy had the decency to wait until they passed through a small town in the foothills, and he stopped there at the side of a collection of shops that had been closed hours ago. They sat dark and silent and still.

By that time, Craig was awake again.

He didn't even ask any questions about what had happened. He just apologized profusely for what he'd done, although Walt got the sense that he wasn't sure what it was that had pissed Roy off. But the man feared Roy. And Roy did not soothe that fear. He fed into it.

When they dropped him on the side of the road, Roy looked at him, pointed at him, and said, "Remember what I told you, Craig. Think about your family."

Then they drove off.

***

Major Pallen was a small, stocky individual with a slab face and a gut that appeared to be creeping up on him in his middle age. The type of man whose arms showed strength, and whose midsection showed stress and food.

He stood now in his quarters, wearing nothing but a tan crew-neck shirt and black PT shorts. His short, gray-brown hair, which was normally neatly combed, was askew in the back. His eyes were red and glaring. His face deeply lined with sleep.

Across from Major Pallen was Marshal Dixon. Flanking Dixon was a pair of soldiers that weren't New Breeds, but looked like they were juicing enough to make a go of it, if only they could gain an additional foot in height.

Pallen kept staring at Dixon for a moment longer. Then he looked to the guard on Dixon's left. "Did you check?"

The soldier nodded. "I sent Sergeant Mason to check, sir."

"And what did he say?"

"They're gone, sir."

"Fuck." Pallen scraped his fingers back across his scalp, then hung his hand at the back of his neck. He closed his eyes in thought for a moment. Spoke while they were still closed. "Is there any reason that we can think of why they would have left Kanawha Three? Without telling me?"

No one said anything.

Dixon cleared his throat after a few seconds. "Well, major, there's something else."

Pallen's eyes opened. Narrowed. "What."

"The Hoffmans," Dixon said. "They're a family that I've long suspected of being loyalist."

Pallen stared, waiting for the other shoe to drop.

"I discovered tonight that they are not in Kanawha Three. Their house is abandoned. That was the original issue that I was going to Roy for."

Pallen released the back of his neck and bared his teeth in a sneer of distaste. "Fucking civilians. This is what you get."

Dixon nodded, as though the term did not apply to him. "The reason I came to you with all of this is because I know for a fact that Roy was friendly with the Hoffmans. I don't think it's such a stretch that he may have helped them get out of Kanawha Three during the shuffling around a few days ago."

"Are you suggesting that Roy Baucom is a loyalist as well?"

Dixon shrugged. "I am simply stating the facts."

"So you *saw* Roy Baucom assist the Hoffmans in getting out?"

"No, sir."

"Then don't tell me you're stating facts," Pallen snapped. "You're offering conjecture. I can give you a fact right here and now, *marshal*"—he said the word with as much disdain as one could conjure—"I may not like the man personally, but Roy Baucom is not a loyalist."

Dixon was unshaken by Major Pallen. Not by his presence, not by his rank, and certainly not by him looking down on Dixon. For all Dixon knew, Pallen himself was two steps away from being a loyalist. Dixon suspected there were a great many soldiers who were somewhat on the fence, but had gone along in order to get along.

When your entire regiment decides to defy orders, do you pick that moment to stand up and risk being one of the ones they kill to get away? Or do you just slide along with it and hope for the best?

Dixon, as you can guess, had his own opinions on that.

"I felt you should know," Dixon stated simply.

Major Pallen made a small chuffing noise. "Yes. Thank you. That'll be all, marshal. You can return to…marshalling."

For a moment, Dixon stood there and stared at Pallen, and in his cold eyes Pallen did not detect a single note of fear. Dixon was looking at him as though he were simply a talking sack of meat, and there was a perennial curl on one side of Dixon's lips, as though he was just barely restraining himself from laughing.

Pallen knew what Dixon had done so far in Kanawha 3. And he realized in that moment that Dixon was not challenging Pallen's authority, or trying to posture. He was simply *evaluating* the military man. He was looking *through* Pallen to determine whether or not the major was as committed to the resistance as he claimed.

Pallen bristled. "You can leave now."

Dixon nodded, that slight smirk at the corner of his lips, and then he turned and walked out the door. Pallen's two guards left with him.

When he was alone in his quarters again, Pallen stalked to his desk. On it, perched upon a cradle, was his PD. Not *his* PD—that had been wiped along with everybody else's right at the start.

He flipped the screen into existence with an aggressive swipe of his hand. The blue glow lit his tired face.

"Call Remus Actual," he commanded.

The screen, flashed, changed. The tone sounded.

A female officer responded. "Remus Actual. Major Pallen?"

Pallen was already grabbing his uniform pants and pulling them on. "Put me through to Colonel Wainwright. Tell him it's urgent."

CHAPTER FIFTEEN

They were loading them onto trucks.

The black sack had come off, but the restraints remained on.

It was late, but Bobbi had no idea of the time. It'd been dark for hours. It was cold. The temperature had steadily been dropping, or maybe it was just that she was standing around in it with nothing to keep her warm but her violent shivering.

It's probably not even that cold, she told herself.

Sometimes, something as mild as 50 degrees can seem bone-achingly cold when you're out in it all night.

They'd formed them into two lines. She was standing in one of those lines. The other line was to her right. The lines were single-file, all the bound people standing almost chest to back, but she didn't think any of them minded. She sure as hell didn't—she could feel the scant body heat from the man in front of her, and it was a nice relief.

She just wished the person behind her would stand a little closer.

There was no talking.

Any time someone spoke, a voice would shout out from behind them, "Quiet on the lines!"

It happened a few more times before there was an explicit warning attached to the command, and then no one spoke after that.

There was also no looking around.

Bobbi had tried to look behind her to see how many other people were in her line. She wanted to count them up. She wasn't sure what an accurate head count would do for her—probably nothing at all—but it gave her something to do besides sit there with what felt like battery acid in her stomach.

When she started to look behind her, the same voice called out, "Eyes forward!"

She snapped her head back. Looking forward over the shoulder of the man in front of her. He was an older man. Stoop shouldered and a little short.

In front of him, she thought she counted ten heads. Which made twelve, including him and her. She wasn't sure how many were behind her. At least the one, she knew, because she could occasionally feel their hot breath on the back of her neck, and they occasionally whimpered. It sounded like a man.

She managed to drag her eyes to the right while keeping her head forward. She counted the line to her right a few times. She could count fifteen, but she knew there was more. She just couldn't see them unless she turned her head. And she didn't want to do that again.

She tried to find Walt.

Rat.

Getty.

Any of them.

But all the faces that she could see were strangers.

Were they somewhere behind her? Had they seen her?

The thought gave her hope. And she could not decide whether to cling to it or to toss it away. It was like finding some fragile bauble in a flea market, one that you wanted very badly for some unknown reason, and you sat there turning it over in your hands, trying to think of what purpose it would serve.

Bobbi was a practical person. She did not like things that served no purpose.

And she thought, *it'll keep you from going mad.*

But she knew that it was only a bandaid. Because when you put your hope in fragile things, eventually that thing would break. And to her, a broken hope was far worse than having no hope at all.

She had heard them call out the name Walter Baucom. Someone had responded to that name. Someone that was now standing in these lines with her. One of these thirty-or-so people.

Could it be that it was simply coincidence? That there were two Walter Baucoms that lived in Agrarian District 89? Two unrelated people?

Perhaps.

Far more likely, they were indeed related.

The Walt that she knew could be a junior.

She considered this for a time, shivering in the darkness.

The two lines, in the middle of a cement field. The more she let her eyes wander about—keeping her head straight forward, of course—the more she realized that the CoAx had commandeered a parcel of District 89's industrial section. This was one of those vast concrete fields where planting and harvesting implements and engines were stored and repaired in the off-season.

The soldiers had erected stands of bright lights all around them, and they lit up the area in the dark of night like a stadium. The lights surrounded them like sentries themselves, and they pried at her eyes and made her brain ache. Just beyond the halo of brightness that they made, she could barely make out tall chain-link fencing.

Yes, she decided. It was most likely that the Walter Baucom that was here with her now was a relative of the Walt that she knew.

The thought that Walt and Rat and Getty had not been captured both filled her with relief and simultaneously made her feel incredibly alone again. She hadn't realized how just the thought of them being with her somewhere in this crowd of unfortunates had given her some mental support.

The night seemed colder. Darker.

She began to look around for older men. People that might've been Walt's father, because that was most likely, right? Fathers named their sons after themselves. That was more likely than sharing a name with an uncle or a cousin.

After a few moments circumspection, she decided that there were three individuals that she could see that could possibly be old enough to be Walt's father. Most of the people in these lines were young. They were her age. Walt's age. Give or take a decade.

Two of the elderly men were in the other line.

The third was directly in front of her.

That was when the trucks came.

Two of them. Big military modulars. Tan painted and as gruff and ugly as a bulldog's face. They were the engines on which the military hung all sorts of things. They could be outfitted with wrecker attachments, cranes for engineering, fuel tanks, or flatbeds for hauling other heavy equipment.

These two trucks appeared to be equipped with personnel modules.

Troop transport modules.

More troops? She thought, as the headlights from the modular engines swept over them.

But she didn't think that was the case.

The two big trucks made a synchronized loop around the cement field, and when their back ends were facing the two lines of prisoners, they began to back up in a cacophony of cautionary beeps.

The engines rumbled loudly in low gear.

For no other reason than she'd been given an opportunity, Bobbi leaned forward and whispered loudly: "Walter!"

She'd barely heard her own whisper over the truck engines.

Surely the guards wouldn't have.

The man in front of her tensed, his shoulders drawing up a bit, and, seemingly on instinct, his head turned just a fraction before he stopped himself and looked forward again.

She continued to stare at the matted, greasy-looking gray hair.

The man said nothing.

Three soldiers marched down between the two lines of prisoners, their battlerifles at the ready. The one in front was focused on the trucks. The two on the sides were paying attention to the lines, eyeing them hard so that anyone thinking of anything might take a moment to reconsider.

Bobbi watched them pass by.

One of the soldiers' eyes caught hers momentarily, but passed on without giving her much attention.

They reached the front of the lines.

The soldier in front had both hands in the air, beckoning the trucks to back up further, further, further. Their beeping growing louder, louder, louder. Until he switched his hands and put both palms up.

There was the hiss and groan of brakes.

The release of exhaust.

The beeping stopped.

The engines went into a high idle.

The lead soldier started calling out commands to other soldiers.

The man in front of her bowed his head. His voice was barely audible.

"What?" he hissed.

Bobbi just stared and didn't say anything.

Up ahead of them, the doors on the back of the personnel unit were opened with a loud and jarring *clank* that made Bobbi jump and her eyes shoot up from the back of the old man's head. Two soldiers were stepping down out of the back of the personnel module. They separated, taking positions to either side, and they began motioning with their arms.

"Step up," they called. "Watch your footing."

Bobbi watched the first prisoner, a small Asian woman with jet black hair, mount the back steps of the personnel module. She looked around uncertainly and the soldier to her right gave her a gentle prod on the shoulder, and she continued in.

The line started moving forward.

***

In Kanawha 3, in an abandoned cistern, there sat a sleeper unit.

Inside that unit was a woman not sleeping.

Dr. Stacy Pogatti lay on her bed with her hands steepled over her chest, staring at the ceiling. It'd been pitch-black when she'd turned out the lights, but as her eyes had adjusted, even the meager glow from a few green diodes at her workstation was enough to show the details of the ceiling. She wasn't even sure where the green diodes were from—perhaps the charging station, showing that the battery cells were fully charged?

She could not sleep.

How could she?

She knew they were coming.

She'd considered trying to leave. Kevin had told her she should. But she knew logically that she had no chance of making it out of Kanawha 3 without being detected. And besides that, it felt wrong. It felt like a betrayal of the cause.

She'd also considered killing herself, but only briefly. Because she wasn't sure what they were going to do when they came for her. She wasn't sure, and that black nebulous future, that's what kept her there in her sleeper unit. Maybe she should've run. But she didn't. Because *maybe* everything would work out in the end.

They came at about three in the morning.

A harsh, clanging knock on her door, and a commanding voice.

"Doctor Pogatti, open the door or we'll let ourselves in."

Stacy stared at the ceiling and actually felt all her veins constrict.

Isn't that funny.

Her heart swelled up with that extra blood.

Then it started slamming. Hard. Fast. Shaking her entire body with each pulse.

"Coming," she said, hollowly at the ceiling.

She got up. She was already dressed.

She slipped on her sandals.

She heard the outside key access being slotted and mutely beeping, granting access to whoever was outside. Apparently she hadn't moved fast enough for him. And admittedly, she did feel like she was moving through molasses.

But she managed to pull the door open before they barged in themselves.

She looked at Sergeant Mason, flanked by two regular soldiers.

"What can I do for you, Sergeant Mason?" she said, with no real curiosity in her voice.

Mason stepped into the room and looked quickly around. The two soldiers slipped around him, around Stacy, and they pulled her arms behind her back and secured them with plastic restraints.

Mason never looked her in the eye the entire time.

Maybe he felt bad.

"Stacy," he said, with a note of regret. "You're being secured for our safety. Major Pallen wants to speak with you."

It didn't take her long to tell Major Pallen everything.

She was loyal to the cause, after all.

CHAPTER SIXTEEN

She was in a basement of some sort.

It was her parent's office at the hotel, but not the same. This was dark. Cavernous.

In the darkness there was a circle of illumination, right in the middle of everything, and in this circle of light there was a sort of quiet celebration. She understood somehow that they were celebrating the defeat of the Coalition.

There were only a few people in this celebration. Her parents were there. A few random people that she did not recognize. John was there too.

And...

She felt her heart rise up in her chest, her throat constricting when she saw him.

She had never felt such relief in her life. She had never felt such joy.

She ran to him, calling his name, "Walter! Walter!"

The celebration grew quiet as she entered the circle of light. She didn't care. She went to Walt and she reached for him, wanting to throw her arms around him, to bury her face in his neck, to smell him, kiss him...

He drew back.

Looked at her strangely.

She felt black, spiny fear. Sudden and dreadful.

"Walt," she said, tears already springing into her eyes, because she could not believe that he would not want to see her as

badly as she wanted to see him. And she could think of nothing to say except, "It's me! It's Carolyn!"

The people around them were very quiet.

Walt took a step back from her.

His eyes were cold and unknowing.

"Baby, it's me," she whispered.

He shook his head. "Your husband is dead," he said. "And I don't know you."

***

Carolyn woke up with her heart pounding in her chest, and the tears still in her eyes, and that horrible, dreadful feeling, of not being known. Of being forgotten. Abandoned. Laid by the wayside. A stranger to everyone.

A fleeting thought: *Who am I?*

Someone was knocking on the door.

She was in a room at the hotel. A crappy hotel called The Royale, in the middle of CoAx County.

A double bed with over-starched sheets and flat pillows.

Not even a pretense of artwork on the beige walls.

She was laying on her side, staring at the door as her pulse thundered.

The room was dim, but not dark.

It was morning. Light was coming in through the drawn privacy shades.

There was light under the door, too. And the shadows of someone's feet.

She threw the covers off and climbed out of bed with the stiffened gait of someone who does not want their movements to be heard. She was wearing only a plain white t-shirt which she'd ripped from the package of three last night, and a pair of panties.

She crept to the door on the tip-toes of her bare feet.

Her mind was cogent enough to think of something besides its initial warning klaxon of *DANGER! DANGER! DANGER!* Now she was wondering who the hell was at her door. Was it friend or foe? Was it the police? Was it an agent? Was it someone who would put a bullet in her the second she opened the door? Maybe some unassuming looking woman like the one they'd murdered yesterday and dumped in the trash…

When she was almost to the door, the knock came again.

And then a voice.

His voice.

"Carolyn," he said. "It's me. It's John."

She didn't relax, although the edge came off of her fear. She stood to the side of the door and leaned over to peek through the peephole.

In the hallway beyond, it was indeed John. He was standing, looking at his shoes.

Distrustfully, she looked as far to the right and left of him as the peephole could afford her. Because why the hell was he knocking on her goddamn door? Was he ever going to leave her the hell alone? Maybe there was someone else with him, hiding around the corner. You never could be too careful.

Jesus, she thought. *No wonder my parents went insane.*

She stepped back from the door and looked down at herself. No bra. Bare legs.

"Hold on," she said huskily, and then finally turned herself from the door.

She found the pants that she'd worn yesterday—the bottom of the legs still had bits of mud on them. They were laying on a chair that was sitting next to the window. She slipped them back on. There were a few bags of clean, new clothes sitting on the floor next to the chair, but she didn't know how they fit, and didn't want to bother right at the moment.

Rather than put her bra back on—her dirty, sweaty bra—she just threw her jacket on and zipped it up. She was not so well-endowed as other women that it would be obvious through a jacket.

Back at the door, she flipped the catch and the deadbolt and opened it.

John was holding a tray that she hadn't seen before. It had a covered platter on it. It was cheap plastic, and at first glance, Carolyn didn't want to eat whatever was under it.

He gave her a once over with his eyes.

"You know there's clean clothes in your room, right?" he asked. He said it nicely enough. "I thought I told you that last night."

Carolyn ignored him. "What is this? They have you running room service around here, too?"

He looked down at the platter and for a moment it almost seemed like he was embarrassed. "I just thought you'd be hungry," he said. "I didn't see you eat anything yesterday."

So. Her parents hadn't sent him to deliver food to her. He'd done it of his own accord.

That was nice. Right?

Carolyn felt a note of guilt. There wasn't much niceness around these days. Why make the man feel bad over trying to be thoughtful?

She moved out of the doorway. "Sorry. Yes. I guess I should eat something."

John entered the room and gave it a glance around. Carolyn let the door swing shut and she watched the man, the way his eyes tracked to the corners of the room. She didn't sense that he felt danger in the room, but rather that it was something he did out of long-born habits.

She felt briefly embarrassed as he stopped at the foot of the bed she'd slept in. She wasn't sure why. It was just one of those things. When someone sees your messy tangled sheets that still smell like your night sweat and morning breath, you feel exposed. A silly thing, really.

He set the platter down on her bed, then regarded the two bags of new clothing sitting on the floor. He sniffed, then looked at her with a touch of a sardonic smile on his lips. "You know, I had to go through the women's department for all of that stuff. It was very awkward."

Carolyn blinked a few times, then crossed her arms over her chest. "Well. That makes me want to wear it even less."

He snorted good-naturedly, and even that little display was odd coming from him. For the last two days he'd been so damn stoic. But Carolyn supposed he had to have a sense of humor lurking in there somewhere.

John gestured to one of the bags. "Did you bother checking through the entire bag?"

"Not all the way."

"You should look on the bottom."

Carolyn peered at the bag, cautiously. Then at John. Then she stepped over to the bag and peeled back a jumble of brand-new pants, looking beneath them like she expected to uncover a creepy item of lingerie, at which point John would leer at her and tell her to try it on.

At the bottom of the bag was a pistol.

She reached for it.

Hesitated.

Then picked it up.

It was nothing fancy. A small, black compact. Serial numbers scraped off.

She cast a look at John. Questioning.

John nodded. "Thought it might make you feel…more secure."

Carolyn still watched him for a moment. Not sure how to take this. Not sure how to feel about it. "That's…thoughtful."

"You're one of us now," he said. "We don't go about unarmed."

"Are we going about?"

"As a matter of fact, we are. I need you to meet me in the lobby in thirty minutes."

Carolyn frowned. "Where are we going?"

John was already heading for the door, but he took a moment to glance over his shoulder at her. "A very important meeting. Wouldn't want to be late."

***

Who am I?

They drove out to the east end of CoAx County in a small, dingy solar that smelled of bubblegum-flavored nicotine vapor. Carolyn couldn't decide whether she thought the smell was pleasant or not.

Same driver as last time—the older man named Brady—but a different car.

She wondered briefly what happened to the old car?

Was it "hot?"

Or had Brady dropped it somewhere to have that woman's blood scrubbed out of it?

Or was it just standard procedure to switch cars every day?

Carolyn was wearing a set of clothes that felt like she'd stolen them, or taken them from another woman's dresser. She'd feared when she dove into the bag that they would be the gaudy, faux-urby shit she'd seen the denizens of CoAx County wearing, but they were all clothes that she would have purchased for herself.

Good job, John.

She wore jeans, a gray cotton shirt, and her jacket, because it was still a bit chilly out, although the day felt like it was warming fast. The little pistol had come with a small belt-clip and this she'd secured inside her waistband, in the front of her pants.

This was based on John's suggestion.

He called it a "no-touch-zone."

But, even though she'd never carried a pistol before, she found it surprisingly comfortable. And John had been right. She felt more secure with it. Like a woobie. Like the matted white giraffe doll that she remembered toting around as a child.

Who am I? She thought again.

Am I Carolyn Baucom, wife of Walter Baucom?

Or am I Stephanie Eudy? Daughter of two of the nation's most feared terrorists?

Resistance, she corrected herself. *Not terrorists.*

But she still did not know who she was supposed to be. She was a just a woman, wearing borrowed clothes, toting an unregistered gun, as brand-new to this life as if she'd been a squalling newborn.

She decided to take a different mental tack to ease herself out of the discomfort she was feeling.

"So, John, how did you get mixed up in all of this?" She looked out the window as she spoke. The low, morning sun flashed dazzlingly between endless rows of buildings. "How did you come to be the Eudy's errand boy?"

He made a chuffing sound.

She looked at him and found him looking back, with an eyebrow raised.

"Wow," he said. "That's a dim appraisal of my skillset."

But he said it in the same easy way he'd handled her joust about the clothes earlier. And then before that, about the food.

Damn, why was she being so prickly?

It really was very rude of her.

She chose not to back down from that particular statement, but she did soften it with a smile and a shrug. "What's your official job title then?"

He smiled broadly, and she saw that he had a handsome face when he wasn't being so dour all the time. He looked up to the front where Brady was listening without listening. "Geez, Brady, what's our official job title?"

Brady smiled and shrugged without taking his eyes off the road. "Errand boys for the Eudys."

John rolled his eyes.

A silence passed, but Carolyn felt that some of the tension was gone.

"I was in GovSec for several years," he stated.

Carolyn considered this. GovSec was not a term she was intimately familiar with, but she knew that it stood for Government Sector and basically meant "people that did things for the Fed." It was a broad term.

"And what did you do in GovSec?"

"I was an analyst," he said, not looking at her.

She waited for more of an explanation, but he didn't provide it.

"And how did my parents get ahold of you?"

"A long and unexciting story."

She felt almost certain that he was fudging, if not flat-out lying.

Brady shifted about in the front seat.

"Something to add, Brady?" she asked him.

Brady smiled at the road. "John don't like to talk about himself is all. Smart man."

"Why don't *you* tell me about John, then?"

"Oh no. Dangerous man, too."

"A dangerous analyst. Seems contradictory."

John issued a long, exasperated sigh. "I may have had a small hand in getting your parents out of DTI. They were appreciative."

Brady nodded, but said nothing.

"Interesting," Carolyn remarked. "And you, Brady?"

"Me?" he asked with a laugh. "I'm just a driver."

"Right," Carolyn said. She went back to looking out the window.

That was the nature of these people, wasn't it? And why shouldn't it be? She couldn't be offended by it. You learned to live with your mouth shut. Never knowing who you could really trust, and never trusting anyone completely. Words led to tips, and tips led to DTI.

Smart man.

Dangerous man.

Maybe she should be taking notes.

It was hard to divorce herself from her previous life, because it was still there, it still hung on her like the feeling of a poignant dream, the way it hangs on you hours after you've awaken. But it wasn't her life anymore, was it? That'd been destroyed when the CoAx had purged District 89. And she wasn't going to get it back.

She missed Walt horribly in that moment. Would have given anything just to speak with him. Just to trade a few words with him. Just to hear him say that he loved her, and to say those words back to him.

It made her chest ache.

She couldn't go on thinking about it.

It would rob her of her strength. It would rob her of her smarts.

And that was what she needed right now.

After all, this wasn't the first time she'd had everything ripped away from her. And when her life had been turned upside down the first time when she was just a kid, she'd done the very same thing that she was going to do now.

She pushed the old stuff down. She devalued it in her mind, because otherwise it paralyzed her. And she could not afford to be paralyzed.

Beside her, John looked around at a passing street sign, and then quickly checked the time on his PD. He straightened his sleeves and turned to Carolyn. "We're just a few minutes out from the meeting spot. For the purposes of operational security, Benjamin and Jean requested that I not brief you until the last minute."

"What, did they think I was gonna call the cops on them?" Carolyn snipped. But surprisingly enough, she wasn't even that offended by it. Which she thought was a good sign. Maybe she was acclimating to this bullshit better than she thought.

John shrugged and moved on without answering her. "The meeting is between your parents and a few other high-tier resistance leaders. Your parents want me to impress upon you that it is their wish that you join them at this meeting because they want you to learn the ropes."

Carolyn just stared. There was a "but" there at the end…

"But they also want you to remain a silent observer during these negotiations."

Carolyn smiled without much humor. Gently ran a finger over her right eyebrow. Tucked her hair behind her ear despite the fact that it hadn't come loose. "Wow. So, sit at the kids table and let the adults talk, but maybe I'll learn enough to one day take over the family business, right?"

John sighed and looked forward again. "Carolyn, don't take offense to it. As an objective observer, I agreed with your parent's decision on this."

"You're their employee. Of course you agreed."

"I'm they're employee, yes. But I am allowed to have my own opinion on things." He glanced at her sidelong. "In fact, they asked me for my opinion on this, and I suggested that I believed you were mature enough to understand the gravity of the situation, and the fact that you are new to this world. No reasonable person would want to interject themselves into something they don't fully understand. Especially when the stakes are this high." He sniffed. "Was I wrong?"

Carolyn pursed her lips and looked out her window. "No," she mumbled to the glass. "You weren't wrong. I'll keep my mouth shut."

Maybe.

"Your parents are very adamant that you learn everything you can learn," John continued. "They want you to take the helm from them. Despite the fact that they have many trusted employees, I suppose it is a kind of dream for you take over what they've built."

Carolyn looked at him with a frown, but kept her mouth shut.

Was he jealous of her?

"We're here," he said.

They pulled up to a section of buildings that was particularly well-adorned with neon lights. Another collection of businesses that went hand-in-hand with eachother: gaming parlors, titty bars, and liquor stores. Brady drove them around back where they dipped down into an underground parking garage. It went down two levels, and Brady found a spot at the bottom.

There were very few cars there.

One homeless man sitting amongst a collection of cardboard and watching them with drunken animal eyes.

Brady stayed in the solar. John and Carolyn got out and walked towards a door. There were three doors on the basement level of the parking garage. None of them were labeled. They went to the one furthest to the right, and nearest to the homeless man who was still watching them.

John gave the man a look. "Wrong place, Jack. Get lost."

The man mumbled something, but decided that this wasn't his time to make a stand. He labored to his feet and sauntered towards a cement set of stairs that led to the topside, still grumbling.

John watched him go with narrowed eyes. He didn't move until the man was on his way up the stairs. Then he turned to the door and knocked.

The door opened immediately.

A tall, grave-looking man, like a mortician, stood there. He wore a loose-fitting tan suit and a turtle-neck. Something that felt out of place by several decades.

"All's well with you?" he asked.

"Right as rain," John answered.

The man nodded, apparently satisfied, and he turned and led them in.

The door drifted closed behind them and the sound of it clacking shut echoed in the hallway they were in. A cement hallway with no other doors on it. A tunnel, more than a hallway.

"The others are here," the mortician said. "They're waiting for you."

John didn't respond.

At the end of the tunnel, the room opened up, and here Carolyn detected the faint sound of throbbing bass somewhere over their heads. If she were to take a guess, she'd say they were in the basement of the titty bar.

In the square room they now found themselves in, there were a set of fake leather couches, on which sat a few large men, similarly dressed as the mortician. They were entertaining themselves at cards. They gave a glance up, but not much else.

Carolyn could see the bulges of weapons under their loose suit jackets.

Not pistols.

Subguns that they had strapped to their chests.

The mortician guided them to the left, to another door. This one he opened and stepped aside. John stood at the side of it and motioned Carolyn to go in. It was apparent that he would not be accompanying her.

In the room beyond, she saw her parents.

And a few other people.

She stepped into the room and the door closed behind her.

There was a table in the center of the room, and around this table there were four people, including her parents. Her mother was seated in her wheelchair, and her father sat beside her, and they were facing Carolyn. The other two people turned in their seats to look at Carolyn.

Her father stood up from his seat. "Stephanie," he said, and the name jarred her again. He gestured to the two other men sitting at the table. "This is Richard Honeycutt and Stephen Linklater. Richard, Stephen, this is my daughter, Stephanie." Her father smiled. "We are here to parlay. Have a seat."

CHAPTER SEVENTEEN

Carolyn—Stephanie—sat stiffly in a seat beside her mother.

So.

The Eudys, the Linklaters, and the Honeycutts.

All three major factions of the resistance, all under one roof.

Her heart did a two-step and she swallowed against a dry throat. She wanted to ask them if this was smart, to have all the heads of the snake in one spot. But she didn't ask that question. She was the newcomer to this world. Surely they had their reasons.

Her mother's simulated voice spoke, calm and smooth: "We would have told you ahead of time," the voice stated. "But things move quickly and quietly around here. You'll learn that."

Carolyn said nothing. She looked across the table at the two other men.

Stephen Linklater was a small man with a pinched expression on his face. He had jet black hair, but the color was too rich for the wear and tear she saw on his face, and she decided that it was a dye job on a man who probably went gray a decade ago. He gave her a curt nod, but otherwise seemed indifferent towards her.

Richard Honeycutt was another matter. He was leaning forward with his elbows on the table and his fingers interlaced and he was looking at her with an undeniably hostile expression. Unlike Linklater, Honeycutt had made no attempts to disguise his age. His face was drawn and craggy and lean, and his hair was nearly white, his goatee salt-and-pepper.

"So," he said with ample irritation in his voice. "This is the one that caused me so much trouble in District Eighty-Nine."

Carolyn was taken aback by the statement.

Her mother was the one that spoke back. That same, calm tone, which did not necessarily agree with the words that she said: "As I heard it, you had troubles enough going into that debacle."

Honeycutt looked up sharply at the woman in the wheelchair.

Her mother smiled poisonously, her lips not moving, but the voice sounding anyways. "As I heard it, you had some individuals that were causing you some issues. Wresting control away from you. Your right hand, Tria. And of course, your nephew, Virgil."

"They were both killed in the fighting," Honeycutt said sharply.

"Then I suspect you're the one who should be the most grateful for what happened in District Eighty-Nine. Otherwise, it might be Tria or Virgil we'd be talking to now."

Carolyn's father cleared his throat loudly. "We're here to parlay," he said, and then put a gentle hand on his wife's withered arm. "Not to argue."

"Yes," Linklater agreed with an imperious sniff. "And our time is valuable. And being here is dangerous. So let's speak and be done."

Benjamin Eudy placed his hands on the table. "Our separation is endangering the cause."

"Your recklessness is endangering the cause," Honeycutt shot back.

Benjamin opened his mouth to speak, but Honeycutt jabbed a finger at him.

"We were doing just fine before you got out of DTI!"

"You weren't doing much at all," Jean Eudy's voice cut in. "The resistance was floundering. The people had backed down. You were sitting on cash flows from information and black market goods. You were—"

"I was using *intelligence* to fight a war!" Honeycutt smacked the table. "Not blowing up every goddamned—"

And in that moment, Carolyn discovered that while Jean Eudy's synthesized voice could not simulate the emotions that she was feeling—could not yell, could not change its tone from the polite, half-smiling voice—Jean was completely capable of controlling the volume of that calm voice.

The voice thundered in the room, but the tone was still polite: "DO NOT INTERRUPT ME."

"Jesus," Honeycutt flinched and half raised his hands to his ears.

Carolyn herself winced as she felt the sound pressing at her eardrums.

"Jean…" Benjamin said with a pained look.

Jean dialed the modulator down to a less throbbing volume, but not fully back to where it had been. "In the internment camps they do not allow us to speak. I have had enough of holding my tongue. I have had enough of being silent." Her lips worked restlessly, the smile gone from them. Now they were a cold slash in her face, moving like she wished she could speak the words, but could only let the modulator do its job. Her eyes were fiery enough to speak volumes, though. "You will not interrupt me again."

"I don't even have to be here," Honeycutt said with a sneer.

"Then leave," Jean replied.

Honeycutt looked surprised, as though he'd expected them to beg him to stay.

"Leave, and see what happens."

Honeycutt frowned. "What's that supposed to mean?"

"You are crumbling, and we are rising," the voice stated. "We did not ask you here to beg for your help. We asked you here to offer you a chance not to die. We are strong and getting stronger. We have elements of defected military, and we expect more to come. You have spies and snitches and drug dealers. We have contacts in every level of the government. You have human traffickers. We do not need you. You need us."

Honeycutt stood up. "I don't have to listen to this nonsense. You've gone mad in DTI. To be expected, I guess." He turned and looked at Linklater. "You can drink the kool-aid if you want, Stephen. But I think I'm done here."

Linklater also stood, his pinched face relaxing into a sort of bland look. "Ayuh. I'd expected more."

"You're all idiots."

The words came out of Carolyn like the popping of an over-filled balloon. She hadn't even meant to speak them at first, but as she'd listened—first to her mother, and then to Honeycutt, and then to Linklater—they continued to build and build and build in her brain until it felt like her head was not big enough to hold them in anymore.

She just kept thinking of Walt.

She kept thinking about the words that she'd seen him say when he'd been staring at that camera and looking like a version of her husband that she never even knew existed—a bloody, smoke-smeared, battle-hardened version. One with something in his eyes that she'd thought was long dead, but it wasn't, because you couldn't really kill it. You could never really kill it.

Our country, our leaders, our government—they've sold you out, he'd said.

And if you were ever thinking about doing something, if you'd ever considered saying 'enough is enough,' then maybe you should do something about it right now. Because the situation is only getting worse. It's only going to get harder and harder to fight them.

And it made her furious to listen to these gathered heads, twitter to each other about their own personal pride, when the lives of millions stood in the balance, and out there in those streets, in those districts, there were poor, dirty-faced people that were clinging to a thread of hope that maybe, just maybe, the resistance would unite and win and they would have a chance to live a free life…

But behind these closed doors, here they were.

Comparing their dick sizes.

And her mother in on it, too.

Carolyn leaned back in her chair and couldn't help the distaste written on her face like she'd just sucked a lemon. "You're all fucking idiots."

Honeycutt waved her off. "Bah," he said, as though that was all he needed to say, and then he turned to the door. "We're through."

Carolyn rocketed out of her chair. "Go then, you fucking traitor."

Somehow, that managed to stop him.

Ah, but offense is usually tied to a chord of truth, now isn't it?

When something is offensive, it is because it is the thing we fear the most, and someone is saying it out loud.

Honeycutt spun on her. "You have no idea what I've sacrificed for this cause."

Carolyn just shrugged and put her hands in the air. "Maybe. Maybe not. I don't know you from Adam. But what I see here is a man walking away from his country, from his people. For something as silly as his pride." She glared at him. "Do you want your country back, or do you just want to keep getting paid?"

And before Honeycutt could answer that question, Carolyn spun and looked at her mother. "And you! Both of you! Acting like you've got the goddamned world on a string. You're awfully proud of the dungheap you've created, aren't you? Do *you* want your country back? Or do you prefer a fucking graveyard?"

"You know—"

And Carolyn was relatively sure that her mother was going to say "you know nothing," but she didn't let her finish. "I know that there are millions of people right now, looking up at you!" she jabbed a finger at her mother, then swept it to Linklater and Honeycutt. "And you! And you! They are looking to the people that are standing in this room, and they are *waiting*, they're just *waiting* to have a fighting chance!

"How many history lessons?" she suddenly demanded of them. "How many?"

They looked confused, but at least Linklater and Honeycutt were standing there, and not walking away. She wasn't sure she truly cared in that moment, but she needed them to hear. She needed to say it, and she needed for it to get through their thick, prideful skulls.

"How many history lessons have you read about the triumph of a factioned-off resistance?" Her eyebrows went up, imploring them, daring them to give her an answer because she knew there wasn't one. "None? Oh, yes. There's not one, is there? Because a factioned resistance is a losing resistance, and history is written by the winners, isn't it? Yes it is.

" 'A house divided cannot stand.' 'Join or die.' 'United we stand, divided we fall.'" She actually laughed, hard, and genuine. "I may just be a dumbfuck grower from the districts, but even I know that. And all of my other dumbfuck grower friends know it too. They know that if they try to fight right now, they're fucking dead, one and all. So they wait. They wait for you three to get your shit together so that they can have a fighting chance. And they *will.* They *will* fight. I know it. I know it because my own husband is doing it, and if there was ever a man that didn't want this fight, it was him. And there are millions just like him. All they need is to see, all they need is to feel that you three factions have come together. And if you can show them that, then you will have such a groundswell that the CoAx will have no hope of ever coming back. Because they cannot fight every man and woman in this country. And that is who they'll have to fight." She paused and stared at each of them, her eyes wide, almost pleading. "*If…if* you can sit down. *If* you can come together. *If* you can think about them, and not about yourselves. Your country. Not your pride."

She threw her hand at the door. "So if you want to walk, then walk. But you *will* be a traitor. Each and every one of you will be a traitor, and myself with you. Because you had a chance. You had a chance right now to actually win. And you pissed it away."

Carolyn sat down, then, and she couldn't look at any of them. Instead, she stared at a spot on the wall, somewhere over Linklater's right shoulder. Her face burned. The back of her neck tingled. It was everything she had in her to not fidget like a kid trapped in a desk just a minute before the bell rings.

She was completely certain that they were going to walk out that door.

But it was Honeycutt that backed down first.

He tugged his shirtsleeves straight and gave his throat a brief clearing, and then he spoke in a low tone that was not completely friendly, but not altogether impudent, as it had been. "Well, there's one Eudy in this room that hasn't gone completely insane."

He bent, as though to take his seat, but then propped his fists on the table and loomed over Carolyn. "Word to the wise," he said. "Coarse language will get you nowhere. But I'll give five minutes based on the merits of your argument, Ms. Eudy. Or do you prefer Mrs. Baucom?"

She looked at him rigidly, and raised her face to him. "I do, as a matter of fact."

Honeycutt sat.

Linklater followed suit with a deep sigh.

Carolyn shot a glance to her parents and saw Benjamin was looking at the men, almost apologetically, while her mother was looking back at her. Her mother's thin fingers hovered next to the voice modulator on her temple, but she didn't touch it. Her eyes were watery and red, and as Carolyn watched, one of them spilled over.

"Speak, Ben," Honeycutt said. "Or will your daughter take command? I wouldn't necessarily mind…"

Benjamin Eudy leaned forward. "Our sources suggest the CoAx is seriously considering a troop surge," he said flatly.

Linklater and Honeycutt both nodded.

"Yes," Linklater said. "I've heard the same."

"Whatever we do," Benjamin continued. "We need to do it before those troops land. We have a window of opportunity to break their hold here. But it's a narrow one. Time is not our friend."

"Assuming that there is a 'we' moving forward," Honeycutt said. "If we move too aggressively, it might just galvanize them *into* the troop surge. Whereas, as it stands right now, it seems that the surge is only a consideration, and not popular in the international community."

Benjamin tilted his head to allow the point, and offered a counter. "If we don't move aggressively enough, we'll lose the small window that we have."

Blessedly, Honeycutt and Linklater just listened, so Benjamin pressed forward.

"We've managed to turn roughly ten percent of the active Fed ground forces. They are currently in hiding and able to mount operations from that hiding, but it's not a matter of *if* the CoAx locates them, but *when*. If we can make strong enough use of them quickly, there are other elements of the Fed command that will make the break to our side. But only if it seems like a winning proposition. If we're not bold enough, or not *successful* enough, those commanders on the fence will remain on the fence."

Honeycutt made a beckoning gesture with his fingers. "Give me numbers, Ben. You have ten percent now—what will 'bold and successful action' get us?"

Carolyn could hear the quotes that Honeycutt put around those words.

"We have promising contact with two additional commanders. Which would net us control of about a third of the Fed military active in the continental United States."

"A third, including the ten percent you have now?" Honeycutt asked.

"Yes."

Linklater made a dubious grumbling sound.

Benjamin held up a hand. "The numbers aren't the only story here. There is an X factor to be counted as well, and that is the power of a movement. Of momentum. Of a groundswell, as she put it." He nodded briefly towards Carolyn. "If a third of the military has turned, that only makes it more likely that others will turn as well. The elements of the Fed that are completely loyal to their CoAx masters are a sad minority. They're holding their fingers in the dyke, and they know it."

"And the people?" Linklater asked suddenly, leaning back and looking across the table, not at Benjamin or Jean, but at Carolyn. "What about them? At what point will they fight?"

Carolyn blinked twice, felt put on the spot, but was determined not to back down. "Some already are. And the rest? Most of them are waiting for a reason. Most of them are just worried about their families. They won't fight if they know the CoAx can come and disappear their loved ones at will." Carolyn glanced at her father. "Like he said, it's a question of winnability. Or even less than that, just the *perception* of winnability. If victory seems real, if it seems attainable, they will start to fight in droves."

"You seem very confident," Linklater said.

"I am," she said back.

"What makes you the voice of the people, Mrs. Baucom?"

"I'm one of them," she stated with as much confidence as she could muster, even as her brain started going silently through a codex of every person she knew, and she began to doubt—would they fight? Was she putting too much faith in them? Most people just wanted to be comfortable. Most people just wanted to be left alone.

Just like her.

Just like Walt.

But Walt was fighting now.

And so was she.

She could not let her doubts show through. She had to have faith in the people. Even if only a small percentage of them picked up the fight, a small percentage of many millions was still a force to be reckoned with. It was still more than she thought the CoAx could handle.

"I'm not a resistance leader," Carolyn said. "I haven't spent my life fighting. I don't have ties to the black market. I'm just another grower, and I lived my life in the Agrarian Districts. That's why I know these people. I know these people because they're all like me. I can speak for them. I can *promise* for them."

"Careful," Honeycutt grumbled. "You should never make promises that you can't keep."

"They'll fight," she said, blocking out her misgivings. "I can promise that."

Linklater and Honeycutt both turned their gaze back to Benjamin.

Carolyn spared a look at her mother and saw that her hand was no longer near the voice modulator. Her eyes were no longer wet, but they were red, and they stared unmovingly at a fixed point on the wall.

Had Carolyn wounded her with her words?

Or had Jean decided to keep her digital mouth shut for the sake of the cause?

Were you truly insane if you could see that your insanity was putting others off?

Carolyn did not think that her mother had truly lost touch with reality. But what she had was a form of insanity all the same. It was an insanity of rage. It was an insanity of grief. It was the madness of obsession.

"And what is it that you need from us?" Honeycutt asked Benjamin. "What is our investment in this?"

Benjamin gathered himself up a bit and lowered his chin as though expecting a blow. "There are three main centers of contention that are currently local to us right now. These are areas where the CoAx is already having to stage troops and work towards calming insurrection. They're all cities, because the CoAx can't control the cities like they can control the Districts—there's too many people, too many ways in, too many ways out, and way too much geography. These places are powder kegs ready to go off."

"Opportunity," Linklater said plainly.

Benjamin nodded. "Yes. One is Pittsburgh, Pennsylvania. South of us right now, in Jacksonville, Florida. And in North Carolina, there is Durham. There are plenty of other locations where small resistance groups have become active, but we don't have high hopes for them. Pittsburgh, Jacksonville, and Durham will be hard for the CoAx to control."

Benjamin folded his hands together. "What we need is to pick one, and begin funneling weapons and agitators into that area. We need one of those places to explode. And we're hedging our bets on Durham, for a variety of reasons. It is the most downtrodden city of the three. It has seen the least economic recovery and therefore has the least reason to love the CoAx. There have been several notable disappearings lately that have garnered support for the resistance and a hatred of the CoAx. And it is close to Raleigh, the state capitol. Which, in time, could prove to be a great symbolic victory, if not an especially strategic one."

The corner of Linklater's mouth turned down a bit. "Honestly, Ben, these cities seem like small potatoes in the grand scheme of things. I'm not sure what strategic motive you see in them aside from causing carnage. I'd like to hear more strategy in general."

"And what if we don't agree with your strategy?" Honeycutt asked.

"Then we figure out another strategy," Benjamin said. "One that we all agree on. But we are dealing with sensitive issues now. I'm sure you can appreciate that. And what's decided behind these closed doors must remain behind these closed doors as much as possible. You both know how close we live to the edge of being found out. If we're going to make a go of this, operational security is a must. Which means I'm not talking specifics until we're pledged and agreed to work together."

Linklater frowned. "When do you expect an answer from us?"

"Now."

Honeycutt chuffed. "That's awfully short term for such a big decision."

And then came again the calm, polite voice of Jean Eudy's modulator. "The time is now."

Carolyn winced and looked at her mother, knowing for certain now that Jean was going to ruin the whole goddamned thing. She and her father had just managed to calm them down and get them talking, and Jean was going to drive them out the door again.

But the words came out slowly, and they were even-keel.

"We have no more time," she said. "You either believe that this is an opportunity that must be taken advantage of, or you don't. You are either convinced that we have a chance now, or you are convinced that we will lose and the CoAx will ultimately own our nation once and for all. There is no other case that we can make to you. We've made our arguments for working together. They've either convinced you, or they haven't. So there is no need for either of you to deliberate, and there isn't time anyways. You either believe, or you do not."

A long moment of silence passed.

Linklater stared at the center of the table, his lips pursed in thought.

Honeycutt stared at Jean, his jaw muscles bunching, his shoulders drawn up into a slouch.

Carolyn looked across at her mother, and found the woman looking back again. She removed her hand from where it hovered near the voice modulator and let it drop to the arm of her wheelchair where it seemed it would rest permanently.

She was done speaking.

She gave a small nod to Carolyn, and Carolyn gave it back.

"Alright," Honeycutt blurted suddenly. He shoved himself back from the table and out of his slouch. "My chips are all in. Let's lay the cards out."

Linklater took another moment of his own counsel. Still staring at the center of the table, he finally nodded. "Ayuh. I'm in. But this won't do."

Carolyn stared at him, questioningly.

He reached into his coat pocket and withdrew a flask, which he uncapped and held up. "No contracts among thieves, but a drink will make it official." He looked at each of them in turn and a small, wry smile tugged at the corner of his mouth. "To being alive and free a year from today."

Then he took a slug of whatever the flask contained.

Then he passed it to Honeycutt, who gave the flask a brief look of distaste, but raised it anyways. "To being alive and free in one year."

He passed it to Carolyn. She didn't hesitate. Refused to show any hesitation, just as she refused to allow her own creeping doubts to manifest. "Alive and free next year," she said, and took a slug. It was bourbon, she thought.

Benjamin took it. "Alive and free next year."

He didn't pass it immediately to Jean. He glanced at his wife and then at Linklater and Honeycutt. "She shouldn't. The medications…"

Jean's wheelchair started forward and bumped the table. A skinny hand shot out and snatched the flask with surprising speed. Jean raised it up with her right hand, and with her left, touched the voice modulator.

"Alive and free. Indefinitely."

Then she drank. A bit deeply.

When Linklater took the flask from her, he was smiling as though they were all friends. And perhaps, in his mind, they were. Or as best of friends they could be after being enemies at the beginning of the day. But there is ceremony in drink, even something so rough as bourbon in a flask. There is a spirituality in spirits that cannot be denied. And very suddenly, the mood in the room shifted, as Linklater put the flask away in his jacket pocket with the finality of a notary stamping a document and making copies for the official record.

It was a piece of ribbon given for bravery.

It was a title given to the one that has earned it.

It was something that held importance only because everyone involved chose to believe that it was so.

They were no longer three hostile parties in a fragile parlay.

They were now three conspirators, planning their freedom.

"Alright," Linklater said in a low voice, drawing himself up close to the table. "Now, for better or worse, we're in this. Let's talk specifics."

So they talked.

CHAPTER EIGHTEEN

The years had not been kind to Durham.

Nor had the last several days.

Walt remembered the night that everything had gone to shit in District 89. He remembered thinking as he'd driven to a quiet little backwoods trailer where a Chicom captain was being held captive, that he could feel the tension in the District.

It did not compare to this.

They drove into the north end of Durham with the rising sun, on a bright and crisp spring morning.

As is usual in the process of gentrification and industrialization and commercialization, the generations had seen the shit-side of Durham shift from one side of the city to the other, like a blob being chased around a ring.

Currently, the northwest corner was the place of poverty.

The center of Durham and the southeast were predominantly owned by the wealthy and by businesses that had hopped on the economic recovery bandwagon at the expense of their country's sovereignty.

In the north end, the buildings had risen and fallen and risen and fallen, and now they were residential. Endless blocks of apartments and townhomes that maybe once had been nice, but the years and neglect had turned them to poverty, the process of gentrification having moved on and leaving the wilds in their wake, like a previously cultivated field being left fallow.

Walt had moved up from the back cargo area to the front passenger seat that Roy had vacated when he'd taken the wheel. From this vantage point, Walt noticed two things immediately that set him on edge.

First, at no point in time was he able to look skyward and see any less than two gunships hovering about. Most of the time he could see the full flight of three. They were not engaged. Nor were they flying around with any sort of purpose, as though to get from one place to another. But simply passing by overhead in a slow, scanning motion.

A warning to the people below.

Second, despite the early hour, on nearly every corner or block of buildings, there was a group of people standing and watching. Their faces were hard and suspicious and it was in those faces that Walt felt the tension—so much worse than he'd felt it in District 89.

"Jesus," Walt whispered. "This place is about to blow."

That was exactly how it felt.

Like they were standing in the cauldron of a volcano, and it was rumbling, dissatisfied, under their feet.

Roy, still at the wheel, said nothing. He drove through deliberately, and he didn't hold the gaze of any of the people that watched them pass.

A few times, Walt spotted a CoAx patrol. Usually three guntrucks, but once it was two guntrucks framing a personnel carrier. But the patrols seemed to know where they were. They didn't waste time. They hauled ass and they weren't stopping. They knew what would happen if they did.

"There's been fighting here," Roy said. "Just spats. Here and there type of shit. But I think the CoAx is gearing up. I think they know what's about to happen around here."

"Why the hell are we in the middle of this, then?" Walt asked.

"I have contacts here. People that can help us."

Walt accepted that. This was Roy's world. He'd do well to remember that.

He leaned over and took a look in the back.

Rat was sound asleep, his head lolling with the gentle motions of the van.

The rest of them were awake, but bleary-eyed. There'd been some sleep in transit, but not much. It was never easy to sleep in a vehicle.

Roy slowed down and pulled into the parking lot of some sort of convenience store. The paving was so broken up that it had almost returned to gravel. The store was a big cube, with one door, but two bright signs projecting into the air. One declared it NORTH MART and the other argued that it was THE FISH MARKET.

Roy backed into a spot. The smell of trashy seafood and the tinge of ammonia came through almost immediately, and Walt decided that it was indeed THE FISH MARKET.

Roy put the van into park and leaned back in his seat.

"What now?" Walt asked.

"We wait."

In the back, Rat began to snore. Getty elbowed him gently awake.

"What?"

Getty nodded towards the windshield. "We're stationary. Look alive."

Rat stretched and yawned and grumbled. "Shit. We're there already?"

In the front passenger seat, Walt fidgeted. He looked around. To the right of the FISH MARKET/NORTH MART was an auto-shop. Then there was an intersection. On the other side of the intersection, a laundromat, and beyond that, apartment high-rises.

To the left and directly across from Walt, there were only more high-rises.

On the other side of the street, and slightly down from them, there was a transit stop. Standing behind the stop were two men and a woman. They stood in a way that suggested they weren't there for the bus. The woman had dusky skin and Walt couldn't tell what her ethnicity was. One of the men was a very dark black. The other was white.

They didn't look happy. They weren't hanging out. They had that look about them that Walt had seen on everyone else's faces coming in.

They were waiting. Watching.

He tried not to stare at them. He didn't want them to see him looking.

But twice he saw the woman turn and begin to speak to the men, and then she would look over her shoulder, just a quick glance, right back at Walt and the van. Then she would go back to talking.

Then one of the men would look up at them.

Then they would all look around, as though there was nothing interesting about the van at all.

After a few iterations of this eye-dance, the light-skinned woman turned on her heel and went directly to the apartment entrance that was behind the group. She went inside and shut the door behind them.

"You see that?" Walt asked, quietly.

"M-hm," Roy said.

Walt started looking up and down the windows of the apartment building that the woman had gone into. There were five stories. The entrance seemed to be in the center, and was likely a common entrance—a stairwell that led to all of those apartments.

Five stories, six windows across. Three to each side of the center entrance.

After about a minute he saw a ghost of movement in one of the upper windows.

"Top floor," Walt said. "Second window from the right."

"Ayuh," Roy said. "Hey, Koz?"

"Yeah?"

"Slide a rifle up to Walt. Discreetly."

Walt looked across the cab at his brother. Roy's eyes were now fixed on the two men at the transit stop. The white one had his back turned. The black one was glancing at them repeatedly. His lips were moving, but there was very little animation in his features. He was trying to speak inconspicuously.

Roy had snaked his hand under his shirt and jacket and had pulled a pistol out, which he held loosely in his lap.

"Walter," Koz said from behind him.

Walt turned and saw that Koz had slid a battlerifle across the floor to him, buttstock first.

"Don't let them see that," Roy said, as Walt took the thing and pulled it up between his legs. He quickly checked the magazine and chamber. It felt good to know how, and then it felt bad.

"If anything happens," Roy continued. "I'm driving, and you're shooting."

"Okay."

"Don't shoot me."

Walt ground his teeth. "Go fuck yourself, Roy."

"If it goes down," Roy said, "She's gonna be shooting out that window. So you just light that fucker up until we're out."

Walt knew damned well that if he were to "light that fucker up," someone was going to catch a round that didn't necessarily deserve to catch one. You couldn't just spray the front of an apartment building and not have collateral damage.

So the wind blows.

He just nodded. Kept staring at that window.

You have to do what you have to do.

Across the street, the white guy turned and suddenly broke off. He walked across the street, heading directly towards them, and there was no disguising his intentions. Shoulders hunched. Hands in his jacket pockets. Eyes right on them.

"One crossing the street," Roy said. "I don't know what he wants, but he's coming to my side."

Koz and Javon were both sitting on the bench directly behind Walt. If someone were at the driver's window, they would be able to see the New Breeds with just a tilt of their head. And that would cause a lot of needless questions.

The two New Breeds shifted to the opposite side, now directly behind Roy.

Koz drew a pistol and held it across his waist, with his shoulder to the wall of the van. He addressed the muzzle of the weapon at the wall, at an angle. If he fired, whoever was standing next to Roy's door stood a good chance of catching something.

"If you want him gone," Koz said in a low voice directed at Roy. "Just ask him about a taxi."

"Taxi, heard," Roy said quietly.

The man was across the street now. On the sidewalk.

Walt didn't like the way the man was walking. His left elbow was swinging with his pace, but his right elbow was pinched to his side. Like you would if you were holding a sawed-off shotgun under your jacket.

"He's holding something in his jacket," Walt said.

"Ayuh," Roy said, and he reached up and pulled the shift lever into drive, and then rolled down the window. "That's close enough," he called sharply.

The man slowed, but kept walking, his body coming up more erect now. He bladed himself just slightly, pulling that pinched right arm away from them.

He was about ten yards away.

"Stop or I blow your fucking head off," Roy said.

The man stopped. He regarded Roy carefully, then looked past Roy to Walt. Walt's eyes kept tracking back to that window in the upper level of the apartment. Then back to the man.

The man hadn't taken his hands out of his pockets.

You see, when someone threatens to blow your head off, and you are innocent, you typically raise up your hands to show that you have nothing to harm them. This isn't something that needs to be trained. This is simple, human body language that dates back thousands of years. It's a part of your DNA, just like a smile, or a sneer.

But when someone tells you they're going to blow your head off, and your hands stay in your pockets, well, then you're trying to reason through whether you think you can take them. You're wondering if you're fast enough. If they're a good enough shot. Or if they're bluffing altogether.

Walt watched all of this play out, and knew it without having to reason it through.

"You got guns pointed at you right now," Walt said. "You ain't that fast. And neither is your girl in that upstairs window."

The man glanced upwards towards the apartments, then seemed to catch himself and looked back at Walt and Roy. Then his face did a complete change, from considering whether he could take them, to considering whether he could *fake* them.

"I was just goin' to the store, man," he said.

But he still hadn't taken his hands out of his pockets.

"No you're not," Roy said.

"I'm not?" The man's face reddened.

"Not right now. You can go to the store later."

"I can go where I want."

"Not today you can't."

"Who the fuck you think you are?"

"I'm the guy that don't bluff."

The man continued to stare at them.

Briefly, he glanced over his shoulder at the black man across the street who was watching, but not approaching. Then his eyes flicked to that upper window—he knew the one, just as well as Walt and Roy did—and then back to Roy.

The man was still standing a few paces off the side of their van. And for a moment it seemed that they'd come to a stalemate. Here, this man neither wanted to cow, nor did he wish to call their bluff. And Roy didn't really want to open up on the guy—not because he'd lose sleep over it, but because it would be noisy, messy, and it would screw up their meeting.

Walt was wondering how long the standoff would last, when a gray car slowed down and pulled in behind the man. It was a nice luxury car, but an older model. Walt could see through the windshield and he could see that the car was full.

Walt tensed again and shifted in his seat.

"We're cool," Roy said quietly to his brother.

The man heard the car pull up behind him. He whirled, but then stiffened. Stared. Then stepped out of the way of the vehicle. The gray luxury vehicle pulled up so it was abreast of the man, and the back window slid down just a bit. The windows were heavily tinted. Walt could see nothing about the man behind that window but his eyes.

The man bent close.

Whoever was inside was saying something that Walt couldn't hear. The man on foot didn't make a response. He simply turned on his heel and headed back across the street to the transit stop.

The eyes above that tinted glass looked over at Roy, and Roy nodded back at them.

The window slid back up, and the gray vehicle drove off.

Roy eased out onto the street and began to follow it.

The gray vehicle led them through a serpentine course of back streets and even a few back alleys, sometimes moving quickly and sometimes going slow. Walt frequently checked their mirrors to see if they had a tail, but whatever the people in the gray vehicle were worried about, he couldn't see it.

Maybe it was simply precautionary.

After about five minutes of this hectic, random driving, they pulled into the back of a warehouse in a cloud of whitish dust. The gray vehicle hauled quickly around the back of the warehouse, and Roy sped after them, as though it was a chase.

At the back of the warehouse there were two loading bays. One of them was open with a man standing there, holding that corrugated sliding door up just high enough to accommodate the two vehicles.

The gray vehicle slid in without hesitation.

Roy tapped the brakes, but followed suit.

The second the rear of the van cleared the doorway, the man let it slide down shut.

The interior of the warehouse was a wide open space with almost cathedral-like ceilings and no windows at all. The light that there was came from work lamps that had been erected in several places around them, and also from the glow of the vehicle's headlamps, which were quickly extinguished.

The circle of light that they found themselves in was surrounded by darkness and, after the bright sunshine of the morning made Walt feel that he'd suddenly been plunged into some miles-deep cave where sunlight dared not wander. It was obvious just from the exterior of the building that the warehouse was large, but with the surrounding darkness it was cavernous.

Roy exited the van, and Walt with him. Then the back door slid open, and the others came out.

It sounded clamorous. Busy. Wailing air wrenches and crackling arc welders and clanging metal on metal. A palpable tension in the air. Workers moving fast to meet an approaching deadline. It smelled like welding rods and garage workshops.

The lighted area that they were now in was roughly twenty yards in diameter. Besides the nice gray vehicle and the shitty old van, there were three other vehicles in that place, and these vehicles were being operated on, the mechanics around them like Frankenstein at his monster, the flashes from their arc welders like the lightning to bring it to life.

All three of those vehicles were older model pickups that had been stripped to their bare bones and were currently being rebuilt. Rebuilt with armor on the sidings. Rebuilt with Lancer canons bolted into the back, although where the hell they'd managed to come across those, Walt had no idea.

They were building technicals.

The chariot of any resistance.

The mechanics weren't the only ones around.

There were men and women that didn't exactly crowd them in, but it was obvious that they were there to surround whoever came out of that van, and each and every one of them was armed with weaponry that was beyond illegal—which was to say, it wasn't a sportsman's shotgun.

Walt did a quick scan and counted ten of these armed "guards"—that was all he could think to call them at the moment. He figured there were a few he couldn't see.

The doors to the gray vehicle opened all at once, and out came a series of individuals. The man that was sitting in the back passenger side—the one that had traded words with the shady young man from the transit stop—was an Asian male dressed in jeans and a canvas jacket with a hood.

None of the four men from the gray vehicle approached them.

The Asian man, who Walt immediately pegged as the one in charge, just stood there watching them.

A woman stepped forward from the loose ring of guards that were around them. She had an unpleasant cast to her face. She looked them each over carefully, up and down, but her eyes rested most suspiciously on the New Breeds.

The arc welders spit and spat.

An air wrench buzzed and whined.

"You'll need to leave your weapons in the van," she said, and her voice, while commanding, was calm and level.

The whole lot of them, including Walt, looked to Roy.

Roy licked his lips, then turned to look at the Asian man that was still standing and watching them. The Asian man nodded. And Roy turned and nodded back to his crew.

Koz and Javon shrugged. They deposited the weapons they had on them into the back of the van. Roy walked over and laid his pistol in. Walt contributed the battlerifle that he was still holding.

Getty and Rat had yet to be armed, so they just held up their hands for a moment, and then let them flop to their sides.

Walt did not particularly want to be disarmed, but he kept a ranging eye on Roy, and it seemed that Roy didn't have too many misgivings about it.

That didn't necessarily mean that Roy was right.

"Is that everything?" the woman asked.

"That's everything," Roy answered.

"Step away from the van."

Javon reached to close the sliding door.

"Leave that open," she said.

Javon hesitated, but then relented and followed the rest of them a few slow steps away from the van.

The woman nodded to a man to her left who was holding a wand, similar to the one that Koz had scanned the van with the previous night.

He approached and began to scan the van.

"We already swept it," Roy said.

"We'll sweep it again," the woman replied.

Roy rolled his eyes but said nothing.

As the van was swept for bugs, two other guards came forward and began to hurriedly pat down the crew. Walt watched them get to the New Breeds, the way they towered over those unfortunate guards, the way the guards kind of cringed moving in, like they were being told to pet a tiger.

Javon just smiled at the one that was patting him down. A great, big, feelingless smile. Perhaps more of a display of teeth than an actual smile.

The man that patted Walt down looked him in the eyes for a moment, and there was a flash of recognition there, but he kept frisking, and when he was done, he moved away and said nothing.

When all of them had been checked, the woman turned and nodded to the Asian man near the gray vehicle. He finally walked over to them. He had no swagger in his walk. His body-language was not that of a person who enjoyed their power over others. He walked with purpose, with his shoulders slightly stooped, as though he felt his power more like a yoke that was weighing him down.

"Roy," he said, and extended his hand.

Roy shook it. “Jimmy. Quite the welcoming committee.”

“Desperate times, my friend. I’m sure you understand.” He looked past Roy to the New Breeds. “And you’re…sure about these two, huh?”

Javon didn’t give a reaction, but Koz bristled a bit.

“They indoctrinate them, Jimmy,” Roy said with a humorless smile. “They don’t brainwash them. They can think for themselves. I’d trust those two with my life, and have. They’re no loyalists, I promise you that.”

“Hm. Well.”

“Did you get the intel that I asked for?”

Jimmy glanced at Walt, and again, there was a flash of recognition there, and Walt wasn’t a fan. Not a fan at all of being recognized. He was quickly realizing that he preferred to be the gray man in the background.

“Yes,” Jimmy said. “The trucks that you described to us, they entered District Eighty-Nine last night around midnight. Left approximately an hour after that. Heading east. Last tabs we had on them, they were just short of Carthage.”

Roy looked at Koz.

The enormous, red-bearded man had taken a step or two closer as Jimmy had spoken. Now, he nodded to Roy. “That sounds about right. I’d guess they made the black site by oh-three-hundred or so. How many of those trucks were there?”

“Two,” Jimmy said.

“That’ll be roughly sixty detainees,” Koz said with a nod of his lion-like head. “But not all of them will be questioned. And they’ll move them at night, to avoid traffic. We need to be in place by twenty-one-hundred tonight. No later.”

Roy looked from Koz to Jimmy. “Do you have the other thing?”

Jimmy nodded. “We do.”

“How much?”

Jimmy waved him off. “We’ll talk prices later. You have only a small amount of time, and I suspect you’ll want to sleep. I have a room for you gentlemen. It’s not much, but it has mattresses.”

At first, Walt thought the idea of sleep at that moment was ludicrous, but after jouncing around in the van all night, the sudden thought of a mattress—even a stained and lumpy second-hand mattress—seemed luxurious. He was suddenly bone-achingly tired.

"Sleep would be a good idea," Koz noted. "We have a long night ahead of us."

Roy nodded marginally. "Okay then."

The man with the scanner wand appeared next to Jimmy. He'd apparently done more than just sweep the van. He'd also searched its contents, and he was holding Roy's backpack. He handed this to Jimmy with a sideways look at Roy.

Jimmy took it and looked inside. The bag was open already.

Roy shifted uncomfortably but said nothing.

"Grenades?" Jimmy said doubtfully.

"Yes," Roy responded, stiffly.

Jimmy reached in and took one out, holding it up like an apple he was inspecting for bruises.

It was the first time that Walt had seen them, but he knew in an instant what it was. A black cylinder with a switch on the side covered by a red safety paddle. The ends were bulbous. Like a small dumbbell.

"Strangest looking grenade I've ever seen," Jimmy remarked.

Roy let out a slow breath and watched the other man.

Jimmy held Roy's gaze. "Never seen a grenade with speakers on it before."

A moment passed with the two of them regarding each other like poker players in an all in hand, waiting for the river card to be placed.

Roy seemed like he was about to say something, but abruptly Jimmy put the object back into the bag and handed it to Roy.

"Rest up now," Jimmy said dismissively. "We'll talk after." He turned to the severe woman who had been in charge of disarming them all. "Mia, show them where they can sleep, please."

CHAPTER NINETEEN

Sleep did not come easy. And when it did, it was half-starts and shallow awakenings.

Walt's body remained drifting in that unrestful place where your mind has gone off to dream world, but your body is still shoveling in all that extraneous data from the physical world around you, so you never truly disconnect and ease out into the peaceful void.

He would roll onto his left side, forgetful in his half-sleep, and the burned side of his face would press against his arm, which he was using as a pillow, and a spike of pain would bring him up again. He would grunt quietly and adjust. Try to sleep again. Fail.

He could not still the gnawing rat of nerves in his gut.

Many times his eyes would shoot open out of a doze, and his heart would take off like a spooked mustang that he'd just barely gotten to eat out of his hand. His thoughts were circling around Carolyn, and around Pops, and all else was somehow forgotten in the slush.

His mind began to obsess. Over seeing his wife again, and the operation to free his father. He felt lost and worried and confused and tense. The way you feel when you are driving in an unfamiliar city and you don't have a map and you don't have a guide, and the cars behind you are honking for you to speed up.

He would open his eyes and his mind would shuck off sleep like a thin rag, and he would check the time and see that only twenty minutes had passed, and he would grudgingly pull that ragged sleep back over him for another twenty minutes.

And then, one time, when he opened his eyes, someone was kneeling there beside his mattress.

Walt jerked fully awake, coming up into a sitting position.

"Easy," Roy said, putting a hand on his shoulder. He spoke quietly, so as not to disturb the others. "It's me."

Walt swallowed down his heart and let out a breath of air. "Shit," he said, expelling the shock. "What's wrong?"

He couldn't really see his brother's face in the darkness, but he could see the stiffness in his shoulders. Roy stood up and made a motion with one of his hands. "Come on," he whispered.

Walt got up out of bed. His body still felt achy with the need for rest, but his mind was already spooling up, off to the races. He followed Roy quietly out of the room.

Outside of that room, they were in a hall, and there were windows that looked out across the back lot of the warehouse. Tinted windows that Walt was sure were one-way. The sun had peaked and begun to fall again. The shadows outside were getting long.

Roy was silent as he walked ahead of Walt, leading him down the hallway to what appeared to be an office. Outside that office, the woman with the stern face—Mia—was standing with her arms crossed over her chest, watching the two of them approach.

She opened the door to the office as they reached her.

Roy went in, then Walt, then Mia.

Inside, Walt found a bare room. Not even a chair to sit in.

Jimmy was standing to one side, flanked by two men with subguns.

He waited until Mia had closed the door behind her before he started talking.

"Did you explain the situation to your brother?" he asked.

Roy shook his head. "I figured I'd let you do the illuminating."

There was a bite to Roy's voice that immediately set Walt on edge. Walt had the distinct feeling that he was walking in on the middle of a conversation. Roy had already been speaking to Jimmy. And something had come up.

Jimmy did not react much to Roy's tone, or his words. He simply faced Walt and gave him a curt nod. He gave no preamble, but went straight to the heart of the matter. "I'm allowing you to use a great tool of ours, per your brother's request. As I understand it, he views it as essential to the mission."

Walt squinted, recalling Roy asking about "the thing" and getting a guarded response about it.

"And what is that?" Walt asked carefully, sensing the awkward footing of his situation, and not really knowing why he was there.

"A directed EMP," Jimmy said. "I don't need to explain to you the amount of manpower and resources that go into building an item like that. All you need to know is that I have one, and I don't simply loan it out to the highest bidder."

Walt pursed his lips but said nothing. His eyes flicked back and forth between Roy and Jimmy, still very unsure of why he was standing in this room. What did any of this have to do with him?

"But I am letting you use it for this operation," Jimmy said. "In exchange for four of those grenades. If they prove as useful as Roy claims they'll be, then the trade-off will be worth it."

"Four," Walt mumbled, then looked at Roy. "That only leaves us with one."

Roy nodded. "You can do the operation with one." He looked sharply at Jimmy, and his voice rose a notch. "But I'd *prefer* two."

"No," Jimmy said flatly. "You get one. Four is the price."

Roy shrugged it off and Walt got the sense that this was simply rehashing the haggling that had occurred while Walt had been sleeping.

Walt allowed a note of confusion to show on his face, and finally had out with it: "Alright. So we can do the operation with one grenade. Roy. Jimmy. What does this have to do with me?"

Jimmy took a breath and launched it out. "The EMP needs to be operated by a professional." He gestured to his right. "Mia is that professional. She will accompany you on your operation. In exchange, I want someone from your crew to remain in my…care."

Roy visibly bristled, but said nothing.

Walt began to bring things together in his mind.

So, Jimmy wanted to hold onto one of Roy's team, like a fucking security deposit. And who had Roy come up with to fill that role? Why, the most useless individual on the team, of course. Walter Lawrence Baucom, Knocker Extraordinaire.

Walt glared sidelong at his brother, then looked back at Jimmy. His voice was stiff when he spoke. "You could just teach me to operate the EMP."

For the first time, something besides flat calm betrayed itself on Jimmy's face. It was a mix of incredulity and amusement. "Do you have any idea of the forces that you're playing with on one of these things? That's like telling a random person off the street to wire a bomb. You might be the brightest man from District Eighty-Nine, Walt, but no. From what I understand, this operation calls for two discharges, which means that it's more than just firing the thing off. It'll need to be re-armed and discharged again." Jimmy was shaking his head. "No. You'll blow it to bits, and your whole team along with you. Mia is the one that has to operate it. And Mia is a very valuable member of my team. So one of you is going to remain behind."

Walt turned to Roy, biting hard down on his lower lip and trying to tell himself that now was not the time to lose his temper. But putting a fist in Roy's suck-hole seemed like an awfully tempting concept at that moment.

"So that's it? I'm off?" Walt spat.

Roy held up a hand. "This isn't about you, Walt. This is about getting Pops back. And that girl, Bobbi, if we can find her."

Jimmy cleared his throat loudly, causing the two brothers to look at him. He wore a pained expression and it was directed at Roy. He held up a hand and dabbed the air with a finger. "I'm sorry, Roy. You must have misunderstood me. I'm not interested in holding your brother as security."

There was a silence of confusion.

Jimmy sucked on his teeth, and then said it, like it was oh-so-obvious. "I'm holding *you*, Roy. You."

"What?" Roy snapped. "You can't—"

"Yes, I can," Jimmy said mildly. "It's my piece of equipment, ergo, I state the terms and conditions for its use. It must be operated by Mia. And in order to secure her safe return to me—and that of the equipment—you will be remaining with me."

Roy thrust a hand at Walt. "Why can't you hold him?"

Walt clenched his fists. "You sonofabitch…"

Jimmy looked Walt over. "I'm sorry, but he's not valuable enough. No offense, Walter."

Walt just glared at him from under his eyebrows. But he really couldn't decide who he wanted to beat more in that moment—his own brother or this stranger? Probably his brother.

Roy seethed at Jimmy. "You can't do this to me."

"I can," Jimmy said coolly. "I am."

"It's my father."

"Your New Breeds are fully capable of executing the mission without your being in the command seat," Jimmy said. Then he gave Walt a nod, as though trying to make a peace offering. "Besides, your brother did get out of District Eighty-Nine alive. We all saw the video. Surely he knows what he's doing."

"What if I don't agree to these terms?" Roy asked.

Jimmy shrugged. "That is fine. You don't have to agree to them. Only if you want the DEMP."

Walt watched his brother in the moment and knew that Roy was mulling it over hard, trying to find a way that the operation could succeed without the DEMP. Hell, Walt hadn't even been given the details of the plan yet. Perhaps he could have helped if he'd known. But Roy had chosen to keep him in the dark.

Gradually, Walt watched the realization dawn on Roy's face that there was no other way to accomplish what he wanted to accomplish. It was the DEMP or bust.

"Fine," Roy said woodenly. "If that's the deal, that's the deal." He looked at Walt. "Koz and Javon are the ones that designed the operation. It's not essential that I be there. Just do what they say. Everything should go fine."

***

"Only one ECHO?" Koz said, referring to the device by its given name. "Well. That's not ideal. But it's not insurmountable."

It was four o'clock in the afternoon, and everybody in the room was now awake, standing in a huddle in the middle of the sprawled out mattresses. Mia was there as well, although Roy was not. He was with Jimmy.

Walt was still struggling with his irritation. He just kept reminding himself that it didn't matter whether or not Roy trusted him. It mattered that the operation got done.

But everything's going down the shitter, Walter thought. And he couldn't help feeling like it was some sort of sign. Which was a strange thought for him, because he'd never been the superstitious type. It was amazing what wagering your life could bring about.

And there was also the feeling.

The feeling that he was getting.

He didn't like what Jimmy had done.

He didn't like that Roy was no longer going.

But he couldn't tell if that's because Roy being in charge was a sort of mental safety blanket, or if it was because he was truly picking up on something.

Sometimes his abilities didn't come through in articulable ways such as *Oh, I just saw his eyebrow twitch, so he must be lying.* Sometimes his subconscious picked up on more than he knew, and it translated into just a bad feeling in general.

Fuck, fuck, fuck.

He rubbed his head, raked fingers through his hair.

"Folks," Walt said, conjuring as much calm and control as he could muster. "Things feel a little wonky right now." He looked around at those gathered. Koz. Javon. Rat. Getty. And the new girl, Mia. "I know we've already kind of had this discussion already, but things have changed, so I just feel like we need to reaffirm what we're doing here."

Some feet shuffled.

No one spoke.

"I'm here to save my Pops," Walter said, looking at the ground, frowning as though thinking out loud. "That's what I came to do. That's still what I'm here to do. And Bobbi too, because I never meant for her to get left behind. I know we have one shot to get this done. And I still want to do it. But…this could also seriously hamper the efforts of the resistance in general." Walter opened his mouth to continue, but then put a hand over it and just issued a frustrated growl.

It wasn't coming out like he wanted.

"What are you saying?" Rat asked, his eyebrows screwing up.

Walter breathed through clenched teeth. “Fuck. I don’t even know, Rat. I guess what I’m saying is that things have gotten real fucking sketchy, and if the group decides that they don’t want to go through with this operation, then…well…fuck…I guess I’d understand.”

Koz straightened up and took a half step forward. “Lemme clarify things for you, Walt.” He began ticking off fingers. “First, nothing has really changed. We have the same amount of people on this op—yeah, we’re down Roy, but we’re up Mia. And I’m told good things about Mia. So, hopefully that equals out. Second, we still have use of the ECHO. Now, we might have to stretch a bit, but again, nothing has changed. The ECHO is a force multiplier. If it works like it’s *supposed* to, the odds of mission success remain largely the same as they were when we started on this thing. Third, if we play this shit smart and clean up after ourselves, there’s no way it comes back to hurt the resistance. If we just leave dead bodies behind, then all the CoAx knows is that we figured out a way to kill New Breeds. If we don’t leave the shell of the ECHO—which is even easier now, since we only have one—and we don’t leave any witnesses, then how the hell is the CoAx going to know how we pulled it off?” Koz shook his great head. “They won’t. Ergo, I don’t think this operation will harm the resistance.”

“If it goes off clean,” Javon pointed out.

“Right,” Koz nodded.

“Which it never does.”

Koz shrugged. “Sometimes it does. In any case, I still don’t think anything has changed. Roy saved my parents from DTI. So I gotta do this. Not even a question in my mind. Not even an option. So I’m with you.”

Javon stretched his arms, as though tired and bored. “The worse the odds, the sweeter the victory.” He yawned. “You know I’m down for this shit.”

Rat and Getty traded a look.

Getty was the one that spoke. “We’re here for Bobbi, but it’s the same difference. Same op. We’re here. We’re not backing down. Can’t do it.”

Walt looked to Koz. “I think it’s about time we heard the plan.”

Koz nodded. "Yeah. I'd agree with you there."

The New Breed turned and nodded to Javon, who was already pulling a small palm computer out of his pocket. He turned it on, and then flipped up the screen, then turned it so that it could be viewed by the others.

"Everybody see that?" Javon asked.

Everyone mumbled their assent.

It was a map. Nothing complicated. The same type of shit you'd see if you were driving from one city to another. There were a few towns named, one of which rang a bell in Walt's mind—Carthage.

Javon set the device on the ground. The projection remained where it was in the air, and Javon stepped around so that he too could see what everyone else was seeing.

Koz stepped up to it. The glowing projection played with a few dust-motes in the air.

"Here's a map," Koz said, with a sort of sardonic simplicity. "But it's a public map. What it doesn't show…" here he paused and reached into the projection, spreading his hands almost as though he were swimming in it, which caused it to zoom in. "…is what's in these woods right about here."

They were looking at a section of highway that looked like it was bordered on both sides by large tracts of forest.

"Javon and I have both been to this location, so we're not yankin' ya. There's a facility here. It's a black site, meaning that it's not for public consumption, not to be known about, never to be talked about, etcetera, etcetera." Koz turned and looked directly at Walt. "Everyone who requires *debriefing* is routed to this location prior to being sent to DTI. That would include high value targets, such as resistance members. Or family of resistance members. And that includes your Pops, our target. And your girl, Bobbi—if she is in fact captured."

Rat shuffled his feet. "So. You guys have detained people there?"

Koz regarded him with one of his broad smiles. "Of course. We were New Breed soldiers. Disappearing folks was a part of our job."

Rat and Getty exchanged a look, but neither of them said anything.

Koz shifted the map by putting his palm into the glowing surface and swiping it over. It followed the cant of the highway, and after a few swipes, Koz stopped it at what appeared to be an overpass. He pointed to it. "That's a bridge. Under that bridge is where we're going to hide. We should be okay, because it's not a road, it's a natural gas pipeline, but it has road access. So there shouldn't be any through traffic. No cops. No pedestrians wondering why a scary van is parked under the bridge. Why are we parking under the bridge?"

"Drones," Getty said simply.

Koz snapped a finger. "Drones. Or *drone*, singular. Ahead of the convoy, there's going to be one drone. This is standard procedure to protect against the very thing that we're trying to do. The drone's job is to fly the route, scouting for trouble. They fly high, and they fly directly above the road, so if we park directly underneath the bridge, the drone shouldn't see us."

Koz clasped his hands together. "We have about thirty seconds from the time that the drone passes over until the convoy hits that bridge. We want them stopped on that bridge." He pointed to Javon. "Javon will be eyes on the sky—he will let us know when the drone has passed over us. The second that he gives the greenlight, the van rolls out from under the bridge, and goes to the road access, right here." Koz pointed at Walt. "You're going to drive the van. And this is very important, so listen carefully."

Walt swallowed and nodded, trying to attune himself to the situation.

"In the back of that van is going to be the EMP device, facing rearward, right up against the doors. Walt, you're driving, and Mia, you're operating that EMP. Walt, your objective is to get that van on the road, right in front of the bridge, which is right where that access road empties out. You face the ass end of that van towards the bridge. Mia kicks the doors, and then lets off with the first charge."

Mia nodded solemnly.

"Walter," Koz continued. "You want your van to be positioned so you're nose to ass with that convoy. This is gonna be tricky, and Mia, you need to trigger that fucker fast, because that lead vehicle is gonna be a guntruck with a Lancer cannon, and the second that Walt pulls out in front of it and slams on the brakes, they're gonna smell an ambush and let loose with that Lancer—turn you all to jelly. So, don't let that happen, okay? Please trigger the EMP before you all get murdered."

Mia nodded again. "I can handle it."

Koz smiled. "I'm sure you can." He took a breath. "The rest of us are under the bridge. That EMP goes off, that convoy is going to be dead. Standard procedure is for all vehicles in the convoy to immediately un-ass and to attempt to assault through the ambush. If the intel we're getting is correct, this convoy is going to be two guntrucks and two personnel modulars. The guntrucks will frame the personnel modulars—one in front, one in back. The guntrucks will be full of New Breeds. The two personnel modulars will likely be manned by regular troops—one driver, and one guard riding shotgun. When the guntrucks un-ass, I'm throwing our one and only ECHO device."

Koz turned and looked at the map, and for the first time, had a look of misgivings cross his broad, red-bearded features. "We have no idea what the effective range of these things is. But I'm going to throw it right in the center of the two personnel modulars. So it's either going to get everybody in the convoy…or nobody at all." He grimaced, then shrugged it off. "Javon and Getty will be on the north side of the bridge, and me and Rat will be on the south side. Once the ECHO goes off, we take the bridge. If it works like it should, the New Breeds in the group will be in La-La Land, freeing us up to slump those four regular guys that *shouldn't* be affected by the ECHO. Me and Javon will make quick work of them. Then we proceed to clean up the New Breeds before they wake up, open up the personnel modulars, locate the target, and get outta Dodge."

"What about the second charge on the EMP?" Mia asked. "You said you'd need a second charge."

Koz clapped his hands. "Right. Yes. So the drone. The second that convoy goes dark, central command is gonna have that drone pilot swing around to do a sit-rep on them, and when it sees what's happened, it's gonna drop ordnance. You're gonna need to bring it down before it does that."

"With a directed EMP," Mia said, a little disbelieving.

"No reason it shouldn't work," Koz said. "But while we're taking care of the convoy, Walt, you're gonna need to swing that van around, so the EMP is facing the opposite direction. These directional devices have a pretty broad scatter, so as long as you're pointing that thing in the general direction, it should take it down. You'll just want to hit it before it releases ordnance."

Mia seemed concerned. "Will it even be in visual range?"

Koz deftly deferred to Javon, who was already producing a large scope, which he handed to Mia. "That's identical to the thermal imager I'll be using to ID the drone when it passes," Javon stated. "When Walt gets that van turned, you just keep your eye to that sky. Don't worry about whatever is happening behind you. I don't care what you hear or if someone is screaming for their mother. You keep your eye—and that scope—on the sky, and you trigger that EMP the second you see that drone." He tapped the device which Mia was now holding in her hands. "Just make sure you keep that thing away from the business end of your first EMP blast. It is an electronic, after all."

Mia blew out a tense breath through pursed lips. "Alright."

"Folks," Koz said, looking at everyone. "I've never operated with any of you people before. So this will be a first for all of us. But I will trust you implicitly, because I expect you to trust me implicitly. And without that, we're probably all going to die."

No one said anything.

Walt looked over at Getty and Rat, and they looked at each other, and then at Walt, and the three of them nodded to each other. They had been through this before. Walt had been a stranger, and he was a stranger no longer. They would trust each other. They would trust Koz and Javon. And dammit, they'd trust Mia too.

Because what other choice did they have?

"Daylight's burning," Koz called out. "Let's load up."

CHAPTER TWENTY

Carolyn buzzed and trembled while she walked, consumed by a mix of fear and anger.

And she knew that she was being followed.

The cruddy buildings of CoAx County drifted past her. The sun was out, and had been all day. It had dried up all the mud, and now everything seemed to have turned to dust. It no longer felt like a cool spring day. Now it felt like summer was creeping in. Hot and humid and insectile.

She dipped down an alley, into shade.

She didn't know exactly where she was, but she knew where she was going.

The alley was a short one, and she walked quickly. She made the corner before her tail did, and came out on another street, which she hung a left on. There were more pedestrians moving about on this street. More of an open-air market feel to it than the previous street.

She walked past a few vendors that tried to get her attention, and then mumbled curses at her when she completely ignored them.

Things had been looking up for her that day.

After the haggling of the meeting, all parties had left mostly on the same page, and Carolyn had felt a burgeoning of hope. Three big organizations were going to come together. They were going to pool their resources to actually get something done.

Nothing like that had happened for generations. And it made her feel like success was finally a possibility.

Of course, she'd also learned some other things.

Her parents had confided in her, seeking to bring her into their fold. Seeking to make her a part of them by trusting her with their true intentions for Durham.

But, all in all, Carolyn had left that meeting feeling the closest to free that she'd ever felt in her life. The closest to being a citizen of a sovereign nation that chose its own course, and was not simply the puppet of other, stronger powers.

But everything in Carolyn's mind had gone to shit when they'd arrived back at the hotel, and her mother and father met with her in their little backroom command bunker.

She had been able to tell instantly that something was wrong.

When the door to the room closed behind her and it was only her parents, and she could see the looks on their faces, she'd known.

Her father was looking at her in a tense, hesitating manner. Barely able to hold eye-contact with her for more than a second.

Her mother seemed stiff, and pensive.

Carolyn stood with her arms at her sides, looking between the two of them, and her mind was already racing, and one thought kept coming up out of the heap of considerations: *Something's happened to Walt. Something's happened to Walt. My God, something has happened to Walt…*

"What?" she asked, her voice flat and emotionless.

"We were contacted," said her mother's maddeningly polite modulator. "By the commander of our renegade troops."

That's where Walt is.

Oh my God.

Something's happened…

"And?" Carolyn managed.

Her mother's finger hovered, palsied, next to her modulator. She was formulating her words. Or second guessing the ones that she'd chosen. But she finally had out with it. "He's informed us that Walt and Roy have disappeared."

"Disappeared?" Carolyn croaked. "As in they *were disappeared*?"

"No," her mother shook her head once. "They left the compound on their own, it seems. They took with them the two resistance fighters that Walt had been with when they'd found him in District Eighty-Nine. As well as two of the top New Breed operators that have been working closely with Roy."

"Where are they?" Carolyn said. Demanded. "Where'd they go?"

"That's not all," her mother replied. Then she looked pointedly at Benjamin Eudy, as though she were irritated at having to do all the explaining herself.

Her father cleared his throat laboriously, then drew himself up. She watched his face, watched his posture, saw him hardening himself, and she did not like that one bit.

"They took something of ours," her father began. "A weapon that we've been developing."

"A weapon? What kind of weapon?"

"A weapon that we sorely need in this fight." Benjamin's hands came together and his fingers interlaced and clutched each other until the blood ran out of them and the knuckles were white. "A weapon that was *supposed* to remain an absolute secret until its hour of use."

Carolyn felt stuck. She could almost see the picture, but not quite, and she was suddenly terrified to ask any more clarifying questions. Abruptly, she didn't want to know. She didn't want to *be here.*

Benjamin continued, coldly. "Certain contacts of ours have led us to believe that Walt and Roy, along with that weapon, are in Durham as we speak. And that they intend to use it. To free their father who was captured during the CoAx purge on District Eighty-Nine."

"Pops," Carolyn muttered, because she'd grown accustomed to calling him by the name that Walt called him. A common enough colloquialism in the districts.

It was only after a few moments of silence that Carolyn noticed the tears in her mother's eyes, and she frowned at her mother, and felt her stomach pulling nauseatingly inside of her, knowing that the tears were sorrow and regret.

"I'm sorry, Stephanie," Jean Eudy said to her daughter. "We need you to hear it from us. Because you would have learned of it eventually. And we wanted to be honest with you. We *have* to be honest with each other. Don't we?"

"Honest about what?" Carolyn said, hearing her voice raise in volume. "What did I need to hear from you?"

Her father suddenly slapped the table, loudly. His eyes darkling with madness. Which set Carolyn on her heels because he had seemed to be the steadier of the two. "He can't be allowed to use that thing!" Benjamin's voice cut through the small room. "That fucking husband of yours could cost us *everything*! And for what? So he can rescue his old man? Who is fucking dying of cancer anyways, isn't he? Isn't he? Red lung, right? Isn't that what the growers call it?"

Carolyn was too stunned to speak.

"No," her father shook his head vehemently. "No, he can't use it. If he uses it, then the CoAx will find a way to counteract it. They won't figure it out immediately, but they might have a solution to it by the time we try to make a push with *actual strategic benefit.* We'll lose everything we've been fighting for. It *has* to remain a secret. It *has* to!"

Carolyn was shaking her head. "What? What are you talking about here?"

But she wasn't dumb. She knew.

Jean Eudy reached over and put a staying hand on Benjamin's arm. "Think about what your father is telling you, Stephanie. You know it's true. You know that it has to—"

Carolyn balled her fists. "My name is not Stephanie."

Her father stood up quickly. "Yes it is," he growled. "Your name is Stephanie Eudy. You are one of *us*. You are not some fucking grower from District Eighty-Nine. You are a *Eudy*!"

Carolyn could feel heat rising on the back of her neck. "You can't be fucking serious with this."

"We have to think unemotionally about this," her mother said, infuriatingly.

"Was it unemotional when you pulled me out of Eighty-Eighty-Nine?" Carolyn demanded. "Or was there some practical purpose to it?"

Benjamin glowered but didn't immediately respond, and for a heartbeat Carolyn thought, *Dear God, they didn't even pull me out to save my ass—they did it for some other reasons...*

"We pulled you out," her mother said. "Because you *are* one of us."

"I may be," Carolyn said, trying to keep her voice from rising any further, wanting to keep it controlled. "But I'm also a Baucom, whether you like it or not. See, there was this whole decade of my life when you all might as well have been dead, and before that, you were just resistance leaders." Carolyn cringed and held up a hand, hating how it sounded like a soul-searching, it-was-all-my-parent's-fault thing to say. "I'm not saying I blame you all for what happened or to complain about my childhood. But you need to understand that I've made a life. I made a life with this man. And *his* family. His Pops was *my* Pops." She shook her head, wide-eyed as she looked between the two people that had brought her into this world. "I've never known either of you as an adult! So you can't seriously sit there in front of me and tell me to be unemotional about this!"

She realized that she was shouting.

She snapped her mouth shut, covered it briefly with a clenched fist.

Her father squared his shoulders and tilted his head back, looking down at her. "This is bigger than some romance story," he said. "This is about our country."

For some reason, Carolyn still felt that there was room to reason them out of this. It seemed that they were so off the rails, but then, did that mean that they were unwilling to get back *on* the rails? Or was it that once you were off, you were gone from them forever? Never to be bound by reason again?

Her father shook his head. "We can't afford to burn this right now. Do you have any idea how valuable it is?"

"No, I don't! I have no idea what it does. What does it do? Why is it so special?"

"It's a weapon to fight the New Breeds," he said. "It uses sound waves to induce them into a…" he waved a hand around, conjuring the right word. "…disassociative state." Then he made a shooing gesture. "But it doesn't matter! It can't be used so soon! It'll ruin everything. You understand that, right? The break that got us out of DTI. The Fed troops defecting. The three resistance organizations coming together. It will ruin all of that."

"Okay," Carolyn said, nodding along with Benjamin as he spoke. "Okay, fine. What about this—what if I went to Durham myself? What if I spoke to Walt? Convinced him not to use it?"

Benjamin and Jean exchanged a slight glance, but Jean shook her head.

"No," Benjamin asserted. "No, it's too late. He plans to use it tonight, according to our intelligence."

"The Maglev could get me there in a few hours, right?" Carolyn said, knowing that she sounded desperate, and not caring. She was, at least, *trying* to come up with a solution, rather than these two assholes who were determined to be stuck in the mud.

"It doesn't matter," her mother said, and the volume of her modulator went up, the sound of it like a slap in the face. "We have people on the ground now in Durham. This situation is going to get handled the way that *we* deem fit to handle it. Because this is what *we've* been working for. Now, you need to take a long hard look at who you are, and who you think you owe in life. Because as I see it, that worthless man has done nothing but bring you into trouble, and we've got you out of it. So why don't you get control of yourself and *think* not only about who you should be loyal to, but how about taking a look at the big picture while you're at it?"

All at once, Carolyn went stiff and cold inside.

She felt a tremor work through her.

Like a shiver that you're trying to restrain.

Benjamin and Jean Eudy stared back at her. Ostensibly, her parents, but what did that mean? She had more feelings for a man that she and her husband called Pops, than for these two. She'd felt the loss of Walt's mother more keenly than she recalled feeling the loss of her parents. Because one had happened in another life, a childhood life, when the totality of things is not fully realized. But she'd lost Mindy Baucom, just as poignantly as Walt had.

Because they were a family.

She was a Baucom.

Not a Eudy.

Not one of these crazies.

All of this she knew, she felt, and it coalesced inside of her, forming a solid foundation that didn't shift like the sands of her parent's whims and paranoias. It held her up. Steadied her. Made her feel for the moment as though her feet were on solid ground.

You can't reason with them, she thought.

But maybe...

She lowered her head. Let the silence sink in.

She felt like a kid again. She felt exactly as she'd felt when she'd been spying on them the night they'd been talking to the man called Jeff. When she'd made the floorboard creak and she'd known she was discovered but then figured she could play it off.

She could play it off.

She'd always been pretty good at manipulating her parents.

She wiped her eyes and set her jaw and her lips. Stern. Solid. Resolute.

She looked up. "I'm sorry. I'm sorry, Mom. I'm sorry, Dad. It's been a difficult time. A very difficult transition for me." She looked away. The emotion she felt wasn't faked. But it wasn't coming from the source that she was making it seem like it was coming from.

She took a long time to gather herself yet again.

Her parents stood patiently watching.

She looked back at them. "I am loyal to this cause," she said, quietly. "But most of all, I'm loyal to this country. And I'm going to prove it to you. I *will* prove it to you."

And then she turned away from them, and she walked out the door, and they did not say anything to her, and she did not say anything to them, and that was how they left each other.

And now?

Now she was walking west, right into the setting sun. And at the end of this long, dusty boulevard, she could see the skeletal gray streak of the Maglev tracks as they approached their stop.

She'd already travelled ten miles across the city in a cab, but she'd noticed the car tailing them, and, not wanting to panic the cabbie, simply told him to pull over, at which point she started hoofing it.

She didn't have that much farther to go anyways.

Maybe a mile. Maybe less.

It felt good to be moving, anyway. Even if she was exposed.

There was a rug store off to the right-hand side of the sidewalk. Its doors were open, and the interior was a confusing profusion of colors and patterns and shapes. It seemed to her in that moment how a thick stand of briars might seem to a deer with dogs on its tail.

She slipped into the rug store and marched towards the back.

A fat, gray-haired man with a golden chain laying luxuriant across a white mane of chest hair watched her come in, then nodded to her, then went back to reading his PD.

All she could think about was the store.

The little store when she'd first got off those Maglev tracks. The store that she and John had run through, and then John had stood to the side of the back door and killed the young lady that followed them out.

Carolyn made it to the back. There was a doorway marked "employees only," but beyond it she could see the exit, so she went through, and no one challenged her. She stepped through that back exit and found herself in another alleyway. She turned left—westward again—walked a few paces, and then turned and reached her hand into the front of her pants, felt the grip of the pistol, warm from being against her.

Just before the back door had a chance to latch again, it burst open.

John came skidding out onto the dusty cement, already looking behind him at either side of the doorway.

Yes, he clearly remembered the young lady too, but he hadn't been expecting Carolyn to be so far down the alley.

He saw her, and started to walk towards her.

"Carolyn," he said, in a warning tone.

She yanked the gun out of her waistband. Pointed it at him.

John stopped, his eyes dropping to the gun in her hand. He frowned, then looked up at her, like a parent who has been disrespected by their child. "Carolyn, you put that fucking thing away. I got a gun too, and I swear to God, if you take a shot at me, I will put you down."

Carolyn wanted so badly to be intimidating in that moment. She wished that she knew how to hold the thing to look scary with it. But it shook in her hand and looked small and unlikely. And she'd never shot a pistol before. And she'd never shot a person, that was for damn sure.

And Jesus, but she was shaking all over!

"Go away," she croaked.

"Stop pointing that thing at me," he said, his voice ratcheting into a high warning tone. "Your parents want you back at the hotel. You're out in the middle of the fucking city right now, and that is not fucking safe, do you understand that? Come on. Quit fucking around."

"I told them that I'm going to prove myself," she said. "And that is what I'm going to do, and I'm not going to let you stop me, John. I'm going to do this. I'm *going* to do this. John, I'm serious."

John started walking towards her, slowly, testing the waters. "It's okay. It's okay. Why don't we go talk to your parents about it?"

"I already did. I'm going to prove myself to them," she repeated. "Stop, John. Stop walking towards me."

"You don't need to prove anything. Put the gun down."

He didn't stop. He was walking slightly faster now.

"John, I'm going to shoot you."

"No one is gonna get shot."

"John, I'm fucking serious!" She hissed. "Are you even listening to me?"

John was about five yards away from her when she shot him.

She punched the gun out reflexively and yanked the trigger back hard and it barked and jumped in her hand so that she almost thought it was going to fly out of her grip, and for maybe a second she wasn't even sure that she had hit John, in fact, she was suddenly hoping that she *hadn't…*

But then his right leg gave out, and as he fell, she saw some blood pulse out of a hole in his pants and hit the sidewalk with a very audible splash that shocked the hell out of her.

Oh my God, what did I do?

As John's right knee hit the ground, his face grimaced and he swept his right hand back, pushing his jacket out of the way and revealing a pistol of his own, which was somehow in his hands in a flash.

And so Carolyn shot him again, and she was surprised at how easy the second shot was. The first had seemed like such a horrible accident, but the second seemed so necessary. And this time she saw the hole appear in his chest, and she realized that she was still pulling the trigger, firing twice more.

The next shot clipped his shoulder, and the last shot was a complete miss.

It didn't matter.

John fell backwards. His knees were bent awkwardly under his body. His back hit the ground, and he was trying to raise his head, trying to raise his gun to get a sight, but his eyes seemed drunken and confused and far away, and Carolyn watched him die over the barrel of her own gun.

She would never recall the next ten minutes of her life in any sort of clarity. It existed like some dark, unexplored nebulae in her brain that simply swirled with toxicity and fear and reproach and guilt, but also some icy things that told her that what she'd done had been necessary.

She knew that she stuffed the pistol back into her waistband and immediately started moving. She would often wonder if John was still alive when she walked away. If he had, maybe, just passed out. Maybe she could have helped him, but that was a silly thought after putting three bullets into someone, wasn't it?

She knew that there were no people in the alleyway when she walked out of it, but that there were a few people on the street that were moving towards that alley with some curiosity. She thought that she had told one of them that, "someone just shot that man," but she wasn't certain whether she'd actually said that to someone or just considered saying it.

Then there'd been a lot of walking and jumping at noises and avoiding eye-contact with people while she dived deeper and deeper into herself and became more and more positive that she had done something to herself, she had not only killed John, she had killed a part of herself, and everyone could see it, and Walt would see, but that would be okay, wouldn't it? He would understand, wouldn't he? Hadn't he had to kill people?

Had to kill people

Had to kill people

Had to

And that thought was perhaps the only source of comfort for her in that moment.

I had to.

And so has Walt.

Eventually, she found herself at the Maglev station, and using fake funds that belonged to a fake person named Jessica Ballantyne, Carolyn Baucom bought herself a one-way ticket to the Raleigh-Durham Maglev station.

CHAPTER TWENTY-ONE

Roy stood outside the van, in the starkly-lit gloom of the garage. The welders were silent at the three technicals. A mechanic was underneath the chassis of one, cranking away with a manual wrench.

The side door and back doors of the van were open.

At the side, Koz and Javon had pulled their big rucksacks to the ground, and were pulling the contents out. They had already equipped themselves. The two New Breeds weren't wearing full suits of hardarmor, but they'd strapped on the chest plates, as well as the helmets. They both had battleshrouds as well, but they had them pulled off to the side for now, their faces exposed.

Koz was handing a set of softarmor each to Rat and Getty, while Javon was fitting Walt into a third set, showing him where to tighten the straps to get the best fit without encumbering his breathing.

At the back of the van, Mia was helping two other men load the DEMP. It was not that large, but given the way they strained at it, he could tell that it was weighty. He had seen more streamlined versions of this device, but it was his understanding that Jimmy's was significantly more powerful than those other, smaller ones. The pulse had more range to it.

The thing shifted just after they'd gotten it propped on the edge of the van's backend. Someone let out a little grunt of semi-panic, and it seemed like the piece was going to drop to the ground.

Walt jumped over beside Mia and grabbed the thing, shoulder to shoulder with her. They hoisted it up and into the van. Pushed it to its berth with a groan of effort.

"Thanks," Mia said, a little breathless from the effort.

Walt just nodded to her, wiping his hands on his pants.

As he turned away from her, he gave her a look over his shoulder, but Roy couldn't see what the expression was. When he turned back around to where Roy could see his face, he saw that Walt wore a slight frown, as though deep in thought.

Behind Roy, Jimmy and his two large bodyguards stood, observing all of this with a certain detachment.

Roy stepped up to his brother's side.

Javon handed a full size combat pistol to Walt. "Stick that shit in your pants." Javon smiled his bright white smile. "Just in case."

Walt hefted the pistol. Big. Big grip. Big slide. Big bore.

He checked the magazine. Saw twenty rounds. One already in the chamber.

He clicked the magazine back into place and stuffed the pistol into his waistband, then held his arms up as though seeking approval from Javon. Like a little kid trying on clothes.

The New Breed gave him a nod and a thumbs up.

Walt turned and looked at Roy. "Wish it was you running this shit."

"You just be very careful," Roy said. "Listen to Koz and Javon and do what they tell you to do."

Walt rolled his eyes. "Thanks, Dad."

Roy grabbed his brother by the shoulder. "Hey."

"What?"

"I'm fucking serious."

Walt's face grew somber. He nodded. "Yeah. I know you are."

Roy removed his hands, and, not knowing what else to do with them, put them on his hips. "You guys will get it done. I know you will."

Walt gave his brother a funny look then. Something that Roy couldn't quite put his finger on, and he wished for a fleeting second that he had Walt's ability to read people.

Walt's eyes slipped over Roy's shoulder for a flash, and Roy knew he was looking at Jimmy. Then he looked at his brother again and forced a fake smile. "Hopefully."

Roy frowned. "What's that supposed to mean?"

But Walt only shook his head, and abruptly the moment was gone. He looked nonchalant, uncaring. He gave a playful punch at Roy's chest. "Don't worry about it, man. We'll handle it." He spread his arms a bit, and looked pointedly at his brother. "You just gotta have faith."

Roy nodded at the use of his own words. But he decided not to say anything else.

Koz stepped up to them. "Everyone's ready. Time's a-wastin'."

Roy took a step back away from them. "Alright. Y'all do your thing. I'll be here. Being useless."

The back doors of the van slammed shut.

Mia walked around to the side door, wiping her hands on her pants. "It's loaded and ready. You guys ready?"

"Hold on," Javon said, shoulder between Koz and Roy and holding a very large plaid shirt up to Walt. "Cover shirt for the driver. Don't want to raise eyebrows rolling around with armor and guns visible, ya know?"

Walt took it and pulled it on. It was practically a robe on him. Walt looked at it doubtfully, but shrugged. "Alright. I'm incognito as fuck now."

Koz and Javon both grinned.

"Alright," Koz twirled a finger in the air. "Let's load up, gents. And lady."

The two New Breeds, Rat, Getty, and Mia piled into the side door, and then Mia slid it shut, casting one last glance over Roy's shoulder to Jimmy, just before the sliding door connected and latched. It didn't escape Roy's notice.

Walt was already on the other side of the van, getting into the driver's seat, and then slamming that door, too.

Roy looked over his shoulder and made eye contact with Jimmy.

Jimmy held his gaze briefly, and then looked away.

Roy felt his stomach do a little shuffle inside of him. But he couldn't explain why. Perhaps it was just that he wasn't in control of the operation. Yes. That had to be it. He was just nervous because it was out of his hands now.

The van started with a creaky rumble.

Walt looked at Roy through the front window and threw him a casual salute, but his mouth was flat and lifeless and grim.

Someone unlatched one of the rolling bay doors and brought it up to waist-height. It rumbled loudly in the space, and bright afternoon sunshine pierced the gloom of the artificial lights.

The van groaned into gear, and then pulled away slowly, carefully. It headed for the light that was pouring in under that door. The man at the door rolled it up further, just high enough for the van to get under, and then it seemed like the van was swallowed by the light as it drove out into that unsure world.

The door closed behind it, leaving them in sun-blinded darkness.

Roy stood there for a moment, his hands still on his hips.

He kept thinking of that look on Walt's face.

He heard footsteps behind him, but didn't bother to look around. He knew it would be Jimmy and his two big goons.

He shook his head. "This is bullshit, Jimmy."

"I know, Roy," the man said, surprisingly close behind him. "But it's the game we play."

Roy felt a spark of irritation and he turned to look at Jimmy.

He didn't get very far.

His arms were suddenly seized in iron grips and it took him so much by surprise that he didn't even fight it. He just looked at the man holding his right arm. And then at the man holding his left arm, and for a second, his mouth just hung open in surprise.

They were pulling his hands behind his back.

"What the fuck…?"

Roy's mind exploded like a firecracker that's gone off in the tube. He started jerking back, but by then, Jimmy's two body guards had too much of a grip on him.

He heard Jimmy's voice, very calm: "Don't fight them, Roy…"

Then he felt his feet come off the ground, and he was upended and then the ground was coming up at his face. He hit the cement floor, chest-first, and the air went out of him in a huff and groan, and he felt heavy, sharp knees going into his back.

His hands, yanked fully behind his back now.

All Roy could do was struggle to breathe.

They were putting restraints on him. He heard the zip of them tightening down, cutting into his skin.

His view of the world was low, and the cement stretched out like an endless landscape. He could see little chunks of gravel and oil stains and bits of granulated carbon that had been used to soak those oils stains up.

"What're you doing?" he finally groaned, once he'd gotten enough air in his lungs.

"Stand him up," Jimmy said.

Roy felt his arms being hauled up, putting painful tension on his shoulders. His body left the ground in one smooth movement and then his feet touched again, and he was standing there, facing Jimmy, gasping for air.

Jimmy's face was as calm and collected as ever. "Sorry, Roy. It's out of my hands. But the good news is that the Eudys want you alive."

Roy bucked against the two men holding him, but he didn't get very far. They jerked him back into place. "What the fuck do you mean?" he shouted at Jimmy. "What about my brother?"

Jimmy just looked away. "Your brother isn't your problem anymore."

***

Walt drove the van.

He was following a small black car. An older model solar that was humming along ahead of them. They were zig-zagging their way through the city, heading for the outer edge, and leading the van around checkpoints and other hazards that they didn't want to come across.

Walt looked into the rearview mirror. He could see most of the back, except for Getty, who was sitting directly behind him. Across from Getty was Rat. Down the wooden bench seat, Mia sat with her elbows on her knees, alternating her gaze to the floor, and then to the machine that she sat next to. Across from her, Koz and Javon were sitting, their bulks taking up a lot of bench.

Walt's jaw muscle was aching, nearly giving him a headache.

He forced himself to stop grinding his teeth together.

Ahead of them, the black solar made a left-hand turn, and Walt followed it.

"So, Mia," Walt began, glancing up at the rearview again to catch her looking up in his direction. "How complicated is that thing?"

She gave him a guarded look.

He had to look back at the road. When his eyes returned to the mirror, she was looking at Koz and Javon, who also appeared to be waiting patiently for her answer.

"Complicated," she said tersely.

Ahead of them the black solar made it through a yellow light and Walt had to gun it to keep from being caught at the red. When they were clear of the intersection, he took a breath and pressed on.

"How long would it take to learn?" he asked.

Mia's shoulders tensed a bit. "I dunno, Walt. How smart are you?"

Walt glanced at Rat, who caught his gaze with a knowing look.

"Well, I guess that depends," Walt replied. "You mean in relation to you? Or just in general?"

Mia looked up at him again. "I mean in relation to an electrical engineering degree."

Walt smiled. "Well, I guess I'm not that smart then."

Mia didn't respond. She leaned back against the wall of the van.

"So, me being the knocker that I am," Walt said. "How long would it take me to figure it out?"

"What's a knocker?"

"A knocker?" Walt said, honestly surprised that the phrase wasn't translating. "You know. Like a line knocker. Unskilled labor. A dumbass."

"Ah."

"So, how long?"

"I dunno, Walt," she said, and he heard the tension in her voice. "A few hours? A day? There's a lot of variables."

"Like what?"

"Like how good can you recall information under stress."

"Pretty good, I think."

Walt watched Mia's feet shuffle back and forth. She crossed her arms, then uncrossed them.

Koz and Javon continued to watch her with blank faces.

Behind him, Getty gently cleared his throat.

Rat rubbed his hands together and found a callus to pick at.

"So, like a day, you think?" Walt asked.

This time, Mia snapped her head in his direction. "What's with all the questions?"

"What do you mean?" Walt asked.

"I mean why are you grilling me about this? It doesn't matter. You're not learning how to run the fucking machine, okay?"

Rat held up his hands, as though it had been him that had been verbally attacked. "Whoa. I thought we were all supposed to be trusting each other here."

"I trust you all to do your jobs," Mia said. "Trust me to do mine."

"I wasn't trying to insult your knowledge," Walt said gently, following the black solar as it made a veering right-hand turn onto a two lane street that seemed to be taking them out of town.

"Well, then why are you asking?" She was looking at him now, full on. One hand propped up on her knee, her elbow jutting up. A position that one might interpret as aggressive, but Walt knew it for what it was. In her case, she was attacking in order to defend.

"Just curious," Walt said, simply. Airily. Like it didn't matter.

And then, almost as an afterthought, he said quietly, "Just watching. Absorbing."

She looked at him, but said nothing.

She settled back against the van wall.

Up ahead of them, the black solar pulled onto an on-ramp, and Walt followed it. The solar immediately began to decelerate, and it pulled to the shoulder of the onramp about halfway down. Walt pulled passed it. He glanced over to see if he could see who the driver of the black solar was, but the windows were tinted. He continued onto the highway.

They were officially out of Durham now.

The tension in the car was like the scent of ozone that rides in on the winds of a coming storm. Not one of the pleasant summer squalls that leave everything fresher, but one of the black, mean ones that darken one side of the sky and cast everything in yellow like the sky has become jaundiced and the sun is discreetly backing out of the room.

He wanted to be in the back of the vehicle.

He wanted to be sitting directly across from Mia.

Because he couldn't do anything from his current position. He had to keep the van on the road. So all he could do was watch and absorb.

As much as possible in the time allotted to him.

Which, for Walt, was never much.

But he never needed much.

"So," Walt said, inwardly cringing as he waded himself out into waters full of biting things. "Jimmy insisted that you come because none of us could learn how to work that thing in a few hours. Complicated machinery, as you've already pointed out."

Now a change came over Mia.

Walt watched it happen.

Her fidgety feet suddenly stopped.

Her hands remained placidly lying on her thighs. She looked directly in front of her at Koz and Javon.

No one was really moving. Not even Rat. He was as still as a stone, even though his posture looked relaxed. Hell, everyone's posture *looked* relaxed. Like someone had swept into a summer barbecue and frozen them all in place. Just oh-so-fucking-relaxed.

But no one was moving.

And that is not relaxed at all.

"Yeah, Walt," Mia said, this time quietly, with a brittle smile on her lips. "That's about the size of it."

Walt nodded amiably, as though he wasn't picking up on any of the tension. He was just cruising along, oblivious. "Sorry. I don't mean to seem like I'm interrogating you. But I'm new to all this stuff, you know? Just trying to learn as I go, I guess."

Mia gave him a weak wave-off that didn't carry much feeling. "No worries," she said.

She crossed her arms again.

Walt watched a car ahead of them change lanes abruptly. It made his heart skitter and he eyeballed the car for a bit, but it went speeding on. Just another impatient driver trying to get home. Driving like an asshole to get to his destination thirty seconds sooner. The normality of it struck Walt oddly in that moment, and made him feel like a fish in a bowl, watching normal life go on outside of his bubble of existence.

This very weird, very tense bubble.

Looking in the rearview again, he noticed that Mia's right hand was tucked against her chest. Just inside her jacket.

His heart redoubled its efforts.

But he kept calm. Kept his face neutral.

Kept his hands on the wheel so no one could see them trembling.

Clear thinking. That's what he needed right now.

Things were off. He could feel it. He'd felt it in the garage. Hell, he'd felt it even prior to that. He'd felt it in the meeting with Jimmy. He'd stood there and he'd watched Jimmy's very minimal body-language, and he couldn't articulate it, but he felt a little something inside of him twist around, like it did when he was just certain on some subconscious level, that someone was trying to pull something over on him.

He was nervous for Roy.

And as he'd driven out, as the garage door had been closing, he'd looked in his sideview mirror and he'd seen Jimmy make a discreet motion to his guards, while Roy stood there, watching the van leave. And then the garage door had rolled shut, cutting him off.

Civilization was melting away from the highway. It was now just two lanes heading east through the countryside. Walt knew very well where he was. If he drove south for a half an hour, he would hit the northern-most edge of District 89. This highway cut east through that no-man's land that was neither city, nor a protected Agrarian District.

Up to the rearview again.

Mia's hand. Was it further under her jacket now?

She caught him staring.

He looked away.

Her feet shifted, slightly.

She was planting them on the floor.

Walt's pulse was hard and sharp, and he was watching the pressure of each burst of blood begin to darkle the edges of his vision.

Clear head, he reminded himself.

"Mia," he said as evenly as he could.

She looked up at him again.

They stared at each other through the mirror.

The road stretched out in front of them. A few cars ahead of them. A few cars behind them. No one driving abreast of them.

"What?" she said, thickly.

"Did Jimmy give you one of the ECHOs?"

Mia's eyes darted at the question. Then she summoned up a confused look. She leaned forward, but it was just a feint—to disguise her hand moving deeper into her jacket.

"What?" she asked him.

But she'd heard him. She knew what he'd said.

"Mia, take your hand out of your jacket," Walt said suddenly.

"There's nothing in my jacket," she replied with a shaky smile.

But her hand went in deeper.

"Take your hand out of your jacket!" Walt blurted.

And suddenly, everything broke.

CHAPTER TWENTY-TWO

Mia lunged her hand into her jacket, still staring at him and saying, "I don't have anything!"

"Getty!" Walt shouted.

Koz and Javon both lurched forward, reaching for her.

Walt felt his seat bump as Getty rocketed into action.

Koz and Javon suddenly froze where they were, halfway across the width of the van, their arms still up as though they intended to grab her, but they'd forgotten what they were doing.

Mia kicked out, connecting one foot to Javon's chest and sending the New Breed sprawling limply backward with a confused look on his face. In the same motion, she ripped her hand out of her jacket and went for the pistol on her side, her teeth bared.

Getty's battlerifle was swinging up.

Rat was grasping his and pivoting towards Mia.

Mia's pistol cleared its holster.

Walt saw fire bloom from her pistol.

Something smacked Walt in his side and he yelped.

The van shook with the heavy punch from Getty's battle rifle.

Mia was slammed back against the wall of the van, off kilter, tilting to one side, her teeth still bared, while holes appeared in her jacket. Her aim was off now and she was trying to get it back on again.

Rat let loose a burst of rounds that scattered across the back of the van and ripped Mia's arm into shreds.

The pistol fell out of her useless hand.

Getty had already crossed the back of the van. He slammed into her with the body of his battlerifle, toppling her back off her seat and onto the floor, wedged between the DEMP and the wall of the van.

Walt heard the roar of his tires on gravel. His eyes darted back to the road, saw that they were skirting the shoulder, and he yanked the van back into his lane with a chirp of tires. Getty almost fell, but maintained his footing by bracing himself against one of the New Breeds.

Everyone was yelling.

Everyone but Koz and Javon.

"Holy fuck!"

"She's down! She's down!"

"Did you kill her?"

"I don't know! I think she's still alive!"

Walt tore his eyes off the road and looked down at his side where a sudden rush of pain was beginning to center itself just above his right hip. He couldn't see the wound past the bulk of the softarmor he wore, but he could see a splash of his own blood, splattered across his right thigh. He felt a wash of faintness, but forced himself to focus. He needed to keep the van on the road.

A million things battered his brain. Thoughts like a hailstorm.

You just murdered her.

So the wind blows.

We do what we have to.

Murderer.

What would Carolyn think?

He strained to focus.

He was hit.

He was bleeding.

"Guys," Walt shouted over them. "I think I'm hit."

"Rat," Getty yelled, as he stepped between Koz and Javon's legs to look at Mia's crumpled form. "Help Walter!"

Rat turned, his eyes wide and bewildered. He slid along the bench seat and came up next to Walt, looking him over. "Where is it? Where'd you get hit?"

Walt momentarily ignored him. "Is she dead?"

Getty was leaning over her. Walt couldn't see her when he looked into the rearview. Only her legs draped over the end of the bench seat. One of her feet was twitching violently. He could hear a loud, rasping, gurgling noise coming from the back.

"Don't worry about her," Getty called back over his shoulder. "How bad are you hit?"

Walt could already feel a cold sweat breaking out all over his face, and he knew without looking at himself that his skin had gone pale. He was going to lose consciousness, which seemed ridiculous to him in that moment—angered him even—because he knew what he'd been through when they'd fought for the Network Hub in District 89, and this couldn't be much worse than that, right?

Right?

But he kept picturing shards of his pelvis perforating his intestines.

Stop thinking about it.

"Where are you hit?" Rat demanded again, his hands shaking in the air in front of him.

"My side," Walt said. Then he took a deep breath and held it. And it hurt his side to hold it, but it focused his head, it pushed the faintness back a bit. "Shit, shit, shit," he mumbled to himself, because he needed to say something. It helped. "Fuck. Fuck. Fuck. I'm okay. I'm okay. I'm gonna be fine."

Rat was bent double, pulling the armrest of the driver's seat out of the way. Pulling the voluminous cover shirt out of the way. He made a face. "Okay, I see it, buddy. I see it. I think you're okay."

Walt pressed himself back into his chair, his deathly-white hands gripping hard on the steering wheel. "Getty! Koz and Javon!"

"Gadamighty. They're fucking out of it," Getty said in a sort of mystified voice.

Rat was beginning to prod the wound.

Walt tried to ignore it. "Getty, she's got an ECHO device in her jacket pocket. You need to shut that shit off, okay? Turn it the fuck off."

In the rear view, Walt could see that Mia's foot wasn't moving anymore. Getty stooped over her, holding his battlerifle out of the way and reaching down. Walt half expected her to come jolting alive again, but no, she was dead. He'd watched no less than six rifle rounds hit her chest.

"Did anyone else get hit?" Walt demanded in a huff of air.

"No," Getty replied. "She got me in the armor, but I'm fine."

Walt went back to muttering curses, trying to center himself.

Getty came up from Mia, one of the ECHO devices in his hand. He clicked the switch off and flipped the red cover over it. "Okay. It's off." Getty turned to the two New Breeds. Both were sitting on their bench, kind of slumped into each other, and their faces looked like the faces of someone who has taken too much of some sort of psychoactive substance and they were not completely *there*.

"Koz? Javon?" Getty spoke to them. "Can you guys hear me?"

"They're gonna be out for a minute," Walt said.

"Hey Getty," Rat yelled as he began to press his palm to the wound. "Get me that Medkit from Javon!" Rat turned and looked up at Walt. "I think you're okay. I'm just gonna try to stop the bleeding."

"How bad is it bleeding?" Walt asked, and he was glad that he didn't sound scared.

Rat looked at it. "Well…it's bleeding."

"The fuck does that mean?"

"It means it's fucking bleeding, okay? I'm not a fucking medic. I don't think it's that bad, but I'm not qualified to make those judgments!" Rat shook his head rapidly. "You're fine. I *think* you're fine."

Getty rustled violently around in the back and came to the front, ripping Javon's Medkit open. "What do you need?"

"The gauze," Rat said, nodding toward the kit. "Gimme the gauze. No. The one in the green packet. No! Fuck-all…the one that says 'HSA' on it!"

Walt took a few rapid breaths. Held the last one. Then turned slightly to look at Getty. "They might freak the fuck out when they come to, okay? Get their weapons off of them. Try to talk to them as they come to."

Getty nodded. "Glad we planned this out ahead of time," he said, and he was only half-sarcastic.

Walt hadn't wanted to be gloom and doom about the operation. But he couldn't deny the feeling that he'd gotten from Jimmy, so he'd gone to Getty and told him about his misgivings. Told him that if he gave the word, Getty needed to be prepared to take Mia out. And then he'd left it at that. Because he just wasn't sure.

But when he'd helped her heft the DEMP into the back of the van, he'd bumped into her side, and he'd felt the cylindrical object in her jacket pocket. There was no way for him to be sure in that moment, but in his brain, only one picture came to mind, and that was one of the ECHO devices.

Walt had known that the one ECHO device they'd been given for this mission was in Koz's care. So what the hell was Mia doing with one?

And then things started to come together.

Well, partially.

He still had no fucking idea *why*.

But he'd learned one thing so far, and that was *not to trust anyone*.

He didn't trust Jimmy. He didn't trust the man's rationalization for insisting Mia be a part of the operation. He didn't trust his reasons for keeping a hold of Roy. The whole thing had just felt completely off to Walt.

And then when he'd felt what he knew to be the ECHO device in Mia's pocket, he became certain that she intended to use it against them. She was dead in the back of the van now, and there was no way he was ever going to get the truth out of her. But that was the only thing that made sense to him. She had the chops to take on Getty and Rat and Walt, but she knew that she'd have to use the ECHO to take the New Breeds out of commission.

If Walt was honest with himself, he knew that she could have done it. The only flaw in Jimmy's plan was that he didn't realize that Walt could see through the deception. If he'd bought it like everyone else did, then somewhere along this road, or perhaps once they reached their destination, Mia would have discreetly triggered the ECHO, and with that, and with surprise on her side, it would have been easy enough to put a bullet in Getty, Rat, and Walt.

Why?

Well, the why didn't fucking matter right now.

It was what it was, and now there was a whole heap of problems to solve.

"Hey, this is gonna hurt," Rat said to him.

Walt held his breath again, and grit his teeth.

Fire and ice poured over his head.

Stay conscious.

It's not that bad.

It's just in my head.

"Just be ready to take the wheel," he told Rat. "In case I pass out."

"Okay. I got it. You'll be okay. Just stay awake. Think about something else."

And with that Rat started shoving the gauze into his wound.

The van jerked as Walt jerked.

Getty stumbled in the back. "Fuck! You guys wanna find a place to park before you do that?"

Rat gave Walt a reprieve, and Walt started nodding vehemently. "Yes," he groaned through his teeth. "That's probably smart."

As Walt looked for a side street to park on, Getty got the battlerifles off of Koz and Javon and passed them over to Rat, who stashed them in the front passenger's seat. Getty stood there a moment, swaying to the rhythm of the van as it drove, staring at the two vacant faces.

Walt blinked hard. Felt the worst of the faintness beginning to subside. "How they lookin'?"

"Creepy," Getty said. "Not all of them had a bad reaction, right?"

Walt thought about the captured New Breeds that the resistance had been doing tests on. "No. But that one guy did."

A road opened up to their right, and Walt took it, getting out of the flow of traffic on the highway. The road dipped back over a set of ancient railroad tracks, and through some woods to what looked like a defunct mill of some sort. Walt had never seen a more welcome sight than that abandoned place.

He pulled to the side of the road, well away from the highway.

"Javon's coming to," Getty said, with an almost scientific curiosity.

"Talk to him."

Getty was standing in the front portion of the van. Koz and Javon were towards the back. It was obvious that Getty didn't want to be within a swinging fist's range of them. A good blow from either of them could cause some serious damage.

"Javon, it's okay," Getty said, slowly, and clearly. "Just be calm. You're okay. You're not hurt. And no one is going to hurt you. Everyone in this van is friendly. We're all friends, okay?"

With the van stopped, Walt turned in his seat, groaning as he did. He could see the back more clearly now. And he could see Javon, and his face wasn't vacant anymore. It was registering a very real sort of fear—an expression he had never seen on Javon's face.

"Be calm," Getty repeated, keeping his own voice low and soothing. "Your friends are here and everyone is okay. Everything will be normal in a minute, you just gotta wait it out. Just wait it out."

As Getty spoke to Javon, Koz came out of it in a sudden rush. He bolted upright out of his seat and immediately started thundering up from the back of the van, like a bull caught in a rodeo cage.

Getty had the presence of mind not to point his weapon at Koz, which would have made it worse. He just raised his hands up, showing his palms, and shouting, "Easy! Be easy! You recognize us? Koz! Koz, we're friends."

Koz stopped short, his huge arms braced, one on each bench, breathing heavily. His eyes looked drunken for a moment, flying back and forth across their faces, his lower teeth exposed. He was making a strange growling noise. But he stayed where he was.

Walt held up a hand. "You good, brother?"

The crazed look melted suddenly out of Koz's face. He straightened a bit and let his knees fall to the floor. "Fuck," he muttered.

Javon swam up to them shortly after that. He blinked rapidly. "The fuck was that? What happened?"

Getty looked at him. "That was the ECHO device."

Javon frowned. "Shit."

"And you know who we are?"

"Coupla scared-lookin' motherfuckers."

Getty nodded. “Yeah, that’s about right.”

Koz turned, shakily, and looked at Mia’s dead form in the back of the van. “Shit. That was unpleasant.” He whirled around to Walt. “You wanna explain to me what the fuck happened here?”

So Walt explained. As best he could, though it was only his suspicions, and he said as much.

Koz listened, then nodded, looking at Mia again. “I’d say those were pretty damn good suspicions,” he grunted. “Why else would she have one of those things if not to take us out and hamstring the op?” He rubbed his beard. “Any idea why?”

“No,” Walt said, cringing as Rat finished dressing his wound. “But Jimmy and his organization are not friends of ours right now.”

“I’m with you on that,” Koz nodded his big head. “What are we going to do about Roy?”

Walt had considered it already. Not much, but it had been on his mind since he’d seen that garage door close behind him. The problem was, now it seemed like he would have to make a choice—between Roy, or his Pops.

Rat spoke up, gesturing to the back of the van. “I mean, the operation is dead anyway, right? We can’t work the DEMP.”

Javon shook his head. “We can probably work it.”

“How so?” Walt asked.

Javon made a flippant gesture at the machine. “It ain’t as complicated as they make it sound. And they teach us this shit, right along with IEDs and the rest of it.” He gave the machine a long look. “I mean, I’m no expert. And it’s been a long time since school. But I’m pretty sure we can work it.”

“So we can still go with the operation,” Getty said.

Koz hoisted himself up onto a bench. “Yeah, I’d say we’re still a go. Need to switch a few moving parts, but…we can do it.” He looked at Walt. “You have any reason to think that Jimmy intends to kill Roy?”

Walt shook his head. “Why go through all the trouble of separating us? If he wanted us all dead, he could’ve iced us while we were sleeping.”

“That’s what I was thinking,” Koz replied. “I don’t think they want to kill Roy. For whatever reason, for whoever’s idea this was—and I can name a few possible names—I think we were the expendable ones."

"Name a name," Walt prodded.

"The Eudys," Koz said, simply enough. "That'd be my guess. I'd bet money that they just didn't want us using Sandman."

"Does Jimmy have ties to the Eudys?"

Koz shrugged. "Couldn't say for certain. But he and Roy knew each other somehow."

Walt rubbed his greasy face with a clammy hand. "Okay. That makes sense."

Getty turned slightly to face Walt. "If we don't think that Roy's life is in immediate danger, and we can still take this opportunity to free your Pops and Bobbi…I say we do it. Because the chance ain't gonna come again."

"Alright," Walt felt shaky, his guts tight and painful. He looked down at his wound. Rat's dressing had stopped the bleeding. It looked like it was a shallow wound. Just meat. No vitals. He looked back to Getty. "Gimme a cigarette."

Getty was already pulling the pack out and he extracted one and handed it to Walt, where it quivered in the air briefly before Walt grabbed it and stuck it in his lips. Getty lit it for him, then lit his own. Walt let the burn and the taste center him. It wasn't exactly pleasant—in fact, it made him feel a little nauseas—but he didn't put it out.

It at least helped to keep him from grinding his teeth.

He pointed to the DEMP. "Javon—or Koz, or whoever is going to do it—start getting familiar with that thing. We're going through with this."

CHAPTER TWENTY-THREE

Surprisingly enough, Carolyn didn't start getting paranoid until a quiet, polite voice came over the speaker in her compartment of the Maglev and announced that they'd just crossed into North Carolina.

The countryside outside of the window was a charcoal gray under a deep blue sky, with strike-throughs of blazing lights as they passed over highways and interstates and small cities whose brightly lit towers blazed defiantly against the darkening sky.

And she began to think. And to wonder.

She began to look anew at the two other occupants of her passenger compartment. One an old man, one a young lady. Both were engrossed in whatever they were reading or watching on their PDs, and they did not look up when the announcement sounded.

Carolyn watched them for a moment, as discreetly as she could.

They were both across from her.

The woman felt eyes on her and glanced up.

Carolyn looked away.

The woman shifted uncomfortably, but said nothing. Went back to her PD.

The old man cleared his throat.

Carolyn knew she should have been looking at her PD. That was what people did when they were amongst strangers. They sat and they stared at projected screens and pretended the strangers did not exist. It was odd of Carolyn to be sitting there, not engrossed in a glowing world of information. But she had tried and found that she couldn't focus on it. So now she just sat.

She'd been in a sort of daze for an hour or so. Passing out of Georgia and into South Carolina—she hadn't even noticed the stops on the way. She tried to remember them now, but they were lost amid a hurricane of thoughts.

She didn't trust the two people across from her. She had no articulable reason for this. Only that she felt that anyone might turn on her in an instant. The world itself seemed to be watching her, like it could smell the guilt on her.

She felt thinly disguised.

By now her parents would know. For sure, they would.

She had left CoAx County. And it would be a safe assumption as to where she was going. And likely, they knew what had happened to John.

What would they think?

What would they *do*?

Would they put a hit out on her? Were they that far gone?

She wasn't sure. She wanted to say no, but then again…they seemed so unstable. In that moment of distrust and misgivings and the soul-sickness that was settling on her like a cold, drenching rain, she felt that Benjamin and Jean Eudy might just order their daughter to be killed.

She considered all of the trouble they had gone through to get her out of District 89. How they claimed it was only because they wanted their daughter with them. But what about now? What about now that they saw her as a liability to their plans?

Give me a chance, she silently wished in their direction, as though they were gods to be prayed to.

She would arrive in Durham with no friends, no contacts, and no idea where to even start looking.

Carolyn had realized this, somewhere in South Carolina.

So, why was she even going? Why had she not gotten off on one of the other stops and caught the next Maglev back to CoAx County?

She stared out the window at an urban expanse that was streaking by in a blaze of light. How quickly these trains moved. One second through quiet countryside and Agrarian Districts, and the next, into a jungle of light and city.

She wrung her hands together, not knowing what to do, or how to proceed, only the very beginnings of a very tenuous thread of thought. Something that might work. Something that might save her ass and buy her some time.

Give me a chance, she wished again.

The voice came over the speaker again and told them they were approaching the Charlotte stop.

She felt the train begin to decelerate smoothly.

Outside, the streaks of light shortened and became rapidly passing pinpoints, and then a second or two later, they were clearly streetlights and the glow of offices high up in glass buildings and cars roaming around in the streets.

The Maglev floated to a stop. A brightly lit station surrounded them. Outside of the windows, people milled about, either with purpose as they headed to board this very train, or absently, as they waited for another—perhaps a southbound one.

You should get off.

But she didn't.

The train dinged a quiet tone and begin to accelerate again. In a moment, the world was streaks of light again, and a few moments later, as they passed out of the city, it was darkness.

The compartment door opened and a man came in. A youngish man dressed in business casual. He swept in with a polite smile and a nod to the passengers that were already in the compartment. He edged passed them. Took a seat next to Carolyn.

He didn't speak. Gave her a short glance, perhaps wondering why she wasn't looking at her PD. When he'd settled into his seat, he flipped his own open. She couldn't see the monitor, as it was adjusted for his eyes only, but from the corner of her eye, she could see the flicker of light on his face and knew he was watching a video of some sort.

He smelled of cologne. Clean laundry.

He reminded her of John.

She had a horrible, striking fear that he *was* John.

Ridiculous, of course.

She snuck a sideways glance at him, wondering if he was watching her. But his eyes were focused on his monitor.

An act, perhaps.

Was he the one that was going to kill her? Would he simply wait until the old man and the young woman had left the compartment? Or would he wait until Carolyn tried to get off the train at Durham? Would he say anything to her? Or would it be a cold and wordless exit from the world?

Give me a chance! she suddenly wanted to scream at him, and knew it was madness, even as it came over her like a stifling shroud.

You have time, she told herself. *You have time, so use it. Think. Think your way out of this.*

You're not just a dumb grower, after all.

Who am I?

And her father's words echoed around in her skull: *You're a Eudy!*

Clever.

Conniving.

Ruthless, even?

That was her genetic inheritance.

Think...

And she did.

She thought all the way to the point that the speaker told them they were approaching the Raleigh-Durham stop. And she had just reached a sudden epiphany when the old man snapped his PD shut and got up with a shuffle and a groan and popping knees.

Carolyn waited for him to exit the compartment first, and then she gave a quick glance to the others, but neither the woman nor the man sitting next to her showed any interest in her.

Carolyn stood up then. Her legs felt stiff and leaden.

She felt the little compact pistol, pressing against her stomach.

How many rounds left in it?

It held ten. She knew. She'd counted them.

How many times had she shot John?

Her stomach flip-flopped unpleasantly. She decided not to try to count.

Several, she thought, and decided to count the rounds in the magazine when she got to a bathroom or some other private place where there were no cameras or people watching.

She went out of the compartment. Closed the door behind her. She felt the Maglev begin to decelerate under her feet. She walked to the rear of the car where the old man was standing with a few others at the exit door.

Carolyn took a spot behind him.

She looked back over her shoulder.

No one followed her out of the compartment.

She was the last person in line to exit.

The train slowed to a stop. The night was gone. Now they were bathed in white, industrial light. Through the insulated walls of the train she could hear the babble of people, but mostly of advertisements for things, and the bright, clamorous flash of them trying to get everyone's attention.

The doors opened.

The station was full of people. People coming. People going. Raleigh was the state capital, after all. And it was a nice city, even if Durham grew off its side like a cancer. All the people here were dressed for business, and they were clean, and they looked pleasant.

Still, as she followed the line of people trundling off the train, she noticed that there were pairs of soldiers stationed at points along the stop. They stood and they watched the crowd with that blank, scanning gaze of someone with an eye out for trouble.

Or looking for someone that they recognized.

Carolyn hunched her shoulders a bit and dipped her head.

The line of people began to disperse to their various points. To lockers that held their belongings. To the exits. To a family member or a friend who greeted them. To business partners who immediately began to harangue them with important questions.

Carolyn chose a direction and went for it, spying the brightly-lit EXIT sign, and figuring it was as good as any.

They were good.

The ones that came for her.

She didn't even see them coming.

She was jostling through a crowd of people that were heading the opposite direction, like a salmon trying to swim upstream, and then, right at the point when she was at the top of the stairs that led down off of the elevated station, she felt someone very close to her.

By the time her brain started shooting off warning signals like fireworks, she felt the shove of something hard being placed against her lower back.

Before she could move her right hand towards the pistol in her waistband, someone seized her by the crook of her elbow.

"Don't," said a voice. A woman's voice.

Then, from the other side, a man suddenly appeared, and as quick as a magician, slipped his hand under her shirt and pulled the pistol from her waist. He palmed it easily and it disappeared into a pocket of his jacket.

"I'll carry this for you," the man said, pleasantly. "Keep walking."

Carolyn could barely feel her feet as they began to descend the stairs. She kept thinking that she was going to fall, even though that was the least of her worries at that point.

The woman on Carolyn's right, prodded her in the back with what Carolyn could only assume was the barrel of a gun. "If you got any other weapons on you, don't try to reach for them, Stephanie. Don't think we won't kill you in public."

And Carolyn went with them, thinking, *This is good. It's a good sign that they haven't killed me yet.*

***

Bobbi knelt on the cement floor, and she wasn't facing anything in particular. A wall. A wall made of large bricks that had been painted with a thick coat of gray. Because that was the motif of this place.

The place was dim and cold. It was gray. Gray floors. Gray pillars holding everything up. Gray walls. Gray ceiling, with industrial pendant lights that hung down on chains and hummed softly above them.

There were others. Other prisoners. She could hear them off to her sides and behind her, sniffing, sighing, groaning. Occasionally coughing or sneezing. But they didn't cry. None of them cried anymore. They'd done all of that, it seemed. They didn't have anything left now.

Now there was an eerie sort of stillness that had overtaken them.

Like they were doomed to die, and they all knew it.

Which was, Bobbie knew, pretty much what was happening.

Death? DTI?

It was all the same in their minds.

There was a reason for the phrase, "Rather die than DTI."

Because DTI was a death in and of itself. You went there, and you never came back. There was no trial. There was no appeal. There was no time served. It was everlasting. It was Hell on earth.

And that was where they were headed next.

This place, this was a purgatory of sorts.

The devils here had questions. They sat in rooms that were just like this room, but smaller. Much smaller. Closed in and tight. And stiflingly hot.

Bobbi knew. She'd already been. Her shirt was still moist from sweat and beginning to cool as the chill night air swept in from the open bay doors to her right. She shivered.

In the small, hot rooms, they'd asked questions. And she'd given the only answer she knew to give, which was "I don't know," or some iteration of that. Something that denied knowledge of anything.

They didn't exactly torture her. They did rough her up a bit. A few open-hand slaps. A punch in the gut. Nothing too terrible.

Some of the others around her looked like they'd gotten it much worse.

Bobbi held no illusions, though.

They would torture her once she got to DTI.

But for now, she denied all knowledge of anything, and they had stopped asking questions after a while, and they had returned her, tired and sweaty and bruised and aching, to her kneeling position, facing this God-forsaken wall. And now she waited. With a sick stomach and a dry tongue. And somehow managing to be hungry through it all.

What type of food did they serve in DTI?

Maybe none at all.

Perhaps that is why no one came back from DTI.

Perhaps they all starved there.

She imagined a smoke stack rising above the security fences with their glittering concertina wire on top, and their high voltage cables running horizontally, every two feet. She pictured that smoke stack belching out thick black smoke all the time. A crematorium in the center of DTI, where all the dead were burned to ashes and claimed never to have existed.

Of course, she had no idea if that was the case.

Probably wasn't.

Or was she giving them too much credit?

"Everyone!" A voice shouted. "On your feet!"

No one replied. There was an eerie silence of voices. Just the shuffle of clothing and the sigh of people's quiet efforts, as they rose up to their feet. Bobbi was among them. Now *standing* and facing the wall.

"Turn and face the garage doors!"

She turned to her left, to where the doors were letting another gust of chilly wind in. The doors were rolled up completely. In the square mouth of the bay was the back of the truck. The same truck that she had boarded to be shipped here. A big personnel modular. Converted for use with prisoners.

It was open, too.

Waiting for them.

Another drive.

And then what?

DTI.

And then what?

Nothing.

Death on earth.

"Board the trucks in an orderly fashion," The voice commanded. "Move!"

There were three people ahead of Bobbi. They began to shuffle forward, towards the open backend of the personnel modular.

Bobbi glanced to the left, where there was an identical line of brain-dead people, heading for an identical door, beyond which sat an identical personnel modular. And looking at them all like sheep to the slaughter she wanted to shout out to them to wake up, to fight back…

But no.

The guards were all around them. If they even had a mind to make a group effort at attacking the guards, they would die in an orgy of gunfire and blood.

It was no use at this point.

And she supposed that was why she was shuffling forward with the rest of them.

The rest of the sheep.

“Eyes forward!” the voice shouted.

Maybe directed at her.

Maybe not.

But before she put her eyes on the back of the person in front of her, she gave a quick glance around and noticed that she did not see Walter Baucom Sr.

CHAPTER TWENTY-FOUR

When they pulled the black sack from Carolyn's face, she found herself face-to-face with Richard Honeycutt.

They were in an office. Sparse. Institutional. It was night. There were windows, but the shades were drawn and beyond them no light came. A set of recessed LEDs hummed from the ceiling. It was quiet enough that she could hear them.

Carolyn realized that her heart was not beating very hard, and she was glad. She was calm. She hadn't been calm initially. But after a while, she'd convinced herself that she'd finally been taken by the Fed and that it was fairly inevitable, seeing as how she'd run off like an idiot.

But…

Instead of a Fed interrogator, laying her out over a rack for some waterboarding, here was a face that she recognized. A compatriot in the cause. Supposedly.

What if he works for the Fed?

Carolyn worked saliva into her dry mouth.

Honeycutt was watching her, scrutinizing her, all the time with that dour expression.

Carolyn's eyes went left and right. Picked up the two people that had grabbed her at the station. They were lounging off to the sides. The man with his hands in his pockets. The woman with her arms crossed over his chest. They were both watching her carefully.

Carolyn herself could not have done anything if she'd wanted to. Except maybe get up and run. Her hands were bound with plastic restraints, but she was not secured to the seat she was sitting in.

Come to think of it…

You could head butt him.

It was an errant thought.

The man and the woman off to the side would just beat her or kill her.

Besides…

The epiphany.

The realization that she'd had on the train.

The culmination of all the conniving and thinking as she travelled between Charlotte and Raleigh-Durham. And what had been the fruit of that labor?

The realization that it didn't matter.

It didn't matter if she got caught on the platform.

There were risks, of course. The risk that they might just kill her outright, or the risk that they might not be associated with the resistance. But the odds were against that. The odds were for them working for her parents, and for them taking her alive. And Carolyn had to play the odds.

Not being caught meant that she would be wandering around aimlessly in a city she knew next to nothing about, with zero resources at her disposal and no friends to help her.

However, if she were caught, there was at least a chance.

To talk.

To manipulate.

She put her eyes back on Honeycutt.

"What the hell is this?" she husked.

Honeycutt's expression didn't change. "This is an abundance of caution."

"Did my parents send you after me?"

"Your parents sent *everyone* after you," Honeycutt replied. "What you did to poor John. That was…not necessary."

She felt her guts lurch around inside of her. Half-guilt, and half-offense. "Fuck you," she growled. "He forced me."

"Remember what I said about foul language."

Carolyn leaned forward this time.

To either side, the two guards tensed.

"Fuck. You."

Honeycutt sneered. "So charming. Perhaps this was a waste of time."

"What?" Carolyn sneered back at him—tit for tat. "Did my parents send you to kill me? Is that what this was? And what? You hoped you could get something out of it before you killed me?"

Honeycutt shrugged minimally. "Why did you come to Durham?"

Carolyn drew back.

Time to be cautious.

She'd let her temper show a bit.

Now it was time to reign it in.

Get control.

You can do this.

"I want to be the point of contact for operations in Durham," she said.

Honeycutt's face remained as flat as a dead man's while he considered this. Then a slight quirk of the eyebrow. "So you killed a man so that you could come to Durham."

"I'd made up my mind."

"That's quite cold."

"Well…there's plenty of Eudy in me. I'm just not as far gone."

Honeycutt broke a smile, but it was a clinical smile. Like a surgeon might have when he's successfully cut out the tumor he's been hunting. "Now, that's the crux of why we're here."

"How's that?"

He waved her off. "First, we need to cut through the bullshit. You go first."

Carolyn eyed him.

He watched her.

No one said anything.

He prompted her with a slow roll of his index finger. "You claim to have shot John because you simply were ravenous for the opportunity to be POC for Durham."

"Yes," she said in a small voice.

"Are you sure it doesn't have anything to do with your renegade husband?"

Carolyn swallowed. Hated that she'd swallowed.

"Honesty," Honeycutt intoned. "Is always the best policy." A pause. "Well, that's actually complete nonsense. However, I do believe that it's like salt. You need a bit of it in every dish, no matter what. So let's put our pinches of salt in this recipe for success, hmm? You came here because you believe that you might save your husband's life. Which makes what you did to John…understandable. And you plan to disguise these efforts by telling your parents that you're just…just *rarin'* to be the point of contact. To get in on the family business. Prove what you can do."

Carolyn's heart was beating hard now. She wasn't calm anymore.

"Am I right?" Honeycutt asked. "See, I was honest *for* you. Now all you have to do is say 'yes.' The hard part is done. Now. Am I right?"

Carolyn felt like she was trying to play simultaneous games of chess with five different champions. She could not keep so many lines of cause-and-effect straight. She was trying to juggle them all and failing miserably.

Finally, she said "Yes."

Honeycutt clasped his hands together. Leaned forward. Became very intense. A single vein popped out under his left eye. "I can help you, Carolyn. Obviously it's not for free. It comes at a price. But I think you'll find that price is not so bad, and the benefit is very great for both of us."

Carolyn felt her throat thickening and fought against it.

You are not weak.

You must be strong. Stronger than you've ever been.

"What do you want?"

"I want you to convince your parents to let you be POC here in Durham."

She frowned.

Honeycutt was very serious. "Plainly spoken, I don't trust your parents. The Eudys are and have always been extremists—no offense to you, as I believe you are not truly one of them. I don't think you *identify* with them. And that is what I want. I want someone who has their ear, someone who they trust, who can…*manipulate* them. Someone who I know is not insane."

"And who owes you," Carolyn said.

Honeycutt nodded forthrightly. "Of course. That is how these things work."

Carolyn held eye contact with the man, but she was in her head, lost in a tangle of thoughts.

It seemed too good to be true, but then, he wasn't asking her to do anything but what she'd already intended to do. She'd arrived in Durham with the very same plan that he wanted her to execute: Get captured, open a line of communication, convince her parents of her loyalty, and then manipulate them. Use the power they gave her to try to find and protect her husband.

God please let him make it through the night!

The only difference between Honeycutt's offer, and her original plan, was that if she worked with Honeycutt she would have someone on the inside. Someone who knew what they were doing.

Still, she hesitated. Only because she was trying to arrange everything in her mind.

Honeycutt seemed to observe this hesitation with the quiet patience of a man who is trying to get a bird to eat from his hand. He leaned back in his chair, slowly, and regarded her with what she could only think of as a *fatherly* expression.

"Carolyn," he said, calling her by her Baucom name. "Do you know why Walter got involved in all of this?"

Carolyn looked away from him. She felt the tears coming, willed them down. Thought of Walt. Fighting. Putting his life in danger. "Because of me," she said. "Because he thought the Fed had taken me."

"Well," Honeycutt bobbled his head slightly. "That's only half the story."

Carolyn blinked rapidly, trying to get her eyes to dry up. Trying to get the lump in her throat to leave her be. She was not weak. She would not show weakness.

"What do you mean?"

"Walter was already involved in the resistance prior to the purge. He would have gotten sucked into this whether you'd been taken or not. But do you know *why* he was involved?"

Carolyn just stared back. She didn't have words.

Walt? Involved even before the purge?

"He was an unwilling participant," Honeycutt continued. "But he helped some of my elements in the district. He helped them interrogate people. He has that…ability, you know. That empathic ability to read people. But he didn't do it for idealism or for patriotism or any of that. You see, he did it because he was trying to earn money, Carolyn. He was trying to earn enough money so that you and he could afford to have a child."

It took a moment.

But then it came up, from the bottom of her gut. Made her lean forward, nearly doubled over, like she'd been hit in the stomach. It clenched her chest, seized everything down, and what came out of her mouth was just a tortured little gasp.

Oh, Walt…

That evening that they'd lain in bed together. When she'd said what she'd said about them. About how she *should* have been happy. He must have heard the longing in her voice. The stupid, stupid longing. For motherhood. For childbearing. For the one thing that they could not have together.

But you had everything else! She railed against herself.

He must have heard the sadness in her when she'd said that stupid thing.

Oh, Jesus, she should have kept her mouth shut!

She clenched her eyes shut. Worked on taking breaths that didn't hitch.

Honeycutt's words kept slamming through her, like a hammer pounding a spike deeper and deeper.

He was trying
To earn enough money
So that you and he
Could afford
To have a child.

She had no option.

She had no recourse.

Honeycutt had outmaneuvered her deftly, and she damn well knew it, but that didn't change things. She had to work with Honeycutt, because without him she would be ineffective in saving Walt. And the only fucking reason Walt was in this position in the first place was because of her.

She had to.

She *had* to.

"Fine," she said. "Get me a line to my parents."

Honeycutt nodded. No smile. No self-gratification.

All business.

He held up a finger. "There's one other thing, before you get on the phone with your parents and convince them, as I know that you are capable of doing—because they *want* to be convinced, don't they? And it's always easy to lie to people that *want* to be lied to. Anyways. I digress. There is another thing."

Of course there is. There's always another thing.

"What is it?"

"I want the truth about Durham," Honeycutt said.

Carolyn stared.

Mind back to those chessboards.

Shit.

She knew. Of course she knew.

Her parents had brought her into their confidences. Which was why she'd decided her half-cocked plan to convince them she wanted to be a part of their bullshit might actually work. They'd already extended the proverbial olive branch. They *wanted* her to work for them. And the killing of John would be a minor thing in their eyes—a minor thing to explain to someone who would murder their own son-in-law because he'd become inconvenient.

But did Honeycutt need to know?

What would the consequences be if he did?

It was difficult in that moment to care about anything other than Walt. The ache in her chest was so strong, it demanded her attention. But Carolyn was a woman with a deep well of strength inside of her, and she forced herself to focus on the big picture.

"Do you promise to stick to the plan?"

It was his turn to frown at her. "You must believe in the deception to ask a question like that."

"You have to stick to the plan. If I tell you the truth about Durham, you have to promise to do what you told them you would do. Besides," she pointed out. "If you do something different they might suspect that I told you. And I wouldn't be much use to you if they don't trust me."

He looked away from her for the first time. A sign of particularly hard thought.

Finally, he nodded, still looking off to the side.

"Okay," he said. "The best deals leave everyone unsatisfied. That is what they say, anyways." He brought his eyes back to her. "I promise that I will stick to the strategy that they laid out—as long as it does not require me to sacrifice men for no reason."

Carolyn shook her head. "It won't. Everyone will sacrifice. But it's for a good reason."

"Speak, then."

"Durham is a feint," she said. "They want to draw attention and troops to Durham. They want to empty out CoAx County. That's the real target. And when all the attention is on Durham, they plan to use the renegade troops to take out CoAx County."

CHAPTER TWENTY-FIVE

Three men and two New Breeds, crammed into the back of a van.

The van stationed under a bridge, in a quiet stretch of highway that went through the middle of nowhere.

In the woods, approximately two hundred yards away from the van, a woman's body lay at the base of a tree, a pile of hastily-scraped-up leaves serving as her only internment. Perhaps she would be found.

There would be other bodies in those woods soon enough.

It was starting to get warm inside the van.

Walt extricated himself from the huddle at the rear of the vehicle, and leaned into the front to turn the ignition and start the air flowing again. The night outside was chilly enough, but between the body heat of five people and their moist breath, the windshield was already beginning to fog over.

As the van came on, the clock on the dash announced that it was 9:20 p.m.

"Shit," Walt said, feeling everything tighten a little bit more. Time was a snake wrapped around his chest, constricting him. "Is that clock right?"

Koz, who was hovering over Javon, but trying not to seem like he was hovering, checked his PD and nodded. "Yeah, that's right." He turned back to his partner. "Come on, Javon."

"Don't 'come on, Javon' me," the other New Breed said, lying sideways on one of the benches so he could get his big head down close enough to the floor to inspect an element of the DEMP that had caused him to hmm-and-haw a few moments prior. "Not my fault they shot this thing up."

Even with the air vents directed at the back of his neck, Walt immediately felt a prickle of hot sweat rise along his hairline. "Shot it up?" He shuffled into the back, gingerly holding his right side where it had been shot and had begun to coalesce into a block of dull, throbbing pain. "Like, bad? Is it bad? Will it work?"

"Well, I don't know," Javon snapped back. "That's what I'm trying to look at."

"What got shot?" Koz said calmly.

"The thing," Javon said back, obviously trying to think of the actual name for it, and coming up blank. "Uh…the thing that regulates the recharge."

"Well, that's not good," Rat observed, quietly.

Getty gave him a look. Decided to go for another cigarette.

"What about firing?" Koz asked. "Will it fire the charge that's already in it?"

"Oh, yeah," Javon said without hesitation. "No doubt. This things loaded up and ready. Setting it off ain't the problem. Getting it to recharge is." He grunted and shimmied his massive bulk further off of the side of the bench seat and down onto the floor. He wore a headlamp to help him work in the dark, and it cast crazy shadows on the ceiling as it blazed up through the contraption's various parts. "I'm trying to…trying to get a better look at it. I can see the bullet hole in the frame of the damn thing, but I can't see where it hit the…the thing we were talking about."

"Just call it a regulator for now," Koz suggested.

"Fine. The regulator."

Walt fidgeted on his feet. "Hey, Koz."

The red-bearded man looked at him.

"Shouldn't we be getting eyes on the sky?"

Koz looked past Walt at the dashboard clock.

9:22 p.m. now.

He nodded. "Javon, where're those thermals?"

"In my bag," Javon replied, his voice muffled and distracted.

Koz squeezed his bulk between Rat and Getty and bent over Javon's bag. "Roll down the windows," he said to Walt. "I need to be able to call it out when I see it."

Walt did as he was told. They had no comms. The under-handed nature of their doings had caused them not to have access to any secure devices. And Roy didn't want to use any unsecured signals.

Koz and Javon had agreed with him. The relative area of operation was small, they reasoned. If everything went as it should, verbal commands would suffice.

"You got those ear pro in?" Walt asked him.

Koz tapped one ear. "It's in."

"Can you hear okay?"

"I can hear just fine. Hopefully they work when the ECHO goes off. Otherwise we're gonna have a bad day."

"It hasn't been a bad day already?"

"Ha. Not even close."

Koz appropriated the thermal scope from the bag, and exited out the side door of the van, closing it quietly behind him and disappearing into the night.

Walt looked out the driver's side window and saw Koz's shadowy shape mounting the steep dirt embankment that led up to the bottom of the bridge.

"Alright, you bastard," Javon mumbled. Then strained with a grunt. Then let out a satisfied sound. He righted himself up from the floor and looked at Walt. The headlamp blinded him until Javon flipped it up and it cast its glow on the ceiling of the van, giving them all a dawn-like illumination.

Javon looked pleased. His dark skin was shimmering with a layer of sweat. "Alright. I think it's okay. There's no penetration on the regulator. The round just dinged it. It should work."

"Should?" Walt asked, doubtfully.

"It *will*," Javon said, more confidently. "No reason for it not to."

Walt hung there at a mental precipice for a moment. He could go on doubting, or he could just accept that Javon knew what he was talking about. And really, at this point, what option did they have? It was time to either go all-in, or fold the cards and call it a day.

And Walt realized immediately that folding was not an option for him.

Time to put his money where his mouth was.

He'd claimed he had the ability to pull this off.

And he would.

They would.

"A'igh," Walt nodded quickly. "You should put those ear pro in."

Javon nodded his assent and pulled the little black devices from his pocket and worked them into his ears.

Walt turned to Getty and Rat. "You guys ready?"

Rat looked tense, his jaw muscles bunching and un-bunching. He had nothing to say, which was more evidence of nerves than anything else.

Getty took a long drag from his cigarette and then stubbed the rest of it out on the floor of the van.

Rat and Getty shared a look, then nodded together, still not speaking.

"Go with Koz, then," Walt said. "Javon, you're with me, brother. You gotta work that thing."

Javon wiped his brow and nodded. "Yeah, man. I got you."

Getty and Rat hefted the battlerifles that they'd been given. Rat took a deep breath and shifted around inside of his softarmor. He pulled the side door of the van open and slipped out.

Getty paused at the doorway and looked back at Walt.

Walt held his gaze, expectantly.

Getty opened his mouth, but then closed it.

He just nodded, then hopped down.

The side door of the van slid closed.

Walt sat in silence for a minute. His chest felt hot. His hands felt cold. His belly was jittery. Momentarily he felt like he might vomit. From nerves, and from the sick feeling that his wound was giving him. But he reminded himself that it wasn't bad. It wasn't bad. And he had to sack up here. He had to get this done.

He wanted to focus on the mission—thinking about getting Pops and Bobbi out of those trucks. But those were just fleeting images. His brain wouldn't let him dwell on it. Wouldn't let him focus. All he could think about was the look on Getty's face as he'd stepped out.

Don't die tonight, he thought, and he wasn't sure whether he was thinking it to himself, or wishing it over Getty and Rat.

Don't die tonight, and that went for Koz and Javon, too.

All of them could die.

It wouldn't take much.

Just a misstep.

Just one thing that went a little too wrong to recover from.

His stomach plummeted with a thought: *This was a horrible idea!*

But he didn't entertain that thought for long. He stuffed it down and away, refused to look at it. Pretended it didn't exist. I can't see you, you can't see me.

Don't die tonight!

He heard the crinkle of a foil wrapper.

He blinked his way out of his dark daydream and looked at Javon.

The man was holding out a mealbar. He already had one open, half of it being chewed.

Walt shook his head.

Javon pushed the mealbar further towards him. "Eat it," he commanded, with no room for argument.

Walt gingerly took the thing. It was a plain, green foil package. Stamped on it were the words MEALBAR – 500Kcal – CHOCOLATE BROWNIE.

He didn't think he was very hungry, even though his stomach hurt.

He tore the package open.

It smelled like brownies…but not quite.

It tasted about the same.

As he chewed, something unexpected crunched in the soft brownie.

Walt frowned. It was like the mealbar had bones in it.

He dipped a finger into his mouth and pulled out a tiny chunk of white, stained brown.

He wasn't exactly sure what the hell that was for a moment, but then he realized…

It's a piece of my tooth.

He ran his tongue across the teeth that he so often ground together, and found a jagged little edge where a bit had broken off. One of his molars on his upper left side.

Momentarily, he felt sick.

He flicked the piece of his tooth off his fingertip and swallowed what was in his mouth. He did not intend to take another bite.

"Better get in that driver's seat," Javon said around his second mouthful of mealbar. "We're getting close to go-time."

"I thought Koz said it'd be closer to eleven o'clock—"

And Walt's thought ended abruptly with the sound of a faint buzz that swooped over their head, and then the sound of Koz's voice calling out: "Shit! That's them! Move! Walt! Fucking *move*!"

***

Getty was barely halfway up the embankment when Koz yelled it out.

"Shit! That's them! Move! Walt! Fucking *move*!"

Getty was a cool hand. But this sent a surge through him like he'd just touched a live wire. It blackened the corners of his vision and made his feet feel like lead blocks and everything else tingled uncomfortably like waking limbs.

He pulled the battlerifle up to his chest and bolted up the cement hill.

Behind them, the van revved, the tires skidding momentarily on the gravel of the access road, and the headlights shifted as the vehicle moved, casting their shadows long and sliding quickly across the ground like wraiths.

At the top of the embankment, just under the big steel girders of the overpass, Koz was crouched now, shoving the thermal optic away from him, not even bothering to repouch it at this point. He was yanking out their one ECHO device.

Koz saw Getty and Rat coming. Holding the ECHO in one hand, he pointed to the opposite side of the bridge with the other. "You two take that side! I'll take this side!"

Getty's heart caught up to him at about that point. Like it had taken a few moments to simply draw all the blood in his body into its chambers and then, at that one moment when Getty turned and looked at the other side of the bridge, and he heard the roar of the convoy's engines now becoming distinct from that of the van's, his heart slammed all that blood out into his arteries with a single vein-stretching pulse, and then it began to throb manically.

Getty ran for the opposite side of the bridge, Rat right behind him, already cursing up a storm.

Getty was used to hit and run. He was used to small unit tactics. He was used to picking at weak targets and sliding through society in disguise, the proverbial wolf in sheep's clothing.

He was not used to assaulting a military convoy.

He was not used to long odds—in fact, had avidly avoided them for most of his life.

The only commonality now with the risks he'd been taking lately was Walt. Now, *that* motherfucker took some risks. Like he didn't think about dying, although Getty could see in his eyes that he did. He thought about it. He just…

He views it as a necessary risk.

The steep angle of the concrete embankment played at the tolerance of Getty's ankles as he took a position under the steel girders and cast a glance over his shoulder. Rat was right there behind him. And on the other side, Koz, clutching the ECHO with both hands, and his eyes staring up, not at the girders, but *through* them. Like he was in the middle of a prayer.

Is this a necessary risk? Getty wondered, the voice of reason very muted behind his animal self that was all ears and eyes and aggression. Hearing the roar of military vehicles. Seeing their headlights splash over the woods down the road. His heart thundering.

If you want Bobbi back it is.

And that was all there was to say about that.

Moment of truth time.

Time to lay down the cards, and see who was walking away with all the chips.

Except, it wasn't like that, was it?

Combat was never a clean win. There was no such thing as a bloodless victory.

And then Getty knew that one of them was going to die tonight.

It was unavoidable.

But that's okay, he told himself, and the realization made him feel better. *Because if I die tonight, at least it was for something bigger than myself. And besides, this world is not so great that I need to cling to it anyway...*

And that was the crux of it, wasn't it?

Getty's coolness. His "bravery."

Isn't it strange how these moments happen so clearly, at the worst possible times?

Watching the blaze from the convoy's headlamps skitter through the trees, illuminating them bright green and gold for brief moments, and then back into blackness, Getty suddenly spewed out the truth: "I'm not brave, Rat."

Rat looked at him, incredulous. Was Getty really going to start talking about this *right now*?

"I just devalue my life and everyone else's life," Getty said simply. "I don't let anything good touch me, because then I'm afraid I might miss it when I die." He shook his head. "That's not brave."

The roar of the engines was overtaking them.

Rat looked like he wanted to say all kinds of things, but he just slapped Getty on the shoulder. "You get the job done. That's what matters right now."

Getty nodded.

On the opposite end of the overpass, the first tires hit the first bridge joint with an audible *thud.*

***

Walt watched it.

Twisted in his driver's seat.

The pain in his side suddenly forgotten.

Not breathing.

Four sets of headlights, just like Koz had said. Two guntrucks, framing two personnel modulars.

The van was stationed at the mouth of the access road. It would be plainly visible to that lead guntruck as it hurtled across the overpass at him. And what were those New Breeds inside thinking?

Ambush.

"You ready?" Walt shouted, not meaning to shout, but that's how it came out.

"Fuckin' ready," Javon answered.

Had the Lancer cannon on that lead guntruck just moved? Was it targeting them?

This is not going to work, something screamed in Walt's head. *They're gonna see it coming!*

The lead guntruck came off the overpass.

Walt stomped on the gas.

He jerked the wheel to the right, aligning the back end of the van with the front of that convoy. The headlights from the lead guntruck bloomed in his mirrors.

"Stopping!" Walt shouted. Then he slammed on the brakes.

The tires skidded.

Javon grunted.

There was the sound of the back doors opening.

The dark dashboard was suddenly lit with headlights.

"Fire it!" he shouted.

There was a deafening BOOM.

A hole the size of a fist appeared in the dashboard.

Fuck!

Then

zzZZ-WHACK

The sound of lightening.

Then the guntruck slammed into the back of them.

***

Everything went suddenly dark and silent.

It worked! Getty thought.

Lights died.

Engines died.

The creak of big machines rolling to a stop. Crunching into each other.

Getty turned, hyper-focused now.

Across from him, Koz was still crouched, staring at the girders, the ECHO clutched in his fist. Waiting.

What's he waiting for? Getty's mind screamed.

Then he heard it.

The sound of doors.

All at once, a clatter of them, all up and down the length of the bridge. There was shouting. A sudden volley of rifle fire shook the night.

Koz rolled out of his position, out from under the bridge, and tossed the ECHO in a hook-shot motion. "Move!" he shouted, without looking at them.

Getty surged out from under the bridge. He put the battlerifle to his shoulder, mounted the dirt. It was uneven. Ruts from rainwash. Patches of stalwart grass that threatened to trip him. He managed to keep his feet. He was moving too slow! He needed to move faster, but he didn't seem to be able to.

Another shout.

He couldn't tell what was said, or who had said it.

He made it to the top. Over the guard rail.

Right there. Right in front of him.

A normal soldier, looking the wrong direction, his attention focused forward.

Getty let out a string of fire and stitched bullets up the soldier's back.

The man grunted, stumbled. Swung quickly in Getty's direction, bringing his battlerifle around in a wobbly grip.

Getty let out another burst and one of the rounds caught him in the face and spilled him backwards.

Getty registered a sudden dampening in the level of gunfire. Now, there were only a few guns firing.

He swung a leg over the guardrail. His throat was already burning. His breathing ragged.

He was broadside to one of the personnel modulars now. The soldier he'd shot had been positioned by the front wheel. The personnel modular—and every other vehicle in the convoy—had accordioned together when their systems had been knocked out, and now they were all nose-to-ass, with no room in between.

Someone fired. Someone cried out. Someone fell down.

Getty swung to his right, looking down the length of the convoy.

He nearly dove for cover.

A big New Breed was standing at the backend of the personnel modular. He had Getty dead to rights, and in that moment, staring at the blank battleshroud that covered the New Breed's face, staring at the black hole in the center of that muzzle, pointed right at Getty, he knew he was going to die.

But he didn't.

The shot never came.

He gulped, felt giddy and unreal.

Another string of shots, hectic and barking, like two dogs fighting.

The two of them were standing, rooted to the roadway.

Getty forced himself to move. "Watch my back," he mumbled, shakily.

As they approached the New Breed at the rear of the personnel modular, he didn't move. He was frozen. Fucking brain-dead. For the moment.

For how long?

How long had it been?

Getty had no idea.

Rat swung around him and approached the New Breed from the side. Without hesitation, Rat swept up to the towering figure, thrust the muzzle of his battlerifle up between the New Breed's battleshroud and the chest plate of his hardarmor, and executed him.

***

Walt woke up with his face mashed against the steering wheel.

When he moved his head, the world swayed lazily to catch up.

How long had he been out?

He could hear gunshots. Screaming.

Panic thundered through him.

He stared at the hole in the dashboard, a thick tendril of white smoke rising from it.

The goddamned Lancer cannon had got a single shot off before Javon had triggered the DEMP. And then the guntruck had rammed into the back of them.

"Javon," Walt tried to say, but his words were just oatmeal in his mouth.

He strained. Grabbed the wheel. Used it to twist himself and look into the back.

Javon was in the back. He was on the bench, his back against the wall of the van. He was moving. Putting something on himself…

"Javon?" Walt tried again, this time with a bit more clarity.

Javon looked at him and his eyes were wide and white in the darkness and his teeth were bared.

Javon was missing an arm.

No, not missing.

It was lying on the floor of the van.

The dark skinned hand was opening and closing freakishly.

Javon was affixing a tourniquet to what remained of his left arm. He had it high and tight up into his left armpit. Walt could hear him ratcheting it down. Walt stared, bewildered, as the steady flow of blood that was dribbling audibly over the bench seat suddenly stopped, like someone had shut off a faucet.

"Oh my God…" Walt attempted to extricate himself out of the driver's seat.

"Stop," Javon said, and his voice was pitched up an octave, and trembling. "Turn the van around. You gotta turn the fucking van around."

Walt stared dumbly for another second or two.

That single round from the Lancer cannon had sheared Javon's left arm off. And still the man had managed to trigger the DEMP.

"Are you gonna bleed to death?" Walt asked.

"Fucking turn the goddamned van around!" Javon shouted back.

Walt blinked, shoved himself back into his seat.

Stop it, he told himself with a sudden blooming of rage. *Stop being a fucking knocker! Stop being a grower! You fight now. That's what you fucking do. You fucking FIGHT.*

He'd never pulled the van out of drive. It was still in gear.

He pushed on the gas and tried to crank the wheel to the left.

Nothing happened.

The gas pedal mushed to the floor.

The steering wheel fought him.

The van was off.

Had he turned the van off? He didn't think so.

He reached down, and turned the keys in the ignition.

The van made a horrible grinding sound. But it didn't do a damn thing.

Walt suddenly fixed his gaze on the hole in the dashboard. It was about midway down. And going in a downward trajectory. Because the Lancer cannon was posted to the roof of the guntruck. And it had fired one, big, armor-piercing round. The kind of round to which an engine block meant very little.

Any second now, a drone pilot was going to realize that the convoy he was attached to had gone dark. And then that drone was going to come back, and it was going to see the aftermath of an ambush, and things were going to get real out of control, real quick.

And here Walt was, in a dead fucking van, with no way to point that DEMP in the direction it needed to be pointed.

Don't be a knocker.

Walt threw his driver's door open and tumbled out, shouting, "We got a problem!"

CHAPTER TWENTY-SIX

Getty didn't waste time staring down at the dead New Breed. The imperative of the situation forced his feet onward. But the image stayed in his brain. It stayed like a background superimposed over everything his eyes were actually seeing.

There was a giddiness that he felt. A sort of feeling like he'd won the lottery.

He'd never killed a New Breed like that.

To stand, not ten feet from the New Breed, and for the New Breed to be the dead one…well, shit. That was something he never thought he'd encounter in his lifetime.

But there was a darkness that went along with it.

It felt…wrong.

At the back of the personnel modular was the last guntruck.

A quick glance over the scene told Getty that the one they had killed had been the driver.

The rear driver's side door was open. That New Breed had not even made it out of the car before his brain had been scrambled. He still sat, one foot on the concrete, the other inside the guntruck, leaning out like he intended to make a break for it. He didn't have his battleshroud pinned up.

Getty stared at the man's face.

The eyes flickered to Getty's, made his heart stop beating for a moment. But there was nothing behind them but an innocent sort of confusion. The person that was sitting there in front of him had no memories. He didn't know he was a New Breed. He didn't know what the Fed or the CoAx was. He didn't even know his own name.

They were the eyes of an infant.

The New Breed's mouth was open, working slightly.

A thin line of drool was spilling over his lower lip, onto the battleshroud that was hanging there against his chest plate.

"Take him out," Rat said, flatly.

Wrong, wrong, wrong.

Getty stepped around the open door, his battlerifle still up, shouldered, pointing at the New Breed's face. There was no comprehension there. The hazy, child-like eyes looked right past that muzzle, fixated on Getty's face.

Getty had heard that infants instinctively fixate on anything that looks like a human face.

Perhaps that was what was happening in the New Breed's brain at that very moment.

He fired once.

He was relieved and ashamed when the eyes disappeared.

The New Breed simply slumped over where he was, tilted a bit, then almost fell out of the guntruck, but his limp head struck the door and stuck there, his body propped up. A waterfall of blood issued out of his head and dribbled on the ground.

Rat was already moving around the backend of the guntruck.

Getty followed him.

On the other side, Koz was working back towards him and Getty almost cranked off a round at the sight of a moving New Breed. He stayed himself at the last minute. Koz made eye-contact with him, and that man was cold.

Another New Breed was standing next to the guard rail.

For a moment, Getty felt guilty under Koz's gaze, as though the man would feel that his kind had been wronged by the ECHO, by being slaughtered like sheep because their brains were too scrambled to defend themselves.

But then he stepped up to the New Breed at the guardrail and dispatched him with a single round, as coolly and thoughtlessly as you might crush an annoying bug underfoot.

Getty looked past Koz, up the line of vehicles that had mashed themselves together.

Bodies littered the concrete. Koz was a cyclone, and they were just the debris he'd left behind.

Koz efficiently scanned the interior of the last guntruck as he pulled up beside Rat and Getty. "Guess Sandman works, huh?" he said.

"Ayuh," Getty replied thickly. "I guess so."

Rat squinted towards the front of the convoy. "Shouldn't Walt be—"

And it was then that they heard Walt yelling: "We got a problem!"

***

Walt rounded the back of the van.

A glance over his shoulder, and an ear that picked up the sudden cessation of gunshots told him that there were no immediate threats. How fantastic. But they had bigger problems now.

The guntrucks came with a beefy grill, which they used almost exclusively for ramming other vehicles out of the way, or, in times of restraint, gently *tapping* them out of the way. So the guntruck that had collided with the rear end of the van had no damage to it.

The backend of the van, however, had not done very well.

Walt yanked the van door out of the way and it protested on bent hinges. He looked up inside the van and could see Javon, edging his way to the back. His face was drenched with a greasy-looking sweat, and his dark skin looked gray, his lips stark and pale on his face.

The fact that he was still conscious, had not been thrown by the impact, and was still operating, was a testament to the supreme mental and physical capabilities of New Breeds.

Walt looked down at the DEMP that was sitting in the back, slightly askew now.

"We gotta get this thing outta the van," Walt huffed.

But both he and Javon could see that the guntruck's grill was blocking that possibility.

Javon dropped his rear end off the bench and braced his back against it. He labored his feet up onto the grill of the guntruck. "Help me push it," he said, his voice a little thready.

"You should—" *take it easy* was what Walt had intended to say, but Javon cut him off.

"Help me fucking *push it*!" he snapped.

Walt rammed himself up against the back of the van. His side screamed at him, but he ignored it. He had about a foot of real estate that wasn't hogged up by the guntruck's grill. He strained against it. Javon pressed out with his legs.

The van rocked, but didn't move.

Javon gasped, and released his effort. He fixed Walt with an intense frown. "Did you put it in neutral?"

"Shit!" Walt jumped off the back of the van and ran for the driver's seat.

Behind him, Javon cursed: "Motherfucker!"

Don't be a fucking knocker! Walt inwardly yelled at himself. *Think! Think your way out of this!*

The driver's door was already open. He reached in and yanked the van into neutral.

It immediately gave up a few loose inches.

He ran to the back again.

Koz and Getty and Rat were running up on the opposite side.

"What do you need?" Koz called out.

"Push the van!" Walt ordered.

All three of them hit a moment after Walt did.

Javon put his legs up against the grill of the guntruck and heaved again.

The van rolled forward. Two feet. Five feet.

Javon lost purchase against the front of the guntruck as the distance grew, and he tumbled out, catching himself with his remaining arm and managing to land on his feet with a weak stumble.

Ten feet.

"That's enough!" Walt said. "Help me get the EMP out!"

No one asked him why. There wasn't time to ask why.

Koz shoved one of the van doors out of his way as it drifted inwards again. He grabbed ahold of one of the metal poles that made up the frame of the machine, and it was then that he saw Javon was missing a limb.

He paused for only a half a second. "You good?" he asked.

Javon nodded, gasping for breath. "I'm good. Keep moving."

Walt seized the other side of the DEMP. Getty and Rat worked their way in and with a single, panicked haul, the machine lurched out. Koz managed to maintain a solid grip on it, but the rest of them grunted and tried to lay it down gently but ended up dropping it to the concrete with a heavy *bang*.

"How much time we got?" Walt asked breathlessly.

"No idea," Koz said back. "Not long."

"Over here," Walt said, grabbing another handhold on the DEMP and yanking it towards the driver's side of the van. They surrounded it and began to push it and pick it up, turning it 180 degrees at the same time.

Javon hovered, swaying on his feet. "Needa recharge it," he mumbled.

"Hold on, hold on," Walt said. They tugged the machine one more time and now it was pointed perfectly downrange. In the direction that the drone would be coming.

"Who's on the thermals?" Walt demanded.

"Here," Javon ripped the scope from where it was tethered to his chest and shoved it into Walt's hands. "Get an eye on that sky."

Walt stepped off to the side and brought the optic to his eyes with shaking hands. It was a monocular platform. He fumbled with the focus. The world came into stark, clear colors. Everything was in shades of green. The roadway was a darker, bluish shade. The van was nearly yellow. The trees to either side, a muted, olive color. The sky was nearly black.

Stars shown out brightly. He stared at them, his heart causing his whole body to move with each pulse. He was trying to see if any of those stars were moving. If any of them looked different from the others. He knew enough that the scope was set to "white-hot"—heat would appear in gradations of white. But that didn't help him when he was looking at white starlight.

"Red-hot," he stated loudly. "How do I change it to red-hot?"

"Switch on the side," Koz called out. "Right there. Next to your index finger."

Walt felt it. Gave it a nudge. It gave a tactile click.

The world changed colors. Still the overall green tones, but that was just the infrared aspect. The thermal aspect had changed the van to a deep, navy blue.

Had one of the stars just disappeared?

He clicked the switch again.

The van turned a mellow orange color.

Reddish, around the engine block and undercarriage.

That's it.

Walt focused on the sky again.

White stars.

White stars.

White stars…

Nothing.

"We're clear," Walt said. Then amended: "I *think* we're clear."

"Do you see anything?" Koz demanded.

"No."

To Walt's side, he could hear the others rustling about. Their breathing. Javon's was audibly more ragged than the others. He was working hard. Trying to stay with them. There was the clank of machinery.

"Still nothing," Walt said.

"Standby," Javon muttered, and it came out "Sta'by."

"What's wrong with the van?" Koz asked.

"Got shot," Walt replied. "Engine block. The Lancer."

"Shit."

Walter looked at him, and instantly his brain made the connection that Koz was getting at. Walt swore under his breath and turned quickly to the others, spewing a half-formed plan as fast as his brain could conjure it. "Getty. Rat."

"Ayuh?"

"Can you steal cars?"

Rat answered: "Certain cars."

"We passed a service station about a mile back," Walt said, speaking rapidly and with absolute focus. "Go. Get us a set of wheels. Steal it. Hijack it. I don't give a fuck. Just get us something that drives."

"Okay," Rat said, tensely.

"When you come back for us, drive slow, with your flashers on, so we know it's you."

"Okay."

"Run."

"Okay."

Rat took off running.

Walter turned back to the skies, to the thermal imager.

"Awright," Javon said drunkenly. "He' we go…"

There was a clacking noise.

Like an engine that was trying to turn over, but failing.

It ended with a sudden, loud *snap.*

Walt pulled the optic off his face. "What the fuck was that?"

Javon was standing there, staring down at the DEMP, as was Koz and Getty.

"Watch the sky," Koz barked at him.

Walt went back to it.

White stars.

White stars.

"What happened?" Koz asked Javon. "What's wrong?"

"Fuck. Fuckfuckfuckfuckfuck," was all Javon said.

"What? Talk to me!"

"Fuckin'…the fuckin' *thing*!" Javon shouted hoarsely, desperately. "The *regulator*!"

The words went right into Walt's chest like a kick from a mule. They turned into yellow-hot fear that went spiraling up his back, around his neck, and into his head. He let out one big breath and then yanked the optic away from his face again.

He looked directly at Koz. "Fuck the EMP," Walt said. "It's busted. We gotta move."

Koz opened his mouth.

Walt didn't wait. He shoved the optic back into Javon's one hand. "Javon, buddy, you with me?"

Javon nodded. He blinked rapidly and squinted, like a drunk man trying to focus. "I'm here. I'm here."

Walt pointed to the sky. "Watch for the drone. Tell us when you see it." Then he turned and began running towards the personnel modulars. "Let's get our people out of those modulars and get the fuck out of here."

Behind him he could hear Koz: "Javon, get in the woodline with that thing! You fucking stay conscious, you hear me?"

If there was a reply from Javon, Walt didn't hear it.

He reached the back of the personnel modular. Getty stumbled to a halt behind him. Walt hurdled quickly up onto the hood of the modular that had run into the back of this one. For a second he was afraid there wouldn't be enough clearance to open the outward-swinging doors, but for a change in luck, he had a few inches of clearance.

He ripped the doors open.

Inside was pitch black.

Walt stood there, staring into the darkness. Then he called out, "Walter Baucom Senior!"

There was a moment of petrified silence, and then the dam broke and he heard a dozen different voices start to shout back at him.

"Help us!"

"What's going on?"

"Are you resistance?"

"Get us the fuck out of here!"

"Come on, man!"

"Let us out!

And the rest of it became a slurry.

Walt took an involuntary step back.

A single voice screamed above the others: "Walter! Is that you?"

Getty vaulted up onto the hood of the modular with Walt. "That's Bobbi!" he said, his voice high-tensile. He clicked on his battlerifle's weapon light. A spear of white shot out into the gloom and several of the voices quieted.

A slew of blinking, desperate faces looked back at them.

They were in two rows, their backs up against the outer walls of the modular. Their hands and feet were manacled together. Each of them shackled to the floor.

Getty plunged into the darkness, his white light leading the way.

The voices started up again, pleading, anxious, demanding.

In the back, one of them was practically writhing out of the restraints. Walt immediately recognized the short-cut, dark hair. But the face was different. It was streaked with smoky dirt and the eyes were not the kind eyes he had remembered, but wide, crazy ones.

"Walter!" someone shouted to his left.

He looked down, saw that Koz was standing there, looking up at him.

“Get in the…”

The rest of it was drowned out by everyone shouting.

Walt ripped the pistol from his waistband and, without a second thought, fired three rounds off to the side. “Everyone shut the fuck up!” he shouted into the modular. “Next person to scream at me gets shot!”

You mean that?

Maybe I fucking do.

He got his silence—sudden and permeating—and he turned back to Koz.

“Get in the modular,” Koz continued. “Close the doors. The drone won’t fire on the modulars, I don’t think. You’ll be relatively safe in there. It’s got two drops of ordnance—I’m gonna try to get it to waste them, and then me and Javon are gonna lead it off away from you guys. Hopefully it’ll track us.”

Walt nodded rapidly. “Okay. Okay.”

“Hey,” Koz said, pointing up at Walt. “You won’t have long. When the drone sees what happened it’s gonna pull the big red handle, okay? You’re gonna have a shit ton of company. Probably a flight of gunships on QRF, and maybe some guntrucks.”

“Okay.”

“Work quickly. Get these people out of here.”

There were a million other questions that ran like spooked horses through Walt’s brain—*You want me to free all of these people? How are we going to provide transportation for all of them? Where the hell am I going to find you and Javon?*—but he never had the chance to ask them.

In the distance, Javon’s voice coughed out, barely audible: “Drone! Inbound!”

CHAPTER TWENTY-SEVEN

Walt jumped across the gap between the hood of the one modular truck and into the back of the next. He reached back and grabbed a hold of the swinging doors and pulled them shut, stopping at the last second before they latched. He held his fingers in the gap. Felt the weight of the doors carrying their momentum and winced as they pressed against his knuckles.

"Getty!" he called out. "Light!"

A second later the bright white beam of light washed over him.

He looked the interior of the two doors over. There were latches. He stuffed the pistol that was still in his hands back into his waistband and pulled at the latch. "Is this thing gonna lock us in?"

"I don't know," Getty answered.

"Yes," someone announced.

Walt looked over his shoulder. A small female with short-cropped hair had edged forward against her restraints. She was looking at Walt boldly, expectantly.

"These are converted for prisoner transport," she said. "They don't open from the inside."

Walt kept his fingers in the gap. They were big, heavy doors. He had the image in his head of a strong gust of wind or some other force causing them to slam shut, cutting his fingers off.

Walt looked further down the row of prisoners to where Getty was standing beside Bobbi.

Getty raised his rifle up so the light illuminated the ceiling and cast them all in a ghostly glow. He gestured emphatically to Bobbi's restraints. "How do you get these things undone?" A look of distress disturbed Getty's normally casual face. "They're fucking electronic."

Walt swallowed.

If the locks were electronic, they would've been toasted by the EMP.

"There's a mechanical override," the woman said.

Walt snapped his gaze back to her and frowned. "How the fuck do you know all this?"

The woman gave a cursory glance around her, as though she was wondering how much to admit in front of all of these people, but she must have decided that there was no time to worry about that right now.

"My group hacked the specs on these things," she said. "In case we ever needed them. Never thought I'd be the one inside."

"Fine," Walt said, making the split second decision to trust what she was saying.

That was the order of the day—split second decisions, and to hell with the consequences.

"Tell me about the override—"

A massive explosion rocked the truck.

The thirty-something people inside of it cried out all at once.

Walt flinched and almost pulled his fingers from the gap in the doors, but restrained himself. Through the crack between the doors, the world blazed brightly for a brief moment, then was yellow, then orange, and then black again.

"Drone's dropping ordnance," Getty said.

Walt stared through the crack.

There was the sound of falling debris. Some smaller chunks peppered the asphalt and the top of the modular like rain on a tin roof. Then a big chunk struck and someone inside let out a little gasp.

Koz, please tell me that you're still alive, he prayed silently.

The New Breeds could handle themselves, but Walt still felt responsible for them being in the situation in the first place. For the fact that they'd gone into battle with him, they deserved a little prayer.

He turned back to the woman who knew about these modulars.

"The locks. Tell me about the locks. Quick."

Another explosion. This one farther away.

Because the drone was tracking Koz and Javon through the woods?

No one cried out this time.

"There's a manual, mechanical override," the woman spoke deliberately, clearly, like someone giving medical instructions over the phone. "Both of the soldiers that drive in the cab have the key to it. It'll be on a chain, probably around their neck. It'll be a round, black piece of rubber with a metal prong coming out of it. The prong has three square teeth."

Her eyes were wide, waiting for Walt to accept what she'd said.

Walt stared, then nodded rapidly.

"Do you understand?" she asked.

"Yes." He turned to Getty. "Getty, I'm goin' out there."

"Is the drone gone?"

"Can't hear it," Walt said, but that didn't mean much, because he hadn't heard it before it'd dropped a missile on them.

But Getty nodded. "Fucking hurry. Your pops might be in the other modular," he added.

Walt just pushed the doors open. Only a few inches at first. He pressed his face out, exposing an ear to the outside world and listening. There was a low, quiet hum, but it sounded far away.

Or was it just high above them, looking straight down?

And how much ordnance did Koz say those things carried?

Two strikes, right?

Shit.

Walt, upon not being vaporized for the ten seconds that his head was out the door, decided that he was safe enough to get his ass in gear.

He slipped through the door and closed it behind him. He heard someone shout to him as the door latched, but he didn't hear what they'd said.

The door clicked shut.

He swung down, feeling his heart still in his throat.

They were probably yelling not to close the fucking door.

Because if he got his ass killed out here, they weren't going to get out until a squad of Fed New Breeds *let* them out.

Too late.

Walt looked briefly around him and saw a body lying against the front tire of the second modular. It was a normal man in softarmor. Not a New Breed. It had to be one of the drivers of the modulars.

He ran to the body and skidded down on his knees, ripping the pants and tearing the skin. He didn't notice.

Walt plunged his hands into the neck of the man's softarmor, diving down until he felt a chain. He pulled it up.

Dogtags.

He dropped the tags and they clattered to the soldier's chest.

Walt went in again, this time getting his fingers underneath the uniform and the undershirt, but he felt no other chain.

He jerked up.

Was that a buzz?

The drone? Or the approach of gunships?

How quick does a Quick Reaction Force move? Walt riddled himself.

He spurred himself back into motion. Maybe that buzzing noise was just the ringing in his ears from the gunshots and the explosions.

He began patting pockets. Sticking his fingers in them. Seething in a half whisper the same words over and over, every time he came up with nothing: "You fuck! You fuck! You fuck!" As though the soldier, even in death, was fighting him.

A small pouch that was attached to the man's belt.

Just a little black thing with a zipper that went all the way around it.

Walt undid the zipper.

A small black object attached to a beaded chain tumbled out and tinkled lightly, almost merrily on the pavement.

Walt snatched it up. Held it to his face like a mine worker that had just found a large diamond.

Black rubber body. A metal prong. Three square teeth.

Winner winner.

He shoved himself standing and pawed his way up onto the modular again. He unlatched the door and slipped inside.

"You shouldn't have let the door latch!" the woman said, before Walt could even get both feet in the door.

Walt didn't even give the comment a second thought.

She was right—he shouldn't have.

"Getty!" he called, then tossed the key down the length of the modular. Getty nabbed it out of the air.

Walt looked at the woman. "How much time before a QRF hits?"

She frowned at him. "You didn't research it yourself?"

"Can you answer the fucking question?"

"Anywhere between five and ten minutes," she said. "Depending on the base they're coming out of and if they're coming from ground or patrol."

Five to ten minutes.

Shit.

How much had they already lost?

Walt stared down the length of the modular.

He had to assume that at least two minutes had passed since the drone had called for QRF. Which meant there was only two or three more minutes left, worst case scenario. And Walt felt comfortable assuming that the worst case scenario was going to be what he got.

There was no way in hell they were going to be able to unlock all thirty of these people *and* find his pops, *and* free the people in the other modular. No way in fucking *hell*.

Bobbi shucked off her restraints and they clattered to the deck. Getty grabbed her by the shoulder and pushed her to the center of the aisle that existed between everyone else's shackled feet.

The prisoners shouted, screamed indignantly, shook their cuffed hands at Getty.

Getty didn't give a shit. He moved past them fluidly, his body, his rifle, always a few inches away from the furthest point their chains would let them reach. His eyes were affixed to the back of Bobbi's head.

Bobbi, however, was looking around desperately at everyone as they pleaded and demanded and offered things. Then she found Walt's eyes. She shouted over everyone else, "Walter, I don't know where your father is! I didn't see him get on any of the trucks!"

"We'll find him," Walt said, grabbing Bobbi and shoving her out of the back end of the modular, like a body guard pulling his client from an angry mob.

"You sonofabitch!" the woman screamed at Walt. "You can't leave us here!"

"I'm not!" Walt belted back at her, hunching so that he was in her face.

She watched him intensely. The cajoling from others continued, but had lost its indignant edge.

Walt bent to her, on one knee like a man with a proposal. He grabbed her hands up so he could see the cuffs and shackles. He unlocked the feet. Then the hands. Then he looked at the woman. "All the soldiers are dead. There should be keys on the drivers, right?"

She nodded.

"Good," Walt said. "Then there should be three more out there. I gotta go."

He backed away from her for a few steps, reasonably concerned that she might try to attack him. For a variety of reasons—his gun being chief among them, but maybe just because she thought he was an asshole.

Asshole or not, Walt had bigger problems.

When he backed into the doors, he turned and quickly slipped out.

Getty and Bobbi were running for the back of the second modular as Walt stamped across the armored hood and jumped down. He could hear Bobbi talking, breathlessly.

"Where's Rat?"

"He's getting us a car."

"You don't have a car?"

"We had one. It got blown up."

Walt sprinted after them. Reached them as they came to the back of the modular. They could hear people inside. Their voices were very faint, but they were audible. And they were stamping their feet or something. There was a rumble in there. The sound of many soft impacts.

"Bobbi, keep an eye on the road, up and down," Walt said. "Let us know if you see anything." He pulled himself up onto the back of the modular. "Getty," he said over his shoulder. "You're with me."

If the interior was as dark in this one as it was in the other, then he would need Getty's weapon light.

He yanked open the heavy doors. Darkness again. But lots of yelling.

The yelling quieted as he flung the doors wide, but then it started up again.

Walt left his pistol in his waistband, although the thought of making the threat again flitted momentarily across his mind. Getty turned on his weapon light again and the same scene showed itself as the last one.

A bunch of chained up people, rattling and yelling to be free.

He dove into the aisle, calling out, "Walter Baucom! Walter Baucom!" and checking faces to his right and to his left. He noticed for the first time that many of these people's faces were battered.

Had that been the case in the first modular?

Now that he was thinking about it, he believed that it was.

Getty echoed the call behind him.

A stream of stranger's faces passed him.

More and more of them.

He was nearly to the back of the modular, and a sick feeling was beginning to coalesce in the center of his stomach.

"Pops!" he started calling. "Pops!"

But Pops didn't answer.

He reached the end of the modular. Almost ran into the wall.

He spun around in a panic, staring at the faces behind him.

Getty was standing there between two waves of clutching, grasping hands, and his head was lowered, his eyes looking up almost guiltily at Walt.

"Did we miss him?" Walt said, gulping air.

Getty didn't respond. He just cast a glance to the left and right again. But Getty didn't really know what Pops looked like, did he? Walt hadn't seen him, but maybe he'd missed him in the hurry. Bobbi had looked different…

He's not here.

But no! He *had* to be here!

"Walter Baucom Senior!" Walt shouted loudly.

The din of the prisoners had downgraded itself to mumbles and an occasional holler that swept over Walt unrecognized, like a foreign language.

They were mostly all just staring at Walt now.

He thought for a bare moment that perhaps his father had been asleep—no, not asleep through all of this noise. Perhaps passed out. But as he looked down the mirrored rows of faces, he saw no one slumped in their seat.

Getty started to shake his head. "Walt, we need to go."

"But…"

"He's not here, Walt. Bobbi said so herself."

"But he was the whole fucking reason we did this!"

"It doesn't matter!" Getty raised his voice, but not harshly. Just to get through to Walt. "We need to get the fuck out of here. And no amount of calling for him or wishing for him is going to make him appear in the back of this truck." Getty reached forward, seized Walt by the shoulder and forced eye-contact. "Come on. You're the one running this show. You know we need to go. I ain't gonna leave without you. But you know we need to go."

Someone shouted, "Your old man probably got iced! Let us out!"

Walter looked for the man that had spoken, his eyes wide and fiery. He was breathing hard. His fists were over-tight on his weapon. He couldn't tell who'd opened their mouth. He wanted to find that motherfucker. Put the pistol in his big mouth and see if he cared to say anything else—

"Walt."

A voice out of the darkness.

Not Getty.

Not Bobbi.

Walter would've known the voice anywhere.

He looked rapidly around as though the darkness itself had spoken and he could not pinpoint a source. The blood was humming in his veins.

"Pops?" his voice cracked. "Pops, was that you?"

"Right here, Walt."

Walter took two steps down the center aisle of the modular and saw a man sitting amongst all the other prisoners, and his shackled hands were waving gently to Walter. When Walter drew abreast of him, his stomach did a little flip-flop and there was a moment when he thought *this guy's lying!*

But then Walter looked closer.

The man that had spoken to him, his face was a swollen, blood-encrusted mass. One eye shut. The other red with broken blood vessels. The nose was bulbous and smashed. Blood like a red goatee down the front of his face. Lips puffy and bluish. Cuts here and there on his face that had long since swollen so bad that they'd cut off their own blood flow.

Nearly unrecognizable.

Nearly.

"Pops?" Walter said again in a shaky, quiet voice.

Pops was crying. Tears were leaking out of his red eye, and from the cracks of his swollen one. Trickling down his ruined face. His hands strained against the shackles, trying to reach for Walter, to touch him.

Walter gasped and fumbled for the keys. "Why didn't you say anything when I walked past?" he demanded. "It's okay! It's okay, we're gonna get you out of here. My God! What they did to your face! I'm so sorry. Just hold on…"

He got the key into the manual override and the cuffs fell off of his father's wrists.

Walter Baucom II reached up and touched his son's face. His hands smelled of dirt and sweat and blood. The son did not recoil. Pops' one good eye traced manically over Walt's face, imprinting a memory.

"Look at you," Pops said huskily. "I never would have thought."

Walt reached forward, grabbed his father by the shoulders and started to hoist him up. "Come on, Pops. We gotta get you out of here."

At first he thought his father was just surprisingly heavy.

Then he realized that Pops was actively resisting.

Halfway out of his seat, Pops lurched back and planted his butt down again.

"Pops? What's wrong?" Walter said sharply. "We gotta go! We have no more time here!"

Pops grabbed Walter's hands, clutched them tight, and Walter could feel his father shaking. "I can't go with you, Walt," Pops said. "You have to leave without me."

CHAPTER TWENTY-EIGHT

Rat came to the service station with ragged lungs, stitches in his sides, cramping hamstrings, and sweaty rings blooming out from his armpits, despite the cool night.

From the tree line just outside the aura of pale light created by the service station canopy, Rat held his battlerifle up to his shoulder and saw that the effort it took to hold it steady was monumental.

It was a medium-sized service station, with several pumps and a decent convenience store.

But there wasn't a goddamned car there.

From his current angle, he couldn't see inside the store. Couldn't see if there was a clerk in there, or if there was a glowing OPEN sign.

Decision time.

Storm in with the battlerifle out?

Or stash the rifle and saunter in like everything was okay?

Except that he was sweaty, breathless, and probably had sticks and leaves in his hair and his pant legs were coated with mud.

You're not fooling anyone.

So go in hard.

He worked his way along the wood line. He'd gotten control of his breathing, but his legs had stiffened up. His arms were twitching and trembling.

He reached the edge of the woods. Now there was a swath of badly-cared-for grass, and then there was cracked and oil-stained parking lot. On the side of the convenience store facing Rat was a dumpster.

There was a back lot, too. Fenced in.

Rat spied two vehicles back there, parked side-by-side. One was a solar. The other a GUV. They both looked like they'd seen better days. Were either of them running?

With no other cars around, they might be his only options.

Rat was about to step out of the tree line and into the light when the front door of the convenience store swung open.

Rat stopped himself in the shadows, his grip tightening on his battlerifle.

A man emerged. Middle aged. Beer gut. Balding.

He carried two, full bags of trash, one in each hand. He was hauling them toward the dumpster.

Now! Do it now!

Rat tore out of the woods, the branches of the last curtain of small trees whipping his face and arms. The rifle was already up. He was staring at the clerk as he advanced quickly, and he didn't say a word, and the clerk didn't know he was there until he was within twenty feet and he caught Rat's movement out of the corner of his eyes.

The clerk jumped and his feet did a little two-step, the trash bags jangling at his sides.

"Don't you fucking move!" Rat said sharply.

The man uttered a little cry of fright and the two trash bags hit the ground. He turned and ran for the store, shockingly quick for an out-of-shape service station worker.

Rat swore and sprinted after him.

For the tiniest of moments, he pictured stitching the man up his back with a burst from the battlerifle, but restrained himself.

If he'd known how this night was going to end, he might have done it.

The clerk hit the doors ahead of him, and Rat knew he wasn't going to catch him. He was too far behind, too winded from the run through the woods. His best hope was to stop him from sounding an alarm, or grabbing a shotgun from under the counter.

Rat hit the doors just as they were swinging closed.

He burst through, into bright, sterile lighting filled with colorful, pre-packaged goods.

An automated advertisement called out to him.

The clerk was huffing, red-faced and wide-eyed, around the counter, disappearing for a moment behind a rack of scratch-offs.

Rat threw himself at the counter. He managed to get his ass up onto the countertop and he leaned, so the muzzle of his rifle cleared the rack of scratch-offs, just as the clerk ran into it. The clerk saw that he'd been cut off a second too late to stop his forward momentum.

Rat hit him in the face with the barrel.

The man fell on his ass, his hands going up to his face as he grunted in pain and looked up with naked fear at Rat.

Rat shook the rifle at him. "I said don't move!" he hissed. "What the fuck were you thinking?" he didn't wait for a response from the clerk. "You fucking idiot! Did you trip an alarm? Did you call anybody?"

"I-I-I—"

"Motherfucker, did you call anybody?" Rat bellowed.

"No," the man squeaked.

"There a gun under this counter?" Rat demanded.

"No."

Rat kept the rifle up with one hand and reached his other hand under the counter, breathing hard again, and sweating even worse now that they were in the still air of the store. He rummaged his fingers around, and the clerk watched him do it with a look of fascination and terror.

His fingers fell across something that didn't take much interpretation.

He grabbed it. Yanked it up.

It was a hunting shotgun—of course.

Rat held it up in the air, but stared at the man who was still seated on the floor. "What the fuck do you call that? A goddamned tennis racquet?"

Rat threw the thing angrily over his shoulder, and it clattered noisily against a shelf full of chips. The whole assembly went down.

The clerk held up his hands, pleading. "I'm sorry, mister! I'm sorry! I don't know what I'm saying! You scared the shit outta me!"

"Did you lie to me about calling someone too?" Rat said, his sides beginning to ache from holding his body in that twisted seated position. He was struggling to get a lungful of air, especially with all this yelling. "Did you call someone? Trigger an alarm?"

The clerk stared, bug-eyed, and swallowed audibly.

"No," he mumbled.

Fucking lie, Rat thought, but it was a moot point now, wasn't it? If he'd managed to set off some alarm or call, then the damage was done. Rat was already operating under that assumption. So now it was time to put things into road gear and get this shit done.

"Keys," Rat ordered. "Keys to those vehicles out back."

The man stared.

Rat kicked the rack of scratch-offs, sending them exploding backward onto the clerk with a satisfying loudness. "Motherfucker, I'm looking for the *keys*! The *keys* to the vehicles out back! The solar and the GUV!"

"Them don't run," the man spluttered.

"Fucking bullshit they don't run," Rat snapped. "One of 'em's gotta run, you asshole. How'd you get here?"

"Wife dropped me off."

"Fuck! What's wrong with them?"

"The solar's got a busted solenoid, and the GUV won't hold a charge."

"Fuck the solar. Tell me about the GUV. Will it keep running if you jump it?"

"For about twenty minutes a-time. The alternator is busted. It just runs that batt'ry dry."

"You got a jump box?"

"I got a few."

"I'm gonna need 'em all," Rat said, nodding quickly.

It was a shit sandwich, that was for damn sure. This had to be the only service station in the state with not a single running vehicle on the premises.

But you had to work with what you had.

And right now he had a GUV with a busted alternator. But at least he had some jump boxes, so all was not lost.

"Those jump boxes backfill?" he asked, scooting his butt of the counter finally, which let him get a full breath.

"Two of 'em do. One of 'em's old."

"Fine, fine." Rat jerked the rifle. "Get up. Come on. Come on. The keys. Don't forget the keys."

The man had calmed a bit during the exchange, but he was still wide-eyed, and still a bit shaky. When he stood up, he seemed a tad unsteady.

Rat opened his mouth to keep ordering the man around, but the roof of the building suddenly rattled violently. The sound thundered over their heads, crescendoed, and then began to fade just as rapidly as it had appeared.

Low flying gunships, if he'd ever heard them.

The clerk was looking at the ceiling. Then he turned his gaping fish mouth to Rat. "Are you resistance?" he almost whispered.

Rat frowned at him, then sneered. "You really wanna know, jackass?"

"I heard the bombs go off," the clerk said excitedly.

"Hey, hey!" Rat took a half a step toward the man as though he might hit him with the barrel again. Then he stopped himself. He looked at the man's name tag. It read STU. "Stu, you need to fucking listen to me, old boy. You're gonna help me get out of here, or we are both going down in a hail of gunfire, do you understand me? That's the only way you get to live tonight—if you get me in one of those vehicles. So quit fucking worrying about who I am and what you heard earlier. All you need to think about is getting me in that *fucking GUV*, so I can get out of your life, so that you can go home and fuck your fat wife tonight, okay?"

"Okay."

"Stu. Go." Rat waved the rifle emphatically. "Go, go, go."

They started towards the back, where it attached to the service garages, but then Rat had a second thought, a second concern, as he began to try to open his mind up about things, and he caught Stu by the shoulder and stopped him.

"Wait a minute," he said.

For a half second Stu looked too terrified to move.

"Lock the front door," Rat said.

"Oh. Okay."

"Quickly."

Rat went with him. Hovered behind him, as they moved around the aisles of shitty food, and stepped gingerly over the toppled rack of chips with the shotgun on the floor—"Don't think about it, Stu. Don't even look at it."—all the way to the door.

With one hand braced on Stu's shoulder, and the other holding the battlerifle to the man's back in a quaking, painful grip, Rat noticed headlights flashing suddenly across the pumps outside.

It all happened so quickly and unexpectedly.

The words "lock the door" died on the tip of Rat's tongue, as he saw the vehicle swing up in front of the store, saw the markings on the side of it—a white GUV with bold, reflective yellow lettering that read SHERIFF.

Rat was caught in the open. Nothing to hide him. Just a bunch of glass.

As the deputy tumbled out of his patrol vehicle, his subgun already up, already yelling commands, Rat snaked his free arm around Stu's neck and started hauling him backwards into the convenience store, using him as a body shield.

Rat's sudden reality crushed his stomach into queasiness.

Well, now I'm stuck in a fucking standoff...

Rat cursed venomously as he dragged Stu backwards, away from the glass front of the convenience store. Out there, the deputy was posted up behind the cover of his engine block, still yelling and sighting at Rat with his subgun.

Rat hoped to God that the deputy wasn't confident enough to take a shot right now. It could totally be done, but the deputy would have to have brass balls to do it. The way the night was shaping up, Rat figured that would be his luck.

They reached the last aisle of foodstuff, which ran like a path back to the door that went out into the service garages. Rat pulled Stu after him, picking up the pace now that they were hidden from the deputy outside.

"You motherfucker!" Rat railed. "You tripped a goddamn alarm!"

"I didn't!" the man squealed like a stuck pig. "I didn't! I swear!"

Rat was now dragging the man after him, rather than using him as a body shield. He kept glancing over his shoulder to make sure that he was still not visible to the deputy. He hit the door to the service garage and ripped it open with the hand that was still holding his battlerifle. But his forearms were gassing out quickly—

his fingers fumbled with the door handle and he almost dropped his weapon.

He got the door open. Hauled Stu through with a harsh shove, and then piled through himself.

Stu went staggering into the service bay.

The bays were empty. No vehicles up on jacks.

It smelled like gasoline and oil and rubber.

Rat pointed the rifle at Stu, relieved to be able to get his support hand up on the weapon again and take some of the pressure off his right arm. He circled Stu, so that his back was to the rear wall of the garage.

"You fucking tripped an alarm," he said again, and he was toying with the idea of killing Stu now.

"No! I didn't!"

"Why's there a fucking cop outside?"

Stu blubbered for a moment. Rat realized he was crying now, wet streaks down his face. "It's Deputy Carson. He comes in almost every night. He just gets coffee. Oh, Jesus, mister! Don't kill him! He's got two little kids!"

Rat swore another streak and looked around the service bay, desperately.

There had to be a way out. There had to be.

But the situation was on a steep fucking spiral at that moment.

The first thing Deputy Carson was going to do would be to call for backup. In fact, he'd probably already done it. And as soon as there was backup here, the chances of Rat managing to talk his way out of it diminished to almost zilch.

Even in the few seconds that he'd spent backpedaling away, he'd been staring at the deputy and thinking, *Maybe he's sympathetic. Maybe he'll collaborate if he knows I'm resistance and not some random thief.*

But when the cavalry arrived, Deputy Carson would make no deals, no matter whether he was sympathetic to the cause or not.

Then things would continue to go downhill.

Because it would only be a matter of time before the Fed picked up on the traffic about a standoff at the service station two miles from where a prisoner convoy had been ambushed. And Rat was dreaming a dream if he thought they wouldn't roll in here and tell the deputies to get lost.

And once there weren't witnesses—or hell, maybe even if there were—they'd drop a payload and level this fucking service station to the ground.

Rat figured all this with the speed of an easy string of kindergarten arithmetic.

One thing led to another.

Rat's life was on a very narrow timeline now.

CHAPTER TWENTY-NINE

Walter stared at Pops.

His guts felt squirmy.

His hands unsteady.

"What do you mean?" he asked, and his voice sounded lost and child-like. "We gotta go, Pops. We came here for you."

Getty and Bobbi were there beside him.

Someone down the line of prisoners was shaking their restraints. "If he don't wanna go, take me! I'll fuckin' go!"

Getty pointed a finger at the man. "I will beat you unconscious."

The man fell silent.

Walter found himself unable to restrain an insane laugh. "Come on, Pops! Me and Roy! We planned this. We did it. Don't you wanna see Roy again? He's out! He's out of DTI!"

Pops closed his one good eye, his face a grimace of pain. Not physical pain. But the news that his eldest son was back from the dead was twisting a knife in his heart. And when Walter saw that expression on his father's face, he knew that it was pain, because Pops knew he would never see that eldest son.

"Come on, Pops," Walter's voice felt creaky. Like a plank bridge with a lot of weak spots.

Pops opened his eyes again. His puffy, split lips were trembling. "Walter," he said, sternly. The voice of a patriarch. Telling a son something very important. "You have to go without me."

"Why?" Walter demanded, suddenly angry.

"Because they're tracking me."

"They're tracking…?" Walter started to look his father's body over. The unwashed, dirty and bloody clothing. "Well, where is it? Let's get that thing off of you!"

Pops was shaking his head. "You can't."

"What do you mean I can't?" Walter was getting mad again.

Pops reached up with his right hand and touched the side of his head. "It's in here. They put it where you can't get it out."

Walter shook his head. Not wanting to believe. "What? I don't…"

Pops took Walt by the shoulders. "Listen to me, son. They knew. They knew that something was gonna happen. I don't know how they knew, or how *much* they knew. But they knew that there was gonna be an ambush on this convoy. And they put a tracker in me. Because they wanted me to go with whoever did the rescue attempt. They wanted me to lead them to a bigger fish. That's all it was. They were just hoping to sacrifice some lowly prisoners to see if they could get to an actual resistance cell."

Pops smiled as he looked into his son's face. "You were right, Walter. You were right all along. So was your brother. We should have fought back. And you are. You *are* fighting back. And I'm so fucking proud of you…" his voice cracked and he stopped. Swallowed. "You have to go. You have to go without me."

Walter was shaking his head again, but he couldn't figure out a way to make all of these facts work. Shit! If he could just stop being a fucking knocker for one second, maybe he could figure out a way around this! Maybe he could solve this problem!

He felt another hand grab his shoulder.

He turned to look at Bobbi.

She looked at him with sympathy in her eyes, and it was almost as though she had the empathic ability to read *Walter*. Like she knew what he was thinking in that moment. Because she raised her chin to him and spoke in a low, comforting voice: "Walter, there's no way around this."

He stared at her. Wanted to deny what she'd said.

But he couldn't.

Because there *wasn't.*

"Walt."

Back to his father.

"Go. You need to get out of here now. You're fighting. You're doing what you should be doing. I only wish I'd done the same thing when I was your age. Then maybe you wouldn't have to be doing it yourself. That is one thing I regret." He shook his head fiercely. "Don't make me regret this moment as well. Don't make me be the reason my son dies."

His grip on Walter's shoulders became almost painful and he shook Walter as he spoke. "Go, Walt. Go where you need to go to get the hell out of here. Get back to Roy. Tell him I love him. And I love you. I'm going to lead them away from you guys, okay?"

"No, no, no…"

Just give me time to come up with a solution!

"Walt!" Pops' voice was like a slap. "You fucking go! Those motherfuckers thought I would sell my son out. Fuck them. I'm going to lead them off. Let me do this for you. Let me help you get away. It's the only way you're getting out of here alive, Walter. You know it. We all know it. Quit bein' a fucking knocker about it."

Like a hurricane wind that suddenly dies.

Like a storm that suddenly quiets.

Quelled.

The words brushed all of Walter's desperate thinking away.

He wasn't a knocker if he couldn't think of anything.

He was a knocker if he couldn't admit the truth.

Pops was right.

It didn't make it hurt less.

But he was right.

Walter suddenly grabbed his father up. He grabbed him by the back of his neck and around his chest and he slammed the older man into his own chest, like he could hug him enough to make up for lost time. Pops squeezed him fiercely back.

And before Pops had to push him away and get him back on track, Walter disengaged.

He looked his father in the eye, and the vision blurred, but he blinked it away.

"Thank you, Pops."

"Give my love to everyone."

"I will. I love you."

Pops' lips trembled again. And then were still. "I love you too, son." And then, just a haggard whisper. "And I'm proud of you."

Walter pressed the manual override key into his father's hand. "Free as many as you can. We're heading west on this road." He pointed to the rear of the vehicle. "That's west." Then to the front of the vehicle. "That's east."

Pops nodded once. "I got it."

The implication was clear.

Walter was going to head west.

Pops was going to draw the QRF east.

There were no other words to say.

Walter bottled it all up and flung it away from him.

He turned away from his father, and with Bobbi and Getty in tow, he slipped out of the back of the modular and into the night.

CHAPTER THIRTY

"Keys," Rat demanded. "I want the keys to the GUV."

The man raised a shaky hand and pointed to a box on the wall. "They're in the key box."

Rat smashed the box in the side with the butt of the battlerifle. The lock was flimsy. The door was nearly ripped off its hinges. There were two sets of keys. Rat recognized the brand of the GUV printed on the key fob, and he seized this and stuffed it into his pants pocket.

"The jump boxes," Rat snapped. "Where are they?"

Stu looked off into the service bay and Rat followed his gaze. There was a red tool cabinet, and jumbled haphazardly on top were the three jump boxes.

"Right there," Stu said. "Look, mister, just take them and go. I'm not gonna do nothing. I'm for the resistance, okay? I am. I swear it. You don't need to kill me or Deputy Carson."

"Shut the fuck up," Rat said, trying to think.

Okay. Three jump boxes.

A dead GUV.

Two of the jump boxes would backfill, meaning that Rat could plug them straight into the power outlet on the GUV's dashboard. That should keep the engine running for a bit. But if the alternator was busted, then it'd suck those damn jump boxes dry in short order.

Still…it would allow Rat to get some distance.

At least, to extricate himself from this shithole.

"Are they all charged?" Rat asked.

"Should be," Stu nodded, seeing a way out for himself as well, and he spoke with mounting hope. "I charge them at the end of every day."

Rat spied a door on the back wall. He nodded towards it. "That go out to the back? Where the GUV is?"

"Ayuh," Stu said quickly. "It sure does. Just take what you need, mister."

"Alright, alright, shut up," Rat said, brain in overdrive now. "Look at me. Look at me, Stu."

Stu met his gaze.

"Do exactly what I fucking tell you."

"Okay."

"I want you to walk out there, okay? Hands up. I want you to walk real fucking slow, okay? Through the convenience store, and you keep your hands up the whole time so that Deputy Carson can see you. *Walk. Slow.*"

"Walk slow. Got it."

"When you get out of the store, you tell Deputy Carson to cancel his backup. Tell him that I'm resistance, and I'm just trying to get out of here alive, okay? I don't want to hurt anyone. You have to tell him that."

"Okay."

"What are you gonna tell him?"

"Uh…cancel his backup. You don't want to hurt anyone."

"And that I'm resistance."

"Right. And that you're resistance."

"Is he sympathetic?"

"Mister, I'm sure I don't know," Stu said, looking worried.

"Fuck it. Tell him anyways, okay?"

"I will."

"Walk slow."

"Ayuh. I got it."

"Go."

Rat motioned Stu towards the door back into the convenience store with his rifle.

Stu started sidestepping, his hands already up to his shoulders, palms out. When he got to the door, he very carefully opened it, and slipped through. Still moving slow, just as Rat had told him to.

But now he turned his body and raised his hands up high, and Rat could hear him call out, "Carson! It's me! It's Stu! Don't shoot!"

Rat watched the door swing closed.

He had no time left.

He sprinted on tired, panicked legs to the tool cabinet with the jump boxes on top. He grabbed them up, trying to get a hold of all three in one hand. They were heavy. The third one slipped out of his grip and clattered to the floor.

He mumbled more curses and slung into his rifle. He was going to get out of this by deception and misdirection anyway, not by shooting his way out. He just hoped to God that Deputy Carson would talk to Stu for long enough to give him a window of escape.

With his rifle slung, Rat grabbed two jump boxes in one hand, and the third in his other.

He stumbled for the back door, the heavy contraptions swinging against his thighs as he moved, his shoulders already burning.

He pushed his way out.

The yard was dimly lit. Oil-stained gravel and dirt. There were stacks of tires, off to the right side, piled up against a chain link fence with razor wire across the top. A few engine parts sat lonely and homeless on wooden pallets. A stripped chassis was parked like a man's skeleton in an anatomy classroom.

Rat tried not to be loud. But he was also trying to be fast.

He wished he could hear if Stu was talking to Deputy Carson yet, but he couldn't hear a damn thing over his own breathing. A reed-less woodwind section, accompanied by the timpani of his heart.

His feet crunched mildly in the dirt as he went for the GUV.

It was positioned towards the right-hand side of the fenced-in lot. Which meant it was close to the gate. Which meant that someone on the corner of the building might see him. He just had to hope that the deputy's backup was still a few minutes out, and he was distracted by Stu.

Still, he decided to go around to the passenger side.

He opened the door. It was unlocked. He jumbled the three jump boxes into the back with a grunt, right behind the center console. Then he climbed in.

Just before he closed the door, he thought for certain he heard the growing wail of a police siren.

Shit, shit, shit...

He clambered over the center console, trying as much as he could to stay low. But even as small a man as he was, it was difficult to contort himself inside the vehicle. These fucking GUV's nowadays. They kept getting smaller and smaller. He remembered when they actually had leg room.

He finally got himself into the driver's seat. He ripped the keys out of his pocket and stuck them in the ignition, but didn't turn them. He didn't know what sort of noises the vehicle would make, but he sure as hell didn't want to call any extra attention to himself before he was completely ready to stomp on the gas and get the fuck out of there.

For sure and certain now—he was definitely hearing sirens.

In fact, he could see the lights, too.

Way down the road. Coming from north of them.

A blue and white, flickering strobe, like some weird comet coming in, burning blue hell fire and magnesium.

Rat ducked a bit more down into his seat. He reached behind him into the back and grabbed the first of the jump boxes. Fumbling around with it, he saw that it was one of the ones with the backfill plug. He pulled it from its storage mount and slammed it carelessly into the outlet in the center console.

Then he turned the jump box on.

Then he waited.

He stared, over the top of the dashboard, at the incoming lights.

The sirens, getting louder.

That wasn't one patrol vehicle, it was two—one right behind the other.

Of course there was two. There'd probably be more. More and more, the longer this went on. And then, it wouldn't be cops. It'd be Fed troops. And then there was no chance for Rat. No chance at all.

But right now. Right now, he still had a chance.

He touched the keys in the ignition, and cringed.

Was now a good time to crank the engine?

The sirens outside were loud. The two patrol vehicles were going to come screeching into that parking lot any second now. If he cranked the engine, there's no way he'd be heard.

Rat cranked it.

It made an encouraging whine, but then died.

He swore. Looked at the jump box.

The charge indicator showed four out of five green lights.

He waited. Hunched. Watching.

The two incoming patrol vehicles roared into the parking lot, killing their sirens as they did.

Great. Now it would be quiet. Now they would hear him try to crank the engine.

And if they heard him crank it, they would come back for him.

Then again, it was possible that Stu had told them what he was planning anyways.

Rat wasn't entirely convinced that Stu hadn't lied to him about everything from the start. That fucker had probably triggered an alarm. And he was probably a Fed collaborator. And he probably knew damn well that Deputy Carson was a collaborator too. He was probably spilling the beans right now.

Shit. Rat should have probably killed the motherfucker when he'd had the chance.

One of the patrol vehicles situated itself so that the headlights were spearing right along the side of the building. Right into Rat's eyes. He could barely make out the actual shape of the vehicle, but he saw the door open, and the deputy inside get out.

Rat sunk down further in his seat. Now uncomfortably compacted.

Try again?

He touched the key in the ignition.

No. Not yet. Not until he was sure that the damn thing would fire up.

But he wasn't sure. *Couldn't* be sure.

This damn thing might suck up all the juice in all three jump boxes and never cough itself to life.

Rat couldn't see the deputy now.

He could see the beam of light from the deputy's weaponlight. It swept over the dashboard, right to left. Then it was gone. Then it swept back again, left to right.

That was long enough.

Surely, that was long enough.

He made his decision, and went for it.

He cranked the key.

The engine stirred. Whirred.

Them rumbled to life.

Sweet Jesus, thank you!

Rat came up in his seat, not waiting for anything, not waiting to see where the deputy was or to put his seatbelt on or do anything but yank that damn thing into drive and stomp on the accelerator.

The engine roared.

The tires churned gravel.

The GUV drifted in place for a moment, then rocketed forward.

Rat yanked the wheel to the left, heading for the chained gate.

The back end of the GUV squirreled out a bit and for a moment Rat was positive that he was going to lose control of the vehicle and sending it into a sidelong collision with the back of the building. He pulled the wheel back straight, and the vehicle righted itself.

They gained just enough speed to smash effortlessly through the gate.

It was a tremendous crash, like clashing cymbals.

Rat's teeth were gritted, eyes squinched down.

He imagined that the deputies outside were yelling, but he couldn't hear them.

What he did hear, very clearly, was the rapid *p-p-p-p-p-p-pop* of their subguns going off on full auto, and the rounds striking the side of the GUV with unpleasant smacking sounds, and pummeling the right windows so that they became gossamer curtains and then exploded with the very next round, sending little round bits of glass scattering everywhere through the vehicle…

Bullets stitched holes in the windshield.

He angled for the road.

Smack-smack-smack

He felt things hitting him.

He could hear the yelling, now that his windows were blown out. But it was indistinct and distant. He just kept that foot hammered down, those tires squealing as they hit pavement and he pulled the steering wheel violently so the GUV hurtled onto the asphalt, nearly sideways.

Smack-smack-smack-smack

Always now the feeling of being right on the edge of losing control of that vehicle. But he got all four tires on the road, and then came the intersection, the intersection of the highway where, two miles down from it, a Fed convoy had been EMP'd to a standstill, and somewhere in those woods were his friends.

Shit, I hope they got Bobbi...

Rounds were going off behind him, he could still hear them.

But now a horrendous pain was beginning to climb up from his thighs, from his belly, from his lower back.

It's nothing.

"It's fuckin' nothing!" he shouted forcefully at himself.

And he didn't look down at himself. He refused. He didn't want to be distracted. He needed to get to his friends. He needed to get this vehicle to them. To Walt. To Getty. To Bobbi.

I hope they got Bobbi.

I hope they didn't die.

He thought he could feel sticky wetness in his seat. In the crotch of his pants. Trickling down his legs.

"It's nothing," he said again.

CHAPTER THIRTY-ONE

Prisoners were scattering everywhere.

They were tumbling out of the backs of the personnel modulars. They would hit the ground, look both ways like thieves caught in the act, and then they would pick a direction and start running. Some of them ran into the woods to the north. Some to the south. Some ran along the road, and Walt watched them and knew that they would die.

But he said nothing.

It was not likely that any of them knew where the hell they were.

They were just running. Running, and figuring it out as they went.

Not too damn different from what Walt was doing.

"Grab weapons!" he shouted to Getty and Bobbi as he ran for the front of the now-defunct convoy. He'd stuffed his pistol into his waistband, and he stopped and scooped up a battlerifle, then ripped a spare magazine from the soldier's chest rig and stuck it in his back pocket.

Getty was already armed, but he also appropriated a magazine.

Bobbi, still in some sort of haze, bent over with a blank face and took a battlerifle from one of the dead New Breeds. Then she looked up at Walt and frowned. "How?"

Walt shook his head. "Long story, I'll explain later."

Someone grabbed him by the shoulders.

Walter didn't think. He just reacted.

He spun away, and then smashed a man's face with the butt of his battlerifle.

The man crumpled to the ground where he twitched for a moment and then looked up at Walt woozily.

"Don't fucking touch me," Walt growled at him, not quite sure why he'd done that.

"Walt," Getty called.

Walt backed away from the man on the ground, and partially turned his attention to Getty. "What?"

"The DEMP," Getty said, nodding towards the smoking ruins of the van.

"It's fucked," Walt said flatly. "If there's anything left, it's just gonna weigh us down." He pointed to the woods to the south. "We need to get in those trees and start moving west along the road." Then he looked at Bobbi. "Bobbi, I'm sorry this is such a cluster fuck."

Bobbi, to Walt's surprise, had tears in her eyes and she threw her arm around Walt's neck and pulled him close. She smelled dirty and unwashed—not at all the prim woman that he'd met in the safehouse in District 89. But he supposed that being three days in Fed captivity will do that to a person.

She separated herself. "Thank you," she said.

In the distance, an unpleasant sound reached them, and it sent tingles down Walt's back.

It must have had the same effect on everyone else, because a collective cry of dismay went up, and the people that were moving quickly for the trees started to move a little quicker.

"Gunships," Walt said. "Let's go."

They ran for the wood line. The wet, dewey grass soaked Walt's pant legs. Down off the shoulder of the road. Over the drainage ditch. Up on the opposite side. Up a steep embankment of scrabbly red clay and rocks.

He glanced over his shoulder, and still, somehow, there were people that were just running along the road. Their minds must have left them in their fear.

He wanted to shout to them to get the hell out of sight, but he had his own problems now.

The three of them dove into the trees as the horrible thumping sound of the gunships began to envelope their entire world, to fill it up, to be the one stimulus they couldn't escape.

The tree tops began to shake as though in a strong wind.

Walt didn't stop running until he was about thirty yards into the woods, and then he hung a hard right, to run east—this was east, right? Yes. He hadn't got himself turned around. The road was to his right.

Blazing white lights suddenly illuminated the road, shaking and trembling all over the place, like flashlights in the hands of palsied giants. A voice boomed over loud speakers.

"STOP WHERE YOU ARE AND LAY DOWN ON THE GROUND."

Walt didn't look. He didn't need to look.

Some would lay down. Some would keep running.

It didn't matter either way.

Somewhere out there, his father was running east, drawing the QRF away from Walter's escape.

The gunships opened up, filling the air with the buzz-saw sound of their cannons cycling at 6,000-rounds-a-minute.

As he ran, he heard Bobbi's voice. When he looked over his shoulder at her, her face caught in the reflected glow of the spotlights, and it had a fierce and stony aspect to it that he'd not seen on her before, and she was breathing the words out through her teeth: "Those motherfuckers! Those mother*fuckers*!"

But this was war, wasn't?

This was why they were fighting.

Walt kept running.

He kept running until he couldn't any more, and he wasn't sure how far they'd come—he could still hear the gunships firing, but it was sporadic now. They were hunting eastwards now. Had his father run into the woods? Had he stayed on the road?

Walt kept moving, but he couldn't get air into his lungs, and his legs burned and ached and cramped. He was already exhausted before all of this began. He wished that he was in better shape, that he could've run farther, faster, but then, when he looked behind him, he realized that it wouldn't have done them any good.

Bobbi and Getty were both trailing behind him, their mouths open, gasping. Looking like they were struggling to keep their feet moving.

"Hold up," Getty coughed out.

"Can't!" Walt wheezed. "Gotta keep moving!"

"Someone's following!"

That stopped Walt.

He spun to look behind them.

Just then, out on the highway, he heard the rumble of engines, and when he glanced in that direction, he could see three sets of headlights tearing down the road in the direction of the ambush. Big diesels. The distinct sound of guntrucks.

The ground QRF had arrived.

He forced himself to look back in the woods, back the way they had come.

Yes, Getty was right.

There wasn't much light to see by now, but he could still see the shadows slipping through the trees, and now that he'd stopped moving, he could hear the rustle of feet moving through the leaves.

Walt mumbled an expletive and thought about what the hell he should do.

Keep going?

Stop and see who was following them?

He didn't get a chance to make a decision.

A voice yelled through the woods: "Hey! Hey you!"

Walt almost jumped at the noise of it. He gripped his rifle tighter and sidled behind a tree. His cramping legs were already seizing up. His lungs felt ragged, like rusted metal.

"That's them," another voice said.

The first voice had been female.

The second had been male.

"Don't shoot!" the female voice called out.

"Shut the fuck up!" Getty hissed back.

The voice quieted some, but kept speaking. "It's me! It's the know-it-all bitch from the truck."

Oh, Jesus…

Walt stayed right where he was until she came fully into view. Then he stepped out, only a bit. His rifle was shouldered, but not pointing right at her. It was indeed the know-it-all from the truck.

She was with two others—both men. And the three of them were standing now, breathless and seemingly unaware that Getty and Bobbi had hemmed them in.

"What the fuck are you doing?" Walt demanded.

"Getting the fuck out of here. What about you?"

"Don't follow us," Walt said.

"We have a safehouse."

Walt's jaw worked. He shifted his weight. "Where?"

"Just outside Durham. You got a ride?"

"Maybe."

"If you can squeeze us in, we can give you a safe place," she said. She swallowed, took a big breath. "If you didn't need a safe place, you wouldn't have even stopped to think about it. Come on. We need a ride. You need a safe place. We need to work together."

Yeah. Work together.

Walt didn't trust this woman as far as he could spit, but he was also desperate.

And what she said was true. What she said went to the heart of why he hated this goddamned resistance so much.

Because no one worked together, and it was going to kill them in the end.

"Fine," Walt blurted. "But until we're at your safe house, you do what the fuck I tell you to do. Understand me? We get on your turf, you can take all the control you want. But out on these roads you shut the fuck up and listen."

"Okay." She didn't even think about it.

Maybe everyone was too winded to do any thinking.

But that was good. If they weren't thinking, they weren't double-crossing.

"Car coming," Bobbi said, faintly. "Flashers on. Is that Rat?"

Walt didn't respond. He just started moving for the edge of the woods. "Come on."

He could see through the trees, down the road.

A vehicle with its flashers on, coming on slow.

And something behind it.

"Ah, shit!" Walt pulled up short of the tree line. "He's got company."

There were two patrol vehicles following, their individual shapes lost in the cacophony of strobing lights. They were a good distance behind, but gaining quickly.

Think quick. Don't be a knocker.

The cops weren't combatants. Likely, they were just two schmoes trying to do a job and catch someone that had just stolen a fucking car.

But they'd also plunged themselves into a bad situation.

Walt could wait until that situation got even worse and he was forced to positively murder them, or he could do something to dissuade them now.

He shot forward to the edge of the woods, flashed Rat with his weapon light, and then shouldered the battlerifle and braced it against a tree.

The vehicle with the flashers began to pull to the side of the road, angling for where Walt had signaled from. But Walt was training the rifle back. Down the road. He put the reticle just below those strobing lights and then he opened up.

He let out three quick bursts, each time, stopping to re-acquire his sight picture before sending another burst.

Tires screeched.

The lead patrol vehicle tried to stop on a dime and angle itself into the road. The rear patrol vehicle didn't see it coming.

There was the crunch of an impact.

The rear patrol vehicle tore off the back end of the lead, and then went careening onto the shoulder in a spray of dirt that momentarily blocked out the headlights.

Walt felt sick and exhilarated. He turned to his right, saw Bobbi, and he pointed at the patrol vehicles, which were still about a two or three hundred yards off. "Keep fire on them!"

Bobbi nodded, posted up, and started letting it rip.

Walt angled around her and ran for the GUV that was parked on the shoulder with its flashers on. The first thing he noticed was that the interior lights were on, illuminating a man in the front seat and for the barest of moments Walt didn't think that it was Rat, because it didn't look like him.

Then he realized that it was indeed Rat, but his face had taken on a feverish pallor and his expression was slack like a man about to pass out. He had the driver's door partially propped open and was struggling to extricate himself.

Something's wrong with him.

The second thing that Walt noticed was that the windows were shot out. The windshield was pock-marked and spider-webbed with bullet holes. And there were bullet holes all along the side of the vehicle.

No, no, no...

Walt ran for the driver's side.

Down the road, the patrol vehicle that had gone off the road was trying to right itself, but was stuck, spinning its wheels. What had been the lead vehicle had tried to back out of the situation, but then the driver had apparently decided not to leave his buddy stuck in the mud.

All the while, Bobbi let loose on them. Evenly spaced bursts of rounds, and after each one, he could hear them impacting down range with heavy, metallic *thwack*s.

Walt made it to the driver's door. Grabbed it. Ripped it fully open.

Rat half tumbled out, but the GUV he was driving was a bit tilted now, being on the shoulder, and he simply slumped forward and held out a weak hand.

His entire lower half was slaked in blood. It covered him like he'd waded into a pool of it. And it stained his seat, and the floorboards, and the center console, and the inside of the door.

"Oh, holy shit, Rat!" Walt grabbed the man's hand and hauled him out.

Rat didn't respond, just made a struggling, wheezy grunt.

Walt pulled his arm to get it over his shoulders, let his own battlerifle hang.

Time, time, time. Time was short. Time to stop the bleeding. Time to get the fuck out of here. There wasn't enough fucking time.

"Somebody help me!" Walt yelled.

Getty was there.

"Into the back!" Walt barked.

How much time until the QRF heard the gunshots and came to investigate?

How much time until the gunships were hovering over their heads?

Once that happened, there would be no escape.

"Someone drive this shit," Walt commanded, out of breath by the time they reached the back of the vehicle.

Someone ran for the driver's seat, but Walt couldn't tell who.

Were they all going to fit in this goddamned thing?

They'd have to.

Getty released his grip on Rat long enough to pull the back gate of the GUV open, revealing a smallish cargo area. Barely enough room for them to lay Rat down, let alone to try and operate on him. It was showered in broken safety glass.

Walt shoved Rat into place, then started rattling the back seats, his hands flying over the levers and switches and buttons that controlled them. His battlerifle, slung to his chest, kept banging into his crotch, but he didn't have time to correct it. There was no time for anything.

"These fucking things…!" Walt found a lever. Yanked it. It did nothing. He found a button. Pushed it. It did nothing. Walt screamed at them.

Getty reached over Rat's body and pulled something on the bottom of the seat. A quiet hydraulic hiss sounded, and the entire back row of seats folded in on themselves and sunk into the floorboards.

"Fine, fine, fine," Walt didn't give it much more than that. He was just happy someone had figured something out. He clambered in, straddled Rat's body, and started pulling the man a little deeper.

Bobbi was getting into the vehicle now, still letting out short sharp bursts of rifle fire, even as she put a leg into the vehicle. Her face was set and grim. Everyone was showing sides of them tonight that Walt had never seen before. But that's what happened to people. That's what these times did.

He was not an exception.

"Get in!" someone shouted from up front. "We gotta go!"

Getty climbed in, tossing his own rifle down on the floor next to Rat. He had to straddle Rat's head, just to get enough room to pull the back gate closed. The three of them crammed into a cargo space meant for a few bags of groceries and maybe a baby stroller.

Odd that Walt would think of that right now.

A baby stroller.

Babies.

Family.

Carolyn.

"Reloading!" Bobbi shouted.

Walt couldn't think of anything else to do except to lean over Rat's body, punch his muzzle through the already-shattered glass of the back gate and begin firing. The concussion in that enclosed area was deafening.

"We're in!" someone else shouted. "Go go go!"

The GUV leapt forward, sending Walt's body slamming into the back gate. He nearly toppled out the shattered window, but Getty caught him by the rifle strap and yanked him back.

Walt realized his knees and feet were all over Rat's wounded midsection. The man screamed weakly.

"I'm sorry," Walt gasped. "Sorry, buddy!"

Whoever was driving yanked the vehicle in a tight U-turn that sent Walt sprawling into Getty. Getty shoved him off, and Walt tried like hell to get his limbs off of Rat's body. In the tiny space, his tired leg muscles suddenly cramped up, but there wasn't enough room to do anything about it except to grit his teeth and groan and try to ignore it.

Bobbi had entered on the passenger's side but had slid over to the driver's side. She finished reloading with a clack from her bolt going forward, and then punched out the window of the door she was against.

"I'm up!" she called, rigidly.

The GUV was now turned in the opposite direction, and picking up speed.

The two patrol vehicles were on Bobbi's side.

"Slow down!" She screamed hoarsely. "Slow, slow, slow!"

The driver obeyed as they drew abreast of the patrol vehicles, and Walt almost told her not to do it, told her to leave the cops be, but it was too late.

She broadsided them with a raking string of fire, and then focused her rounds on their doors, on their windshields. All the rounds directed at the driver's seat.

Walt couldn't see much.

He thought he saw one of the cops trying to climb over the center console to escape out the passenger door. That passenger door never opened. Bobbi kept up her unrelenting fire until her rifle went dry again and there was not a shred of movement from either patrol vehicle, and then she pounded the back of the driver's seat.

"Go! Get us out!"

Walt was prepared for the acceleration this time. He braced himself as the GUV took off again, heading up to top speed. He looked around, looked out the shattered windows, to see if those patrol vehicles would pursue, but they didn't.

He looked to the sky, to see if he could see any gunships, but there was nothing.

Just a lot of dark sky, and dark highway.

He yanked his battlerifle off and set it, smoking, on the floor.

Getty was crouched over Rat, undoing his soaked pants.

"I'm not gonna look," Rat was saying, his voice thin and reedy. "Not gonna look, okay? Don't say anything about it. Just do it. Do what you gotta do, okay? I don't give a fuck. I don't care. I don't care. It's nothing. Nothing."

Getty yanked the man's pants down off his ass.

A layer of blood swept off with them, leaving the pale skin momentarily exposed, but then Walt watched it well quickly out of several holes. Too many holes. Holes through Rat's legs. Holes though his hips. Holes through his belly.

Walt stared for a few solid, heavy beats of his heart, and all he could think was, *He can't live through that.*

They didn't have a medpack. Those had been attached to Koz and Javon's gear. There'd been extra in the van, but that had been blown up. Even if they had a medpack, the wounds were centered around his pelvis. They couldn't tourniquet them, even if they had one. All they could do was rip cloth and stuff wounds.

Getty was already doing that. He had yanked out a knife and was piecing away at Rat's shirt, which was the only thing not completely soaked through already. As he cut strips, he nodded to Rat's pelvis.

"Walter! Hold pressure!"

The energy had gone out of Walt. He felt like he was stuck in a tub of grease. He moved forward, unwillingly sluggish, and he stared at all those holes. He couldn't even see them anymore. They were just fountains now. Welling up and covering everything. He couldn't hold the pressure on the wounds. There were too many.

So he just picked two and pressed the heels of his palms down on them.

He could feel hot blood pulsing against his hands.

Bobbi had pulled herself into the back, crowding the space even further, all of their heads, all of their bodies so close that Walt could feel the heat from them, could smell their breath, could smell their sweat, the stink of gunsmoke on their skin.

Bobbi huddled over Rat's face, cradled his head with her arms. "Rat. Rat. Hey, buddy," she said.

Rat looked up at her and actually smiled. "Oh, shit," he said weakly. "They got you out. That's great, hon."

"Yeah," She nodded, and Walt watched a tear drip off her nose. "Yeah, they got me out. *You* got me out."

Rat reached up a hand and placed it on her shoulder, holding it with a weak grip. "Hey. Sorry we left you. It wasn't…wasn't our choice."

"It's okay," Bobbi shook her head forcefully. "Everyone did what they had to do. That's the name of the game. We just gotta keep doing what we have to do."

A distressed look passed over Rat's face and he let out a shaky breath. "Shit…I think I'm gonna pass out."

"Don't pass out, Rat," Walt said sternly, as though he could order the man's body around.

Rat started taking short, sharp breaths. His eyes looked around, momentarily panicked, scanning the ceiling, like he was searching for some reprieve. His face had suddenly started to pour sweat. He looked more green now than white.

To his side, Getty had managed to make two strips. He immediately began to stuff one of the wounds.

Pointless, Walt thought, as he watched. *Don't they see it's pointless?*

Rat squirmed under the pain, but the movement wasn't much. He didn't have much left.

After about ten seconds, he didn't seem to notice at all.

His eyes looked half-empty, like a house that's in the process of being vacated. He looked at Bobbi. "Kiss me, hon," he said. "I always wanted to kiss you."

Bobbi smiled a gutted smile.

"Come on," Rat whispered. "Grant an ugly fuck his dying wish."

Bobbi bent down and kissed him on the lips. One, long, slow kiss. Like a heartfelt goodbye into a night they both knew wouldn't end.

Rat's eyes were closed when she pulled away.

"That's nice," he mumbled.

And the tail end of his words bled off into a low, groaning sound. His back arched weakly and it had the feel of reflex, and nothing more. A tremor went through Rat's body. His hands twitched, shook in the air, then melted down, curling in on themselves. His whole body curling up.

Getty just continued to doggedly stuff wounds.

Walt watched the man. His eyes jagged over to Rat's face, then back to his work. He seemed to know. But he didn't want to stop working. He finished stuffing one of the wounds. Then he reached for the second strip he'd cut, thought better of it, and started to hold pressure on the wound he'd packed.

The vehicle took a right-hand turn on some road. Some dark road that was heading north.

Walt barely noticed the movement of the car anymore.

His leg cramps were gone. Powered out.

Getty held pressure on that wound with both hands, his face blank. He looked up and made eye-contact with Walt. Getty's eyes were clear. Dry. Dead. He held Walt's gaze for a long time, the two of them with their hands stuffed in Rat's blood.

The blood was not pulsing against Walt's hands anymore.

Beside them, Bobbi sniffed, but said nothing.

Eventually, Walt watched Getty's strength ebb out of him. The pressure that he held slackened, and then he just appeared to give it up. He leaned away and put his bloody hands on his thighs, resting for a few breaths.

"Sorry, Bobbi," he said, levelly.

Bobbi said nothing.

Getty reached to his side, pulled up the other strip.

"Anyone else wounded?" he asked loudly, and his voice cracked at the last word. "No one needs this shit?" He said with sudden bitterness, and he flung the strip of cloth away from him.

He pulled his legs out from under himself and laid them across Rat's body. Then he pulled his knees up. Buried his face in his bloody hands and did not say a word or utter a sound.

CHAPTER THIRTY-TWO

Koz plunged through darkness.

His footsteps splashing through the shallow, mildewy water, echoed around him, running forward and then back to him along the length of the pipe. He could feel the webs from spiders that lurked in places where the sun never went, and he did not want to imagine what those spiders might look like.

Strange that a big, indomitable New Breed could still have a hang up like that.

But the body mods didn't remove old childhood fears, and Koz was borderline arachnaphobic. Hated the things. Broke out into cold sweat when confronted with them. Logically, he knew they weren't a threat, and that was what kept him moving forward through this impenetrable darkness. Because he knew that the real threat was behind them.

This tunnel, this culvert—it was a one way ticket. Once inside, the only way out was on the other end.

He had no idea where that other end went.

But he knew that the drones and the gunships couldn't see inside this tunnel.

He also knew that if anyone had seen him make his exit by disappearing into the culvert, they'd figure out where it *did* come out. Eventually. And they'd be waiting for him. So it behooved him to move in what the growers would call "road gear."

He slowed his pace a bit, and turned his head, although he could see absolutely nothing.

"Javon, you still with me?" he said into the oily blackness.

Holding his breath to listen, he could hear Javon's labored breathing.

"Yeah," the man wheezed. "I'm still here."

"Fuck right you're still here," Koz said back. "You got this. Easy day. Now put your hand back on my shoulder."

Javon was supposed to be holding onto Koz so that Koz would notice if he lost him, and also so Koz could sort of tug-boat him along, lending the wounded man some of his own strength. Unfortunately, Koz had gone about fifty yards without noticing that Javon's hand had fallen off.

There were a few splashing, dragging footsteps, the sound of a stumble being caught and corrected, and then a hand touched him in the darkness, rough and cold. It practically slapped Koz's face, then roamed over his neck, his shoulder, and finally found the drag strap of his hardarmor.

Koz turned then and continued on, but slowed his pace a little bit.

He didn't *want* to slow his pace.

But Javon was nearing the end of his physical capabilities, if he hadn't reached them already. The wounded man was running completely on willpower at that moment, and Koz knew it. He simply wasn't quitting…because.

Because you never fucking quit.

Because a battlerifle's buttstock is reinforced with steel for a reason.

So when they found you on the battlefield, with not a round of ammunition on your person, you'll be lying in a pile of spent casings, and the last motherfucker to try you got his skull knocked in.

After that, you always had your knife.

You always had your hands.

You always had your teeth.

Tooth and nail was easy to say. Not so easy to live.

But Koz had lived it. So had Javon. And now they were both living it again.

After another interminable time, the darkness began to feel woozy.

Koz had a light on his rifle. He just didn't want to use it. He didn't want to waste the battery life. And also, he didn't want to see the spiders that lived this deep in the dark.

But he clicked it on at that moment.

It seared his retinas.

He blinked, painfully.

The tunnel continued on into infinity, swallowing a beam that Koz knew could illuminate up to two hundred yards out.

Koz used the momentary illumination to take a glance at his friend.

Javon's eyes were squinted in the light, but they looked buggy and tired. His lips were cracked and chapped and frothed and oddly pale. He had stopped sweating now. That wasn't a good sign. But then, it was cold down here. Cold enough to see their breath.

Pale strands of cobwebs hung from Javon's head and shoulders.

Something spindly and white and freakishly large crawled away from them, toward the ceiling of the tunnel.

Koz refused to look directly at it. Decided that it didn't exist.

"Lookin' strong," he lied.

Lights off.

They continued into the darkness.

***

Roy sat in the very same room of that abandoned warehouse where he and Walt had talked with Jimmy and made their deal. Except, now he was sitting on his butt, on the ground, with his wrists bound together with flex ties.

They'd done him the courtesy of switching them to the front. So that was nice.

Two of Jimmy's men stood in the room with him. Their backs were to the opposite wall, facing Roy, and framing the one and only entry point. Both of them were armed. Both of them were ready. Neither spoke. They looked like they were more than willing to kill him if he made a wrong move.

So he didn't.

He sat.

And he brooded.

And he felt sick to his damn stomach.

His brain kept coming back to the same thing, the same phrase, the same words: *That motherfucker*, he kept thinking, and in his mind he would picture Jimmy with his cool, practical face, and his calm, unfrazzled tone.

That motherfucker.

They'd provided him with a combat meal kit that had expired the previous year. He'd picked at it sullenly and then tossed it off to the side without touching the entrée—lofty name, anyways. Call it a hunger strike. He preferred to occupy himself by staring at the guards for long periods of time, and imagining ramming a live welding rod through Jimmy's eye socket.

But for all of that, Jimmy had spoken the truth, hadn't he?

When Roy had been lying on the ground, being taken into custody only moments after he watched his brother disappear behind that closing garage door, Jimmy had said, "It's out of my hands."

And it had been, hadn't it?

This was above Jimmy's head.

Above Roy's head.

This was the Eudys.

This was the nature of the beast that he called master. And he wrestled with that. He wrestled with his sense of loyalty to them that he somehow still clung to. And why? Well, because they'd gotten him out of hell.

There was nothing that Roy could say to really put into words what it had been like in DTI. And he'd been asked. And he usually answered with a single syllable: Bad.

But "bad" didn't sum it up. Not by a long shot.

And Benjamin and Jean Eudy had taken him out of that hell. They'd saved him. They'd saved his life. Given him a new one. Given him a gun. Given him a chance to fight back. A chance to hurt the people who had hurt him. And that meant something, didn't it?

He'd gone behind their back. He'd only wanted to keep his Pops from having to go to that same hell that he'd managed to get out of. But he'd done it in the worst possible way. He'd taken the thing that they'd been developing for years—those damn ECHO devices—and he'd turned them into a cheap trick.

Like a chess game where you wasted your queen to knock off an opponent's pawn.

He understood all this. He put it together. It wasn't hard to do.

He knew why he was being held.

And he also knew that if they'd wanted him dead, they would have sent him out with Walt in that van. Because that's why Mia had gone along, wasn't it? So she could kill them, or trip something, or blow them up, or who in the fuck knew what, but that's what made sense to Roy at the moment.

Jimmy wanted everyone in that van dead.

And he wanted Roy alive.

Roy clung to one thing and one thing only. It was his tether. It was a life preserver—the only thing keeping him from going mad and making a suicide run at the guards.

Walt's got some steel in him, Roy kept telling himself. *And he's smart. And he sees things that other people don't see. And Jimmy doesn't know that, does he? Neither does Mia. If something was going down, Walt would see it coming like a neon billboard.*

That was what he kept telling himself anyway.

But when there was a harsh knock on the door to the room, and it immediately swung open, the words that came to his lips were, "Did you kill my brother? Is he still alive?"

Roy never said those words, though.

They flew away like ashes in the wind.

Because it wasn't Jimmy standing there in the doorway.

Roy blinked a few times, half-convinced he was mistaken.

"Carolyn?" he mumbled, eyebrows creasing over widening eyes.

Walt's wife, Roy's sister-in-law, and daughter to Benjamin and Jean Eudy, stepped into the room with a cold, authoritative gait. And she was followed by Jimmy. Followed by him the way the secretary follows their boss.

Jimmy closed the door and stood there with his back to it. His arms folded across his chest. His chin lowered. Watching. Listening. Introspective.

Carolyn took two steps forward, now in the very center of the room. The fulcrum that stood between Jimmy and Roy. She looked down at him, and her eyes were not kind, and it confused Roy. It truly confused him.

"What are you doing here?" he mumbled.

But his mind was racing. Racing ahead. Connecting dots. Filling in blanks with half-answers.

Carolyn shook her head once, slow. "What were you thinking?" she whispered.

Roy sputtered, dancing next to the edge of anger for a moment, but not quite able to commit to it. "I…I was trying to save my Pops," he said. "Same way your parents saved you."

"My parents didn't burn through the only chance to beat the New Breeds in order to get me," Carolyn said sternly. "They got me in order to protect what they'd built. They got me because that was what needed to happen. They weren't wasting resources to rescue one old man who's already sick."

"He was your father, too," Roy snapped at her.

He knew it was true. He knew that Pops had been the closest thing she'd ever had to a father. And he knew the words would hit her, and that was all he wanted. He just wanted to see something there besides this cold callousness, because it seemed so very different from what Walt described as his wife.

Why was she being this way?

They got their hooks in her, Roy thought. *Those crazy fucks have poisoned her.*

Carolyn knelt down so they were at eye level. Her face was still hard, but there was a glimmer in her eyes now, and her lips had a tiny tremble in them.

"I know," she said, softly. "But this is bigger than us. This is bigger than family. You understand that, don't you? Mothers against daughters. Fathers against sons. Brothers against brothers. That is how things have to be. Because the stakes are so much higher."

Roy stared at her, not liking the words. Wanting to spit them back in her face. "What are you saying right now? Why are you even here?"

Carolyn leaned even closer to him, and her face remained stolid, but somewhere underneath there—or was he imagining it?—there was this wild desperation. "I can't. Help you. Or him."

Roy realized his heart had picked up its pace. Hard, heavy hits against the inside of his chest. An angry pulse. Blood like rage. "You fucking bitch," Roy whispered. "Everything Walt did he did in order to be with you again. You're the whole reason he's fighting in the first place."

Carolyn reared back, stood up. She looked down at Roy, and blinked rapidly, and after a moment, that tiny glimmer of wetness was gone. She was ice-cold. "I can't help him now. This is bigger than all of us. You know that. Or at least, my parents believe that you do. Which is why they decided to keep you alive."

"Walt's alive," Roy blurted. "You know he is. You know he didn't fall for that stupid trick. We both fucking know it."

"Ayuh," Carolyn whispered, and in that single breath there came a torrent of pain that seemed to blast out of her and then was gone again.

Was Roy imagining all of this? Was Carolyn as stalwart as she appeared?

Or was she on the edge of crumbling? Or breaking?

He could not tell.

"He's on the news," Carolyn said, hollowly. "They did the raid. They went ahead with it. But now he's lost out there. And I don't know how much time he has left…" She stopped, as though she'd caught herself saying something she shouldn't. As she'd spoken, her shoulders had seemed to curl in around her chest, like she'd been wounded there.

Now, she straightened. Drew herself up.

"But I can't do anything for him," She said. "I am here…" she swallowed. "To provide my parents with a trusted point of contact for the operations that are about to begin here in Durham. I am in command of the elements operating in their name. Which includes you. And I am sending you back to CoAx County, where you can explain yourself to them in person."

"What about Walt?" Roy insisted.

"Benjamin and Jean," she said stiffly. "Have put a notification out to their local elements. If he is found…he is to be dealt with. He has no protection from them now." Her eyes were like hollow little blue orbs. They looked to Roy like the water in an ornamental pond that's been dyed blue to give the impression of depth.

"I thought you were in charge," Roy said bitterly.

"I can do nothing for him," Carolyn repeated.

"You're his wife!"

"I'm a Eudy," she replied, with no more feeling than she'd said anything else. No feeling. No conviction.

Who the hell was this person?

Carolyn turned to exit the room, but before she did, she appeared to look at Jimmy, and something passed between them, something strained and unpleasant, and Carolyn stopped and turned her head to speak to Roy over her shoulder.

"I'm Stephanie Eudy," she said.

***

After the door closed behind her, rigid-spined and stone-lipped, Carolyn excused herself and went to the only bathroom that was still operational in this dingy warehouse.

Jimmy watched her go, but did not question her.

It was not his place to question her.

In the bathroom, Carolyn closed the door, gently, almost as though it were the middle of the night and she did not want to wake anyone. Then she locked it.

She turned to the right. To the sink. She stared at herself in the mirror.

The mask cracked, her face suddenly full of fault-lines.

She gasped as it hit her, all at once, like a physical blow.

She grabbed the sides of the sink with both hands, almost cut in half, it felt like. Almost doubled over by it. But her eyes didn't leave the reflection of themselves. Standing there, hanging on, staring into her own cold eyes and watching them suddenly blur, just as the veins began to stand out.

She let out a gasp, then, terrified, she clapped one clammy hand over her mouth.

Her eyes wrinkled, and then shut, almost convulsively, blocking out that horrible image of herself. Her chest hitched uncontrollably. Everything coming down now. Everything falling. And her just being buried under the weight of it.

She slapped the faucet on, so the water would run. Hide some of the noise.

And then she melted away from that sink, her legs losing their strength to hold her upright. She held to the lip of the sink with one hand, the other still clenched over her mouth. She put her back to the door and slid down, down, until she was folded in on herself.

She put her face against her legs and wept as quietly as she was able.

CHAPTER THIRTY-THREE

Three of the four remaining members of Koz's team sat at the picnic table in the little common area between their triangle of sleeper units. The fourth slipped into the common area and stood, looking over them.

"It's true," he said, quietly.

Chief Tye Gibbs. Once upon a time, a pencil-necked nerd with glasses. Now seven feet tall and four hundred pounds with eyes like a hawk. Dressed in his PT shorts, sandals, and a t-shirt that would have been a tent on anyone else.

Looking back at him from their seats around the picnic table were chiefs Clayburn, Montgomery, and Harris.

Clay, Monty, and…well, they just called Harris "Harris."

"Sergeant Mason is on his way here now," Gibbs continued. "Major Pallen sent him."

"They're gonna try to lock us down," Monty said in a warning tone. "They think we're in on it."

"I think we *should* be in on it," Harris pointed out, quietly. "If Koz and Javon are out there with their asses in the wind, we need to be doing something about it."

Monty nodded. So did Clay.

Finally, Gibbs nodded too.

"When we agreed to do this," Gibbs said. "We agreed to have each other's backs, no matter what. It's always been us against the world. Now's no different. It might get us in a whole hell of a heap of trouble, but right now Koz and Javon need us. And I can't let that lie."

"What are we going to do about Mason?" Clay asked.

"You let me handle Mason," Gibbs said. Then he nodded to the sleepers. "Why don't yall get some game clothes on and grab your shit? If we're gonna roll, we need to roll now."

"What are you gonna do to him?" Monty asked.

The others were already splitting for their sleeper units.

"I'm gonna pacify the sonofabitch."

"Alright then."

Gibbs sat on the tabletop, facing out, with his legs up on the bench seat. He waited there for a few moments. The door to Clay's sleeper unit closed behind him. Gibbs stretched his legs. Stretched his shoulders and neck. Limbered his wrists.

It was important to keep the muscles supple.

He didn't have to wait long.

Sergeant Mason entered the little common area. He had two armed soldiers with him. But they were regulars. The sergeant looked about the empty space and a slight frown creased his brow.

"Mister Gibbs," he said, with a curt nod. "Where is the rest of your team?"

Gibbs just stared at him, impassively. "They're sleeping. What can I do for you?"

Mason visibly swallowed. But he stayed there, standing erect.

"Major Pallen sent me…for you and your team."

"What for?"

Mason's jaw worked. "That's between you and the Major. It's his orders."

"Well," Gibbs stretched his neck. "They're sleeping."

"You'll need to wake them."

"No."

All three of the soldiers standing in front of Gibbs squirmed a bit as the last word reached them. Their feet shuffled, making their bodies more bladed. Their hands tensed towards the subguns strapped to their chests.

"But the orders—"

"My boys have had a long-ass weekend. They've earned a bit of sleep. Now, if Major Pallen wants to talk, he can talk to me." Gibbs stood up and walked toward Sergeant Mason, his voice softening, becoming placating. He was even holding his hands up in a sort of "surrender" position. "I'll be happy to talk to him. Besides, I'm sure that by the time he's done grilling me, the others will be up and about."

Gibbs was now standing a bit *over* Sergeant Mason, smiling.

"This is about Koz and Javon, right?" Gibbs asked, quietly. "About them runnin' off and helpin' Roy steal that shit from the Sleep Lab?"

Sergeant Mason half-nodded, then corrected himself and shrugged. "I don't know. All I know is that—"

Gibbs slapped him across the face with an open hand, hard enough to knock him senseless, but he followed it up with an immediate elbow to the jaw that cracked bone and Mason was out cold.

In the same movement, while the two soldiers were still processing what the fuck had just happened, Gibbs hugged Sergeant Mason to his body—a meager shield, for sure, but it would have to do—and he shot out with a right hook that obliterated the soldier to his right, and then pivoted and brought his leg across in a blur, smashing his shin into the last soldier's thigh.

The soldier cried out, nearly fainting as his common peroneal nerve was crushed.

While the soldier was still standing, Gibbs released his grip on Sergeant Mason, stepped into that last soldier, plowed a fist into his solar plexus and then put him out with another elbow—this one catching his temple instead of the jaw, but doing the job just as good as it had done it to Mason.

Gibbs had time to watch all three bodies hit the ground.

The two soldiers were groaning and trembling, the way unconscious people will do.

Sergeant Mason wasn't even moving.

It was possible he was dead or in a coma.

Gibbs appropriated their weapons.

The sound of sleeper units opening.

He looked up, cradling the three subguns that they'd been carrying.

Without a word, Clay, Monty, and Harris scooped up the limp bodies, and then they carried them into their respective sleeper units. Probably to be stowed in a footlocker for the time being.

Absently, Gibbs genuinely hoped that Sergeant Mason wasn't dead.

But it was the price of doing business.

And you never send a man to do a New Breed's business.

***

Fifteen minutes later, four New Breeds dressed in street clothes, with large packs on their backs, exited the slurry cistern. The night was still deep and it was many hours until dawn. The moon was still high, just a half-moon, but bright enough in this clear mountain air to illuminate their way.

Silently the four of them walked down the gravel utility road to the edge of the Kanawha 3 town proper. They split into two pairs—Monty and Gibbs, and Clay and Harris. They took both sides of the street.

It didn't take them long to find what they were looking for.

They popped the lock on the old pickup truck—it actually belonged to the natural gas company that ran Kanawha 3—and then they all piled in. It was a crew cab, so it was big enough for all of them. "Enough" being a relative term.

Gibbs took the driver's seat. He was the senior man amongst them, and he preferred to be at the wheel. He popped the ignition and inserted a dialing wand into the place where the manual starter would go. A few seconds of blinking lights and then the pickup truck started up with a rumble.

Gibbs extracted the dialing wand and pocketed it.

They pulled out onto the main drag and started driving towards the checkpoint.

They made one little stop, just before the road curved and brought them in view of the checkpoint. Then Gibbs continued on.

As they rounded the curve, he could see that the checkpoint was occupied, which was no surprise, but that Marshal Dixon was also there, his marshal's car parked to the side, the lights on, still running.

"Jesus," Monty said to Gibbs. "This prick ever sleep?"

"'Parently not."

They approached the checkpoint slowly.

Two guards.

One inside the guard booth, controlling the arm—which had only just been repaired—and the spike strip that glittered in the moonlight.

The other guard stood with Marshal Dixon, watching the pickup truck approach.

Marshal Dixon had a look on his face that said he'd just gotten a big whiff of shit.

He and the guard were standing on the driver's side.

Dixon, one hand on his sidearm, raised the other hand, signaling them to stop.

Gibbs rolled to a slow and leisurely stop.

Dixon hovered outside of his window, glaring in.

Gibbs rolled the window down, smiling cordially.

"Yes, marshal?"

"No one's approved to leave," Dixon snapped.

"Mission's classified," Gibbs replied in a tone of infinite patience. "We don't go putting classified missions on printed itineraries and distributing them to checkpoint guards. It's something called *operational security.*"

Dixon continued to glare. His eyes coursed over the truck. Into the back. Then back to Gibbs. "An operation? With just the two of you?"

Gibbs nodded. "Yes. Just the two of us. And we have a very narrow window, marshal. So if you could be so kind as to buzz us through, I'm sure the powers that be—you know, the people that planned this mission in the first place—will be very pleased."

Dixon was still not convinced. "I have a direct line to Major Pallen."

"Congratulations."

"It was given to me this evening. After some *other* issues."

"Do tell."

"Apparently two of your team members, Roy, his brother, and the two assholes that showed up with him, slipped out of Kanawha 3 with an item of value to the Eudys. And the Eudys are not pleased."

"Heavens help us."

"I don't think you understand the gravity of the situation."

"I'm sure you're about to explain it to me."

And Dixon was, indeed going to explain it to him. But right about the time that he was opening his mouth to speak, he heard a voice behind him, say, "Nobody moves or I blow your fuckin' head off."

Dixon jerked and turned.

Clay and Harris, who they'd let out just before arriving at the checkpoint, were there. Clay had a suppressed battlerifle covering Dixon and the guard that was with him, and Harris had taken the guard in the shack.

"You," Clay said, nodding to the guard. "Put that subgun on the ground and back away."

As the guard complied, looking confused, Gibbs reached out and snatched Marshal Dixon's sidearm from his belt. He then switched his grip and held it, pointed at Dixon's chest. Gibbs could have used his own weapon, but he thought it would be more insulting this way.

At the guard shack, Harris was pulling the disarmed guard out and proning him onto the ground.

"Get on the ground," Clay instructed both the guard and Marshal Dixon.

Dixon was staring between Clay and Gibbs, as though he was thinking of trying something.

"Dear God," Gibbs said, smiling. "Please do it. Please jump, you froggy motherfucker. Nothing would make me happier."

While Dixon was hyper-focused on Gibbs, and the guard was already face-down on the pavement, Clay rammed into Dixon's back, slamming his head into the side window of the pickup truck and then planting the skinny bastard on the concrete.

Dixon coughed and spluttered.

Harris had deactivated the crossing arm and the spike strip. He ran out of the guard shack and piled into the truck, behind Monty.

Clay held his battlerifle, trained on the back of Dixon's head. "You want me to?" he asked Gibbs.

Gibbs shook his head. "Nah. Come on."

Clay sneered, but said nothing else. He ported his rifle up, and climbed into the pickup truck, sitting behind Gibbs.

Gibbs put the truck into reverse and cut the wheel hard to the right. Then he backed up. There was the *thump-thump* of the front wheels going over the dual speed bumps of Marshal Dixon's ankles, and then a lot of screaming.

He straightened the truck out, put it back into drive. He considered driving over Dixon's legs again, but the marshal had curled into a fetal position. Gibbs would have to run his entire body over. It didn't seem worth the trouble.

He then considered stopping and passing onto Dixon some piece of advice, but then he figured Dixon was likely in too much pain to hear it and take it to heart.

"Pearls before swine," Gibbs remarked.

Then they drove through the checkpoint, headed for Durham.

CHAPTER THIRTY-FOUR

Agent Goring arrived in a black GUV. It parked at the edge of the carnage. The driver didn't want to get the tires bloody, or dodge all the chewed up bodies in the road. Besides, the gunship's cannons had fucked up the concrete. It'd be a bumpy ride.

Goring preferred to walk.

He needed to walk.

He needed to get some of this irritation out.

Anger? No, not anger.

He was not the type of person to get angry.

He was the type of person to get even.

He was dressed in a nice gray suit. Not black. Black was for guys that liked to look like company men. Goring didn't like to look like a company man. He didn't like anyone to think anything about him at all. And a gray suit is…well…gray.

He stalked along the road. The hard leather heels of his dress shoes clicked on the concrete, stern and businesslike. He wove between the bodies. There were a lot of them. Well. Not bodies anymore. Just parts. Bits and pieces. They reminded him of the action figures he would blow to pieces as a kid.

He avoided little rivers of blood.

Wouldn't want the shoes to get dirty.

He arrived at the back of the ambushed convoy. Continued on.

He checked his PD as he walked around a dead New Breed soldier. He was unsurprised by the fact that the New Breed was dead. Goring knew they weren't demigods like the populace thought. There were weaknesses. There were ways to take them out. And it just so happened that apparently whatever little thing the resistance had been developing…well, apparently it worked.

He arrived at the front of the ambush.

Highly interesting.

A crater in the concrete that still had that sharp odor of high explosives. There was wreckage around the crater where the drone had dropped their first piece of ordnance. He'd reviewed the footage already. Knew that it had been a van, and what appeared to be a Directed EMP off to the side.

Neither of those items existed any more, except in abstract jumbles of parts scattered across a hundred foot radius.

Just past the crater, there sat a guntruck at idle.

At the rear of the guntruck were three figures.

Two New Breeds—live ones, this time—were standing on either side of an old man with a battered face.

Goring stopped in front of them. Then he adjusted his suit jacket. His belt line. Making sure everything was straight and proper.

"Mr. Baucom," he said, peeved, as he tugged at the French cuffs of his shirt.

The man said nothing. He was kneeling. Staring up at Goring.

He only had one eye to do it with—the other was still hideously swollen.

Goring, finally settled in his suit, clasped his hands in front of him in a gentle, interviewer's stance, and looked at Walter Baucom II.

"Why are you still here?" he asked.

Mr. Baucom snorted, then spit.

Goring moved his right foot so the bloody loogy wouldn't hit his nice shoes.

"I thought…" Goring paused to take a deep breath. "…we had an understanding."

"Ain't gon' betray my own son, y'knocker."

Goring pinched the bridge of his nose, his eyes cinched shut for a moment. "No, Walt. *You're* the knocker, whatever the fuck that means in your hick language." He released the bridge of his nose and blinked rapidly at the man kneeling before him. "Do you realize what you could have prevented? You could have prevented hundreds, maybe even thousands, of unnecessary deaths. I put a tracking device on you for a fucking *reason*, you brain-fucked farmer. Jesus Christ."

Another deep breath.

He was getting angry.

Angry didn't do.

"If you'd've gone with the plan," Goring continued, more evenly. "You could have led us straight to the resistance in Durham and we could have made a surgical strike. Cut the head off the fucking snake. Nobody would die that didn't need to die." He shoved a palm at the old man. "Now look what you've done. We're going to have to bomb half the fucking city now. I hope you're happy."

"Fuck you, you loyalist piece of shit."

Goring made an exasperated raspberry noise. "Fine. Have it your way."

He drew his pistol and executed Walter Baucom II with a single shot to his forehead.

He stood over him, looking at the body, but he was thinking about other things.

He'd told the Baucom man that they would have to bomb half of Durham to locate the resistance cells.

Well…that wasn't *entirely* true.

They had other resources.

The Baucom man was just one of several.

He could still make it work.

Goring reholstered.

Sniffed.

Looked around.

"We're done here."

CHAPTER THIRTY-FIVE

They arrived at the back of some tumbledown brick building that looked like it was on the verge of being condemned, or perhaps had been already.

It stood on a small, industrial back street that was surrounded by shops and business that were dark, a few of them looking abandoned, as did the brick building itself.

Walt wasn't sure at all what the hell the place had been.

But now it was a safe house, apparently.

Walt had barely pulled his aching, blood-covered body out of the stolen GUV before a door slammed open and a man came running out.

Walt's immediate reaction was to grab his weapon, but he didn't raise it.

The woman—whose name was Mel, they'd discovered—was walking towards the newcomer, her hand upraised in greeting.

The greeting was not returned, Walt noticed.

The man did not look happy to see her, which was odd.

"The fuck is this shit?" the man practically yelled. He was thrusting his hand at the vehicle. "That shit is hot! Don't bring it in here!" he grabbed Mel by the shoulders and threw her into the most awkward and rushed embrace that Walt had ever witnessed, and it seemed to him that the man had done it as an afterthought, perhaps realizing that he should express some joy that his comrade had escaped.

"Well, good to see you too, fuckhead," Mel snapped. "Jesus..."

"I'm sorry," the man's words were rushed. "I can't believe you got out. None of us can. We've been waiting for you. It's just..."

"How'd you hear about it?" Walt said, stepping forward.

He wasn't sure if he was welcome to barge into this conversation, but he was tired, he was worn, he was raw. He didn't care.

The man looked up at Walt and frowned. "Who the hell is this?"

Mel turned and gestured to him. "He's the one that hit the convoy."

"How?"

"Later," Walt said, feeling that thing inside of him bucking up, starting to surge against its leash, and he was just so goddamned tired, he didn't know if he cared to restrain it any longer. "How did you know about the op?"

The man released his faux-affectionate grip on Mel and flipped his PD into life in a brusque manner that Walter didn't care for. The monitor sprang into the air and the man spun it to be viewed publicly.

It was a newscast. Of course.

It was showing security footage.

In that footage, Walt saw Rat. Armed with a battlerifle. Giving orders to a stranger. The clerk of a store, it looked like.

"It's all over the fucking news!" the man said. "Is that you? Is that one of your people? Because his *face* is fucking *everywhere*!" The man was ardently shaking his head. "He can't be here. This fucking *car* can't be here. I'm not sure *any of you*—"

Walt watched him as he talked, watched his mouth moving. Watched his scared little eyes, beaming out his ignorance of everything.

Who did he think he was?

Who *the fuck* did he think he was?

Walter didn't broadcast it at all.

He was just done.

Done listening.

Done being told to shut up.

Done being told what to do.

Done being shitted on.

Just…

Done.

He grabbed the man by the throat. And no one moved to stop him. Maybe they were done too. And maybe that's as far as Walter would have gone—just stand there and choke off the idiot's belligerent words—but when he had his fingers hooked into the man's larynx, the man started to fight back.

Who the fuck does he think he is?

Walter put a leg behind him and threw the man over his hip. The man's body left the earth. Went back. Met the earth again. Hard. Cracking.

Still, no one moved to restrain Walter.

He didn't choke the man to death.

The thought crossed his mind.

But he didn't.

He just held him there, gasping and clawing ineffectively at his neck.

Held him there and looked at him right in the eyes and he hoped that for the man's sake, if he valued his life, that he was seeing what was inside of Walter. That he was seeing that there was something in there that wanted destruction.

"I'll fucking kill you," Walter grated into the man's face. Not loudly. But harshly.

The man simply kept gagging. Staring into Walter's eyes. Scared.

So scared.

Finally, someone cared enough to put a hand on Walter's shoulder.

It was Mel.

"Let him up, Walter."

Walter did not immediately comply.

For a second longer, he held the man down.

"You hear that?" he asked the man on the ground. "You remember that name. Walter Lawrence Baucom. The third. Remember it."

Then he gave the man a final shove to the throat that he hoped, in the darkest parts of him, would crush the man's larynx. It didn't.

And he released the man to gasp and try to get air past his swollen throat.

Walter stood up and he looked at Mel, who was looking at him strangely now. But not angrily. Just…differently.

He pointed at her. “I’ll listen to you. This is your house. But fuck that guy. You keep him away from me.”

The man on the ground was getting to his knees, finding his voice, which was wheezy and high-pitched. “He fucking tried to kill me! You trust this fucking psychopath?”

Mel was, as it turned out, also done.

She turned to the man. “You shut your fucking mouth. You deserved what you got. The man in that video was one of their friends. And he died to get us out of there. Which is more than I can say of you. That dead man is sitting in the back of the car right now. And I’m pretty sure that Walter would’ve killed you if he fucking wanted to.” She spat on the ground. “As for trust? They killed New Breeds. Did it fast, too. Every single one of ‘em in the convoy. So yeah. I trust he’s not a fucking Fed.”

The man was standing there, hunched like a spurned dog. Rubbing his neck and working his jaw. He was alternately eyeing Mel and Walt. Eyes watering. “Yeah? What about the psycho part?”

“Maybe we could use a little bit of that around here,” Mel said, coldly. Then she pointed to the building. “Go get yourself together, Twigs. Send Bryce and Pablo to ditch that car and burn it. I want them to use the thermite. I want that thing to be unrecognizable.”

Twigs stood there, looking twiggy, and glaring. An angry twig.

Walter wanted to snap him.

Mel leaned towards him. “Twigs. Do what I fuckin’ told you to do.”

After another willful moment, Twigs turned and went inside the building.

Mel spun on Walter. “You put me in a bad position,” she said, sternly. “I backed your play because I appreciate what you did for me and my people. And also, Twigs is a fuck. But let’s not do that shit again. I don’t want to have to choose between you and my people.”

Walter nodded to her, marginally. "Didn't mean to put you in a spot." He lifted his head. "You mind if I ask who your people are? You guys a rogue cell? Or part of a bigger organization?"

Mel looked at him for a moment, and Walter knew he was being further evaluated. And he also knew, just from the set of her mouth, that she was only rehashing the decision that she'd already made. Which was, of course, to trust them.

"You familiar with the Honeycutt outfit?"

Walter felt his blood get a bit hotter.

Or maybe it was colder.

Hard to tell sometimes.

Out of the corner of his eye, he could tell that Bobbi and Getty were both standing suddenly very still. Their eyes were on him. They were watching. Waiting. Wondering what he was going to say that.

"Passing familiar," Walter said.

Mel watched him for another moment.

Walt gave her absolutely nothing.

Eventually, she just nodded.

To the side, Getty tapped out a cigarette.

Bobbi remained silent.

Mel opened her mouth to say something else.

And then the ground rumbled underneath their feet.

Walter felt it like electricity shooting up from his toes to the top of his head, arcing down his fingertips. A sudden surge of adrenaline.

"The fuck…?"

Walter looked around him, in the sky, along what he could see of the horizon.

There.

He pointed, but didn't speak.

A fireball was roaring up into the sky to the north.

Where the city was. Where Durham lay.

Another boom that rumbled under their feet.

Another fireball.

Then another.

And another.

Then the sky shook and the air exploded around them.

In unison they all ducked like they were under fire.

"Holy shit!" Mel shouted. "What the hell was that?"

Walter looked skyward. Just out of the corner of his vision, he could see the fiery arcs of two jet engines burning hot, streaking across the sky towards the city.

"Fast movers," Walt said. "Broke the sound barrier over our heads."

Mel had already turned to another one of her crew. "Get on the horn. Get everybody. I want them all down here and locked and loaded A-S-A-fucking-P!"

To the north, a string of tracer fire burst from the heavens, from some unknown source in the darkness, and it spewed across the cityscape.

A second string of tracers answered, arcing upwards into the sky.

"My God," Getty said, the cigarette forgotten in his lips. "It's gonna be a fuckin' warzone."

Walter grabbed Bobbi and Getty by the shoulder and started pushing them for the entrance to the building. "We should get inside. This is gonna get nasty."

As they moved toward the door, people began to spill out of it, eyes to the sky, wide and shocked and morbidly curious.

"Back inside!" Mel was yelling. "Get the fuck back inside! If you don't have a fucking rifle in your hands then you're wrong!"

There was a confusion of bustling.

In a dark corridor.

There was a lot of alarmed yelling.

Walter did not like being in this scrum of bodies, but he found himself going with them, with the flow of people. He kept a hand on Bobbi and a hand on Getty, and it seemed that they were being herded deeper into the building.

"I don't like this!" Bobbi shouted.

"Me neither!" Getty confirmed.

"Stick with me," Walter replied.

Deeper in the building, it wasn't so dark. The disorientation faded with the glow of the artificial lights. They spilled out into a massive room. There were tables. Cages. Lots of people. Lots of bustling. The words "bombing" and "invade" and "attack" and "counterattack" were being tossed around, thick in the air.

The tables were crammed full of gear.

Everything from bottles of water to cases of bullets.

Walter thought he saw a man-pack mortar tube on one table.

Off to the right, there was a sort of command section. There were monitors glowing on people's faces, and there were several techs staring urgently at those monitors, and people hanging over their shoulders, some of them talking on comms, others pacing urgently in the background, talking on their PDs.

Someone got on a bullhorn.

They were standing on one of the steel tables.

"This is what we've been training for, people! This is no-bullshit-time. Quit having a goddamned panic attack and do what you came here to do." The man speaking started pointing to different areas. "Rifle teams, form up over here! Techies, get into the command center and wait for orders. Heavy weapons, form up over here!"

Walter backed himself up against a wall, managing to drag Getty and Bobbi along with him.

"Well, what the hell are we supposed to do?" Bobbi asked.

Walter frowned, staring into the mad rush that was starting to coalesce into something marginally more orderly. It seemed that people were grabbing ammunition and supplies from the tables and there wasn't much checking about who was grabbing what.

Strangely, the concept of free grenades really appealed to Walter.

He looked around, but couldn't find Mel in all the hubbub.

"Fuck it," he said. "Grab what you can. I have no idea what we'll be doing, but I imagine we're gonna want lots of ammunition. And explosives."

"Fuck," Getty sighed, barely audible over the amplified orders. "So much for getting some goddamned sleep."

Walter started pushing them towards the tables with the ammunition. "Sleep when you're dead, ayuh?"

"Don't tempt the devil, Walt."

CHAPTER THIRTY-SIX

In the confusion, Mel managed to slip away.

She moved through the confusing labyrinth of this building's halls and interconnecting rooms. When she'd been caught in the middle of District 89, when they'd sealed the place off, she'd thought it was over. Thought she'd never see this place again.

It wasn't that it held fond memories for her.

Nothing quite that nice.

But it was a place from which she could fight.

And so it held a special spot in her heart.

Now, though, she did not feel good about being here.

There was no warmth to it. Not the warmth of homecoming. Not the warmth of rage, either.

She felt cold and sick to her stomach.

The shooting and the driving and the tension had distracted her. But now, as she moved quickly through these halls, with the sound of all that yelling and clamoring in the weapons room fading to a dull murmur that seemed to just ooze out of the walls…now she was scared again.

Scared, and guilty.

This is what a murderer must feel like, immediately after committing their crime.

Wondering how they're going to hide it.

Trying to figure out what their life looks like moving forward.

But everything changes.

Everything is different.

She found the door that she was looking for.

She slipped in, closed the door behind her. Locked it.

The lights were out. They regularly kept them out so as not to attract attention. The lights should not be on in an abandoned building, after all.

She activated the weaponlight on her stolen battlerifle.

The cold glow illuminated the room.

It was formerly an office.

No windows.

It served as her quarters.

She walked stiffly to the cot that was her bed. The covers were still rumpled from the last time she'd slept in it several days ago. Everything was as she'd left it before she'd gone to District 89.

There was a personal bag underneath the cot.

She took the rifle from her shoulders and laid it on her cot. Bent down. Grabbed the personal bag and began rummaging through it. In the bottom of one of the small pockets, she felt what she was looking for and pulled it out.

It was her old PD.

Wiped, obviously. It had no service.

But the applications on it would still work. And the battery was still charged.

She flipped it open. It came readily to life, bathing her in monitor light.

She glanced at the door to her quarters, but it was closed. Secured.

Had she locked it?

She wasn't sure.

She sat on the edge of the cot and selected an application.

It took a moment. But then the monitor became an image of her face. A mirror image.

She looked at her eyes, saw the haunted nature of them, and hated it. She needed to fix that. Those eyes were a dead-fucking-giveaway. She put her face into neutral. Watched the fear lines disappear. Her mouth relaxed. Her eyebrows slackened.

That was better.

Now…

She turned her head slightly.

Held the PD with her right hand.

Brought her left hand up to her temple.

She kept her hair short. Not buzzed-short, but short enough so that it didn't get in the way. She was, after all, first and foremost a soldier for the resistance. All other aspects of life had long ago taken a backseat.

She pressed her hand to the side of her head and swept up, so that the hair parted, showing the scalp beneath. And as she swept up, the hair fell, the part moving up, like a scan of her scalp.

She stopped.

Frowned.

Looked closer at the mirror image of herself.

Yes. There it was.

She poked at it.

It was still tender.

A slightly raised bump.

A little red mark on her scalp.

She let the hair fall back into place. Brushed it over a few times.

Turned her head this way and that.

No, you couldn't see it.

No one would know.

She snapped her PD shut.

Stared at the wall.

How long?

How long did they have?

The PD fell out of her shaky fingers and clattered to the floor.

She stared at it. Didn't pick it up again. She put her hands on her face and wiped down, smelling the dirty, sweaty stink of herself in her palms. After her hands had passed over her eyes, they looked haunted again.

She held both her hands against her nose and mouth. Like a mask that she was trying to hide herself behind.

"What are you gonna do, Mel?" she whispered into the hollow of her hands. "What the fuck are you gonna do?"

ROGUE CELL

A GROWER'S WAR
BOOK 3

Coming Soon!

DJ MOLLES is the *New York Times* bestselling author of The Remaining series. He published his first short story, "Darkness," while still in high school. Soon after, he won a prize for his short story "Survive." He got started self-publishing the first books in The Remaining series while working full time as a police officer for a major metropolitan city. Since then he's had the good fortune to retire, and lives a semiquiet life with his wife and children in the southeast.

Follow him at facebook.com/djmolles

Want more from DJ Molles?

Try the Bestselling *The Remaining* series:

The Remaining
The Remaining: Aftermath
The Remaining: Refugees
The Remaining: Fractured
The Remaining: Allegiance
The Remaining: Extinction

Also by DJ Molles:

Wolves

Made in the USA
Monee, IL
24 January 2021